# The Ladies' Delight

# The Ladies' Delight

Émile Zola

MINT EDITIONS

*The Ladies' Delight* was first published in 1883.

This edition published by Mint Editions 2021.

ISBN 9781513282121 | E-ISBN 9781513287140

Published by Mint Editions®

 MINT
EDITIONS

minteditionbooks.com

Publishing Director: Jennifer Newens
Design & Production: Rachel Lopez Metzger
Project Manager: Micaela Clark
Translated By: Ernest Alfred Vizetelly
Typesetting: Westchester Publishing Services

# Contents

# I

Denise had come on foot from the Saint-Lazare railway station, where a Cherbourg train had landed her and her two brothers, after a night spent on the hard seat of a third-class carriage. She was leading Pépé by the hand, while Jean followed her; all three of them exhausted by their journey, frightened and lost in that vast city of Paris, their eyes raised to the house fronts and their tongues for ever inquiring the way to the Rue de la Michodière, where their uncle Baudu lived. However, as she at last emerged into the Place Gaillon, the girl stopped short in astonishment.

"Oh! just look there, Jean," said she; and they remained stock still, nestling close to one another, dressed from head to foot in black, the old mourning bought at their father's death. Denise, rather puny for her twenty years, was carrying a small parcel in one hand, while on the other side, her little brother, five years old, clung to her arm, and in the rear her big brother in the flower of his sixteen summers stood erect with dangling arms.

"Well I never," said she, after a pause, "that *is* a shop!"

They were at the corner of the Rue de la Michodière and the Rue Neuve-Saint-Augustin, in front of a draper's shop, whose windows displayed a wealth of bright colour in the soft, pale October light. Eight o'clock was striking at the church of Saint-Roch; and only the early birds of Paris were abroad, a few clerks on their way to business, and housewives flitting about on their morning shopping. Before the door of the drapery establishment, two shopmen, mounted on a step-ladder, were hanging up some woollen goods, whilst in a window facing the Rue Neuve-Saint-Augustin another young man, kneeling with his back to the pavement, was delicately plaiting a piece of blue silk. In the shop, which was as yet void of customers, and whose employees were only just beginning to arrive, there was a low buzz as in a bee hive just awakening.

"By Jove!" said Jean, "this beats Valognes. Yours wasn't such a fine shop."

Denise shook her head. She had spent two years at Valognes, with Cornaille, the principal draper in the town; and this Parisian shop so suddenly encountered and to her so vast made her heart swell and detained her there, interested, impressed, forgetful of everything else. The lofty plate-glass door in a corner facing the Place Gaillon reached the first storey amidst a medley of ornaments covered with gilding. Two allegorical female figures, with laughing faces and bare bosoms unrolled a scroll bearing the inscription "The Ladies' Paradise"; then, on either side, along the Rue de la Michodière and the Rue Neuve-Saint-Augustin, stretched the windows of the establishment, not limited merely to the corner house but comprising four others—two on the right and two on the left which had been recently purchased and fitted up. It all appeared endless to Denise, thus seen in perspective, with the display down below and the plate glass windows above, through which a long line of counters was to be perceived. Upstairs a young lady, dressed in silk, could be espied sharpening a pencil, while two others, beside her, were unfolding some velvet mantles.

"The Ladies' Paradise," read Jean, with a soft laugh, like a handsome youth who already has thoughts of women. "That's a pretty name—that must draw customers—eh?"

But Denise was absorbed by the display at the principal entrance. There, in the open street, on the very pavement, she beheld a mass of cheap goods—doorway temptations, bargains to attract the passer-by. Pieces of woollen and cloth goods, merinoes, cheviots, and tweeds, hung from above like bunting, with their neutral, slate, navy-blue, and olive-green tints relieved by large white price-tickets. Close by, on either side of the doorway, dangled strips of fur, narrow bands for dress trimmings, ashen-hued Siberian squirrel-skin, swansdown of spotless snowiness, and rabbit-skin transformed into imitation ermine and imitation sable. Below, in boxes and on tables, amidst piles of remnants, appeared a quantity of hosiery which was virtually given away; knitted woollen gloves, neckerchiefs, women's hoods, cardigan waistcoats, a complete winter show with colours in mixtures, patterns and stripes and here and there a flaming patch of red. Denise saw some tartan at nine sous, some strips of American bison at a franc the mètre, and some mittens at five sous a pair. An immense clearance sale was apparently going on; the establishment seemed to be bursting with goods, blocking up the pavement with the surplus of its contents. Uncle Baudu was forgotten. Even Pépé, clinging tightly to his sister's hand, opened his big eyes in wonder. However a vehicle in coming up forced them to quit the roadway, and they mechanically turned into the Rue Neuve-Saint-Augustin, following the windows and stopping at each fresh display. At first they were captivated by an intricate arrangement: up above a number of umbrellas, placed obliquely, seemed to form a rustic roof; upon rods beneath them hung a quantity of silk stockings displaying neat ankles and well rounded calves, some of them dotted with rosebuds, others of divers hues, the black ones open-worked and the red ones elegantly clocked; whilst those which were of a flesh tint, looked, with their satiny texture, as soft as skin itself. Then, on the baize covering of the show-stage, came a symmetrical array of gloves with extended fingers and narrow palms recalling the hands of Byzantine Virgins, all the rigid and, as it were, adolescent grace which characterises feminine frippery before it is worn. However, it was especially the last window which detained their eyes. An exhibition of silks, satins and velvets, in a supple, vibrating scale of colour, here set, as in full bloom, the most delicate hues of the floral world. At the top were the velvets, deeply black, or white as curds; lower down came the satins, pinks and blues, bright at their folds, then fading into paler and paler tints of infinite delicacy; and lower still were silks, the rainbow's variegated scarf, the several pieces cocked shell-wise, plaited as though round some female waist, endowed, as it were, with life by the skilful manipulation of the employees; and between each *motif*, each glowing phrase of the display ran a discreet accompaniment, a light, puffy roll of creamy *foulard*. Here too at either end of the window, were huge piles of the two silks which were the exclusive property of the establishment, the "Paris Delight" and the "Golden Grain"—articles of exceptional quality destined to revolutionize the silk trade.

"Oh! look at that *faille* at five francs sixty!" murmured Denise, transported with astonishment at sight of the "Paris Delight".

Jean, however, was getting bored and stopped a passer-by. "Which is the Rue de la Michodière, please, sir?"

On hearing that it was the first on the right they all turned back, making the tour of the establishment. But just as she was entering the street, Denise was again attracted by a window in which ladies' mantles were displayed. At Cornaille's the mantles had been her department, but she had never seen anything like this, and remained rooted to the spot with admiration. At the rear a large scarf of Bruges lace, of considerable value, was spread out like an altar-veil, with its two creamy wings extended; then there were flounces of Alençon, grouped in garlands; and from the top to the bottom, like falling snow, fluttered lace of every description—Malines, Valenciennes, Brussels, and Venetian-point. On each side pieces of cloth rose up in dark columns imparting distance to the background. And the mantles were here, in this sort of chapel raised to the worship of woman's beauty and grace. In the centre was a magnificent article, a velvet mantle trimmed with silver fox; on one side of it appeared a silk cloak lined with miniver, on the other a cloth cloak edged with cocks' plumes; and, last of all, some opera cloaks in white cashmere and quilted silk trimmed with swansdown or chenille. There was something for every taste, from the opera cloaks at twenty-nine francs to the velvet mantle which was marked eighteen hundred. The round busts of the dummies filled out the stuff, the prominent hips exaggerating the slimness of the waists and the absent heads being replaced by large price-tickets pinned on the necks, whilst the mirrors, on each side of the window, reflected and multiplied all these forms, peopling the street, as it were, with beautiful women for sale, each bearing a price in big figures in lieu of a head.

"How stunning they are!" murmured Jean, finding no other words to express his emotion.

This time he himself had become motionless, and stood there gaping. All this female luxury turned him rosy with pleasure. He had a girl's beauty—a beauty which he seemed to have stolen from his sister—a fair white skin, ruddy curly hair, lips and eyes overflowing with tenderness. By his side Denise, with her rather long face, large mouth, fading complexion and light hair, appeared thinner still. Pépé, who was also fair, with the fairness of infancy, now clung closer to her, as if anxious to be caressed, perturbed and delighted as he was by the sight of the beautiful ladies in the window. And those three fair ones, poorly clad in black, that sad-looking girl between the pretty child and the handsome youth, looked so strange yet so charming standing there on the pavement, that the passers-by glanced back smilingly.

For some minutes a stout man with grey hair and a large yellow face had been looking at them from a shop-door on the other side of the street. He had been standing there with bloodshot eyes and contracted mouth, beside himself with rage at the display made by The Ladies' Paradise, when the sight of the girl and her brothers had completed his exasperation. What were those three simpletons doing there, gaping in front of the cheap-jack's show booth?

"What about uncle?" asked Denise, suddenly, as if just waking up.

"We are in the Rue de la Michodière," replied Jean. "He must live somewhere about here."

They raised their heads and looked round; and just in front of them, above the stout man, they perceived a green sign-board on which in yellow letters, discoloured by the rain was the following inscription:

"The Old Elbeuf. Cloths and Flannels. Baudu, late Hauchecorne." The house, coated with ancient rusty paint, and quite flat and unadorned amidst the surrounding mansions of the Louis XIV period, had only three front windows up above, square and shutterless windows simply provided with handrails supported by two iron bars placed crosswise. But what most struck Denise, whose eyes were full of the bright display of The Ladies' Paradise, was the low ground-floor shop, surmounted by an equally low storey with half-moon windows, of prison-like appearance. Right and left, framed round by wood work of a bottle-green hue, which time had tinted with ochre and bitumen, were two deep windows, black and dusty, in which pieces of cloth heaped one on another could vaguely be seen. The open doorway seemed to conduct into the darkness and dampness of a cellar.

"That's the house," said Jean.

"Well, we must go in," declared Denise. "Come on, Pépé."

All three, however, grew somewhat troubled, as if seized with fear. When their father had died, carried off by the same fever which a month previously had killed their mother, their uncle Baudu, in the emotion born of this double bereavement, had certainly written to Denise, assuring her that there would always be a place for her in his house whenever she might like to try fortune in Paris. But this had taken place nearly a year ago, and the young girl was now sorry that she should have so impulsively left Valognes without informing her uncle. The latter did not know them, never having set foot in the little town since the day when he had left it as a boy, to enter the service of the draper Hauchecorne, whose daughter he had subsequently married.

"Monsieur Baudu?" asked Denise, at last making up her mind to speak to the stout man who was still eyeing them, surprised by their appearance and manners.

"That's me," he replied.

Then Denise blushed deeply and stammered: "Oh, I'm so pleased! I am Denise. This is Jean, and this is Pépé. You see, we have come, uncle."

Baudu seemed lost in amazement. His big eyes rolled in his yellow face; he spoke slowly and with difficulty. He had evidently been far from thinking of this family which now suddenly dropped down upon him.

"What—what, you here?" he several times repeated. "But you were at Valognes. Why aren't you at Valognes?"

In her sweet but rather faltering voice she then explained that since the death of her father, who had spent every penny he possessed in his dye-works, she had acted as a mother to the two children; but the little she had earned at Cornaille's did not suffice to keep the three of them. Jean certainly worked at a cabinet-maker's, a repairer of old furniture, but didn't earn a sou. Still, he had got to like the business, and had even learned to carve. One day, having found a piece of ivory, he had amused himself by carving it into a head, which a gentleman staying in the town had seen and praised; and this gentleman it was who had been the cause of their leaving Valognes, as he had found Jean a place with an ivory-carver in Paris.

"So you see, uncle," continued Denise, "Jean will commence his apprenticeship at his new master's to-morrow. They ask no premium, and will board and lodge him. And so I felt sure that Pépé and I would be able to jog along. At all events we can't be worse off than we were at Valognes."

She said nothing about a certain love affair of Jean's, of certain letters which he had written to the daughter of a nobleman of the town, of the kisses which the pair had exchanged over a wall—in fact, quite a scandal which had strengthened her in her determination to leave. And if she was so anxious to be in Paris herself it was that she might be able to look after her brother, feeling, as she did, quite a mother's tender anxiety for this gay and handsome youth, whom all the women adored. Uncle Baudu, however, couldn't get over it, but continued his questions.

"So your father left you nothing," said he. "I certainly thought there was still something left. Ah! how many times did I write advising him not to take those dye-works! He was a good-hearted fellow certainly, but he had no head for business And you were left with those two youngsters to look after—you've had to keep them, eh?"

His bilious face had now become clearer, his eyes were not so bloodshot as when he had stood glaring at The Ladies' Paradise. All at once he noticed that he was blocking up the doorway. "Well," said he, "come in, now you're here. Come in, that'll be better than gaping at a parcel of rubbish."

And after addressing a last pout of anger to The Ladies' Paradise, he made way for the children by entering the shop and calling his wife and daughter: "Elizabeth, Geneviève, come down; here's company for you!"

Denise and the two boys, however, hesitated at sight of the darkness of the shop. Blinded by the clear outdoor light, they blinked as on the threshold of some unknown pit, and felt their way with their feet with an instinctive fear of encountering some treacherous step. And drawn yet closer together by this vague fear, the child still holding the girl's skirts, and the big boy behind, they made their entry with a smiling, anxious grace. The clear morning light outlined the dark silhouettes of their mourning clothes; and an oblique ray of sunshine gilded their fair hair.

"Come in, come in," repeated Baudu.

Then, in a few sentences he explained matters to his wife and daughter. The former was a little woman, consumed by anæmia and quite white—white hair, white eyes and white lips. Geneviève, the daughter, in whom the maternal degeneracy appeared yet more marked, had the sickly, colourless appearance of a plant reared in the shade. However, a thick, heavy crop of magnificent black hair, marvellously vigorous for such poor soil, gave her, as it were, a mournful charm.

"Come in," said both the women in their turn; "you are welcome." And they at once made Denise sit down behind a counter.

Pépé then jumped upon his sister's lap, whilst Jean leant against the panelling beside her. They were regaining their assurance and looking round the shop where their eyes had grown used to the obscurity. They could now distinctly see it all, with its low and smoky ceiling, its oaken counters polished by use, and its old-fashioned nests of drawers with strong iron fittings. Bales of dark goods reached to the beams above; a smell of wool and dye—a sharp chemical smell—prevailed, intensified it seemed by the humidity of the floor. At the further end two young men and a young woman were putting away some pieces of white flannel.

"Perhaps this young gentleman would like to take something?" said Madame Baudu, smiling at Pépé.

"No, thanks," replied Denise, "we each had a cup of milk at a café opposite the station." And as Geneviève looked at the small parcel she had laid on the floor near her, she added: "I left our box there too."

She blushed as she spoke feeling that she ought not to have dropped down on her friends in this way. Even in the train, just as she was leaving Valognes, she had been assailed by regrets and fears; and this was why she had left the box at the station and given the children their breakfast immediately on arriving in Paris.

"Well, well," suddenly said Baudu, "let's come to an understanding. 'Tis true that I wrote to you, but that was a year ago, and since then business hasn't been flourishing, I can assure you, my girl."

He stopped short, choked by an emotion he did not wish to show. Madame Baudu and Geneviève, had cast down their eyes with an air of resignation.

"Oh," continued he, "it's a crisis which will pass, no doubt, I'm not uneasy; but I have reduced my staff; there are only three here now, and this is not the moment to engage a fourth. In short, my poor girl, I cannot take you as I promised."

Denise listened, aghast and very pale. He repeated his words, adding: "It would do no good to either of us."

"All right, uncle," at last she replied, with a painful effort, "I'll try to manage all the same."

The Baudus were not bad sort of people. But they complained of never having had any luck. In the flourishing days of their business, they had had to bring up five sons, of whom three had died before attaining the age of twenty; the fourth had gone wrong, and the fifth had just started for Mexico, as a captain. Geneviève was the only one now left at home. From first to last, however, this large family had cost a deal of money, and Baudu had made things worse by buying a great lumbering country house, at Rambouillet, near his wife's father's place. Thus, a sharp, sour feeling was springing up in the honest old tradesman's breast.

"You might have warned us," he resumed, gradually getting angry at his own harshness. "You might have written and I should have told you to stay at Valognes. When I heard of your father's death I said what is right on such occasions, but you drop down on us without a word of warning. It's very awkward."

He raised his voice, as he thus relieved himself. His wife and daughter still kept their eyes on the floor, like submissive persons who would never think of interfering. Jean, however, had turned pale, whilst Denise hugged the terrified Pépé to her bosom. Hot tears of disappointment fell from her eyes.

"All right, uncle," she said, "we'll go away."

At that he ceased speaking, and an awkward silence ensued. Then he resumed in a surly tone: "I don't mean to turn you out. As you are here you can sleep upstairs to-night; after that, we'll see."

Then, as he glanced at them, Madame Baudu and Geneviève understood that they were free to arrange matters. And all was soon settled. There was no need to trouble about Jean, as he was to enter on his apprenticeship the next day. As for Pépé, he would be well looked after by Madame Gras, an old lady who rented a large ground floor in the Rue des Orties, where she boarded and lodged young children for forty francs a month. Denise said that she had sufficient to pay for the first month, and, so the only remaining question was to find a place for herself. Surely they would be able to discover some situation for her in the neighbourhood.

"Wasn't Vinçard in want of a saleswoman?" asked Geneviève.

"Of course, so he was!" cried Baudu; "we'll go and see him after lunch. There's nothing like striking the iron while it's hot."

Not a customer had come in to interrupt this family discussion; the shop remained dark and empty as before. At the far end, the two young men and the young woman were still working, talking in low sibilant whispers amongst themselves. At last, however, three ladies arrived, and Denise was then left alone for a moment. She kissed Pépé with a swelling heart, at the thought of their approaching separation. The child, affectionate as a kitten, hid his little head without saying a word. When Madame Baudu and Geneviève returned, they remarked how quiet he was, and Denise assured them that he never made any more noise than that, but remained for days together without speaking, living solely on kisses and caresses. Then until lunch-time the three women sat and talked together about children, housekeeping, life in Paris and life in the country, in curt, cautious sentences, like relations whom ignorance of one another renders somewhat awkward. Jean meantime had gone to the shop-door, and stood there watching all the outdoor life and smiling at the pretty girls. At ten o'clock a servant appeared. As a rule the cloth was then laid for Baudu, Geneviève, and the first-hand; a second lunch being served at eleven o'clock for Madame Baudu, the other young man, and the young woman.

"Come to lunch!" exclaimed the draper, turning towards his niece; and when they sat ready in the narrow dining-room behind the shop, he called the first-hand who had lingered behind: "Colomban lunch!"

The young man entered apologising; he had wished to finish arranging the flannels, he said. He was a big fellow of twenty-five, heavy but crafty, for although his face, with its large weak mouth, seemed at first sight typical of honesty there was a veiled cunning in his eyes.

"There's a time for everything," rejoined Baudu, who sat before a piece of cold veal, carving it with a master's skill and prudence, calculating the weight of each thin slice to within a quarter of an ounce.

He served everybody, and even cut up the bread. Denise had placed Pépé near her to see that he ate properly; but the dark close room made her feel uncomfortable. She thought it so small, after the large, well-lighted rooms to which she had been accustomed in the country. A single window overlooked a small back-yard, which communicated with the street by a dark passage running along the side of the house. And this yard, dripping wet and evil-smelling, was like the bottom of some well into which fell a circular glimmer of light. In the winter they were obliged to keep the gas burning all day, and when the weather enabled them to do without it the room seemed more melancholy still. Several seconds elapsed before Denise's eyes got sufficiently used to the light to distinguish the food on her plate.

"That young chap has a good appetite," remarked Baudu, observing that Jean had finished his veal. "If he works as well as he eats, he'll make a fine fellow. But you, my girl, you are not eating. And, I say, now that we can talk a bit, tell us why you didn't get married at Valognes?"

At this Denise almost dropped the glass she held in her hand. "Oh! uncle—get married! How can you think of it? And the little ones!"

She ended by laughing, it seemed to her such a strange idea. Besides, what man would have cared to take her—a girl without a sou, no fatter than a lath, and not at all pretty? No, no, she would never marry, she had quite enough children with her two brothers.

"You are wrong," said her uncle; "a woman always needs a man. If you had found an honest young fellow over there you wouldn't have dropped on to the Paris pavement, you and your brothers, like a party of gipsies."

He paused in order to apportion with a parsimony full of justice, a dish of bacon and potatoes which the servant had just brought in. Then, pointing to Geneviève and Colomban with his spoon, he added: "Those two will get married next spring, if we have a good winter season."

Such was the patriarchal custom of the house. The founder, Aristide Finet, had given his daughter, Désirée, to his first-hand, Hauchecorne; he, Baudu, who had arrived in the Rue de la Michodière with seven francs in his pocket, had married old Hauchecorne's daughter, Elizabeth; and in his turn he intended to hand over Geneviève and the business to Colomban as soon as trade should improve. If he still delayed the marriage which had been decided on three years previously, it was because a scruple had come to him, a fixed resolve to act in all honesty. He himself had received the business in a prosperous state, and did not wish to pass it on to his son-in-law with fewer customers or doubtful sales. And, continuing his talk, he formally introduced Colomban, who came from Rambouillet, like Madame Baudu's father; in fact they were distant cousins. A hard-working fellow was Colomban, said he; for ten years he had slaved in the shop, fairly earning all his promotions!

Besides, he was far from being a nobody; his father was that noted toper, Colomban, the veterinary surgeon so well known all over the department of Seine-et-Oise, an artist in his line, but so addicted to the flowing bowl that his money fast slipped through his fingers.

"Thank heaven!" said the draper in conclusion, "if the father drinks and runs after women, the son at all events has learnt the value of money here."

Whilst he was thus speaking Denise began to examine Geneviève and Colomban. Though they sat close together at table, they remained very quiet, without a blush or a smile. From the day of entering the establishment the young man had counted on this marriage. He had passed through the various stages of junior hand, salesman, etc., at last gaining admittance into the confidence and pleasures of the family circle, and all this patiently, whilst leading a clock-work style of life and looking upon his marriage with Geneviève as a legitimate stroke of business. The certainty of having her as his wife prevented him from feeling any desire for her. On her side the girl had got to love him with the gravity of her reserved nature, full of a real deep passion of which she was not aware, in the regulated monotony of her daily life.

"Oh! it's quite right, when folks like each other, and can do it," at last said Denise, smiling, with a view to making herself agreeable.

"Yes, it always finishes like that," declared Colomban, who, slowly masticating, had not yet spoken a word.

Geneviève gave him a long look, and then in her turn remarked: "When people understand each other, the rest comes naturally."

Their affection had sprung up in this gloomy nook of old Paris like a flower in a cellar. For ten years past she had known no one but him, living by his side, behind the same bales of cloth, amidst the darkness of the shop; and morning and evening they had found themselves elbow to elbow in the tiny dining-room, so damp and vault-like. They could not have been more concealed, more utterly lost had they been far away in the country, under the screening foliage of the trees. Only the advent of doubt, of jealous fear, could make it plain to the girl, that she had given herself, for ever, amidst this abetting solitude, through sheer emptiness of heart and mental weariness.

As it was, Denise, fancied she could detect a growing anxiety in the look Geneviève had cast at Colomban, so she good-naturedly replied: "Oh! when people are in love they always understand each other."

Meantime Baudu kept a sharp eye on the table. He had distributed some "fingers" of Brie cheese, and, as a treat for the visitors, called for a second dessert, a pot of red-currant jam, a liberality which seemed to surprise Colomban. Pépé, who so far had been very good, behaved rather badly at the sight of the jam; whilst Jean, his attention attracted by the conversation about his cousin Geneviève's marriage, began to take stock of the girl, whom he thought too puny and too pale, comparing her in his own mind to a little white rabbit with black ears and pink eyes.

"Well, we've chatted enough, and must make room for the others," said the draper, giving the signal to rise from table. "Just because we've had a treat there is no reason why we should want too much of it."

Madame Baudu, the other shopman, and the young lady then came and took their places at table. Denise, again left to herself, sat down near the door waiting until her uncle should be able to take her to Vinçard's. Pépé was playing at her feet, whilst Jean had resumed his post of observation on the threshold. And Denise sat there for nearly an hour, taking interest in what went on around her. Now and again a few customers came in; a lady, then two others appeared, the shop meanwhile retaining its musty odour and its half light, in which old-fashioned commerce, simple and good natured, seemed to weep at finding itself so deserted. What most interested Denise, however, was The Ladies' Paradise opposite, whose windows she could see through the open doorway. The sky remained cloudy, a sort of humid mildness warmed the air, notwithstanding the season; and in the clear light, permeated, as it were, by a hazy diffusion of sunshine, the great shop acquired abundant life and activity.

To Denise it seemed as if she were watching a machine working at full pressure, setting even the window-shows in motion. They were no longer the cold windows she had seen in the early morning; they seemed to have been warmed and to vibrate with all the activity within. There were folks before them, groups of women pushing and squeezing against the sheets of glass, a perfect crowd excited with covetousness. And in this passionate atmosphere the stuffs themselves seemed endowed with life; the laces quivered, drooped, and concealed the depths of the shop with a disturbing air of mystery; even the thick square-cut lengths of cloth breathed, exhaling a tempting odour, while the tailor-made coats seemed to draw themselves up more erectly on the dummies, which acquired souls, and the velvet mantle expanded, supple and warm, as if falling from real shoulders, over a heaving bosom and quivering hips. But the factory-like glow which pervaded the house came above all from the sales, the crush at the counters, which could be divined behind the walls. There was the continual roaring of a machine at work, an engulfing of customers close-pressed against the counters, bewildered amidst the piles of goods, and finally hurled towards the pay-desks. And all went on in an orderly manner, with mechanical regularity, force and logic carrying quite a nation of women through the gearing of this commercial machine.

Denise had felt tempted ever since early morning. She was bewildered and attracted by this shop, to her so vast, which she saw more people enter in an hour than she had seen enter Cornaille's in six months; and with her desire to enter it was mingled a vague sense of danger which rendered her seduction complete. At the same time her uncle's shop made her feel ill at ease; she felt unreasonable disdain, instinctive repugnance for this cold, icy place, the home of old-fashioned trading. All her sensations—her anxious entry, her relatives' cold reception, the dull lunch partaken of in a prison-like atmosphere, her spell of waiting amidst the sleepy solitude of this old establishment doomed to speedy decay—all these became concentrated in mute protest, in a passionate longing for life and light. And despite her good heart, her eyes ceaselessly turned to The Ladies' Paradise, as if, saleswoman as she was, she felt the need of warming herself in the glow of that immense business.

"Plenty of customers over there at all events!" was the remark which at last escaped her.

But she promptly regretted these words on seeing the Baudus near her. Madame Baudu, who had finished her lunch, was standing there, quite white, with her pale eyes fixed on the monster; and resigned though she tried to be, she could never catch sight of that place across the road, without mute despair filling her eyes with tears. As for Geneviève, she was anxiously watching Colomban, who, unaware that he was being observed, remained in ecstasy, looking at the young saleswomen in the mantle department of the Paradise, whose counter was visible through the first floor window. Baudu, for his part, though his anger was written on his face, merely remarked: "All is not gold that glitters. Patience!"

The members of the family evidently kept back the flood of rancour rising in their throats. A feeling of self-esteem prevented them from displaying their temper before these children, who had only that morning arrived. At last the draper made an effort, and tore himself away from the spectacle of The Paradise and its sales.

"Well!" he resumed, "we'll go and see Vinçard. Situations are soon snatched up and it might be too late to-morrow."

However, before starting, he ordered his junior salesman to go to the railway station to fetch Denise's box. On her side Madame

Baudu, to whom the girl had confided Pépé, decided to run over to see Madame Gras in order to arrange about the child. Jean on the other hand promised his sister not to stir from the shop.

"It's two minutes' walk," explained Baudu as he went down the Rue Gaillon with his niece: "Vinçard has a silk business, and still does a fair trade. Oh, of course he has his worries, like every one else, but he's an artful fellow, who makes both ends meet by his miserly ways. I fancy, though, he wants to retire, on account of his rheumatics."

Vinçard's shop was in the Rue Neuve-des-Petits-Champs, near the Passage Choiseul. It was clean and light, well fitted up in the modern style, but rather small, and contained but a poor stock. Baudu and Denise found Vinçard in consultation with two gentlemen.

"Never mind us," called out the draper; "we are in no hurry; we can wait." And discreetly returning to the door he whispered to Denise: "That thin fellow is second in the silk department at The Paradise, and the stout man is a silk manufacturer from Lyons."

Denise gathered that Vinçard was trying to sell his business to Robineau of The Paradise. With a frank air, and open face, he was giving his word of honour, with the facility of a man whom assurances never troubled. According to him, his business was a golden one; and albeit in the splendour of robust health he broke off to whine and complain of those infernal pains of his which prevented him from remaining in business and making his fortune. Robineau who seemed nervous and uneasy interrupted him impatiently. He knew what a crisis the trade was passing through, and named a silk warehouse which had already been ruined by the vicinity of The Paradise. Then Vinçard, inflamed, raised his voice.

"No wonder! The downfall of that big booby Vabre was a foregone conclusion. His wife spent everything he earned. Besides, we are more than five hundred yards away, whilst Vabre was almost next door to The Paradise."

Gaujean, the silk manufacturer, then chimed in, and their voices fell again. He accused the big establishments of ruining French manufactures; three or four laid down the law, reigning like masters over the market; and he gave it as his opinion that the only way to fight them was to favour the small traders; above all, those who dealt in specialties, for to them the future belonged. For that reason he offered Robineau plenty of credit.

"See how you have been treated at The Paradise," said he. "No notice has been taken of your long service. You had the promise of the first-hand's place long ago, when Bouthemont, an outsider without any claim at all, came in and got it at once."

Robineau was still smarting under this act of injustice. However, he hesitated to start business on his own account, explaining that the money came from his wife, who had inherited sixty thousand francs, and he was full of scruples regarding this money, saying that he would rather cut off his right hand than compromise it in a doubtful affair.

"No," said he, "I haven't yet made up my mind; give me time to think over it. We'll have another talk about it."

"As you like," replied Vinçard, concealing his disappointment under a smiling countenance. "My interest, you know, is not to sell; and I certainly shouldn't were it not for my rheumatics—"

Then stepping to the middle of the shop, he inquired: "What can I do for you, Monsieur Baudu?"

The draper, who had been slily listening, thereupon introduced Denise, telling Vinçard as much as he thought necessary of her story and adding that she had two years' country experience. "And as I heard you are wanting a good saleswoman—" he added.

But Vinçard, affecting extreme sorrow, cut him short: "How unfortunate!" said he. "I had, indeed, been looking for a saleswoman all this week; but I've just engaged one—not two hours ago."

A silence ensued. Denise seemed to be in consternation. Robineau, who was looking at her with interest, probably inspired with pity by her poverty-stricken appearance, ventured to remark: "I know they're wanting a young person at our place, in the mantle department."

At this Baudu could not restrain a fervent outburst: "At your place indeed! Never!"

Then he stopped short in embarrassment. Denise had turned very red; she would never dare to enter that great shop, and yet the idea of belonging to it filled her with pride.

"Why not?" asked Robineau, surprised. "It would be a good opening for the young lady. I advise her to go and see Madame Aurélie, the first-hand, to-morrow. The worst that can happen to her is to be refused."

The draper, to conceal his inward revolt, then began talking vaguely. He knew Madame Aurélie, or, at least, her husband, Lhomme, the cashier, a stout man, who had had his right arm crushed by an omnibus. Then suddenly turning to Denise, he added: "However, it's her business, it isn't mine. She can do as she likes."

And thereupon he went off, after wishing Gaujean and Robineau "good-day". Vinçard accompanied him as far as the door, reiterating his regrets. The girl meantime had remained in the middle of the shop, intimidated yet desirous of asking Robineau for further particulars. However she could not muster the courage to do so, but in her turn bowed, and simply said: "Thank you, sir."

On the way back, Baudu said nothing to his niece, but as if carried away by his reflections walked on very fast, forcing her to run in order to keep up with him. On reaching the Rue de la Michodière, he was about to enter his establishment when a neighbouring shopkeeper, standing at his door, called to him.

Denise stopped and waited.

"What is it, Père Bourras?" asked the draper.

Bourras was a tall old man, with a prophet's head, bearded and hairy, with piercing eyes shining from under bushy brows. He kept an umbrella and walking-stick shop, did repairs, and even carved handles, which had won for him an artistic celebrity in the neighbourhood. Denise glanced at the windows of his shop where the sticks and umbrellas were arranged in straight lines. But on raising her eyes she was astonished by the appearance of the house—it was an old hovel squeezed in between The Ladies' Paradise and a large Louis XIV mansion; you could hardly conceive how it had sprung up in the narrow slit where its two low dumpy storeys displayed themselves. Had it not been for the support of the buildings on either side it must have fallen; the slates of its roof were old and rotten, and its two-windowed front was cracked and covered with stains, running down in long rusty lines to the worm-eaten sign-board over the shop.

"You know he's written to my landlord, offering to buy the house?" said Bourras, looking steadily at the draper with his fiery eyes.

Baudu became paler still, and bent his shoulders. There was a silence, during which the two men remained face to face, looking very serious.

"We must be prepared for anything," murmured Baudu at last.

Thereupon Bourras flew into a passion, shaking his hair and flowing beard while he shouted: "Let him buy the house, he'll have to pay four times the value for it! But I swear that as long as I live he shan't touch a stone of it. My lease has twelve years to run yet. We shall see! we shall see!"

It was a declaration of war. Bourras was looking towards The Ladies' Paradise, which neither of them had named. For a moment Baudu

ÉMILE ZOLA

remained shaking his head in silence, and then crossed the street to his shop, his legs almost failing him as he repeated: "Ah! good Lord! ah! good Lord!"

Denise, who had listened, followed her uncle. Madame Baudu had just come back with Pépé, whom Madame Gras had agreed to receive at any time. Jean, however, had disappeared, and this made his sister anxious. When he returned with a flushed face, talking in an animated way of the boulevards, she looked at him with such a sad expression that he blushed with shame. Meantime their box had arrived, and it was arranged that they should sleep in the attic.

"Ah! By the way, how did you get on at Vinçard's?" inquired Madame Baudu.

The draper thereupon gave an account of his fruitless errand, adding that Denise had heard of a situation; and, pointing to The Ladies' Paradise with a scornful gesture, he exclaimed: "There—in there!"

The whole family felt hurt at the idea. The first dinner was at five o'clock. Denise and the two children sat down to it with Baudu, Geneviève, and Colomban. A single gas jet lighted and warmed the little dining-room which reeked with the smell of food. The meal passed off in silence, but at dessert Madame Baudu, who was restless, left the shop, and came and sat down behind Denise. And then the storm, kept back all day, broke out, one and all seeking to relieve their feelings by abusing the "monster".

"It's your business, you can do as you like," repeated Baudu. "We don't want to influence you. But if you only knew what sort of place it is—" And in broken sentences he commenced to relate the story of that Octave Mouret to whom The Paradise belonged. He had been wonderfully lucky! A fellow who had come up from the South of France with the smiling audacity of an adventurer, who had no sooner arrived in Paris than he had begun to distinguish himself by all sorts of disgraceful pranks, figuring most prominently in a matrimonial scandal, which was still the talk of the neighbourhood; and who, to crown all, had suddenly and mysteriously made the conquest of Madame Hédouin, who had brought him The Ladies' Paradise as a marriage portion.

"That poor Caroline!" interrupted Madame Baudu. "We were distantly related. If she had lived things would be different. She wouldn't have let them ruin us like this. And he's the man who killed her. Yes, with that very building! One morning, when she was visiting the works, she fell into a hole, and three days after she died. A fine, strong, healthy woman, who had never known what illness was! There's some of her blood in the foundations of that house."

So speaking she pointed to the establishment opposite with her pale and trembling hand. Denise, listening as to a fairy tale, slightly shuddered; the sense of fear which had mingled with the temptation she had felt since morning, was due, perhaps, to the presence of that woman's blood, which she fancied she could now detect in the red mortar of the basement.

"It seems as if it brought him good luck," added Madame Baudu, without mentioning Mouret by name.

But the draper, full of disdain for these old women's tales, shrugged his shoulders and resumed his story, explaining the situation commercially. The Ladies' Paradise had been founded in 1822 by two brothers, named Deleuze. On the death of the elder, his daughter, Caroline, had married the son of a linen manufacturer, Charles Hédouin; and, later on, becoming a widow, she had married Mouret. She thus brought him a half share in the business. Three months after the marriage, however, the second brother Deleuze died childless; so that when Caroline met her death, Mouret became sole heir, sole proprietor of The Ladies' Paradise. Yes, he had been wonderfully lucky!

"He's what they call a man of ideas, a dangerous busybody, who will overturn the whole neighbourhood if he's left to himself!" continued Baudu. "I fancy that Caroline, who was rather romantic also, must have been carried away by the gentleman's extravagant plans. In short, he persuaded her to buy the house on the left, then the one on the right; and he himself, on becoming his own master, bought two others; so that the establishment has kept on growing and growing to such a point that it now threatens to swallow us all up!"

He was addressing Denise, but was in reality speaking for himself, feeling a feverish longing to recapitulate this story which continually haunted him. At home he was always angry and full of bile, always violent, with fists ever clenched. Madame Baudu, ceasing to interfere, sat motionless on her chair; Geneviève and Colomban, with eyes cast down, were picking up and eating the crumbs off the table, just for the sake of something to do. It was so warm, so stuffy in that tiny room that Pépé had fallen asleep with his head on the table, and even Jean's eyes were closing.

"But wait a bit!" resumed Baudu, seized with a sudden fit of anger, "such jokers always go to smash! Mouret is hard-pushed just now; I know that for a fact. He's been forced to spend all his savings on his mania for extensions and advertisements. Moreover, in order to raise additional capital, he has induced most of his shop-people to invest all they possess with him. And so he hasn't a sou to help himself with now; and, unless a miracle be worked, and he manages to treble his sales, as he hopes to do, you'll see what a crash there'll be! Ah! I'm not ill-natured, but that day I'll illuminate my shop-front, I will, on my word of honour!"

And he went on in a revengeful voice; to hear him you would have thought that the fall of The Ladies' Paradise would restore the dignity and prestige of commerce. Had any one ever seen such doings? A draper's shop selling everything! Why not call it a bazaar at once? And the employees! a nice set they were too—a lot of puppies, who did their work like porters at a railway station, treating both goods and customers as if they were so many parcels; taking themselves off or getting the sack at a moment's notice. No affection, no morals, no taste! And all at once he appealed to Colomban as a witness; he, Colomban, brought up in the good old school, knew how long it took to learn all the cunning and trickery of the trade. The art was not to sell much, but to sell dear. And then too, Colomban could tell them how he had been treated, carefully looked after, his washing and mending done, nursed in illness, considered as one of the family—loved, in fact!

"Of course, of course," repeated Colomban, after each statement made by his governor.

"Ah, you're the last of the old stock, my dear fellow," Baudu ended by declaring. "After you're gone there'll be none left. You are my sole consolation, for if all that hurry and scurry is what they now call business I understand nothing of it and would rather clear out."

Geneviève, with her head on one side as if her thick hair were weighing down her pale brow, sat watching the smiling shopman; and in her glance there was a gleam of suspicion, a wish to see whether Colomban, stricken with remorse, would not blush at all this praise. But, like a fellow well acquainted with every trick of the old style of trade, he retained his sedateness, his good-natured air, with just a touch of cunning about his lips. However, Baudu still went on, louder than ever, accusing the people opposite—that pack of savages who murdered each other in their struggle for existence—of even destroying all family ties. And he mentioned his country neighbours, the Lhommes—mother, father, and son—all employed in the infernal shop, people who virtually had no home but were always out and about, leading a hotel, *table d'hôte* kind of existence, and never taking a meal at their own place excepting on Sundays. Certainly his dining-room wasn't over large or too well aired or lighted; but at least it spoke to him of his life, for he had lived there amidst the affection of his kith and kin. Whilst speaking, his eyes wandered about the room; and he shuddered at the unavowed idea that if those savages should succeed in ruining his trade they might some day turn him out of this hole where he was so comfortable with his wife and child. Notwithstanding the seeming assurance with which he predicted the utter downfall of his rivals, he was in reality terrified, feeling at heart that the neighbourhood was being gradually invaded and devoured.

"Well, I don't want to disgust you," he resumed, trying to calm himself; "if you think it to your interest to go there, I shall be the first to say, 'go.'"

"I am sure of that, uncle," murmured Denise in bewilderment, her desire to enter The Ladies' Paradise, growing keener and keener amidst all this display of passion.

Baudu had put his elbows on the table, and was wearying her with his fixed stare. "But look here," he resumed; "you who know the business, do you think it right that a simple draper's shop should sell everything? Formerly, when trade was trade, drapers sold nothing but drapery. But now they are doing their best to snap up every branch of trade and ruin their neighbours. The whole neighbourhood complains of it, every small tradesman is beginning to suffer terribly. This man Mouret is ruining them. For instance, Bédoré and his sister, who keep the hosiery shop in the Rue Gaillon, have already lost half their customers; Mademoiselle Tatin, who sells under-linen in the Passage Choiseul, has been obliged to lower her prices, to be able to sell at all. And the effects of this scourge, this pest, are felt as far as the Rue Neuve-des-Petits-Champs, where I hear that Messrs. Vanpouille Brothers, the furriers, cannot hold out much longer. Ah! Drapers selling fur goods—what a farce! another of Mouret's ideas!"

"And gloves," added Madame Baudu; "isn't it monstrous? He has even dared to add a glove department! Yesterday, when I passed down the Rue Neuve-Saint-Augustin, I saw Quinette, the glover, at his door, looking so downcast that I hadn't the heart to ask him how business was going."

"And umbrellas," resumed Baudu; "that's the climax! Bourras is convinced that Mouret simply wants to ruin him; for, in short, where's the rhyme between umbrellas and drapery? But Bourras is firm on his legs, and won't let himself be butchered! We shall see some fun one of these days."

Then Baudu went on to speak of other tradesmen, passing the whole neighbourhood in review. Now and again he let slip a confession. If Vinçard wanted to sell it was time for the rest to pack up, for Vinçard was like the rats who make haste to leave a house when it threatens ruin. Then, however, immediately afterwards, he contradicted himself, and talked of an alliance, an understanding between the small tradesmen to enable them to fight the colossus. For a moment, his hands shaking, and his mouth twitching nervously, he hesitated as to whether he should speak of himself. At last he made up his mind to do so.

"As for me," he said, "I can't complain as yet. Of course he has done me harm, the scoundrel! But up to the present he has only kept ladies' cloths, light stuffs for dresses and heavier goods for mantles. People still come to me for men's goods, velvets and velveteens for shooting suits, cloths for liveries, without speaking of flannels and *molletons*, of which I defy him to show so complete an assortment as my own. But he thinks he will annoy me by placing his cloth department right in front of my door. You've seen his display, haven't you? He always places his finest mantles there, surrounded by a framework of cloth in pieces—a cheapjack parade to tempt the hussies. Upon my word, I should be ashamed to use such means! The Old Elbeuf has been known for nearly a hundred years, and has no need of any such catchpenny devices at its door. As long as I live, it shall remain as I took it, with its four samples on each side, and nothing more!"

The whole family was becoming affected; and after a spell of silence Geneviève ventured to make a remark:

"Our customers know and like us, papa," said she. "We mustn't lose heart. Madame Desforges and Madame de Boves have been to-day, and I am expecting Madame Marty for some flannel."

"For my part," declared Colomban, "I took an order from Madame Bourdelais yesterday. 'Tis true she spoke of an English cheviot marked up opposite ten sous cheaper than ours, and the same stuff, it appears."

"Fancy," murmured Madame Baudu in her weak voice, "we knew that house when it was scarcely larger than a handkerchief! Yes, my dear Denise, when the Deleuzes started it, it had only one window in the Rue Neuve-Saint-Augustin; and such a tiny one, there was barely room for a couple of pieces of print and two or three pieces of calico.

There was no room to turn round in the shop, it was so small. At that time The Old Elbeuf, after sixty years' trading, was already such as you see it now. Ah! all has greatly changed, greatly changed!"

She shook her head; the drama of her whole life was expressed in those few words. Born in the old house, she loved each of its damp stones, living only for it and by it; and, formerly so proud of that house, the finest, the best patronised in the neighbourhood, she had had the daily grief of seeing the rival establishment gradually growing in importance, at first disdained, then equal to her own and finally towering above it, and threatening all. This was to her an ever-open sore; she was slowly dying from sheer grief at seeing The Old Elbeuf humiliated; if she still lived it was, as in the case of the shop itself, solely by the effect of impulsion; but she well realised that the death of the shop would be hers as well, and that she would pass away on the day when it should close.

Silence fell. Baudu began softly beating a tattoo with his fingers on the American cloth on the table. He experienced a sort of lassitude, almost a regret at having once more relieved his feelings in this way. The whole family shared his despondency, and with dreamy eyes chewed the cud of his bitter story. They never had had any luck. The children had been brought up and fortune had seemed at hand, when suddenly this competition had arisen and ruined all their hopes. And there was, also, that house at Rambouillet, that country house to which the draper had been dreaming of retiring for the last ten years—a bargain, he had thought when he acquired it, but it had proved a sorry old building, always in want of repairs, and he had let it to people who never paid any rent. His last profits were swallowed up by this place—the only folly he had been guilty of in his honest, upright career as a tradesman stubbornly attached to the old ways.

"Come, come!" he suddenly exclaimed, "we must make room for the others. That's enough of this useless talk!"

It was like an awakening. The gas was hissing in the lifeless, stifling air of the tiny room. They all jumped up, breaking the melancholy silence. Pépé, however, was sleeping so soundly that they decided to lay him on some bales of cloth. Jean had already returned to the street door yawning.

"In short," repeated Baudu to his niece, "you can do as you like. We have explained the matter to you, that's all. You know your own business best."

He gave her an urgent glance, waiting for a decisive answer. But Denise, whom these stories had inspired with a still greater longing to enter The Ladies' Paradise, instead of turning her from it, retained her quiet gentle demeanour beneath which lurked a genuine Norman obstinacy. And she simply replied: "We'll see, uncle."

Then she spoke of going to bed early with the children, for they were all three very tired. But it had only just struck six, so she decided to stay in the shop a little longer. Night had now come on, and she found the street quite dark, drenched by a fine close rain, which had been falling since sunset. It came on her as a surprise. A few minutes had sufficed to fill the roadway with puddles, a stream of dirty water was running along the gutters, the pavement was sticky with a thick black mud; and through the beating rain she saw nothing but a confused stream of umbrellas, pushing along and swelling in the gloom like great black wings. She started back at first, feeling very cold, oppressed at heart by the badly-lighted shop, now so extremely dismal. A moist breeze, the breath of that old quarter of Paris, came in from the street; it seemed as if the rain, streaming from the umbrellas, was running right up to the counters, as if the pavement with its mud and its puddles was coming into the shop, putting the finishing touch to the mouldiness of that ancient, cavernous ground-floor, white with saltpetre. It was quite a vision of old Paris in the wet, and it made her shiver with distressful astonishment at finding the great city so cold and so ugly.

But across the road The Ladies' Paradise glowed with its deep, serried lines of gas jets. She moved nearer, again attracted and, as it were, warmed by that ardent blaze. The machine was still roaring, active as ever, letting its steam escape with a last roar, whilst the salesmen folded up the stuffs, and the cashiers counted the receipts. Seen through the hazy windows, the lights swarmed vaguely, revealing a confused factory-like interior. Behind the curtain of falling rain, the vision, blurred and distant, assumed the appearance of a giant furnace-house, where the shadows of firemen passed black against the red glare of the furnaces. The displays in the windows likewise became indistinct: you could only distinguish the snowy lace, its whiteness heightened by the ground glass globes of a row of gas jets, and against this chapel-like background the ready-made goods stood out vigorously, the velvet mantle trimmed with silver fox setting amidst them all the curved silhouette of a headless woman who seemed to be running through the rain to some entertainment in the unknown shades of nocturnal Paris.

Denise, yielding to the fascination, had gone to the door, heedless of the raindrops dripping upon her. At this hour, The Ladies' Paradise, with its furnace-like brilliancy, completed its conquest of her. In the great metropolis, black and silent beneath the rain—in this Paris, to which she was a stranger, it shone out like a lighthouse, and seemed to be of itself the life and light of the city. She dreamed of her future there, working hard to bring up the children, with other things besides—she hardly knew what—far-off things however, the desire and fear of which made her tremble. The idea of that woman who had met her death amidst the foundations came back to her; and she felt afraid, fancying that the lights were tinged with blood; but the whiteness of the lace quieted her, a hope, quite a certainty of happiness, sprang up in her heart, whilst the fine rain, blowing on her, cooled her hands, and calmed the feverishness within her, born of her journey.

"It's Bourras," all at once said a voice behind her.

She leant forward, and perceived the umbrella-maker, motionless before the window containing the ingenious roof-like construction of umbrellas and walking-sticks which she had noticed in the morning. The old man had slipped up there in the dark, to feast his eyes on that triumphant show; and so great was his grief that he was unconscious of the rain beating down on his bare head, and streaming off his long white hair.

"How stupid he is, he'll make himself ill," resumed the voice.

Then, turning round, Denise again found the Baudus behind her. Though they thought Bourras so stupid, they also, despite themselves, ever and ever returned to the contemplation of that spectacle which rent their hearts. It was, so to say, a rageful desire to suffer. Geneviève, very pale, had noticed that Colomban was watching the shadows of the saleswomen pass to and fro on the first floor opposite; and, whilst Baudu almost choked with suppressed rancour, Madame Baudu began silently weeping.

"You'll go and see, to-morrow, won't you, Denise?" asked the draper, tormented with uncertainty, but feeling that his niece was conquered like the rest.

She hesitated, then gently replied: "Yes, uncle, unless it pains you too much."

ÉMILE ZOLA

# II

The next morning, at half-past seven, Denise was outside The Ladies' Paradise, wishing to call there before taking Jean to his new place, which was a long way off, at the top of the Faubourg du Temple. But, accustomed as she was to early hours, she had come down too soon; the employees were barely arriving and, afraid of looking ridiculous, overcome by timidity, she remained for a moment walking up and down the Place Gaillon.

The cold wind that blew had already dried the pavement. From all the surrounding streets, illumined by a pale early light, falling from an ashen sky, shopmen were hurriedly approaching with their coat-collars turned up, and their hands in their pockets, taken unawares by this first chill of winter. Most of them hurried along alone, and vanished into the warehouse, without addressing a word or look to their colleagues marching along around them. Others however came up in twos and threes, talking fast, and monopolising the whole of the pavement; and all, with a similar gesture, flung away their cigarettes or cigars before crossing the threshold.

Denise noticed that several of the gentlemen took stock of her in passing. This increased her timidity; and she no longer had courage to follow them, but resolved to wait till they had entered, blushing at the mere idea of being elbowed at the door by all these men. However the stream of salesmen still flowed on, and in order to escape their looks, she took a walk round the Place. When she came back again, she found a tall young man, pale and awkward, who appeared to be waiting like herself.

"I beg your pardon, mademoiselle," he finished by stammering, "but perhaps you belong to the establishment?"

She was so troubled at hearing a stranger address her that she did not at first reply.

"The fact is," he continued, getting more confused than ever, "I thought of applying to see if I could get an engagement, and you might have given me a little information."

He was as timid as she was, and had probably risked speaking to her because he divined that she was trembling like himself.

"I would with pleasure, sir," she at last replied. "But I'm no better off than you are; I'm just going to apply myself."

"Ah, very good," said he, quite out of countenance.

Thereupon they both blushed deeply, and still all timidity remained for a moment face to face, affected by the striking similarity of their positions yet not daring to openly express a desire for each other's success. Then, as nothing further fell from either and both became more and more uncomfortable, they parted awkwardly, and renewed their wait, one on either side at a distance of a few steps.

The shopmen continued to arrive, and Denise could now hear them joking as they passed, casting side glances towards her. Her confusion increased at finding herself thus on exhibition, and she had decided to take half an hour's walk in the neighbourhood, when the sight of a young man approaching rapidly by way of the Rue Port-Mahon, detained her for another moment. He was probably the manager of a department, thought she, for all the others raised their hats to him. Tall, with a clear skin and carefully trimmed beard, he had eyes the colour of old gold and of a velvety softness, which he fixed on her for a moment as he crossed the Place. He was already entering the shop with an air of indifference, while she remained motionless, quite upset by that glance of his, filled indeed with a singular emotion, in which there was more uneasiness than pleasure. Without doubt, fear was gaining on her, and, to give herself time to collect her courage, she began slowly walking down the Rue Gaillon, and then along the Rue Saint-Roch.

The person who had so disturbed her was more than the manager of a department, it was Octave Mouret in person. He had been making a night of it, and his tightly buttoned overcoat concealed a dress suit and white tie. In all haste he ran upstairs to his rooms, washed himself and changed his clothes, and when he at last seated himself at his table, in his private office on the first floor, he was at his ease and full of strength, with bright eyes and cool skin, as ready for work as if he had enjoyed ten hours' sleep. The spacious office, furnished in old oak and hung with green rep, had but one ornament, the portrait of that Madame Hédouin, who was still the talk of the whole neighbourhood. Since her death Octave ever thought of her with tender regret, grateful as he felt to her for the fortune she had bestowed on him with her hand. And before commencing to sign the drafts laid upon his blotting-pad he darted upon her portrait the contented smile of a happy man. Was it not always before her that he returned to work, after the escapades of his present single-blessedness?

There came a knock however, and before Mouret could answer, a young man entered, a tall, bony fellow, very gentlemanly and correct in his appearance, with thin lips, a sharp nose and smooth hair already showing signs of turning grey. Mouret raised his eyes, then whilst still signing the drafts, remarked:

"I hope you slept well, Bourdoncle?"

"Very well, thanks," replied the young man, walking about as if he were quite at home.

Bourdoncle, the son of a poor farmer near Limoges, had begun his career at The Ladies' Paradise at the same time as Mouret, when it only occupied the corner of the Place Gaillon. Very intelligent and very active, it then seemed as if he would easily supplant his comrade, who was much less steady, and far too fond of love-affairs; but he had neither the instinctive genius of the impassioned Southerner, nor his audacity, nor his winning grace. Besides, by a wise instinct, he had, from the first bowed before him, obedient without a struggle. When Mouret had advised his people to put their money into the business, Bourdoncle had been one of the first to do so, even investing in the establishment the proceeds of an unexpected legacy left him by an aunt; and little by little, after passing through all the various stages, such as salesman, second, and then first-hand in the silk department, he had become one of Octave's most cherished and influential lieutenants, one of the six intéressés[1] who assisted him to govern The Ladies' Paradise—forming something like a privy council under an absolute king. Each one watched over a department or province. Bourdoncle, for his part, exercised a general surveillance.

"And you," resumed he, familiarly, "have you slept Well?"

When Mouret replied that he had not been to bed, he shook his head, murmuring: "Bad habits."

"Why?" replied the other, gaily. "I'm not so tired as you are, my dear fellow. You are half asleep now, you lead too quiet a life. Take a little amusement, that'll wake you up a bit."

This was their constant friendly dispute. Bourdoncle who professed to hate all women, contented himself with encouraging the extravagance of the lady customers, feeling meantime the greatest disdain for the frivolity which led them to ruin themselves in stupid gewgaws. Mouret, on the contrary, affected to worship them, ever showed himself delighted

---

1. In the great Paris magasins de nouveautés such as the Louvre and Bon Marché there have been at various stages numerous intéressés, that is partners of a kind who whilst entitled to some share of the profits, exercise but a strictly limited control in the management of the establishment's affairs.—*Trans.*

and cajoling in their presence and was ever embarking in fresh love-affairs. This served, as it were, as an advertisement for his business; and you might have said that he enveloped all women in the same caress the better to bewilder them and keep them at his mercy.

"I saw Madame Desforges last night, she was looking delicious at that ball," said he, beginning to relate his evening experiences. But then, abruptly breaking off, he took up another bundle of drafts, which he began to sign whilst Bourdoncle continued to walk about, stepping towards the lofty plate-glass windows whence he glanced into the Rue Neuve-Saint-Augustin. Then, retracing his steps, he suddenly exclaimed: "You know they'll have their revenge."

"Who will?" asked Mouret, who had lost the thread of the conversation.

"Why, the women."

At this, Mouret became quite merry, displaying, beneath his adorative manner, his really brutal character. With a shrug of the shoulders he seemed to declare he would throw them all over, like so many empty sacks, as soon as they should have finished helping him to make his fortune. But Bourdoncle in his frigid way obstinately repeated: "They will have their revenge; there will be one who will some day avenge all the others. It's bound to be."

"No fear," cried Mouret, exaggerating his Southern accent. "That one isn't born yet, my boy. And if she comes, you know, why there—"

So saying he raised his penholder, brandishing it and pointing it in the air, as if he were bent on stabbing some invisible heart with a knife. Bourdoncle thereupon resumed his walk, bowing as usual before the superiority of the governor, whose genius, with all its lapses, disconcerted him. He, himself so clear-headed, logical and passionless, incapable of falling into the toils of a syren, had yet to learn the feminine character of success, all Paris yielding herself with a kiss to her boldest assailant.

A silence fell, broken only by the sound of Mouret's pen. Then, in reply to his brief questions, Bourdoncle gave him various information respecting of the great sale of winter novelties, which was to commence on the following Monday. This was an important affair, the house was risking its fortune in it; for the rumours of the neighbourhood had some foundation, Mouret was throwing himself into speculation like a poet, with such ostentation, such desire to attain the colossal, that everything seemed likely to give way under him. It was quite a new style of doing business, a seeming commercial phantasy which had formerly made Madame Hédouin anxious, and even now, notwithstanding certain successes, quite dismayed those who had capital in the business. They blamed the governor in secret for going too quick; accused him of having enlarged the establishment to a dangerous extent, before making sure of a sufficient increase of custom; above all, they trembled on seeing him put all the available cash into one venture, filling the departments with a pile of goods without leaving a copper in the reserve fund. Thus, for this winter sale, after the heavy sums recently paid to the builders, the whole capital was exhausted and it once more became a question of victory or death. Yet Mouret in the midst of all this excitement, preserved a triumphant gaiety, a certainty of gaining millions, like a man so worshipped by women, that there could be no question of betrayal. When Bourdoncle ventured to express certain fears with reference to the excessive development given to several departments of doubtful profit he gave vent to a laugh full of confidence, and exclaimed:

"Pooh, pooh! my dear fellow, the place is still too small!"

The other appeared dumbfounded, seized with a fear which he no longer attempted to conceal. The house too small! an establishment which comprised nineteen departments, and numbered four hundred and three employees!

"Of course," resumed Mouret, "we shall be obliged to enlarge our premises again before another eighteen months are over. I'm seriously thinking about the matter. Last night Madame Desforges promised to introduce me to some one who may be useful. In short, we'll talk it over when the idea is ripe."

Then having finished signing his drafts, he rose, and tapped his lieutenant on the shoulder in a friendly manner, but the latter could not get over his astonishment. The fright displayed by the prudent people around him amused Mouret. In one of those fits of brusque frankness with which he sometimes overwhelmed his familiars, he declared that he was at heart a greater Jew than all the Jews in the world; he took, said he, after his father, whom he resembled physically and morally, a fellow who knew the value of money; and, if his mother had given him that dash of nervous fantasy which he displayed, it was, perhaps, the principal element of his luck, for he felt that his ability to dare everything was an invincible force.

"Oh! You know very well that we'll stand by you to the last," Bourdoncle finished by saying.

Then, before going down into the shop to give their usual look round, they settled certain other details. They examined a specimen of a little book of account forms, which Mouret had just invented for the use of his employees. Having remarked that the old-fashioned goods, the dead stock, went off the more rapidly the higher the commission allowed to the employees, he had based on this observation quite a new system, that of interesting his people in the sale of all the goods, giving them a commission on even the smallest piece of stuff, the most trumpery article they sold. This innovation had caused quite a revolution in the drapery trade, creating between the salespeople a struggle for existence of which the masters reaped the benefits. To foment this struggle was indeed Mouret's favourite method, the principle which he constantly applied. He excited his employees' passions, pitted one against the other, allowed the stronger to swallow up the weaker ones, and for his own part battened on this struggle of conflicting interests. The sample account book was duly approved of; at the top of each leaf on both counterfoil and bill form, appeared particulars of the department and the salesman's number; then also in duplicate came columns for the measurement, the description of the goods sold, and their price. The salesman simply signed the bill form before handing it to the cashier; and in this way an easy account was kept: it was only necessary to compare the bill-forms delivered by the cashier's department to the clearing-house with the salesmen's counterfoils. Every week the latter would receive their commission, without any possibility of error.

"We shan't be robbed so much," remarked Bourdoncle, with satisfaction. "This was a very good idea of yours."

"And I thought of something else last night," explained Mouret. "Yes, my dear fellow, at supper. I have an idea of giving the clearing-house clerks a little bonus for every error they detect while checking the bills. You understand, eh? Like this we shall be sure that they won't pass any, for rather than do that they'll be inventing mistakes!"

He began to laugh, whilst the other looked at him admiringly. This new application of the struggle-for-existence theory delighted Mouret; he had a real genius for administrative functions, and dreamed of so organizing the establishment as to trade upon the selfish instincts of his employees, for the greater satisfaction of his own appetites. He often said that to make people do their best, and even to keep them fairly honest, it was first of all necessary to excite their selfish desires.

"Well, let's go downstairs," he resumed. "We must look after this sale. The silk arrived yesterday, I believe, and Bouthemont must be getting it in now."

ÉMILE ZOLA

Bourdoncle followed him. The receiving office was in the basement on the side of the Rue Neuve-Saint-Augustin. There, on a level with the pavement, was a kind of glazed cage, into which the vans discharged the goods. They were weighed, and then shot down a rapid slide, whose oak and iron work was polished by the constant chaffing of bales and cases. Everything entered by this yawning trap; it was a continuous swallowing up, a niagara of goods, falling with a roar like that of a torrent. At the approach of big sale times especially, the slide brought down an endless stream of Lyons silks, English woollens, Flemish linens, Alsatian calicoes, and Rouen prints. The vans were sometimes obliged to wait their turn along the street; and as each bale rushed down to the basement there arose a sound as of a stone thrown into deep water.

On his way Mouret stopped for a moment before the slide, which was in full activity. Rows of cases were coming down of themselves, falling like rain from some upper stream. Then bales appeared, toppling over in their descent like rolling stones. Mouret looked on, without saying a word. But this wealth of goods rushing in to his establishment at the rate of thousands of francs each minute, made his clear eyes glisten. He had never before had such a clear, definite idea of the struggle he was engaged in. It was this falling mountain of goods which he must cast to the four corners of Paris. He did not open his mouth, however, but continued his inspection.

By the grey light which came in through the large vent-holes, a squad of men were receiving the goods, whilst others removed the lids of the cases and opened the bales in presence of the managers of different departments. A dockyard kind of bustle filled this basement, whose vaulted roofing was supported by wrought-iron pillars and whose bare walls were simply cemented.

"Have you got everything there, Bouthemont?" asked Mouret, approaching a broad-shouldered young fellow who was checking the contents of a case.

"Yes, everything seems all right," replied he, "but the counting will take me all the morning."

Then the manager of the silk department ran down an invoice he held, standing the while before a large counter on which one of his salesmen deposited, one by one, the pieces of silk which he took from an open case. Behind them ran other counters, also littered with goods which a small army of shopmen was examining. It was a general unpacking, a seeming confusion of stuffs, inspected, turned over, and marked, amidst a continuous buzz of voices.

Bouthemont who was becoming a celebrity in the trade, had the round, jovial face of a right good fellow, with a coal-black beard, and fine hazel eyes. Born at Montpellier, noisy, and over fond of pleasure, he was not of much good for the sales, but in buying he had not his equal. Sent to Paris by his father, who kept a draper's shop in his native town, he had absolutely refused to return home when the old fellow, thinking that he ought to know enough to succeed him in his business, had summoned him to do so; and from that moment a rivalry had sprung up between father and son, the former, absorbed in his little country business and shocked to see a simple shopman earning three times as much as he did himself, and the latter joking at the old man's humdrum routine, chinking his money, and throwing the whole house into confusion at every flying visit he paid. Like the other managers, Bouthemont drew, besides his three thousand francs regular pay, a commission on the sales. Montpellier, surprised and respectful, whispered that young Bouthemont had made fifteen thousand francs the year before, and that that was only a beginning—people prophesied to the exasperated father that this figure would certainly increase.

Meantime Bourdoncle had taken up one of the pieces of silk, and was examining the texture with the eye of a connoisseur. It was a faille with a blue and silver selvage, the famous Paris Delight, with which Mouret hoped to strike a decisive blow.

"It is really very good," observed Bourdoncle.

"And the effect it produces is better than its real quality," said Bouthemont. "Dumonteil is the only one capable of manufacturing such stuff. Last journey when I fell out with Gaujean, the latter was willing to set a hundred looms to work on this pattern, but he asked five sous a yard more."

Nearly every month Bouthemont went to Lyons, staying there days together, living at the best hôtels, with orders to treat the manufacturers with open purse. He enjoyed, moreover, a perfect liberty, and bought what he liked, provided that he increased the yearly business of his department in a certain proportion, settled beforehand; and it was on this proportion that his commission was based. In short, his position at The Ladies' Paradise, like that of all the managers, was that of a special tradesman, in a grouping of various businesses, a sort of vast trading city.

"So," resumed he, "it's decided we mark it at five francs twelve sous? It's barely the cost price, you know."

"Yes, yes, five francs twelve sous," said Mouret, quickly; "and if I were alone, I'd sell it at a loss."

The manager laughed heartily. "Oh! I don't mind, its cheapness will treble the sales and my only interest is to secure heavy receipts—"

But Bourdoncle remained grave, biting his lips. For his part he drew his commission on the total profits, and it was not to his advantage that the prices should be lowered. As it happened, a part of his duties was to exercise a control over the prices fixed upon in order to prevent Bouthemont from selling at too small a profit for the sole purpose of increasing the sales. Moreover, all his former anxiety reappeared in the presence of these advertising combinations which he did not understand, and he ventured to display his repugnance by remarking:

"If we sell it at five francs twelve sous, it will be like selling it at a loss, as we must allow for our expenses, which are considerable. It would fetch seven francs anywhere."

At this Mouret got angry. Striking the silk with his open hand he exclaimed excitedly: "I know that, that's why I want to give it to our customers. Really, my dear fellow, you'll never understand women's ways. Don't you see that they'll fight together over this silk?"

"No doubt," interrupted the other, obstinately, "and the more they buy, the more we shall lose."

"We shall lose a few sous on the stuff, very likely. But what can that matter, if in return we attract all the women here, and keep them at our mercy, fascinated, maddened by the sight of our goods, emptying their purses without thinking? The principal thing, my dear fellow, is to inflame them, and for that purpose you must have an article which will flatter them and cause a sensation. Afterwards, you can sell the other articles as dear as they are sold anywhere else, they'll still think yours the cheapest. For instance, our Golden Grain, that taffetas at seven francs and a half, sold everywhere at the same price, will go down as an extraordinary bargain, and suffice to make up for the loss on the Paris Delight. You'll see, you'll see!"

He was becoming quite eloquent. "Don't you understand?" he resumed, "In a week's time from to-day I want the Paris Delight to effect a revolution in the market. It's our master-stroke, which will save us and send our name everything. Nothing else will be talked of; that blue and silver selvage will be known from one to the other end of

France. And you'll hear the furious complaints of our competitors. The small traders will lose another wing by it. Yes, we shall have done for all those slop-sellers who are dying of rheumatism in their cellars!"

The shopmen checking the goods round-about were listening and smiling. Mouret liked to talk in this way without contradiction. Bourdoncle yielded once more. However, the case of silk was now empty and two men were opening another.

"It's the manufacturers who are vexed," now said Bouthemont. "At Lyons they are all furious with you, they pretend that your cheap trading is ruining them. You are aware that Gaujean has positively declared war against me. Yes, he has sworn to give long credits to the little houses rather than accept my prices."

Mouret shrugged his shoulders. "If Gaujean doesn't behave sensibly," he replied, "Gaujean will be floored. What do they all complain of? We pay ready money and we take all they can make; it's strange if they can't work cheaper at that rate. Besides, the public gets the benefit, and that's everything."

The shopman now began emptying the second case, whilst Bouthemont checked the pieces by the invoice. Another employee at the end of the counter then marked them in plain figures, and the checking finished, the invoice, signed by the manager, had to be sent to the chief cashier's office. For another minute Mouret continued looking at the work, at all the activity around this unpacking of goods which threatened to drown the basement; then, never adding a word but with the air of a captain satisfied with his men, he went off, again followed by Bourdoncle.

They slowly crossed the basement floor. The air-holes placed at intervals admitted a pale light; while in the dark corners, and along the narrow corridors, gas was constantly burning. In these corridors were the reserves, large vaults closed with iron railings, containing the surplus goods of each department. As he passed along Mouret glanced at the heating apparatus which was to be lighted on the following Monday for the first time, and at the firemen guarding a giant gas-meter enclosed in an iron cage. The kitchen and dining-rooms, old cellars turned into habitable apartments, were on the left near the corner of the Place Gaillon. At last, right at the other end of the basement, he arrived at the delivery office. Here, all the purchases which customers did not take away with them, were sent down, sorted on tables, and placed in compartments each of which represented a particular district of Paris; then by a large staircase opening just opposite The Old Elbeuf, they were sent up to the vans standing alongside the pavement. In the mechanical working of The Ladies' Paradise, this staircase in the Rue de la Michodière was ever disgorging the goods devoured by the slide in the Rue Neuve-Saint-Augustin, after they had passed through the mill of the counters up above.

"Campion," said Mouret to the delivery manager, a retired sergeant with a thin face, "why weren't six pairs of sheets, bought by a lady yesterday about two o'clock, delivered in the evening?"

"Where does the lady live?" asked the employee.

"In the Rue de Rivoli, at the corner of the Rue d'Alger—Madame Desforges."

At this early hour the sorting tables were yet bare and the compartments only contained a few parcels left over night. Whilst Campion was searching amongst these packets, after consulting a list, Bourdoncle looked at Mouret, reflecting that this wonderful fellow knew everything, thought of everything, even when he was supposed to be amusing himself. At last Campion discovered the error; the cashiers' department had given a wrong number, and the parcel had come back.

"What is the number of the pay-desk that debited the order?" asked Mouret: "No. 10, you say?" And turning towards his lieutenant, he added: "No. 10; that's Albert, isn't it? We'll just say two words to him."

However, before starting on a tour round the shops, he wanted to go up to the postal order department, which occupied several rooms on the second floor. It was there that all the provincial and foreign orders arrived; and he went up every morning to see the correspondence. For two years this correspondence had been increasing daily. At first occupying only a dozen clerks, it now required more than thirty. Some opened the letters and others read them, seated on either side of the same table; others again classified them, giving each one a running number, which was repeated on a pigeon-hole. Then when the letters had been distributed to the different departments and the latter had delivered the articles ordered, these articles were placed in the pigeon-holes as they arrived, in accordance with running numbers. Nothing then remained but to check and pack them, which was done in a neighbouring room by a squad of workmen who were nailing and tying up from morning to night.

Mouret put his usual question: "How many letters this morning, Levasseur?"

"Five hundred and thirty-four, sir," replied the chief clerk. "After the new sale has begun on Monday, I'm afraid we sha'n't have enough hands. Yesterday we were driven very hard."

Bourdoncle expressed his satisfaction by a nod of the head. He had not reckoned on five hundred and thirty-four letters arriving on a Tuesday. Round the table, the clerks continued opening and reading the letters, the paper rustling all the time, whilst before the pigeon-holes the various articles ordered began to arrive. This was one of the most complicated and important departments of the establishment, and the rush was continual, for, strictly speaking, all the orders received in the morning ought to be sent off the same evening.

"You shall have whatever more hands you want," replied Mouret, who had seen at a glance that the work of the department was well done. "When there's work," he added, "we never refuse the men."

Up above, under the roof, were the bedrooms occupied by the saleswomen. However, Mouret went downstairs again and entered the chief cash office, which was near his own. It was a room with a glazed partition in which was a metal-work wicket, and it contained an enormous safe, fixed in the wall. Two cashiers here centralised the receipts which Lhomme, the chief cashier of the sales' service, brought in every evening; and with these receipts they discharged the current expenses, paid the manufacturers, the staff, all the people indeed who lived by the house. Their office communicated with another, full of green cardboard boxes, where some ten clerks checked the innumerable invoices. Then came yet a third office, the clearing-house, so to say, where six young men bending over black desks, with quite a collection of registers behind them, made up the commission accounts of the salesmen, by checking the debit notes. This department but recently organized did not as yet work particularly well.

Mouret and Bourdoncle crossed the cashier's office and the invoice room and when they passed into the third office the young men there, who were laughing and joking together, started with surprise. Mouret, without reprimanding them, thereupon explained his scheme of giving them a little bonus for each error they might detect in the debit notes; and when he went out the clerks, quite cured of all inclination for idle laughter, set to work in earnest, hunting for errors.

On reaching the ground-floor, occupied by the shops, Mouret went straight to pay-desk No. 10, where Albert Lhomme was polishing his nails, pending the arrival of customers. People currently spoke of "the

ÉMILE ZOLA

Lhomme dynasty," since Madame Aurélie, first-hand in the mantle department, after helping her husband to secure the post of chief cashier, had further managed to get a pay desk for her son, a tall, pale, vicious young man who had been unable to remain in any situation, and had caused her an immense deal of anxiety. On reaching his desk, Mouret, who never cared to render himself unpopular by performing police duty, and from policy and taste preferred to play the part of a benign Providence, retired into the back ground, after gently nudging Bourdoncle with his elbow. It was Bourdoncle, the infallible and impeccable, whom he generally charged with the duty of reprimanding.

"Monsieur Albert," said Bourdoncle, severely, "you have again taken an address wrong; the parcel has come back. It is unbearable!"

The cashier, thinking it advisable to defend himself, called as a witness the assistant who had tied up the packet. This assistant, named Joseph, also belonged to the Lhomme dynasty, for he was Albert's foster brother, and likewise owed his place to Madame Aurélie's influence. Albert sought to make him say that the mistake had been made by the customer herself, but all Joseph could do was to stutter and twist the shaggy beard that ornamented his scarred face, struggling the while between his conscience and his gratitude to his protectors.

"Let Joseph alone," Bourdoncle exclaimed at last, "and don't say any more. It's a lucky thing for you that we are mindful of your mother's good services!"

However, at this moment Lhomme senior came running up. From his office near the door he could see his son's pay-desk, which was in the glove department, and doubtless the colloquy had alarmed him. Quite white-haired already, deadened by his sedentary life, he had a flabby, colourless face, blanched and worn, as it were, by the reflection of the money he was continually handling. The circumstance that he had lost an arm did not at all incommode him in this work, and indeed people would go to his office out of curiosity to see him verify the receipts, so rapidly did the notes and coins slip through his left hand, the only one remaining to him. The son of a tax-collector at Chablis, he had come to Paris as clerk to a merchant of the Port-aux-Vins. Then, whilst lodging in the Rue Cuvier, he had married the daughter of his doorkeeper, a petty Alsatian tailor, and from that day onward he had bowed submissively before his wife, whose commercial ability filled him with respect. She now earned more than twelve thousand francs a year in the mantle department, whilst he only drew a fixed salary of five thousand francs. And the deference he felt for this wife who brought such large sums into the household was extended to their son, whom he also owed to her.

"What's the matter?" he murmured; "is Albert in fault?"

Then, according to his custom, Mouret reappeared on the scene, to play the part of an indulgent prince. When Bourdoncle had made himself feared, he looked after his own popularity.

"Oh! nothing of consequence!" he answered. "My dear Lhomme, your son Albert is a careless fellow, who should take an example from you." Then, changing the subject, showing himself more amiable than ever, he continued: "And by the way, how about that concert the other day—did you get a good seat?"

A blush spread over the white cheeks of the old cashier. Music was his only vice, a secret vice which he indulged in solitarily, frequenting theatres, concerts and recitals. Moreover, despite the loss of his arm, he played on the French horn, thanks to an ingenious system of claws; and as Madame Lhomme detested noise, before playing his instrument of an evening he would wrap it in cloth, and then draw from it all sorts of weird muffled sounds which delighted him to the point of ecstasy. In the forced irregularity of their domestic life he had made himself an oasis of his passion for music—that, his cash receipts and his admiration for his wife, summed up his whole existence.

"A very good seat," he replied with sparkling eyes. "You are really too kind, sir."

Mouret, who took a personal pleasure in satisfying other people's passions, sometimes gave Lhomme the tickets forced upon him by lady patronesses and he put the finishing touch to the old man's delight by remarking: "Ah, Beethoven! ah, Mozart! What music!" Then, without waiting for a reply, he went off, rejoining Bourdoncle, who had already started on his tour of inspection through the departments.

In the central hall—an inner courtyard with a glass roof—was the silk department. At first Mouret and his companion turned into the Rue-Saint-Augustin gallery occupied by the linen department, from one end to the other. Nothing unusual striking them, they passed on slowly through the crowd of respectful assistants. Next they turned into the cotton and hosiery departments, where the same good order reigned. But in the department devoted to woollens, occupying the gallery which ran towards the Rue de la Michodière, Bourdoncle resumed the part of executioner, on observing a young man seated on the counter,

ÉMILE ZOLA

looking quite knocked up by a sleepless night; and this young man, a certain Liénard, son of a rich Angers draper, bowed his head beneath the reprimand, for in the idle, careless life of pleasure which he led his one great fear was that he might be recalled from Paris by his father. And now reprimands began to shower down on all sides like hail, and quite a storm burst in the gallery of the Rue de la Michodière. In the drapery department a salesman, a fresh hand, who slept in the house, had come in after eleven o'clock and in the haberdashery department, the second counterman had allowed himself to be caught smoking a cigarette downstairs. But the tempest attained its greatest violence in the glove department, where it fell upon one of the few Parisians in the house, handsome Mignot, as he was called, the illegitimate son of a music-mistress. His crime was that of causing a scandal in the dining-room by complaining of the food. As there were three tables, one at half-past nine, one at half-past ten, and another at half-past eleven, he wished to explain that, belonging as he did to the third table, he always had the leavings, the worst of everything for his share.

"What! the food not good?" asked Mouret, with a naive air, opening his mouth at last.

He only allowed the chief cook, a terrible Auvergnat, a franc and a half a head per day, out of which small sum this man still contrived to make a good profit; and indeed the food was really execrable. But Bourdoncle shrugged his shoulders: a cook who had four hundred luncheons and four hundred dinners to serve, even in three series, had no time to waste on the refinements of his art.

"Never mind," said the governor, good-naturedly, "I wish all our employees to have good and abundant food. I'll speak to the cook." And thus Mignot's complaint was shelved.

Then returning to their point of departure, standing near the door, amidst the umbrellas and neckties, Mouret and Bourdoncle received the report of one of the four inspectors, who were charged with the police service of the establishment. The inspector in question, old Jouve, a retired captain, decorated for his bravery at Constantine and still a fine-looking man with his big sensual nose and majestic baldness, drew their attention to a salesman, who, in reply to a simple remonstrance on his part, had called him "an old humbug," and the salesman was immediately discharged.

Meantime, the shop was still without customers, that is, except a few housewives of the neighbourhood who were passing through the almost deserted galleries. At the door the time-keeper had just closed his book, and was making out a separate list of the late arrivals. The salesmen on their side were taking possession of their departments, which had been swept and brushed by the assistants before their arrival. Each young man put away his hat and over-coat as he arrived, stifling a yawn, still half asleep as he did so. Some exchanged a few words, gazed about the shop and sought to pull themselves together for another day's work; while others leisurely removed the green baize with which they had covered the goods over night, after folding them up. Then the piles of stuffs appeared symmetrically arranged, and the whole shop looked clean and orderly, brilliant in the gay morning light pending the rush of business which would once more obstruct it, and, as it were, reduce its dimensions by the unpacking and display of linen, cloth, silk, and lace.

In the bright light of the central hall, two young men were talking in a low voice at the silk counter. One of them, short but well set and good looking, with a pinky skin, was endeavouring to blend the colours of some silks for an indoor show. His name was Hutin, his father kept a café at Yvetot, and after eighteen months' service he had managed to become one of the principal salesmen, thanks to a natural flexibility of character and a continual flow of caressing flattery, under which were concealed furious appetites which prompted him to grasp at everything and devour everybody just for the pleasure of the thing.

"Well, Favier, I should have struck him if I had been in your place, honour bright!" said he to his companion, a tall bilious fellow with a dry yellow skin, who had been born at Besançon of a family of weavers, and concealed under a cold graceless exterior a disquieting force of will.

"It does no good to strike people," he murmured, phlegmatically; "better wait."

They were both speaking of Robineau, the "second" in the department, who was looking after the shopmen during the manager's absence in the basement. Hutin was secretly undermining Robineau, whose place he coveted. To wound him and induce him to leave, he had already introduced Bouthemont to fill the post of manager which had been previously promised to Robineau. However, the latter stood firm, and it was now an hourly battle. Hutin dreamed of setting the whole department against him, of hounding him out by dint of ill-will and vexation. Still he went to work craftily, ever preserving his amiable air. And it was especially Favier whom he strove to excite against the "second"—Favier, who stood next to himself as salesman, and who

ÉMILE ZOLA

appeared willing to be led, though he had certain brusque fits of reserve by which one could divine that he was bent on some private campaign of his own.

"Hush! seventeen!" he all at once hastily remarked to his colleague, intending by this peculiar exclamation to warn him of the approach of Mouret and Bourdoncle. These two, still continuing their inspection, were now traversing the hall and stopped to ask Robineau for an explanation respecting a stock of velvets, the boxes of which were encumbering a table. And as Robineau replied that there wasn't enough room to store things away, Mouret exclaimed with a smile:

"Ah! I told you so, Bourdoncle, the place is already too small. We shall soon have to knock down the walls as far as the Rue de Choiseul. You'll see what a crush there'll be next Monday."

Then, respecting the coming sale, for which they were preparing at every counter, he asked further questions of Robineau and gave him various orders. For some minutes however, whilst still talking, he had been watching Hutin, who was slowly arranging his silks—placing blue, grey, and yellow side by side and then stepping back to judge of the harmony of the tints. And all at once Mouret interfered: "But why are you endeavouring to please the eye?" he asked. "Don't be afraid; blind the customers! This is the style. Look! red, green, yellow."

While speaking he had taken up some of the pieces of silk, throwing them together, crumpling them and producing an extremely violent effect of colour. Every one allowed the governor to be the best "dresser" in Paris albeit one of a revolutionary stamp, an initiator of the brutal and the colossal in the science of display. His fancy was a tumbling of stuffs, heaped pell-mell as if they had fallen by chance from the bursting boxes, and glowing with the most ardent contrasting colours, which heightened each other's intensity. The customers, said he, ought to feel their eyes aching by the time they left the shop. Hutin, who on the contrary belonged to the classic school whose guiding principles were symmetry and a melodious blending of shades, watched him lighting this conflagration of silk on the table, without venturing to say a word; but on his lips appeared the pout of an artist whose convictions were sorely hurt by such a debauch of colour.

"There!" exclaimed Mouret, when he had finished.

"Leave it as it is; you'll see if it doesn't fetch the women on Monday."

Just then, as he rejoined Bourdoncle and Robineau, there arrived a woman, who stopped short, breathless at sight of this show. It was Denise, who, after waiting for nearly an hour in the street, a prey to a violent attack of timidity, had at last decided to enter. But she was so beside herself with bashfulness that she mistook the clearest directions; and the shopmen, of whom in stammering accents she asked for Madame Aurélie, in vain directed her to the staircase conducting to the first floor; she thanked them, but turned to the left if they told her to turn to the right; so that for the last ten minutes she had been wandering about the ground-floor, going from department to department, amidst the ill-natured curiosity and boorish indifference of the salesmen. She longed to run away, but was at the same time retained by a wish to stop and admire. She felt herself lost, so little in this monstrous place, this machine which was still at rest, and trembled with fear lest she should be caught in the movement with which the walls already began to quiver. And in her mind the thought of The Old Elbeuf, so black and narrow, increased the immensity of this vast establishment, which seemed bathed in a golden light and similar to a city with its monuments, squares, and streets, in which it seemed impossible she should ever find her way.

However, she had previously not dared to venture into the silk hall whose high glass roof, luxurious counters, and cathedral-like aspect frightened her. Then when she did venture in, to escape the shopmen of the linen department, who were grinning at her, she stumbled right on Mouret's display; and, despite her bewilderment, the woman was aroused within her, her cheeks suddenly flushed, and she forgot everything in looking at the glow of this conflagration of silk.

"Hullo!" said Hutin in Favier's ear; "there's the drab we saw on the Place Gaillon."

Mouret, whilst affecting to listen to Bourdoncle and Robineau, was at heart flattered by the startled look of this poor girl, just as a marchioness might be by the brutal admiration of a passing drayman. But Denise had raised her eyes, and her confusion increased at the sight of this young man, whom she took for the manager of a department. She thought he was looking at her severely. Then not knowing how to get away, quite lost, she once more applied to the nearest shopman, who happened to be Favier.

"Madame Aurélie, if you please?"

However Favier, who was disagreeable, contented himself with replying sharply: "On the first floor."

Then, Denise, longing to escape the looks of all these men, thanked him, and was again turning her back to the stairs she ought to have ascended when Hutin, yielding naturally to his instinctive gallantry, stopped her with his most amiable salesman's smile albeit he had just spoken of her as a drab.

"No—this way, mademoiselle, if you please," said he.

And he even went with her a little way, as far indeed as the foot of the staircase on the left-hand side of the hall. There he bowed, and smiled at her, as he smiled at all women.

"When you get upstairs turn to the left," he added. "The mantle department will then be in front of you."

This caressing politeness affected Denise deeply. It was like a brotherly hand extended to her; she raised her eyes and looked at Hutin, and everything in him touched her—his handsome face, his smiling look which dissolved her fears, and his voice which seemed to her of a consoling softness. Her heart swelled with gratitude, and she gave him her friendship in the few disjointed words which her emotion allowed her to utter.

"Really, sir, you are too kind. Pray don't trouble to come any further. Thank you very much."

Hutin was already rejoining Favier, to whom he coarsely whispered: "What a bag of bones—eh?"

Upstairs the young girl suddenly found herself in the midst of the mantle department. It was a vast room, with high carved oak cupboards all round it and clear glass windows overlooking the Rue de la Michodière. Five or six women in silk dresses, looking very coquettish with their frizzy chignons and crinolines drawn back, were moving about and talking. One of them, tall and thin, with a long head, and a run-away-horse appearance, was leaning against a cupboard, as if already knocked up with fatigue.

"Madame Aurélie?" inquired Denise.

The saleswoman did not reply but looked at her, with an air of disdain for her shabby dress; then turning to one of her companions, a short girl with a sickly white skin and an innocent and disgusted expression of countenance, she asked: "Mademoiselle Vadon, do you know where Madame Aurélie is?"

The girl, who was arranging some mantles according to their sizes, did not even take the trouble to raise her head. "No, Mademoiselle Prunaire, I don't know at all," she replied in a mincing tone.

Silence fell. Denise stood still, and no one took any further notice of her. However, after waiting a moment, she ventured to put another question: "Do you think Madame Aurélie will be back soon?"

Thereupon, the second-hand, a thin, ugly woman, whom she had not noticed before, a widow with a projecting jaw-bone and coarse hair, cried out from a cupboard, board, where she was checking some tickets: "You'd better wait if you want to speak to Madame Aurélie herself." And, addressing another saleswoman, she added: "Isn't she downstairs?"

"No, Madame Frédéric, I don't think so," was the reply. "She said nothing before going, so she can't be far off."

Denise, thus meagrely informed, remained standing. There were several chairs for the customers; but as she had not been asked to sit down, she did not dare to take one although her perturbation well nigh deprived her legs of strength. All these young ladies had evidently guessed that she was an applicant for the vacancy, and were taking stock of her, ill-naturedly pulling her to pieces with the secret hostility of people at table who do not like to close up to make room for hungry outsiders. Then Denise's confusion increasing, she slowly crossed the room and looked out of the window into the street, for the purpose of keeping countenance. Over the way, The Old Elbeuf, with its rusty front and lifeless windows, appeared to her so ugly and so wretched, thus viewed from amidst the luxury and life of her present standpoint, that a sort of remorse filled her already swollen heart with grief.

"I say," whispered tall Mdlle. Prunaire to little Mdlle. Vadon, "have you seen her boots?"

"And her dress!" murmured the other.

With her eyes still turned towards the street, Denise divined that she was being devoured. But she was not angry; she did not think them handsome, neither the tall one with her carroty chignon falling over her horse-like neck, nor the little one with her curdled-milk complexion, which gave her flat and, as it were, boneless face a flabby appearance. Clara Prunaire, daughter of a clogmaker of the woods of Vivet had begun to misconduct herself at the time when she was employed as needlewoman at the Château de Mareuil. Later on she had come to Paris from a shop at Langres, and was avenging herself in the capital for all the kicks with which her father had regaled her when at home. On the other hand Marguerite Vadon, born at Grenoble, where her parents kept a linen shop, had been obliged to come to Paris, where she had entered The Ladies' Paradise, in order to conceal a misfortune due to her frailty. Since then, however, she had ever been a well-conducted girl, and intended to return to Grenoble to take charge of her parents' shop, and marry a cousin who was waiting for her.

ÉMILE ZOLA

"Ah! well," resumed Clara, in a low voice, "that girl won't be of much account here even if she does get in."

But they all at once stopped talking, for a woman of about forty-five was coming in. It was Madame Aurélie, very stout and tightly laced in her black silk dress, the body of which, strained over her massive shoulders and full bust, shone like a piece of armour. Under dark folds of hair, she had big fixed eyes, a severe mouth, and broad and rather drooping cheeks; and in the majesty of her position as manageress her face seemed to swell with pride like the puffy countenance of a Cæsar.

"Mademoiselle Vadon," said she, in an irritated voice, "you didn't return the pattern of that mantle to the workroom yesterday, it seems?"

"There was an alteration to be made, madame," replied the saleswoman, "so Madame Frédéric kept it."

The second-hand thereupon took the pattern out of a cupboard, and the explanation continued. Every one gave way to Madame Aurélie, when she thought it expedient to assert her authority. Very vain, even to the point of objecting to be called by her husband's name, Lhomme, which annoyed her, and of denying the humble position of her father to whom she always referred as a regularly established tailor, she only proved gracious towards those young ladies who showed themselves flexible and caressing and bowed down in admiration before her. Formerly, whilst trying to establish herself in a shop of her own, her temper had been soured by continual bad luck; the feeling that she was born to fortune and encountered nothing but a series of catastrophes had exasperated her; and now, even after her success at The Ladies' Paradise, where she earned twelve thousand francs a year, it seemed as if she still nourished a secret spite against every one. She was in particular very hard with beginners, even as life had shown itself hard for her at first.

"That will do!" said she, sharply; "You are not more reasonable than the others, Madame Frédéric. Let the alteration be made immediately."

During this explanation, Denise had ceased looking into the street. She had no doubt this was Madame Aurélie; but, frightened by her sharp voice, she remained standing, still waiting. The two saleswomen, delighted to have set their two superiors at variance, had returned to their work with an air of profound indifference. A few minutes elapsed, nobody being charitable enough to extricate the young girl from her uncomfortable position. At last, Madame Aurélie herself perceived her, and astonished to see her standing there motionless inquired what she wanted.

"Madame Aurélie, please."

"I am Madame Aurélie."

Denise's mouth was dry and parched, her hands were cold; she felt some such fear as when she was a child and trembled at the thought of being whipped. At last she stammered out her request, but was obliged to repeat it to make herself understood. Madame Aurélie gazed upon her with her large fixed eyes, not a line of her imperial countenance deigning to relax.

"How old are you?" she eventually inquired.

"Twenty, madame."

"What, twenty years old? you don't look sixteen!"

The saleswomen again raised their heads. Denise hastened to add: "Oh, I'm very strong!"

Madame Aurélie shrugged her broad shoulders and then coldly remarked: "Well! I don't mind entering your name. We enter the names of all who apply. Mademoiselle Prunaire, give me the book."

But the book could not be found; Jouve, the inspector, had probably got it. And just as tall Clara was about to fetch it, Mouret arrived, still followed by Bourdoncle. They had made the tour of the other departments on the first floor—they had passed through the lace, the shawls, the furs, the furniture and the under-linen, and were now winding up with the mantles. Madame Aurélie left Denise for a moment to speak to them about an order for some cloaks which she thought of giving to one of the large Paris houses. As a rule, she bought direct, and on her own responsibility; but, for important purchases, she preferred to consult the chiefs of the house. Bourdoncle then told her of her son Albert's latest act of carelessness, which seemed to fill her with despair. That boy would kill her; his father, although not a man of talent, was at least well-conducted, careful, and honest. All this dynasty of the Lhommes, of which she was the acknowledged head, very often caused her a great deal of trouble. However, Mouret, surprised to come upon Denise again, bent down to ask Madame Aurélie what that young person was doing there; and, when the first-hand replied that she was applying for a saleswoman's situation, Bourdoncle, with his disdain for women, seemed suffocated by such pretension.

"You don't mean it," he murmured; "it must be a joke, she's too ugly!"

"The fact is, there's nothing handsome about her," replied Mouret, not daring to defend her, although he was still moved by the rapture she had displayed downstairs before his arrangement of the silks.

However, the book having been brought, Madame Aurélie returned to Denise, who had certainly not made a favourable impression. She looked very clean in her thin black woollen dress; still the question of shabbiness was of no importance, as the house furnished a uniform, the regulation silk dress; but she appeared weak and puny, and had a melancholy face. Without insisting on handsome girls, the managers of the house liked their assistants to be of agreeable appearance. And beneath the gaze of all the men and women who were studying her, estimating her like farmers would a horse at a fair, Denise lost what little countenance had still remained to her.

"Your name?" asked Madame Aurélie, standing at the end of a counter, pen in hand, ready to write.

"Denise Baudu, madame."

"Your age?"

"Twenty years and four months." And risking a glance at Mouret, at this supposed manager, whom she met everywhere and whose presence troubled her so much, she repeated: "I don't look like it, but I am really very strong."

They smiled. Bourdoncle showed evident signs of impatience; her remark fell, moreover, amidst a most discouraging silence.

"What establishment have you been at, in Paris?" resumed Madame Aurélie.

"I've just arrived from Valognes, madame."

This was a fresh disaster. As a rule, The Ladies' Paradise only engaged as saleswomen such girls as had had a year's experience in one of the small houses in Paris. Denise thought all was lost; and, had it not been for the children, had she not been obliged to work for them, she would have brought this futile interrogatory to an end by leaving the place.

"Where were you at Valognes?" asked Madame Aurélie.

"At Cornaille's."

"I know him—good house," remarked Mouret.

It was very seldom that he interfered in the engagement of the employees, the manager of each department being responsible for his or her staff. But with his fine appreciation of women, he divined in this girl a hidden charm, a wealth of grace and tenderness of which she herself was ignorant. The good reputation of the establishment in which the candidate had started was of great importance, often deciding the question in his or her favour. Thus even Madame Aurélie continued in a kinder tone: "And why did you leave Cornaille's?"

"For family reasons," replied Denise, turning scarlet. "We have lost our parents, I have been obliged to follow my brothers. Here is a certificate."

It was excellent. Her hopes were reviving, when another question troubled her.

"Have you any other references in Paris? Where do you live?"

"At my uncle's," she murmured, hesitating to name him for she feared that they would never engage the niece of a competitor. "At my uncle Baudu's, opposite."

At this, Mouret interfered a second time. "What! are you Baudu's niece?" said he, "is it Baudu who sent you here?"

"Oh! no, sir!" answered Denise; and she could not help laughing as she spoke for the idea appeared to her so singular. That laugh was like a transfiguration; she became quite rosy, and the smile playing round her rather large mouth lighted up her whole face. Her grey eyes sparkled with a soft flame, her cheeks filled with delicious dimples, and even her light hair seemed to partake of the frank and courageous gaiety that pervaded her whole being.

"Why, she's really pretty," whispered Mouret to Bourdoncle.

The latter with a gesture of boredom refused to admit it. Clara on her side bit her lips, and Marguerite turned away; Madame Aurélie alone seemed won over, and encouraged Mouret with a nod when he resumed: "Your uncle was wrong not to bring you here; his recommendation sufficed. It is said he has a grudge against us. We are people of more liberal minds, and if he can't find employment for his niece in his house, why we will show him that she has only had to knock at our door to be received. Just tell him I still like him very much, and that if he has cause for complaint he must blame, not me, but the new circumstances of commerce. Tell him, too, that he will ruin himself if he insists on keeping to his ridiculous old-fashioned ways."

Denise turned quite white again. It was Mouret; no one had mentioned his name, but he revealed himself, and she guessed who he was, and understood why the sight of him had caused her such emotion in the street, in the silk department, and again here. This emotion, which she could not analyze, pressed more and more upon her heart like an unbearable weight. All the stories related by her uncle came back to her, increasing Mouret's importance in her eyes, surrounding him with a sort of halo in his capacity as the master of the terrible machine between whose wheels she had felt herself all the morning.

ÉMILE ZOLA

And, behind his handsome face, with its well-trimmed beard, and eyes the colour of old gold, she beheld the dead woman, that Madame Hédouin, whose blood had helped to cement the stones of the house. The shiver she had felt the previous night again came upon her; and she thought she was merely afraid of him.

However, Madame Aurélie had closed the book. She only wanted one saleswoman, and she already had ten applications. True, she was too anxious to please the governor to hesitate for a moment, still the application would follow its course, inspector Jouve would go and make inquiries, send in his report, and then she would come to a decision.

"Very good, mademoiselle," said she majestically, as though to preserve her authority; "we will write to you."

Denise stood there, unable to move for a moment, hardly knowing how to take her leave in the midst of all these people. At last she thanked Madame Aurélie, and on passing Mouret and Bourdoncle, she bowed. The gentlemen, however, were examining the pattern of a mantle with Madame Frédéric and took no further notice of her. Clara looked in a vexed way towards Marguerite, as if to predict that the new-comer would not have a very pleasant time of it in the establishment. Denise doubtless felt this indifference and rancour behind her, for she went downstairs with the same troubled feeling that had possessed her on going up, asking herself whether she ought to be sorry or glad at having come. Could she count on having the situation? She doubted it, amidst the uneasiness which had prevented her from clearly understanding what had been said. Of her various sensations, two remained and gradually effaced all others—the emotion, almost fear, with which Mouret had inspired her, and the pleasure she had derived from the amiability of Hutin, the only pleasure she had enjoyed the whole morning, a souvenir of charming sweetness which filled her with gratitude. When she crossed the shop on her way out she looked for the young man, happy in the idea of thanking him again with her eyes, and she was very sorry not to see him.

"Well, mademoiselle, have you succeeded?" inquired a timid voice, as she at last reached the pavement. She turned round and recognised the tall, awkward young fellow who had spoken to her in the morning. He also had just come out of The Ladies' Paradise, and seemed even more frightened than herself, still bewildered by the examination through which he had just passed.

"I really don't know as yet, sir," she replied.

"You're like me, then. What a way they have of looking at you and talking to you in there—eh? I'm applying for a place in the lace department. I was at Crevecœur's in the Rue du Mail."

They were once more standing face to face; and, not knowing how to take leave, they again began to blush. Then the young man, by way of saying something, timidly ventured to ask in his good-natured, awkward way: "What is your name, mademoiselle?"

"Denise Baudu."

"My name is Henri Deloche."

Then they smiled, and, yielding to a fraternal feeling born of the similarity of their positions, shook each other by the hand.

"Good luck!" said Deloche.

"Yes, good luck!" was Denise's reply.

# III

Every Saturday, between four and six, Madame Desforges offered a cup of tea and a few sweet biscuits to those friends who were kind enough to visit her. She occupied the third floor of a house at the corner of the Rue de Rivoli and the Rue d'Alger; and the windows of her two drawing-rooms overlooked the gardens of the Tuileries.

That Saturday, just as a footman was about to introduce him into the principal drawing-room, Mouret from the anteroom perceived, through an open doorway, Madame Desforges crossing the smaller salon. She stopped on seeing him, and he went in that way, bowing to her with a ceremonious air. But when the footman had closed the door, he quickly caught hold of the young woman's hand, and tenderly kissed it.

"Take care, I have company!" she remarked, in a low voice, glancing towards the door of the larger room. "I've just come to fetch this fan to show them," and so saying she playfully tapped him on the face with the tip of the fan she held. She was dark and inclined to stoutness, and had big jealous eyes.

However, he still held her hand and inquired: "Will he come?"

"Certainly," she replied: "I have his promise."

They both referred to Baron Hartmann, the director of the Crédit Immobilier. Madame Desforges, daughter of a Councillor of State, was the widow of a speculator, who had left her a fortune, underrated to the point of nothingness by some and greatly over-estimated by others. During her husband's lifetime she had already known Baron Hartmann, whose financial tips had proved very useful to them; and later on, after her husband's death, the connection had been kept up in a discreet fashion; for she never courted notoriety in any way, and was received everywhere in the upper-middle class to which she belonged. Even now too when she had other lovers—the passion of the banker, a sceptical, crafty man, having subsided into a mere paternal affection—she displayed such delicate reserve and tact, such adroit knowledge of the world that appearances were saved, and no one would have ventured to openly express any doubt of her conduct. Having met Mouret at a mutual friend's she had at first detested him; but had been carried away by the violent love which he professed for her, and since he had begun manœuvring to approach Baron Hartmann through her, she had gradually got to love him with real and profound tenderness, adoring him with all the violence of a woman of thirty-five, who only acknowledged the age of twenty-nine, and distressed at feeling him younger than herself, which made her tremble lest she should lose him.

"Does he know about it?" he resumed.

"No, you'll explain the affair to him yourself," was her reply.

Meantime she looked at him, reflecting that he couldn't know anything or he would not employ her in this way with the baron, whom he appeared to consider simply as an old friend of hers. However, Mouret still held her hand and called her his good Henriette, at which she felt her heart melting. Then silently she presented her lips, pressed them to his, and whispered: "Remember they're waiting for me. Come in behind me."

A murmur of voices, deadened by the heavy hangings, came from the principal drawing-room. Madame Desforges went in, leaving the folding doors open behind her, and handed the fan to one of the four ladies who were seated in the middle of the room.

"There it is," said she; "I didn't know exactly where it was. My maid would never have found it." And turning round she added in her cheerful way: "Come in, Monsieur Mouret, come through the little drawing-room; it will be less solemn."

Mouret bowed to the ladies, whom he knew. The drawing-room, with its Louis XVI furniture upholstered in flowered brocatel, its gilded bronzes and large green plants, had a pleasant, cozy, feminine aspect, albeit the ceiling was so lofty; and through the two windows could be seen the chestnut trees of the Tuileries Gardens, whose leaves were blowing about in the October wind.

"But this Chantilly isn't at all bad!" exclaimed Madam Bourdelais, who had taken the fan.

She was a short fair woman of thirty, with a delicate nose and sparkling eyes. A former school-fellow of Henriette's, married to a chief clerk at the Ministry of Finances, and belonging to an old middle-class family, she managed her household and three children with rare activity, good grace, and exquisite knowledge of practical life.

"And you paid twenty-five francs for it?" she resumed, examining each mesh of the lace. "At Luc, I think you said, to a country-woman? No, it isn't dear; still you had to get it mounted, hadn't you?"

"Of course," replied Madame Desforges. "The mounting cost me two hundred francs."

Madame Bourdelais began to laugh. And that was what Henriette called a bargain! Two hundred francs for a plain ivory mount, with a monogram! And that for a mere piece of Chantilly, over which she had perhaps saved five francs. Similar fans could be had, ready mounted, for a hundred and twenty francs, and she named a shop in the Rue Poissonnière where she had seen them.

However, the fan was handed round to all the ladies. Madame Guibal barely glanced at it. She was a tall, slim woman, with red hair, and a face full of indifference, in which her grey eyes, belying her unconcerned air, occasionally cast a hungry gleam of selfishness. She was never seen out with her husband, a barrister well-known at the Palais de Justice, who led, it was said, a pretty free life between his briefs and his pleasures.

"Oh," she murmured, passing the fan to Madame de Boves, "I've scarcely bought one in my life. One always receives too many of such things."

"You are fortunate, my dear, in having a gallant husband," answered the countess in a tone of delicate irony. And bending over to her daughter, a tall girl of twenty, she added: "Just look at the monogram, Blanche. What pretty work! It's the monogram that must have increased the price of the mounting like that."

Madame de Boves had just turned forty. She was a superb woman, with the neck and shoulders of a goddess, a large regular face, and big sleepy eyes. Her husband, an Inspector-General of the State Studs, had married her for her beauty. She appeared quite moved by the delicacy of the monogram, seized indeed by a desire which so stirred her as to make her turn pale; and suddenly turning she continued: "Give us your opinion, Monsieur Mouret. Is it too dear—two hundred francs for this mount?"

Mouret had remained standing among the five women, smiling and affecting an interest in what interested them. He took the fan, examined it, and was about to give his opinion, when the footman opened the door and announced:

"Madame Marty."

There then entered a thin, ugly woman, disfigured by small-pox but dressed with elaborate elegance. She seemed of uncertain age, her five-and-thirty years sometimes appearing equal to thirty, and sometimes to forty, according to the intensity of the nervous fever which so often agitated her. A red leather bag, which she had not been willing to leave in the anteroom, hung from her right hand.

"Dear madame," said she to Henriette, "you will excuse me bringing my bag. Just fancy, as I was coming, along I went into The Paradise, and as I have again been very extravagant, I did not like to leave it in my cab for fear of being robbed." Then, having perceived Mouret, she resumed laughing: "Ah! sir, I didn't mean to give you an advertisement, for I didn't know you were here. But you really have some extraordinarily fine lace just now."

This turned the attention from the fan, which the young man laid on the table. The ladies were now all anxious to see what Madame Marty had bought. She was known to be very extravagant, totally unable to resist certain temptations. Strict in her conduct, incapable of any sexual transgression she proved weak and cowardly before the least bit of finery. Daughter of a clerk of small means, she was ruining her husband, the fifth-class professor at the Lycée Bonaparte, who in order to meet the constantly increasing expenses of the household was compelled to double his income of six thousand francs by giving private lessons. However, she did not open her bag, but held it tightly on her lap, and began to talk about her daughter Valentine, a girl of fourteen whom she dressed like herself, in all the fashionable novelties to whose irresistible fascination she succumbed.

"You know," said she, "they are making girls' dresses trimmed with narrow lace this winter. So when I saw a very pretty Valenciennes—"

Thereupon she at last decided to open her bag; and the ladies were craning their necks, when, amidst the silence, the door-bell was heard.

"It's my husband," stammered Madame Marty, in great confusion. "He promised to call for me on leaving the Lycée Bonaparte."

Forthwith she shut her bag again, and instinctively hid it away under her chair. All the ladies set up a laugh. This made her blush for her precipitation, and she took the bag on her knees again, explaining, however, that men never understood matters and that they need not know everything.

"Monsieur de Boves, Monsieur de Vallagnosc," announced the footman.

It was quite a surprise. Madame de Boves herself did not expect her husband. The latter, a fine man, wearing a moustache and an imperial in the correct military fashion so much liked at the Tuileries, kissed the hand of Madame Desforges, whom he had known as a young girl at her father's. And then he made way so that his companion, a tall, pale fellow, of an aristocratic poverty of blood, might in his turn make his bow to the lady of the house. However, the conversation had hardly been resumed when two exclamations rang out.

"What! Is that you, Paul?"

"Why, Octave!"

Mouret and Vallagnosc thereupon shook hands, much to Madame Desforges's surprise. They knew each other, then? Of course, they had grown up side by side at the college at Plassans, and it was quite by chance they had not met at her house before. However, jesting together and with their hands still united they stepped into the little drawing-room, just as the servant brought in the tea, a china service on a silver waiter, which he placed near Madame Desforges, on a small round marble table with a light brass mounting. The ladies drew up and began talking in louder tones, raising a cross-fire of endless chatter; whilst Monsieur de Boves, standing behind them leant over every now and then to put in a word or two with the gallantry of a handsome functionary. The spacious room, so prettily and cheerfully furnished, became merrier still with these gossiping voices interspersed with laughter.

"Ah! Paul, old boy," repeated Mouret.

He was seated near Vallagnosc, on a sofa. And alone in the little drawing-room—which looked very coquettish with its hangings of buttercup silk—out of hearing of the ladies, and not even seeing them, except through the open doorway, the two old friends commenced grinning whilst they scrutinized each other and exchanged slaps on the knees. Their whole youthful career was recalled, the old college at Plassans, with its two courtyards, its damp class-rooms, and the dining-hall in which they had consumed so much cod-fish, and the dormitories where the pillows flew from bed to bed as soon as the monitor began to snore. Paul, who belonged to an old parliamentary family, noble, poor, and proud, had proved a good scholar, always at the top of his class and continually held up as an example by the master, who prophesied a brilliant future for him; whereas Octave had remained at the bottom, amongst the dunces, but nevertheless fat and jolly, indulging in all sorts of pleasures outside. Notwithstanding the difference in their characters, a fast friendship had rendered them inseparable until they were examined for their bachelor's degrees, which they took, the one with honours, the other in just a passable manner after two vexatious rebuffs. Then they went out into the world, each on his own side, and had now met again, after the lapse of ten years, already changed and looking older.

"Well," asked Mouret, "what's become of you?"

"Nothing at all," replied the other.

Vallagnosc indeed, despite the pleasure of this meeting, retained a tired and disenchanted air; and as his friend, somewhat astonished, insisted, saying: "But you must do something. What do you do?" he merely replied: "Nothing."

Octave began to laugh. Nothing! that wasn't enough. Little by little, however, he succeeded in learning Paul's story. It was the usual story of penniless young men, who think themselves obliged by their birth to choose a liberal profession and bury themselves in a sort of vain mediocrity, happy even when they escape starvation, notwithstanding their numerous degrees. For his part he had studied law by a sort of family tradition; and had then remained a burden on his widowed mother, who already hardly knew how to dispose of her two daughters. Having at last got quite ashamed of his position he had left the three women to vegetate on the remnants of their fortune, and had accepted a petty appointment at the Ministry of the Interior, where he buried himself like a mole in his hole.

"What do you get there?" resumed Mouret.

"Three thousand francs."

"But that's pitiful pay! Ah! old man, I'm really sorry for you. What! a clever fellow like you, who floored all of us! And they only give you three thousand francs a year, after having already ground you down for five years! No, it isn't right!" He paused and then thinking of his own good fortune resumed: "As for me, I made them a humble bow long ago. You know what I'm doing?"

"Yes," said Vallagnosc, "I heard you were in business. You've got that big place on the Place Gaillon, haven't you?"

"That's it. Counter-jumper, my boy!"

Mouret raised his head, again slapped his friend on the knee, and repeated, with the sterling gaiety of a man who did not blush for the trade by which he was making his fortune:

"Counter-jumper, and no mistake! You remember, no doubt, I didn't nibble much at their baits, although at heart I never thought myself a bigger fool than the others. When I took my degree, just to please the family, I could have become a barrister or a doctor quite as easily as any of my school-fellows, but those trades frightened me, for one sees so many chaps starving at them. So I just threw the ass's skin away—oh! without the least regret and plunged head-first into business."

Vallagnosc smiled with an awkward air, and ultimately muttered: "It's quite certain that your degree can't be of much use to you in selling linen."

"Well!" replied Mouret, joyously, "all I ask is, that it shan't stand in my way; and you know, when one has been stupid enough to burden one's self with such a thing, it is difficult to get rid of it. One goes at a tortoise's pace through life, whilst those who are bare-footed run like madmen." Then, noticing that his friend seemed troubled, he took his hand in his, and continued: "Come, come, I don't want to hurt your feelings, but confess that your degrees have not satisfied any of your wants. Do you know that my manager in the silk department will draw more than twelve thousand francs this year. Just so! a fellow of very clear intelligence, whose knowledge is confined to spelling, and the first four rules of arithmetic. The ordinary salesmen in my place make from three to four thousand francs a year, more than you can earn yourself; and their education did not cost anything like what yours did, nor were they launched into the world with a written promise to conquer it. Of course, it is not everything to make money; only between the poor devils possessed of a smattering of science who now block up the liberal professions, without earning enough to keep themselves from starving, and the practical fellows armed for life's struggle, knowing every branch of their trade, I don't hesitate one moment, I'm for the latter against the former, I think they thoroughly understand the age they live in!"

His voice had become impassioned and Henriette, who was pouring out the tea, turned her head. When he caught her smile, at the further end of the large drawing-room, and saw two other ladies listening, he was the first to make merry over his own big phrases.

"In short, old man, every counter-jumper who commences, has, at the present day, a chance of becoming a millionaire."

Vallagnosc indolently threw himself back on the sofa, half-closing his eyes and assuming an attitude of mingled fatigue and disdain in which a dash of affectation was added to his real hereditary exhaustion.

"Bah!" murmured he, "life isn't worth all that trouble. There is nothing worth living for." And as Mouret, quite shocked, looked at him with an air of surprise, he added: "Everything happens and nothing happens; a man may as well remain with his arms folded."

He then explained his pessimism—the mediocrities and the abortions of existence. For a time he had thought of literature, but his intercourse with certain poets had filled him with unlimited despair. He always came to the conclusion that every effort was futile, every hour equally weary and empty, and the world incurably stupid and dull. All enjoyment was a failure, there was even no pleasure in wrong-doing.

"Just tell me, do you enjoy life yourself?" asked he at last.

Mouret was now in a state of astonished indignation, and exclaimed: "What? Do I enjoy myself? What are you talking about? Why, of course I do, my boy, and even when things give way, for then I am furious at hearing them cracking. I am a passionate fellow myself, and don't take life quietly; that's what interests me in it perhaps." He glanced towards the drawing-room, and lowered his voice. "Oh! there are some women who've bothered me awfully, I must confess. Still I have my revenge, I assure you. But it is not so much the women, for to speak truly, I don't care a hang for them; the great thing in life is to be able to will and do—to create, in short. You have an idea; you fight for it, you hammer it into people's heads, and you see it grow and triumph. Ah! yes, my boy, I enjoy life!"

All the joy of action, all the gaiety of existence, resounded in Mouret's words. He repeated that he went with the times. Really, a man must be badly constituted, have his brain and limbs out of order, to refuse to work in an age of such vast undertakings, when the entire century was pressing forward with giant strides. And he railed at the despairing ones, the disgusted ones, the pessimists, all those weak, sickly offsprings of our budding sciences, who assumed the lachrymose airs of poets, or the affected countenances of sceptics, amidst the immense activity of the present day. 'Twas a fine part to play, decent and intelligent, that of yawning before other people's labour!

"But yawning in other people's faces is my only pleasure," said Vallagnosc, smiling in his cold way.

At this Mouret's passion subsided, and he became affectionate again. "Ah, Paul, you're not changed. Just as paradoxical as ever! However, we've not met to quarrel. Each man has his own ideas, fortunately. But you must come and see my machine at work; you'll see it isn't a bad idea. And now, what news? Your mother and sisters are quite well, I hope? And weren't you supposed to get married at Plassans, about six months ago?"

A sudden movement made by Vallagnosc stopped him, and as his friend had glanced into the larger drawing-room with an anxious expression, he also turned round, and noticed that Mademoiselle de Boves was closely watching them. Blanche, tall and sturdy, resembled her mother; but her face was already puffed out and her features seemed large—swollen, as it were, by unhealthy fat. Then, in reply to a discreet question, Paul intimated that nothing was yet settled; perhaps nothing would be settled. He had made the young person's acquaintance at

Madame Desforges's, where he had visited a good deal the previous winter, but whither he now very rarely came, which explained why he had not met Octave there before. In their turn, the Boves invited him, and he was especially fond of the father, an ex-man about town who had retired into an official position. On the other hand there was no money, Madame de Boves having brought her husband nothing but her Juno-like beauty as a marriage portion. So the family were living poorly on their last mortgaged farm, to the little money derived from which were fortunately added the nine thousand francs a year drawn by the count as Inspector-General of the State Studs. Certain escapades, however, continued to empty his purse; and the ladies, mother and daughter, were kept very short of money, being at times reduced to turning their dresses themselves.

"In that case, why marry?" was Mouret's simple question.

"Well! I can't go on like this for ever," said Vallagnosc, with a weary movement of the eyelids. "Besides, there are certain expectations, we are waiting for the death of an aunt."

However, Mouret still kept his eye on Monsieur de Boves, who, seated next to Madame Guibal, proved most attentive to her, laughing softly the while, with an amorous air. Thereupon Octave turned to his friend with such a significant twinkle of the eye that the latter added:

"Not that one—at least not yet. The misfortune is, that his duties call him to the four corners of France, to the breeding dépôts, so that he has frequent pretexts for absenting himself. Last month, whilst his wife supposed him to be at Perpignan, he was simply carrying on in Paris, in an out-of-the-way neighbourhood."

There ensued a pause. Then the young man, who was also watching the count's gallantry towards Madame Guibal, resumed in a low tone: "Really, I think you are right. The more so as the dear lady is not exactly a saint, if all people say be true. But just look at him! Isn't he comical, trying to magnetize her with his eyes? The old-fashioned gallantry, my dear fellow! I adore that man, and if I marry his daughter, he may safely say it's for his sake!"

Mouret laughed, greatly amused. He questioned Vallagnosc again, and when he found that the first idea of a marriage between him and Blanche had come from Madame Desforges, he thought the story better still. That dear Henriette took a widow's delight in marrying people, so much so, that when she had provided for the girls, she sometimes allowed their fathers to choose friends from her company.

At that moment she appeared at the door of the little drawing-room, followed by a gentleman apparently about sixty years old, whose arrival had not been observed by the two friends, absorbed as they were in the conversation they were carrying on, to the accompaniment of the ladies' voices. These voices at times rang out in a shriller key above the tinkling of the small spoons in the china cups; and from time to time, during a brief silence you heard a saucer being harshly laid down on the marble table. A sudden gleam of the setting sun, which had just emerged from behind a thick cloud, gilded the crests of the chestnut-trees in the gardens, and streamed through the windows in a red, golden flame, whose glow lighted up the brocatel and brass-work of the furniture.

"This way, my dear baron," said Madame Desforges. "Allow me to introduce to you Monsieur Octave Mouret, who is longing to express the admiration he feels for you." And turning round towards Octave, she added: "Baron Hartmann."

A smile played on the old man's lips. He was short, and vigorous, with a large Alsatian head, and a heavy face, which lighted up with a gleam of intelligence at the slightest curl of his mouth, the slightest movement of his eyelids. For the last fortnight he had resisted Henriette's wish that he should consent to this interview; not that he felt any immoderate jealousy of Mouret, but because this was the third friend Henriette had introduced to him, and he was afraid of becoming ridiculous at last. And so on approaching Octave he put on the discreet smile of one who, albeit willing to behave amiably, is not disposed to be a dupe.

"Oh! sir," said Mouret, with his Provençal enthusiasm, "the Crédit Immobilier's last operation was really astonishing! You cannot think how happy and proud I am to know you."

"Too kind, sir, too kind," repeated the baron, still smiling.

Henriette, robed in a lace dress, which revealed her delicate neck and wrists, looked at them with her clear eyes without any sign of embarrassment; standing between the two, raising her head, and going from one to the other she indeed appeared delighted to see them so friendly together.

"Gentlemen," said she at last, "I leave you to your conversation." And, turning towards Paul, who had risen from the sofa, she resumed: "Will you accept a cup of tea, Monsieur de Vallagnosc?"

"With pleasure, madame," he replied, and they both returned to the larger drawing-room.

Mouret resumed his seat on the sofa, when Baron Hartmann likewise had sat down on it; and forthwith the young man broke into renewed praise of the Crédit Immobilier's operations. From that he went on to the subject so near his heart, speaking of the new thoroughfare, a lengthening of the Rue Réaumur, a section of which running from the Place de la Bourse to the Place de l'Opéra was about to be opened under the name of the Rue du Dix-Décembre. It had been declared a work of public utility eighteen months previously; the expropriation jury had just been appointed; and the whole neighbourhood was excited about this new street, anxiously awaiting the commencement of the works, and taking a keen interest in the houses condemned to disappear. For three years Mouret had been waiting for this work—first, in the expectation of an increase of his own business; secondly, for the furtherance of certain schemes of enlargement which he dared not openly avow, so extensive were his ideas. As the Rue du Dix-Décembre was to cut through the Rue de Choiseul and the Rue de la Michodière, he pictured The Ladies' Paradise occupying the whole block of building which these streets and the Rue Neuve-Saint-Augustin surrounded; and he already imagined it with a princely frontage in the new thoroughfare, dominating everything around like some lord and master of the conquered city. Hence his strong desire to make Baron Hartmann's acquaintance, as soon as he had learnt that the Crédit Immobilier had contracted with the authorities to open and build this Rue du Dix-Décembre, on condition that it should receive the frontage ground on each side of the street.

"Really," he repeated, trying to assume a naive look, "you'll hand over the street ready made, with sewers, pavements, and gas lamps. And the frontage ground will suffice to compensate you. Oh! it's curious, very curious!"

At last he came to the delicate point. He was aware that the Crédit Immobilier was secretly buying up the houses forming part of the same block as The Ladies' Paradise, not only those which were to fall under the demolishers' pickaxes, but the others as well, those which were to remain standing; and he suspected the existence of a project for founding some great establishment, which made him anxious about those enlargements of his own premises of which he was ever dreaming, seized with fear at the idea that he might one day come into collision with a powerful company owning property which they certainly would not sell. It was precisely this fear which had prompted him to seek an alliance between himself and the Baron under Henriette's auspices. No doubt he could have seen the financier at his office, and have there talked the affair over at his ease; but he felt that he would be stronger in Henriette's house. To be near her, within the beloved perfume of her presence, to have her ready to convince them both with a smile, seemed to him a certain guarantee of success.

"Haven't you bought the former Hôtel Duvillard, that old building next to my place?" he suddenly inquired.

The baron hesitated for a moment, and then denied it. But Mouret looked him straight in the face and smiled, from that moment beginning to play the part of an open-hearted young man who was always straightforward in business.

"Look here, Monsieur le Baron," said he, "as I have the unexpected honour of meeting you, I must make a confession. Oh, I don't ask you for any of your secrets, but I am going to entrust you with mine, for I'm certain that I couldn't place them in better hands. Besides, I want your advice. I have long wished to call and see you, but dared not do so."

He did make his confession, and related his debut in life, not even concealing the financial crisis through which he was passing in the midst of his triumph. Everything was brought up, the successive enlargements of his premises, the continual reinvestments of all profits in the business, the sums contributed by his employees, the existence of the establishment risked at every fresh sale, in which the entire capital was staked, as it were, on a single throw of the dice. However, it was not money he wanted, for he had a fanatic's faith in his customers; his ambition ran higher; and he proposed to the baron a partnership, in which the Crédit Immobilier should contribute the colossal palace which he pictured in his dreams, whilst for his part he would give his genius and the business he had already created. Everything would be properly valued, nothing appeared to him easier to realise.

"What are you going to do with your land and buildings?" he asked persistently. "You have a plan, no doubt. But I'm quite certain that your idea is not so good as mine. Think of it. We build fresh galleries on the vacant ground, we pull the houses down or re-arrange them and open the most extensive establishment in Paris—a bazaar which will bring in millions." And then he let this fervent, heartfelt exclamation escape him: "Ah! if I could only do without you! But you hold everything now. Besides, I shall never have the necessary capital. Come, we must come to an understanding. It would be a crime not to do so."

"How you go ahead, my dear sir!" Baron Hartmann contented himself with replying. "What an imagination you have!"

He shook his head, and continued to smile, resolved not to return confidence for confidence. In point of fact the idea of the Crédit Immobilier was to found in the Rue du Dix-Décembre a huge rival to the Grand Hôtel, a luxurious hostelry whose central position would attract foreigners. At the same time, however, as the hotel was only to occupy a certain frontage, the baron might also have entertained Mouret's idea, and have treated for the rest of the block of houses, which still represented a vast surface. However, he had already advanced funds to two of Henriette's friends, and he was getting tired of his lavishness. Besides, despite his passion for activity, which prompted him to open his purse to every fellow of intelligence and courage, Mouret's commercial genius astonished rather than captivated him. Was not the founding of such a gigantic shop a fanciful, imprudent scheme? Would he not court certain failure by thus enlarging the drapery trade beyond all reasonable bounds? In short, he didn't believe in the idea and refused his support.

"No doubt the idea is attractive," said he, "but it's a poet's idea. Where would you find the customers to fill such a cathedral?"

Mouret looked at him for a moment in silence, as if stupefied by the refusal which these words implied. Was it possible?—a man of such foresight, who divined the presence of money at no matter what depth! And suddenly, with an extremely eloquent gesture, he pointed to the ladies in the drawing-room and exclaimed: "Customers?—why look there!"

The sun was paling and the golden-red flame was now but a yellowish gleam, dying away on the silk of the hangings and the panels of the furniture. At this approach of twilight, the large room was steeped in warm cosy pleasantness. While Monsieur de Boves and Paul de Vallagnosc stood chatting near one of the windows, their eyes wandering far away into the gardens, the ladies had closed up, forming in the middle of the room a small circle of skirts whence arose bursts of laughter, whispered words, ardent questions and replies, all woman's passion for expenditure and finery. They were talking about dress, and Madame de Boves was describing a gown she had seen at a ball.

"First of all, a mauve silk skirt, covered with flounces of old Alençon lace, twelve inches deep."

"Oh! is it possible!" exclaimed Madame Marty. "Some women are very fortunate!"

Baron Hartmann, who had followed Mouret's gesture, was looking at the ladies through the doorway which was wide open. And he continued listening to them with one ear, whilst the young man, inflamed by his desire to convince him, went yet deeper into the question, explaining the mechanism of the new style of drapery business. This branch of commerce was now based on a rapid and continual turning over of capital, which it was necessary to convert into goods as often as possible in the same year. For instance, that year his capital, which only amounted to five hundred thousand francs, had been turned over four times, and had thus produced business to the amount of two millions. But this was a mere trifle, which could be increased tenfold, for later on, in certain departments, he certainly hoped to turn the capital over fifteen or twenty times in the course of the twelvemonth.

"You understand, baron, the whole system lies in that. It is very simple, but it had to be found out. We don't need an enormous working capital; the sole effort we have to make is to get rid of the stock we buy as quickly as possible so as to replace it by other stock which each time will make our capital return interest. In this way we can content ourselves with a very small profit; as our general expenses amount to as much as sixteen per cent., and as we seldom make more than twenty per cent. on our goods, there is only a net profit of four per cent. at the utmost; only this will finish by representing millions when we can operate on large quantities of goods incessantly renewed. You follow me, don't you? nothing can be clearer."

The baron again shook his head doubtfully. He who had entertained the boldest schemes and whose daring at the time of the introduction of gas-lighting was still spoken of, remained in the present instance uneasy and obstinate.

"I quite understand," said he; "you sell cheap in order to sell a quantity, and you sell a quantity in order to sell cheap. But you must sell, and I repeat my former question: Whom will you sell to? How do you hope to keep up such a colossal sale?"

A loud exclamation, coming from the drawing-room, interrupted Mouret just as he began to reply. It was Madame Guibal declaring that she would have preferred the flounces of old Alençon simply round the upper skirt of the dress.

"But, my dear," said Madame de Boves, "the upper skirt was covered with it as well. I never saw anything richer."

"Ah, that's a good idea," resumed Madame Desforges, "I've got several yards of Alençon somewhere; I must look them up for a trimming."

Then the voices fell again, sinking into a murmur. Prices were quoted, a feverish desire to buy and bargain stirred all the ladies; they were purchasing lace by the mile.

"Why?" declared Mouret, when he could at last speak, "one can sell what one likes when one knows how to sell! Therein lies our triumph."

And then with his southern enthusiasm, he pictured the new business at work in warm, glowing phrases which brought everything vividly before the eyes. First came the wonderful power resulting from the assemblage of goods, all accumulated on one point and sustaining and facilitating the sale of one another. There was never any stand-still, the article of the season was always on hand; and from counter to counter the customer found herself caught and subjugated, at one buying the material for a gown; at another cotton and trimming, elsewhere a mantle, in fact everything necessary to complete her costume; while in addition there were all the unforeseen purchases, chases, a surrender to a longing for the useless and the pretty. Next he began to sing the praises of the plain figure system. The great revolution in the business sprang from this fortunate inspiration. If the old-fashioned small shops were dying out it was because they could not struggle against the low prices which the tickets guaranteed. Competition now went on under the very eyes of the public; a look in the windows enabled people to contrast the prices of different establishments; and each shop in turn was lowering its rates, contenting itself with the smallest possible profit. There could be no deceit, no long prepared stroke of fortune by selling an article at double its value; there were simply current operations, a regular percentage levied on all goods, and success depended solely on the skilful working of the sales which became the larger from the very circumstance that they were carried on openly and honestly. Was it not altogether an astonishing development? And it was already revolutionizing the markets and transforming Paris, for it was made of woman's flesh and blood.

"I have the women, I don't care a hang for the rest!" exclaimed Mouret, with a brutal frankness born of his passion.

At this cry Baron Hartmann appeared somewhat moved. His smile lost its touch of irony and he glanced at the young man, gradually won over by the confidence he displayed and feeling a growing friendship for him.

"Hush!" he murmured, paternally, "they will hear you."

But the ladies were now all speaking at once, so excited that they did not even listen to each other. Madame de Boves was finishing the description of an evening-dress; a mauve silk tunic, draped and caught up by bows of lace; the bodice cut very low, with similar bows of lace on the shoulders.

"You'll see," said she. "I am having a bodice made like it, with some satin—"

"For my part," interrupted Madame Bourdelais, "I was bent on buying some velvet. Oh! such a bargain!"

Then suddenly Madame Marty asked: "How much did the silk cost?"

And off they started again, all together. Madame Guibal, Henriette, and Blanche were measuring, cutting out, and making up. It was a pillage of material, a ransacking of all the shops, an appetite for luxury seeking satisfaction in toilettes envied and dreamed of—with such happiness at finding themselves in an atmosphere of finery, that they buried themselves in it, as in warm air necessary to their existence.

Mouret had glanced towards the larger drawing-room, and in a few phrases, whispered in the baron's ear, as if he were confiding to him one of those amorous secrets which men sometimes venture to reveal among themselves, he finished explaining the mechanism of modern commerce. And, above all that he had already spoken of, dominating everything else, appeared the exploitation of woman to which everything conduced, the capital incessantly renewed, the system of assembling goods together, the attraction of cheapness and the tranquillizing effect of the marking in plain figures. It was for woman that all the establishments were struggling in wild competition; it was woman whom they were continually catching in the snares of their bargains, after bewildering her with their displays. They had awakened new desires in her flesh; they constituted an immense temptation, before which she fatally succumbed, yielding at first to reasonable purchases of articles needed in the household, then tempted by her coquetry, and finally subjugated and devoured. By increasing their business tenfold and popularizing luxury, they—the drapers—became a terrible instrument of prodigality, ravaging households, and preparing mad freaks of fashion which proved ever more and more costly. And if woman reigned in their shops like a queen, cajoled, flattered and overwhelmed with attentions, she was one on whom her subjects traffic, and who pays for each fresh caprice, with a drop of her blood. From beneath the very gracefulness of his gallantry, Mouret thus allowed the baron to divine the brutality of a Jew who sells woman by the pound weight. He raised a temple to her, caused her to be steeped in incense by a legion of shopmen, prepared the ritual of a new cultus, thinking of nothing but woman and ever seeking to imagine more powerful fascinations. But, behind her back, when he had emptied her purse and shattered her nerves, he remained full of the secret scorn of a man to whom a woman has been foolish enough to yield.

"Once have the women on your side," he whispered to the baron, laughing boldly, "and you could sell the very world."

Now the baron understood. A few sentences had sufficed, he guessed the rest, and such a gallant exploitation inflamed him, stirring up the memories of his past life of pleasure. His eyes twinkled in a knowing way, and he ended by looking with an air of admiration at the inventor of this machine for devouring the female sex. It was really clever. And then he made precisely the same remark as Bourdoncle, a remark suggested to him by his long experience: "They'll make you suffer for it, by and by, you know," said he.

But Mouret shrugged his shoulders with an air of overwhelming disdain. They all belonged to him, they were his property, and he belonged to none of them. After deriving his fortune and his pleasures from them he intended to throw them all over for those who might still find their account in them. It was the rational, cold disdain of a Southerner and a speculator.

"Well! my dear baron," he asked in conclusion, "will you join me? Does this affair appear possible to you?"

Albeit half conquered, the baron did not wish to enter into any engagement yet. A doubt remained beneath the charm which was gradually operating on him; and he was going to reply in an evasive manner, when a pressing call from the ladies spared him the trouble. Amidst light bursts of laughter voices were repeating "Monsieur Mouret! Monsieur Mouret!"

And as the latter, annoyed at being interrupted, pretended not to hear, Madame de Boves, who had risen a moment previously, came as far as the door of the little drawing-room.

"You are wanted, Monsieur Mouret. It isn't very gallant of you to bury yourself in a corner to talk over business."

Thereupon he decided to join the ladies, with an apparent good grace, a well-feigned air of rapture which quite astonished the baron. Both of them rose and passed into the other room.

"But I am quite at your service, ladies," said Mouret on entering, a smile on his lips.

He was greeted with an acclamation of triumph and was obliged to step forward; the ladies making room for him in their midst. The sun had just set behind the trees in the gardens, the daylight was departing, delicate shadows were gradually invading the spacious apartment. It was the emotional hour of twilight, that quiet voluptuous moment which reigns in Parisian flats between the dying brightness of the street and the lighting of the lamps in the kitchen. Monsieur de Boves and Vallagnosc, still standing before a window, cast shadows upon the carpet: whilst, motionless in the last gleam of light which came in by the other window, Monsieur Marty, who had quietly entered, shewed his poverty-stricken silhouette, his worn-out, well-brushed frock coat, and his pale face wan from constant teaching and the more haggard as what he had heard of the ladies' conversation had quite upset him.

"Is your sale still fixed for next Monday?" Madame Marty was just asking.

"Certainly, madame," replied Mouret, in a flute-like voice, an actor's voice, which he assumed when speaking to women.

Henriette thereupon intervened. "We are all going, you know. They say you are preparing wonders."

"Oh! wonders!" he murmured, with an air of modest fatuity. "I simply try to deserve your patronage."

But they pressed him with questions: Madame Bourdelais, Madame Guibal, even Blanche wanted to know something.

"Come, give us some particulars," repeated Madame de Boves, persistently. "You are making us die of curiosity."

And they were surrounding him, when Henriette observed that he had not even taken a cup of tea. At this they were plunged into desolation and four of them set about serving him, stipulating however that he must answer them afterwards. Henriette poured the tea out, Madame Marty held the cup, whilst Madame de Boves and Madame Bourdelais contended for the honour of sweetening it. Then, when he had declined to sit down, and began to drink his tea slowly, standing up in the midst of them, they all drew nearer, imprisoning him in the circle of their skirts; and with their heads raised and their eyes sparkling, they smiled upon him.

"And what about silk, your Paris Delight which all the papers are talking of?" resumed Madame Marty, impatiently.

"Oh!" he replied, "it's an extraordinary article, large-grained faille, supple and strong. You'll see it, ladies, and you'll see it nowhere else, for we have bought the exclusive right to it."

"Really! a fine silk at five francs sixty centimes!" said Madame Bourdelais, enthusiastic. "One can hardly believe it."

Ever since the advertisements and puffs had appeared, this silk had occupied a considerable place in their daily life. They talked of it, promising themselves some of it, all agog with desire and doubt. And, beneath the inquisitive chatter with which they overwhelmed the young man, one could divine their different temperaments as purchasers. Madame Marty, carried away by her rage for spending money, bought everything at The Ladies' Paradise without selecting, just as things chanced to be placed in the windows or on the counters. Madame Guibal on the other hand walked about the shop for hours without ever buying anything, happy and satisfied in simply feasting her eyes; Madame de Boves, short of money and always tortured by some immoderate desire, nourished a feeling of rancour against the goods she could not carry away with her; Madame Bourdelais, with the sharp eyes of a careful and practical housewife, made straight for the bargains, availing herself of the big establishments with such skill that she saved a lot of money; and lastly, Henriette, having very elegant tastes, only purchased certain articles there, such as gloves, hosiery, and her coarser linen.

"We have other stuffs of astonishing cheapness and richness," continued Mouret, in his musical voice. "For instance, I recommend you our Golden Grain, a taffeta of incomparable brilliancy. In the fancy silks there are some charming lines, designs specially chosen from among thousands by our buyer; and in velvets you will find an exceedingly rich collection of shades. I warn you, however, that cloth will be greatly worn this year; you'll see our *matelassés* and our cheviots."

They had ceased to interrupt him, and drew yet closer, their lips parted by vague smiles, their faces eagerly out-stretched as if their whole beings were springing towards the tempter. Their eyes grew dim, and slight quivers ran through them but he meantime retained his calm, conquering air, amidst the intoxicating perfumes which their hair exhaled; and between each sentence he continued to sip a little of his tea, the aroma of which softened those sharper odours. At sight of such a power of fascination, so well controlled, strong enough to play with woman without being overcome by the intoxication which she diffuses, Baron Hartmann, who had not ceased to look at Mouret, felt his admiration increasing.

"So cloth will be worn?" resumed Madame Marty, whose rugged face sparkled with coquettish passion. "I must have a look at it."

Madame Bourdelais, who kept a cool look-out, in her turn remarked: "Your remnant sales take place on Thursdays, don't they? I shall wait. I have all my little ones to clothe." And turning her delicate blonde head towards the mistress of the house, she asked: "Sauveur is still your dressmaker, I suppose?"

"Yes," replied Henriette, "Sauveur is very dear, but she is the only person in Paris who knows how to make a dress-body. Besides, Monsieur Mouret may say what he likes but she has the prettiest designs, designs that are not seen anywhere else. I can't bear to see the same dresses as mine on every woman's back."

At first Mouret slightly smiled. Then he intimated that Madame Sauveur bought her material at his shop; no doubt she went to the manufacturers direct for certain designs of which she acquired the sole right of sale: but for black silks, for instance, she watched for The Paradise bargains, laying in a considerable stock, which she disposed of at double and treble the price she gave. "Thus I am quite sure that her buyers will snap up our Paris Delight. Why should she go to the manufacturers and pay dearer for this silk than she would at my place? On my word of honour, we shall sell it at a loss."

This was a decisive blow for the ladies. The idea of getting goods below cost price awoke in them all the natural greed of woman, whose enjoyment in purchasing is doubled when she thinks that she is robbing the tradesman. He knew the sex to be incapable of resisting anything cheap.

"But we sell everything for nothing!" he exclaimed gaily, taking up Madame Desforges's fan, which lay behind him on the table. "For instance, here's this fan. How much do you say it cost."

"The Chantilly cost twenty-five francs, and the mounting two hundred," said Henriette.

"Well, the Chantilly isn't dear. However, we have the same at eighteen francs; as for the mount, my dear madame, it's a shameful robbery. I should not dare to sell one like it for more than ninety francs."

"Just what I said!" exclaimed Madame Bourdelais.

"Ninety francs!" murmured Madame de Boves, "one must be very poor indeed to go without one at that price."

She had taken up the fan, and was again examining it with her daughter Blanche; and, over her large regular face and in her big, sleepy eyes, spread an expression of suppressed and despairing longing which she could not satisfy. The fan once more went the round of the ladies, amidst various remarks and exclamations. Monsieur de Boves and Vallagnosc, meantime, had left the window, and whilst the former returned to his place behind Madame Guibal, whose charms he again began to admire, with his correct and superior air, the young man leant over Blanche, endeavouring to think of some agreeable remark.

"Don't you think it rather gloomy, mademoiselle, that white mount and the black lace?"

"Oh," she replied, gravely, not a blush colouring her inflated cheeks, "I saw one made of mother-of-pearl and white feathers. Something truly virginal!"

Then Monsieur de Boves, who had doubtless observed the distressful glances with which his wife was following the fan, at last added his word to the conversation. "Those flimsy things soon break," said he.

"Of course they do!" declared Madame Guibal, with a pout, affecting an air of indifference. "I'm tired of having mine mended."

For several minutes, Madame Marty, very much excited by the conversation, had been feverishly turning her red leather bag about on her lap, for she had not yet been able to show her purchases. She was burning with a sort of sensual desire to display them; and, suddenly forgetting her husband's presence, she opened the bag and took out of it a few yards of narrow lace wound on a piece of cardboard.

"This is the Valenciennes for my daughter," said she. "It's an inch and a half wide. Isn't it delicious? One franc ninety centimes the metre."

The lace passed from hand to hand. The ladies were astonished. Mouret assured them that he sold these little trimmings at cost price. However, Madame Marty had closed the bag, as if to conceal certain things she must not show. But after the success obtained by the Valenciennes she was unable to resist the temptation of taking out a handkerchief.

"There was this handkerchief as well. Real Brussels, my dear. Oh! a bargain! Twenty francs!"

And after that the bag became inexhaustible. She blushed with pleasure, at each fresh article she took out. There was a Spanish blonde-lace cravat, thirty francs: she hadn't wanted it, but the shopman had sworn it was the last one in stock, and that in future the price would be raised. Next came a Chantilly veil: rather dear, fifty francs; if she didn't wear it she could make it do for her daughter.

"Really, lace is so pretty!" she repeated with her nervous laugh. "Once I'm inside I could buy everything."

"And this?" asked Madame de Boves, taking up and examining some guipure.

"That," replied she, "is for an insertion. There are twenty-six yards—a franc the yard. Just fancy!"

"But," asked Madame Bourdelais, in surprise, "What are you going to do with it?"

"I'm sure I don't know. But it was such a funny pattern!"

At that moment however, she chanced to raise her eyes and perceived her terrified husband in front of her. He had turned paler than ever, his whole person expressive of the patient, resigned anguish of a powerless man, witnessing the reckless expenditure of his dearly earned salary. Every fresh bit of lace to him meant disaster; bitter days of teaching, long journeys to pupils through the mud, the whole constant effort of his life resulting in secret misery, the hell of a necessitous household. And she, perceiving the increasing wildness of his look, wanted to catch up the veil, cravat and handkerchief and put them out of sight, moving her feverish hands about and repeating with forced laughter: "You'll get me a scolding from my husband. I assure you, my dear, I've been very reasonable; for there was a large lace flounce at five hundred francs, oh! a marvel!"

"Why didn't you buy it?" asked Madame Guibal, calmly. "Monsieur Marty is the most gallant of men."

The poor professor was obliged to bow and say that his wife was quite free to buy what she liked. But at thought of the danger to which that large flounce had exposed him, an icy shiver sped down his back; and as Mouret was just at that moment affirming that the new shops increased the comfort of middle-class households, he glared at him with a terrible expression, the flash of hatred of a timid man who would like to throttle the destroyer but dares not.

But the ladies had still retained possession of the lace. They were intoxicating themselves with their prolonged contemplation of it. The several pieces were unrolled and then passed from one to the other, drawing them all still closer together, linking them, as it were, with delicate meshes. On their laps there was a continual caress of this wondrously delicate tissue amidst which their guilty fingers fondly lingered. They still kept Mouret a close prisoner and overwhelmed him with fresh questions. As the daylight continued to decline, he was now and again obliged to bend his head, grazing their hair with his beard, as he examined a mesh, or indicated a design. Nevertheless in this soft voluptuousness of twilight, in this warm feminine atmosphere, Mouret still remained the master whatever the rapture he affected. He seemed

ÉMILE ZOLA

to be a woman himself, they felt penetrated, overcome by the delicate sense of their secret passions which he possessed, and surrendered themselves to him quite captivated; whilst he, certain that he had them at his mercy, appeared like the despotic monarch of finery, enthroned above them all.

"Oh, Monsieur Mouret! Monsieur Mouret!" they stammered in low, rapturous voices, amidst the increasing gloom of the drawing-room.

The last pale gleams of the heavens were dying away on the brass-work of the furniture. The laces alone retained a snowy reflection against the dark dresses of the ladies, who in a confused group around the young man had a vague appearance of kneeling, worshipping women. A final glow still shone on one side of the silver teapot, a gleam like that of a night-light, burning in an alcove balmy with the perfume of tea. But suddenly the servant entered with two lamps, and the charm was destroyed. The drawing-room awoke, light and cheerful once more. Madame Marty replaced her lace in her little bag and Madame de Boves ate another sponge cake, whilst Henriette who had risen began talking in a low tone to the baron, near one of the windows.

"He's a charming fellow," said the baron.

"Isn't he?" she exclaimed, with the involuntary impulse of a woman in love.

He smiled, and looked at her with paternal indulgence. This was the first time he had seen her so completely conquered; and, too high-minded to suffer from it, he experienced nothing but compassion at seeing her in the hands of this handsome fellow, seemingly so tender and yet so cold-hearted. He thought he ought to warn her, and so in a joking way he muttered: "Take care, my dear, or he'll eat you all up."

A flash of jealousy darted from Henriette's fine eyes. Doubtless she understood that Mouret had simply made use of her to get at the baron; but she vowed that she would render him mad with passion, he whose hurried style of love-making was instinct with the facile charm of a song thrown to the four winds of heaven. "Oh," said she, affecting to joke in her turn, "the lamb always finishes by eating up the wolf."

Thereupon the baron, greatly amused, encouraged her with a nod. Could she be the woman who was to avenge all the others?

When Mouret, after reminding Vallagnosc that he wanted to show him his machine at work, came up to take his leave, the baron retained him near the window opposite the gardens, now steeped in darkness. He was at last yielding to the young man's power of fascination; confidence had come to him on seeing him amidst those ladies. Both conversed for a moment in a low tone, and then the banker exclaimed: "Well, I'll look into the affair. It's settled if your Monday's sale proves as important as you expect."

They shook hands, and Mouret, delighted, took his leave, for he never enjoyed his dinner unless before sitting down at table he had been to glance at the day's receipts at The Ladies' Paradise.

# IV

On the following Monday, the 10th of October, a bright sun of victory pierced through the grey clouds which had darkened Paris during the previous week. There had even been a drizzle throughout the previous night, a sort of watery mist whose moisture had dirtied the streets; but in the early morning, thanks to the sharp breezes driving the clouds away, the pavement had become drier; and now the blue sky displayed a limpid, spring-like gaiety.

Thus, already at eight o'clock, The Ladies' Paradise blazed forth beneath the clear sun-rays in all the glory of its great sale of winter novelties. Flags were flying at the door, pieces of woollens were flapping about in the fresh morning air, animating the Place Gaillon with the bustle of a country fair; whilst along both streets the windows developed symphonious displays whose brilliant tones were yet heightened by the clearness of the glass. It was like a debauch of colour, a street pleasure bursting forth, a wealth of purchasable articles publicly displayed, on which everybody could feast their eyes.

But at this early hour very few people entered, a few customers pressed for time, housewives of the neighbourhood, women desirous of avoiding the afternoon crush. Behind the stuffs which decorated the shop, one could divine that it was empty, under arms and waiting for customers, with its waxed floors and its counters overflowing with goods.

The busy morning crowd barely glanced at the windows, as it passed without slackening its steps. In the Rue Neuve-Saint-Augustin and on the Place Gaillon, where the vehicles were to take their stand, there were at nine o'clock only two cabs. The inhabitants of the district, and especially the small traders, stirred up by such a show of streamers and decorations, alone formed little groups in the doorways and at the street corners, gazing at the Paradise and venting bitter remarks. What most filled them with indignation was the sight of one of the four delivery vans just introduced by Mouret, which was standing in the Rue de la Michodière, in front of the delivery office. These vans were green, picked out with yellow and red, their brilliantly varnished panels gleaming with gold and purple in the sunlight. This particular one with its brand-new medley of colours, and the name of the establishment painted on either side, whilst up above appeared an announcement of the day's sale, finished by going off at the fast trot of a splendid horse, after being filled with parcels left over from the previous night; and Baudu, who was standing on the threshold of The Old Elbeuf, watched it rolling off towards the boulevard, where it disappeared to spread amid a starry radiance the hated name of The Ladies' Paradise all over Paris.

Meantime, a few cabs were arriving and forming in line. Each time a customer entered, there was a movement amongst the shop messengers, who dressed in livery consisting of a light green coat and trousers, and red and yellow striped waistcoat were drawn up under the lofty doorway. Jouve, the inspector and retired captain, was also there, in a frock-coat and white tie, wearing his decoration as a mark of respectability and probity, and receiving the ladies with a gravely polite air. He bent over them to point out the departments, and then they vanished into the vestibule, which had been transformed into an oriental saloon.

From the very threshold it was a marvel, a surprise, which enchanted all of them. It was to Mouret that this idea had occurred. Before all others, he had been the first to purchase at very advantageous rates in the Levant a collection of old and new carpets, articles then but seldom seen and only sold at curiosity shops, at high prices; and he intended to flood the market with them, selling them at but little more than cost price, and simply utilizing them as a splendid decoration which would attract the best class of art customers to his establishment. From the centre of the Place Gaillon you could see this oriental saloon, composed solely of carpets and door-curtains hung up under his direction. The ceiling was covered with a quantity of Smyrna carpets, whose intricate designs stood out boldly on red grounds. Then from each side there hung Syrian and Karamanian door-curtains, streaked with green, yellow, and vermilion; Diarbekir hangings of a commoner type, rough to the touch, like shepherds' cloaks; and carpets which could also be used as door-curtains—long Ispahan, Teheran, and Kermancha rugs, broader ones from Schoumaka and Madras, a strange florescence of peonies and palms, fantastic blooms in a garden of dreamland. On the floor too were more carpets, a heap of greasy fleeces: in the centre was an Agra carpet, an extraordinary article with a white ground and a broad, delicate blue border, through which ran a violet-coloured pattern of exquisite design. And then, here, there and everywhere came a display of marvels; Mecca carpets with velvety reflections, prayer carpets from Daghestan with the symbolic points, Kurdistan carpets covered with blooming flowers; and finally, in a corner a pile of cheap goods, Gherdes, Koula, and Kirchur rugs from fifteen francs a-piece.

This seeming and sumptuous tent, fit for a caliph, was furnished with divans and arm-chairs, made of camel sacks, some ornamented with variegated lozenges, others with primitive roses. Turkey, Arabia, Persia and the Indies were all there. They had emptied the palaces, looted the mosques and bazaars. A tawny gold prevailed in the weft of the old carpets, whose faded tints retained still a sombre warmth, like that of an extinguished furnace, a beautiful mellow hue suggestive of the old masters. Visions of the East floated before you at sight of all the luxury of this barbarous art, amid the strong odour which the old wool retained of the land of vermin and of the rising sun.

In the morning at eight o'clock, when Denise, who was to enter on her duties that very Monday, crossed the oriental saloon, she stopped short, lost in astonishment, unable to recognise the shop entrance, and quite overcome by this harem-like decoration planted at the door. A messenger having shown her to the top of the house, and handed her over to Madame Cabin, who cleaned and looked after the rooms, this person installed her in No. 7, where her box had already been placed. It was a narrow cell, opening on the roof by a skylight, and furnished with a small bed, a walnut-wood wardrobe, a toilet-table, and two chairs. Twenty similar rooms ran along the yellow-painted convent-like corridor; and, of the thirty-five young ladies in the house, the twenty who had no relations in Paris slept there, whilst the remaining fifteen lodged outside, a few with borrowed aunts and cousins. Denise at once took off her shabby woollen dress, worn thin by brushing and mended at the sleeves, the only gown that she had brought from Valognes; and then donned the uniform of her department, a black silk dress which had been altered for her and which she found ready on the bed. This dress was still too large, too wide across the shoulders; but she was so flurried by her emotion that she paid no heed to petty questions of coquetry. She had never worn silk before; and when rigged out in this unwonted finery she went downstairs again and looked at her shining skirt, she felt quite ashamed of the noisy rustling of the silk.

Down below, as she was entering her department, a quarrel burst out and she heard Clara exclaim in a shrill voice:

"Madame, I came in before her."

"It isn't true," replied Marguerite. "She pushed past me at the door, but I had already one foot in the room."

The matter in dispute was their inscription on the list of turns, which regulated the sales. The girls wrote their names on a slate in the order of their arrival, and whenever one of them had served a customer, she re-inscribed her name beneath the others. Madame Aurélie finished by deciding in Marguerite's favour.

"Always some injustice here!" muttered Clara, furiously.

However Denise's entry reconciled these young ladies. They looked at her, then smiled at each other. How could a person truss herself up in that way! The young girl went and awkwardly wrote her name on the list, where she found herself last. Meanwhile, Madame Aurélie examined her with an anxious pout and could not help saying:

"My dear, two like you could get into your dress; you must have it taken in. Besides, you don't know how to dress yourself. Come here and let me arrange you a bit."

Then she placed her before one of the tall glasses alternating with the massive doors of the cupboards containing the dresses. The spacious apartment, surrounded by these mirrors and carved oak wood-work, its floor covered with red carpet of a large pattern, resembled the commonplace drawing-room of an hotel, traversed by a continual stream of travellers. The young ladies dressed in regulation silk, and promenading their charms about, without ever sitting down on the dozen chairs reserved for the customers, completed the resemblance. Between two button-holes of their dress bodies they all wore a long pencil, with its point in the air; and protruding from their pockets, you could see the white leaves of a book of debit-notes. Several ventured to wear jewellery—rings, brooches and chains; but their great coquetry, the point of display in which, given the forced uniformity of their dress they all struggled for pre-eminence, was their hair, hair ever overflowing, its volume augmented by plaits and chignons when their own did not suffice, and combed, curled, and decked in every possible fashion.

"Pull the waist down in front," said Madame Aurélie to Denise. "There, you now have no hump on your back. And your hair, how can you massacre it like that? It would be superb, if you only took a little trouble."

This was, in fact, Denise's only beauty. Of a beautiful flaxen hue, it fell to her ankles: and when she did it up, it was so troublesome that she simply rolled it in a knot, keeping it together with the strong teeth of a bone comb. Clara, greatly annoyed by the sight of this abundant hair, affected to laugh at it, so strange did it look, twisted up anyhow with savage grace. She made a sign to a saleswoman in the under-linen department, a girl with a broad face and agreeable manner. The two departments, which adjoined one another, were ever at variance, still the young ladies sometimes joined together in laughing at other people.

"Mademoiselle Cugnot, just look at that mane," said Clara, whom Marguerite was nudging, also feigning to be on the point of bursting into laughter.

But Mademoiselle Cugnot was not in the humour for joking. She had been looking at Denise for a moment and remembered what she had suffered herself during the first few months after her arrival in the establishment.

"Well, what?" said she. "Everybody hasn't got such a mane as that!"

And thereupon she returned to her place, leaving the two others crestfallen. Denise, who had heard everything, followed her with a glance of gratitude, while Madame Aurélie gave her a book of debit-notes with her name on it, remarking:

"To-morrow you must get yourself up better; and now, try and pick up the ways of the house, and wait your turn for selling. To-day's work will be very hard; we shall be able to judge of your capabilities."

Despite her prophecies, the department still remained deserted; very few customers came to buy mantles at this early hour. The young ladies husbanded their strength, prudently preparing for the exertion of the afternoon. Denise, intimidated by the thought that they were watching her, sharpened her pencil, for the sake of something to do; then, imitating the others, she stuck it in her bosom, between two buttonholes, and summoned up all her courage, for it was necessary that she should conquer a position. On the previous evening she had been told that she was accepted as a probationer, that is to say, without any fixed salary; she would simply have the commission and allowance on what she sold. However, she fully hoped to earn twelve hundred francs a year even in this way, knowing that the good saleswomen earned as much as two thousand, when they liked to take the trouble. Her expenses were regulated; a hundred francs a month would enable her to pay Pépé's board and lodging, assist Jean, who did not earn a sou, and procure some clothes and linen for herself. Only, in order to attain to this large amount, she would have to prove industrious and pushing, taking no notice of the ill-will displayed by those around her but fighting for her share and even snatching it from her comrades if necessary. While she was thus working herself up for the struggle, a tall young man, passing the department, smiled at her; and when she saw that it was Deloche, who had been engaged in the lace department on the previous day, she returned his smile, happy at the friendship which thus presented itself and accepting his recognition as a good omen.

At half-past nine a bell rang for the first luncheon. Then a fresh peal announced the second; and still no customers appeared. The second-hand, Madame Frédéric, who, with the sulky harshness of widowhood, delighted in prophesying disasters, declared curtly that the day was lost, that they would not see a soul, that they might close the cupboards and go away; predictions which clouded the flat face of Marguerite who was eager to make money, whilst Clara, with her runaway-horse appearance, already began dreaming of an excursion to the woods of Verrières should the house really fail. As for Madame Aurélie, she remained silent and serious, promenading her Cæsarian countenance about the empty department, like a general who has responsibility whether in victory or in defeat.

About eleven o'clock a few ladies appeared; and Denise's turn for serving had arrived when the approach of a customer was signalled.

"The fat old girl from the country—you know whom I mean," murmured Marguerite to Clara.

It was a woman of forty-five, who occasionally journeyed to Paris from the depths of some out-of-the-way department where she saved her money up for months together. Then, hardly out of the train, she made straight for The Ladies' Paradise, and spent all her savings. She very rarely ordered anything by letter for she liked to see and handle the goods, and would profit by her journeys to lay in a stock of everything, even down to needles, which she said were extremely dear in her small town. The whole staff knew her, was aware that her name was Boutarel, and that she lived at Albi, but troubled no further about her, neither about her position nor her mode of life.

"How do you do, madame?" graciously asked Madame Aurélie, who had come forward. "And what can we show you? You shall be attended to at once." Then, turning round she added: "Now, young ladies!"

Denise approached; but Clara had sprung forward. As a rule, she was very careless and idle, not caring about the money she earned in the shop, as she could get plenty outside. However, the idea of doing the newcomer out of a good customer spurred her on.

"I beg your pardon, it's my turn," said Denise, indignantly.

Madame Aurélie set her aside with a severe look, exclaiming: "There are no turns. I alone am mistress here. Wait till you know, before serving our regular customers."

The young girl retired, and as tears were coming to her eyes, and she wished to conceal her sensibility, she turned her back and stood up before the window, pretending to gaze into the street. Were they going to prevent her selling? Would they all conspire to deprive her of the important sales, like that? Fear for the future came over her, she felt herself crushed between so many contending interests. Yielding to the bitterness of her abandonment, her forehead against the cold glass, she gazed at The Old Elbeuf opposite, thinking that she ought to have implored her uncle to keep her. Perhaps he himself regretted his decision, for he had seemed to her greatly affected the previous evening. And now she was quite alone in this vast house, where no one cared for her, where she found herself hurtled, lost. Pépé and Jean, who had never left her side, were living with strangers; she was parted from everything, and the big tears which she strove to keep back made the street dance before her in a sort of fog. All this time, the hum of voices continued behind her.

"This one makes me look a fright," Madame Boutarel was saying.

"You really make a mistake, madame," said Clara; "the shoulders fit perfectly—but perhaps you would prefer a pelisse to a mantle?"

Just then Denise started. A hand was laid on her arm. Madame Aurélie addressed her severely:

"Well, you're doing nothing now, eh? only looking at the people passing? Things can't go on like this, you know!"

"But since I'm not allowed to sell, madame?"

"Oh, there's other work for you, mademoiselle! Begin at the beginning. Do the folding-up."

In order to please the few customers who had called, they had already been obliged to ransack the cupboards, and on the two long oaken tables, to the right and left, lay heaps of mantles, pelisses, and capes, garments of all sizes and materials. Without replying, Denise began to sort and fold them carefully and arrange them again in the cupboards. This was the lowest work, generally performed by beginners. She ceased to protest, however, knowing that they required the strictest obedience, and prepared to wait until the first-hand should be good enough to let her sell, as she seemed at first to have the intention of doing. She was still folding, when Mouret appeared upon the scene. To her his arrival came as a shock, she blushed without knowing why, and again seized by a strange fear, thinking that he was going to speak to her. But he did not even see her; he no longer remembered the little girl whom a momentary impression had induced him to support.

"Madame Aurélie," he called curtly.

He was rather pale, but his eyes were clear and resolute. In making the tour of the departments he had found them empty, and the possibility of defeat had suddenly presented itself before him amidst all his obstinate faith in fortune. True, it was only eleven o'clock; he knew by experience that as a rule the crowd never arrived much before the afternoon. But certain symptoms troubled him. On the inaugural days of previous sales a general movement had manifested itself even in the morning; besides, he did not see any of those bareheaded women, customers living in the neighbourhood, who usually dropped into his shop as into a neighbour's. Despite his habitual resolution, like all great captains, he felt at the moment of giving battle a superstitious weakness growing on him. Things would not succeed, he was lost, and he could not have explained why; yet he thought he could read his defeat on the faces of the passing ladies. Just at that moment, Madame Boutarel, she who always bought something, turned away, explaining, "No, you have nothing that pleases me. I'll see, I'll decide later on."

Mouret watched her depart. Then, as Madame Aurélie ran up at his call, he took her aside, and they exchanged a few rapid words. She waved her hands despairingly and was evidently admitting that things were bad. For a moment they remained face to face, overcome by one of those doubts which generals conceal from their soldiers. But at last, in his brave way, he exclaimed aloud: "If you want any assistance, take a girl from the workroom. She'll be a little help to you."

Then he continued his inspection, in despair. He had avoided Bourdoncle all the morning, for his assistant's anxious doubts irritated him. However, on leaving the under-linen department, where business was still worse than in the mantle gallery, he suddenly came upon him, and was obliged to listen to the expression of his fears. Still he did not hesitate to send him to the devil, with the brutality which he did not spare even his principal employees when things were looking bad.

"Do keep quiet!" said he, "Everything is going on all right. I shall end by pitching the tremblers out of doors."

Then, alone and erect, he took his stand on the landing overlooking the central hall, whence he commanded a view of almost the entire shop; around him were the first-floor departments; beneath him those of the ground-floor. Up above, the emptiness seemed heart-breaking; in the lace department an old woman was having every box searched and yet buying nothing; whilst three good-for-nothing minxes in the under-linen department were slowly choosing some collars at eighteen sous a-piece. Down below, in the covered galleries, in the rays of light which come in from the street, he noticed that customers were gradually becoming more numerous. There was a slow, intermittent procession wending its way past the counters; in the mercery and the haberdashery departments some women of the commoner class were pushing about, still there was hardly a soul among the linens or the woollens. The shop messengers, in their green swallow-tails with bright brass buttons, were waiting for customers with dangling hands. Now and again there passed an inspector with a ceremonious air, very stiff in his white choker. And Mouret was especially grieved by the mortal silence which reigned in the hall, where the light fell from a ground-glass roofing through which the sunrays filtered in a white diffuse hovering dust, whilst down below the silk department seemed to be asleep, in a quivering, church-like quietude. A shopman's footstep, a few whispered words, the rustling of a passing skirt, were the only faint sounds; and these the warm air of the heating apparatus almost stifled. However, carriages were beginning to arrive, the sudden pulling up of the horses was heard, followed by the banging of the doors of the vehicles. Outside, a distant tumult was commencing to rise, inquisitive folks were jostling in front of the windows, cabs were taking up their positions on the Place Gaillon, there were all the appearances of a crowd's approach. Still on seeing the idle cashiers leaning back on their chairs behind their wickets, and observing that the parcel-tables with their boxes of string and reams of blue packing-paper remained unlittered, Mouret, though indignant with himself for being afraid, thought he could feel his immense machine ceasing to work and turning cold beneath him.

"I say, Favier," murmured Hutin, "look at the governor up there. He doesn't seem to be enjoying himself."

"Oh! this is a rotten shop!" replied Favier. "Just fancy, I've not sold a thing yet."

Both of them, on the look-out for customers, from time to time whispered such short remarks as these, without looking at each other. The other salesmen of the department were occupied in piling up pieces of the Paris Delight under Robineau's orders; whilst Bouthemont, in full consultation with a thin young woman, seemed to be taking an important order. Around them, on light and elegant shelves, were heaps of plain silks, folded in long pieces of creamy paper, and looking like pamphlets of an unusual size; whilst, encumbering the counters, were fancy silks, moires, satins and velvets, resembling beds of cut flowers, quite a harvest of delicate and precious tissues. This was the most elegant of all the departments, a veritable drawing-room, where the goods, so light and airy, seemed to be simply so much luxurious furnishing.

"I must have a hundred francs by Sunday," said Hutin. "If I don't make an average of twelve francs a day, I'm lost. I reckoned on this sale."

"By Jove! a hundred francs; that's rather stiff," retorted Favier. "I only want fifty or sixty. You must go in for swell jollifications, then?"

"Oh, no, my dear fellow. It's a stupid affair; I made a bet and lost. So I have to stand a dinner for five persons, two fellows and three girls. Hang me! I'll let the first that passes in for twenty yards of Paris Delight!"

They continued talking for a few minutes, relating what they had done on the previous day, and what they intended to do on the ensuing Sunday. Favier followed the races while Hutin did a little boating, and patronized music-hall singers. But they were both possessed by the same eager desire for money, fighting for it throughout the week, and spending it all on Sunday. It was their sole thought in the shop, a thought which urged them into an incessant and pitiless struggle. And to think that cunning Bouthemont had just managed to get hold of Madame Sauveur's messenger, the skinny woman with whom he was talking! That meant good business, three or four dozen pieces, at least, for the celebrated dressmaker always gave large orders. A moment before too, Robineau had taken it into his head to trick Favier out of a customer.

"Oh! as for that fellow, we must settle his hash," said Hutin, who took advantage of the slightest incidents to stir up the salesmen against the man whose place he coveted. "Ought the first and second hands to sell? 'Pon my word! my dear fellow, if ever I become second you'll see how well I'll act with the others."

Thereupon, with his plump, amiable little Norman person he began energetically playing the good-natured man. Favier could not help casting a side glance at him; however he retained his phlegmatic air and contented himself with replying:

"Yes, I know. For my part I should be only too pleased." Then, as a lady came up, he added in a lower tone: "Look out! Here's one for you."

It was a lady with a blotchy face, wearing a yellow bonnet, and a red dress. Hutin immediately divined in her a woman who would buy nothing; so in all haste he stooped behind the counter, pretending to be doing up his boot-lace: and, thus concealed, he murmured: "No fear, let some one else take her. I don't want to lose my turn!"

ÉMILE ZOLA

However, Robineau was calling him: "Whose turn, gentlemen? Monsieur Hutin's? Where's Monsieur Hutin?"

And as that gentleman still gave no reply, it was the next salesman who served the lady with the blotches. Hutin was quite right, she simply wanted some patterns with the prices; and she detained the salesman more than ten minutes, overwhelming him with questions. However, Robineau had seen Hutin get up from behind the counter; and so when another customer arrived, he interfered with a stern air, and stopped the young man just as he was rushing forward.

"Your turn has passed. I called you, and as you were there behind—"

"But I didn't hear you, sir."

"That'll do! write your name at the bottom. Now, Monsieur Favier, it's your turn."

Favier, greatly amused at heart by this adventure, gave his friend a glance, as if to excuse himself. Hutin, with pale lips, had turned his head away. What particularly enraged him was that he knew the customer very well, an adorable blonde who often came to their department, and whom the salesmen called amongst themselves "the pretty lady," knowing nothing of her except her looks, not even her name. She always made a good many purchases, instructed a messenger to take them to her carriage, and then immediately disappeared. Tall, elegant, dressed with exquisite taste, she appeared to be very rich, and to belong to the best society.

"Well! and your hussy?" asked Hutin of Favier, when the latter returned from the pay-desk, whither he had accompanied the lady.

"Oh! a hussy!" replied the other. "No, she looks far too lady-like. She must be the wife of a stockbroker or a doctor, or something of that sort."

"Don't tell me! All the women get themselves up so much alike now-a-days that it's impossible to tell what they are!"

Favier glanced at his debit book. "I don't care!" he resumed, "I've stuck her for two hundred and ninety-three francs. That makes nearly three francs for me."

Hutin bit his lips, and vented his spleen on the debit books. Another invention for cramming their pockets! There was a secret rivalry between these two. Favier, as a rule, pretended to consider himself of small account and to recognise Hutin's superiority, but in reality devoured him all the while behind his back. Thus, Hutin was wild at the thought of the three francs pocketed so easily by a salesman whom he considered his inferior in business-talent. A fine day's work! If it went on like this, he would not earn enough to pay for the seltzer water for his Sunday guests. And in the midst of the battle, which was now becoming fiercer, he walked along the counters with hungry eyes, eager for his share, jealous even of his superior, who was just showing the thin young woman out, and saying to her:

"Very well! it's understood. Tell her I'll do my best to obtain this favour from Monsieur Mouret."

Mouret had quitted his post up above some time before. Suddenly he reappeared on the landing of the principal staircase which communicated with the ground floor; and here again he commanded a view of the whole establishment. His face was regaining its colour, his faith was coming back and increasing at sight of the crowd which was gradually filling the place. It was the expected rush at last, the afternoon crush, which in his feverishness he had for a moment despaired of. All the shopmen were at their posts, a last ring of the bell had announced the end of the third lunch; the disasters of the morning, due no doubt to a shower which had fallen about nine o'clock, could still be repaired, for the blue sky of daybreak had come back with its victorious gaiety. Now that the first-floor departments were growing animated, he was obliged to stand back to make way for the women who were coming up to the under-clothing and mantle departments; whilst, behind him, in the lace and the shawl departments, he heard shopmen and customers talking of large sums. But the sight of the galleries on the ground-floor especially reassured him. There was a crowd among the haberdashery, and even the linen and woollen departments were invaded. The procession of buyers had closed up; and now nearly all of them wore hats or bonnets, it was only here and there that you espied the white caps of a few belated housewives. In the yellow light streaming down into the silk hall, ladies had taken off their gloves to feel the Paris Delight on which they commented in whispers. And there was no longer any mistaking the noises which came from outside, the rolling of cabs, the banging of carriage-doors, all the increasing tumult of a growing crowd. Mouret felt that his machine was again setting to work beneath him, getting up steam and reviving to activity, from the pay-desks where gold was jingling, and the tables where messengers were hurriedly packing up goods, to the delivery-room in the basement, which was quickly filling with the parcels sent down to it, its subterraneous rumble seeming to shake the whole house. And in the midst of the crowd was inspector Jouve, walking about gravely, on the look-out for thieves.

"Hullo! is that you?" said Mouret, all at once recognising Paul de Vallagnosc whom a messenger was conducting to him. "No, no, you are not in my way. Besides, you've only to follow me if you want to see everything, for to-day I stay in the breach."

He still felt a little anxious. No doubt there were plenty of people, but would the sale prove to be the triumph he hoped for? However, he laughed with Paul and gaily carried him off.

"Things seem to be picking up a bit," said Hutin to Favier. "But somehow I've no luck; there are some days that are precious bad, my word! I've just made another miss, that old frump hasn't bought anything."

As he spoke he glanced towards a lady who was walking off, casting looks of disgust at all the goods. He was not likely to get fat on his thousand francs a year, unless he sold something; as a rule he made seven or eight francs a day in commission, which with his regular pay gave him an average of ten francs a day. Favier never made much more than eight, and yet now that animal was literally taking the bread out of his mouth, for he had just sold another dress. To think of it, a cold-natured fellow who had never known how to amuse a customer! It was exasperating.

"Those chaps over there seem to be doing very well," remarked Favier, speaking of the salesmen in the hosiery and haberdashery departments.

But Hutin, who was looking all round the place, suddenly inquired: "Do you know Madame Desforges, the governor's sweetheart? Look! that dark woman in the glove department, who is having some gloves tried on by Mignot." He paused, then resumed in a low tone, as if speaking to Mignot, on whom he continued to direct his eyes: "Oh, go on, old man, you may pull her fingers about as much as you like, that won't do you any good! We know your conquests!"

There was a rivalry between himself and the glove-man, the rivalry of two handsome fellows, who both affected to flirt with the lady-customers. As a matter of fact neither had any real conquests to boast about, but they invented any number of mysterious adventures, seeking to make people believe in all sorts of appointments given them by titled ladies between two purchases.

"You ought to get hold of her," said Favier, in his sly, artful way.

"That's a good idea!" exclaimed Hutin. "If she comes here I'll let her in for something extensive; I want a five-franc piece!"

In the glove department there was quite a row of ladies seated before the narrow counter covered with green velvet and edged with nickel silver; and before them the smiling shopmen were heaping up flat boxes of a bright pink, taken out of the counter itself, and resembling the ticketed drawers of a secrétaire. Mignot, in particular, was bending his pretty doll-like face forward, and striving to impart tender inflections to his thick Parisian voice. He had already sold Madame Desforges a dozen pairs of kid gloves, the Paradise gloves, one of the specialties of the house. She had then asked for three pairs of Suèdes, and was now trying on some Saxon gloves, for fear the size should not be exact.

"Oh! the fit is perfect, madame," repeated Mignot. "Six and a quarter would be too large for a hand like yours."

Half-lying on the counter, he held her hand, taking her fingers one by one and slipping the glove on with a long, renewed, persistently caressing touch, looking at her the while as if he expected to see in her face some sign of pleasure. But she, with her elbow on the velvet counter and her wrist raised, surrendered her fingers to him with the same unconcerned air as that with which she gave her foot to her maid so that she might button her boot. For her indeed he was not a man; she utilized his services with the disdain she always showed for servants and did not even look at him.

"I don't hurt you, madame?" he inquired.

She replied "No," with a shake of the head. The smell of the Saxon gloves—a savage smell resembling sugared musk—troubled her as a rule, but seated at this commonplace counter she did not notice it.

"And what next, madame?" asked Mignot.

"Nothing, thanks. Be good enough to carry the parcel to pay-desk No. 10, for Madame Desforges."

Being a constant customer, she gave her name at a pay-desk, and had each purchase sent there without requiring a shopman to follow her. When she had gone away, Mignot turned towards his neighbour and winked, and would have liked him to believe that some wonderful things had just taken place.

Meanwhile, Madame Desforges continued her purchases. She turned to the left, stopping in the linen department to procure some dusters; then she walked round and went as far as the woollen department at the further end of the gallery. As she was well pleased with her cook, she wanted to make her a present of a dress. The woollen department overflowed with a compact crowd; all the lower middle-class women were there, feeling the stuffs and absorbed in mute calculations; and she was obliged to sit down for a moment. The shelves were piled up with great rolls of material which the salesmen took down one by one, with a sudden pull. They were indeed getting confused with all the litter on the counters, where stuffs were mingling and slipping down. It was a sea of neutral tints, the dull hues of woollens—iron-greys, yellow-greys and blue-greys, with here and there a Scotch tartan and a blood-red flannel showing brightly. And the white tickets on the pieces looked like a scanty shower of snow flakes, dotting a dark December soil.

Behind a pile of poplin, Liénard was joking with a tall bare-headed girl, a work-girl of the neigbourhood, sent by her mistress to match some merino. He detested these big-sale days, which tired him to death, and endeavoured to shirk his work, getting plenty of money from his father and not caring a fig about the business but doing only just enough to avoid being dismissed.

"Listen to me, Mademoiselle Fanny," he was saying; "you are always in a hurry. Did the striped vicuna suit the other day? I shall come and see you, and ask for my commission, mind."

But the girl ran off, laughing, and Liénard found himself before Madame Desforges, whom he could not help asking: "What can I serve you with, madame?"

She wanted a dress, not too dear but yet of strong stuff. Liénard, with the view of sparing his arms, which was his principal thought, manœuvred so as to make her take one of the stuffs already unfolded on the counter. There were cashmeres, serges and vicunas there, and he declared that there was nothing better to be had, for you could never wear them out. However, none of these seemed to satisfy her. On one of the shelves she had observed a blue shalloon, which she wished to see. So he made up his mind at last, and took down the roll, but she thought the material too rough. Then he showed her a cheviot, some diagonals, some greys, every sort of woollens, which she felt out of curiosity, just for the pleasure of doing so, decided at heart to take no matter what. The young man was thus obliged to empty the highest shelves; his shoulders cracked and the counter vanished under the silky grain of the cashmeres and poplins, the rough nap of the cheviots and the tufty down of the vicunas; there were samples of every material and every tint. Though she had not the least wish to buy any, she even asked to see some grenadine and some Chambéry gauze. Then, when she had seen enough, she remarked:

"Oh! after all, the first is the best; it's for my cook. Yes, the narrow ribbed serge, the one at two francs." And when Liénard had measured it, pale with suppressed anger, she added: "Have the goodness to take that to pay-desk No. 10, for Madame Desforges."

Just as she was going away, she recognised Madame Marty near her, accompanied by her daughter Valentine, a tall girl of fourteen, thin and bold, who already cast a woman's covetous looks on the materials.

"Ah! it's you, dear madame?"

"Yes, dear madame; what a crowd—is it not?"

"Oh! don't speak of it, it's stifling. And such a success! Have you seen the oriental saloon?"

"Superb—wonderful!"

Thereupon, amidst all the jostling, pushed hither and thither by the growing crowd of modest purses rushing upon the cheap woollen goods, they went into ecstasies over the exhibition of Eastern carpets. And afterwards Madame Marty explained that she was looking for some material for a mantle; but she had not quite made up her mind and wanted to see some woollen *matelassé*.

"Look, mamma," murmured Valentine, "it's too common."

"Come to the silk department," then said Madame Desforges, "you must see their famous Paris Delight."

Madame Marty hesitated for a moment. It would be very dear, and she had faithfully promised her husband to be reasonable! She had been buying for an hour, quite a pile of articles was following her already: a muff and some quilling for herself and some stockings for her daughter. She finished by saying to the shopman who was showing her the *matelassé*:

"Well—no; I'm going to the silk department; you've nothing to suit me."

The shopman then took up the articles already purchased and walked off before the ladies.

In the silk department there was also a crowd, the principal crush being opposite the inside display arranged by Hutin, to which Mouret had given the finishing touches. This was at the further end of the hall, around one of the slender wrought-iron columns which supported the glass roof. A perfect torrent of material, a billowy cascade fell from above, spreading out more and more as it neared the floor. The bright satins and soft-tinted silks—the Reine and Renaissance satins with the pearly tones of spring water; the light silks, Nile-green, Indian-azure, May-pink, and Danube-blue all of crystalline transparency—flowed forth above. Then came the stronger fabrics: warm-tinted Merveilleux satins, and Duchess silks, rolling in waves of increasing volume; whilst at the bottom, as in a fountain-basin, the heavy materials, the figured armures, the damasks, and brocades, the beaded silks and the silk embroidered with gold and silver, reposed amidst a deep bed of velvet of every sort—black, white, and coloured—with patterns stamped on silk and satin grounds, and spreading out with their medley of colours like a still lake in which reflections of sky and scenery were seemingly dancing. The women, pale with desire, bent over as if to look at themselves in a mirror. And before this gushing cataract they all remained hesitating between a secret fear of being carried away by such a flood of luxury, and an irresistible desire to jump in and be lost in it.

"Here you are, then!" said Madame Desforges, on finding Madame Bourdelais installed before a counter.

"Ah! good day!" replied the latter, shaking hands with the other ladies. "Yes, I've come to have a look."

"What a prodigious exhibition! It's like a dream. And the oriental saloon! Have you seen the oriental saloon?"

"Yes, yes; extraordinary!"

But beneath this enthusiasm, which was decidedly to be the fashionable note of the day, Madame Bourdelais retained her practical housewifely coolness. She was carefully examining a piece of Paris Delight, for she had come on purpose to profit by the exceptional cheapness of this silk, if she found it really advantageous. She was doubtless satisfied with it, for she bought five-and-twenty yards, hoping that this quantity would prove sufficient to make a dress for herself and a cloak for her little girl.

"What! you are going already?" resumed Madame Desforges. "Take a walk round with us."

"No, thanks; they are waiting for me at home. I didn't like to risk bringing the children into this crowd."

Thereupon she went away, preceded by the salesman carrying the twenty-five yards of silk, who led her to pay-desk No. 10, where young Albert was getting confused by all the demands for invoices with which he was besieged. When the salesman was able to approach, after having inscribed his sale on a debit-note, he called out the item, which the cashier entered in a register; then it was checked, and the leaf torn out of the salesman's debit book was stuck on a file near the receipting stamp.

"One hundred and forty francs," said Albert.

Madame Bourdelais paid and gave her address, for having come on foot she did not wish to be troubled with a parcel. Joseph had already received the silk behind the pay-desk, and was tying it up; and then the parcel, thrown into a basket on wheels, was sent down to the delivery department, which seemed to swallow up all the goods in the shop with a sluice-like roar.

Meanwhile, the block was becoming so great in the silk department that Madame Desforges and Madame Marty could not find a salesman disengaged. So they remained standing, mingling with the crowd of ladies who were looking at the silks and feeling them, staying there for hours without making up their minds. However the Paris Delight proved the great success; around it pressed one of those crowds whose feverish infatuation decrees a fashion in a day. A host of shopmen were engaged in measuring off this silk; above the customers' heads you could see the pale glimmer of the unfolded pieces, as the fingers of the employees came and went along the oak yard measures hanging from brass rods; and you could hear the noise of scissors swiftly cutting the silk, as fast as it was unwound, as if indeed there were not shopmen enough to suffice for all the greedy outstretched hands of the purchasers.

"It really isn't bad for five francs sixty centimes," said Madame Desforges, who had succeeded in getting hold of a piece at the edge of the table.

Madame Marty and her daughter experienced some disappointment, however. The newspapers had said so much about this silk, that they had expected something stronger and more brilliant. However, Bouthemont had just recognised Madame Desforges, and anxious to pay his court to such a handsome lady, who was supposed to be all-powerful with the governor, he came forward, with rather coarse amiability. What! no one was serving her! it was unpardonable! He begged her to be indulgent, for really they did not know which way to turn. And then he began to look for some chairs amongst the neighbouring skirts, laughing the while with his good-natured laugh, full of a brutal love for the sex, which did not seem to displease Henriette.

"I say," murmured Favier, as he went to take some velvet from a shelf behind Hutin, "there's Bouthemont making up to your mash."

Beside himself with rage with an old lady, who, after keeping him a quarter of an hour, had finished by buying a yard of black satin for a pair of stays, Hutin had quite forgotten Madame Desforges. In busy moments they took no notice of the turns, each salesman served the customers as they arrived. And he was answering Madame Boutarel, who was finishing her afternoon at The Ladies' Paradise, where she had already spent three hours in the morning, when Favier's warning made him start. What! was he going to miss the governor's sweetheart, from whom he had sworn to extract a five-franc piece for himself? That would be the height of ill-luck, for he hadn't made three francs as yet with all those other chignons who were mooning about the place!

Bouthemont was just then calling out loudly: "Come gentlemen, some one this way!"

Thereupon Hutin passed Madame Boutarel over to Robineau, who was doing nothing. "Here's the second-hand, madame. He will answer you better than I can."

And he rushed off to take Madame Marty's purchases from the woollen salesman who had accompanied the ladies. That day a nervous excitement must have interfered with his usually keen scent. As a rule, the first glance told him if a customer meant to buy, and how much. Then he domineered over the customer, hastened to serve her so as to pass on to another, imposing his choice upon her and persuading her that he knew better than herself what material she required.

"What sort of silk, madame?" he asked, in his most gallant manner and Madame Desforges had no sooner opened her mouth than he added: "I know, I've got just what you want."

When the piece of Paris Delight was unfolded on a corner of the counter, between heaps of other silks, Madame Marty and her daughter approached. Hutin, rather anxious, understood that it was at first a question of serving these two. Whispered words were exchanged, Madame Desforges was advising her friend. "Oh! certainly," she murmured. "A silk at five francs twelve sous will never equal one at fifteen, or even ten."

"It is very light," repeated Madame Marty. "I'm afraid that it has not sufficient body for a mantle."

This remark induced the salesman to intervene. He smiled with the exaggerated politeness of a man who cannot make a mistake. "But flexibility, madame, is the chief quality of this silk. It will not crimple. It's exactly what you require."

Impressed by such an assurance, the ladies said no more. They had taken the silk up, and were again examining it, when they felt a touch on their shoulders. It was Madame Guibal, who had been slowly walking about the shop for an hour past, feasting her eyes on all the assembled riches but not buying so much as a yard of calico. And now there was another explosion of gossip.

"What! Is that you?"

"Yes, it's I, rather knocked about though."

"What a crowd—eh? One can't get about. And the oriental saloon?"

"Ravishing!"

"Good heavens! what a success! Stay a moment, we will go upstairs together."

"No, thanks, I've just come down."

Hutin was waiting, concealing his impatience beneath a smile that did not quit his lips. Were they going to keep him there long? Really the women took things very coolly, it was like stealing money out of his pocket. At last, however, Madame Guibal went off to resume her stroll, turning round the large display of silks with an enraptured air.

"Well, if I were you I should buy the mantle ready-made," said Madame Desforges, suddenly returning to the Paris Delight. "It won't cost you so much."

"It's true that the trimmings and making-up—" murmured Madame Marty. "Besides, one has more choice."

All three had risen; Madame Desforges, turning to Hutin, said to him: "Have the goodness to show us to the mantle department."

He remained dumbfounded, unaccustomed as he was to such defeats. What! the dark lady bought nothing! Had he made a mistake then? Abandoning Madame Marty he thereupon attacked Madame Desforges, exerting all his ability as a salesman on her. "And you, madame, would you not like to see our satins, our velvets? We have some extraordinary bargains."

"Thanks, another time," she coolly replied, looking at him no more than she had looked at Mignot.

Hutin had to take up Madame Marty's purchases and walk off before the ladies to show them to the mantle department. But he also had the grief of seeing that Robineau was selling Madame Boutarel a large quantity of silk. Decidedly his scent was playing him false, he wouldn't make four sous! Beneath the amiable propriety of his manners his heart swelled with the rage of a man robbed and devoured by others.

"On the first floor, ladies," said he, without ceasing to smile.

It was no easy matter to reach the staircase. A compact crowd of heads was surging under the galleries and expanding like an overflowing river in the middle of the hall. Quite a battle of business was going on, the salesmen had this population of women at their mercy, and passed them on from one to another with feverish haste. The moment of the formidable afternoon rush, when the over-heated machine led its customers such a feverish dance, extracting money from their very flesh, had at last arrived. In the silk department especially a gust of folly seemed to reign, the Paris Delight had brought such a crowd together that for several minutes Hutin could not advance a step; and Henriette, half-suffocated, having raised her eyes to the summit of the stairs there beheld Mouret, who ever returned thither as to a favourite position, from which he could view victory. She smiled, hoping that he would come down and extricate her. But he did not even recognise her in the crowd; he was still with Vallagnosc, showing him the establishment, his face beaming with triumph the while.

The trepidation within was now stifling all outside noise; you no longer heard the rumbling of the vehicles, nor the banging of their doors; apart from the loud buzzing of the sales nought remained but a consciousness that the immensity of Paris stretched all around, an immensity which would always furnish buyers. In the heavy still air, in which the fumes of the heating apparatus heightened the odours of the stuffs, there was an increasing hubbub compounded of all sorts of noises, of continual tramping, of phrases a hundred times repeated around the counters, of gold jingling on the brass tablets of the pay-desks, which a legion of purses besieged, and of baskets on wheels laden with parcels which were constantly disappearing into the gaping cellars. And, amidst the fine dust, everything finished by getting mixed, it became impossible to recognise the divisions of the different departments; the haberdashery department over yonder seemed submerged; further on, in the linen department, a ray of sunshine, entering by a window facing the Rue Neuve-Saint-Augustin, looked like a golden dart in a mass of snow; while, among the gloves and woollens, a dense mass of bonnets and chignons hid the background of the shop from view. Even the toilettes could no longer be distinctly seen, the head-gear alone appeared, decked with feathers and ribbons, while a few men's hats here and there showed like black spots, and the woman's complexions, pale with fatigue and heat, assumed the transparency of camelias. At last, Hutin—thanks to his vigorous elbows—was able to open a way for the ladies, by keeping in front of them. But on reaching the landing, Henriette no longer found Mouret there, for he had just plunged Vallagnosc into the midst of the crowd in order to complete his bewilderment, he himself, too, feeling the need of a dip into this bath of success. He lost his breath with rapture, feeling the while a kind of continuous caress from all his customers.

"To the left, ladies," said Hutin, still attentive despite his increasing exasperation.

Up above, however, there was the same block. People invaded even the furnishing department, usually the quietest of all. The shawl, the fur, and the under-clothing departments literally swarmed with customers; and as the ladies crossed the lace gallery another meeting took place. Madame de Boves was there with her daughter Blanche, both buried amidst the articles which Deloche was showing them. And again Hutin had to make a halt, parcel in hand.

"Good afternoon! I was just thinking of you."

"I've been looking for you myself. But how can you expect to find any one in this crowd?"

"It's magnificent, isn't it?"

"Dazzling, my dear. We can hardly stand."

"And you're buying?"

"Oh! no, we're only looking round. It rests us a little to be seated."

As a fact, Madame de Boves, with scarcely more than her cab-fare in her purse, was having all sorts of laces handed down, simply for the pleasure of seeing and handling them. She had guessed Deloche to be a new salesman, slow and awkward, who dared not resist a customer's whims; and she had taken advantage of his bewildered good-nature, to keep him there for half an hour, still asking for fresh articles. The counter was covered, and she plunged her hands into an increasing mountain of lace, Malines, Valenciennes, and Chantilly, her fingers trembling with desire, her face gradually warming with a sensual delight; whilst Blanche, close to her, agitated by the same passion, was very pale, her flesh inflated and flabby. However, the conversation continued; and Hutin, standing there waiting their good pleasure, could have slapped their faces for all the time they were making him lose.

"Ah!" said Madame Marty, "you're looking at some cravats and handkerchiefs like those I showed you the other day."

This was true; Madame de Boves, tormented by Madame Marty's lace ever since the previous Saturday, had been unable to resist the desire to at least handle some like it, since the meagre allowance which her husband made her did not permit her to carry any away. She blushed slightly, explaining that Blanche had wished to see the Spanish-blonde cravats. Then she added: "You're going to the mantles. Well! we'll see you again. Shall we say in the oriental saloon?"

"That's it, in the oriental saloon—Superb, isn't it?"

Then they separated enraptured, amidst the obstruction which the sale of insertions and small trimmings at low prices was causing. Deloche, glad to be occupied, again began emptying the boxes before the mother and daughter. And amidst the groups pressing close to the counters, inspector Jouve slowly walked about with his military air, displaying his decoration and watching over all the fine and precious goods, so easy to conceal up a sleeve. When he passed behind Madame de Boves, surprised to see her with her arms plunged in such a heap of lace he cast a quick glance at her feverish hands.

"To the right, ladies," said Hutin, resuming his march.

He was beside himself with rage. Was it not enough that he had missed a sale down below? Now they kept on delaying him at each turn of the shop! And with his annoyance was blended no little of the rancour that existed between the textile and the ready-made departments, which were in continual hostility, ever fighting for customers and stealing each other's percentages and commissions. Those of the silk hall were yet more enraged than those of the woollen department whenever a lady decided to take a mantle after looking at numerous taffetas and failles and they were obliged to conduct her to Madame Aurélie's gallery.

"Mademoiselle Vadon!" said Hutin, in an angry voice, when he at last arrived in the department.

But Mademoiselle Vadon passed by without listening, absorbed in a sale which she was conducting. The room was full, a stream of people were crossing it, entering by the door of the lace department and leaving by that of the under-clothing department, whilst on the right were customers trying on garments, and posing before the mirrors. The red carpet stifled all noise of footsteps here, and the distant roar from the ground-floor died away, giving place to a discreet murmur and a drawing-room warmth, increased by the presence of so many women.

"Mademoiselle Prunaire!" cried out Hutin. And as she also took no notice of him, he added between his teeth, so as not to be heard: "A set of jades!"

He was certainly not fond of them, tired to death as he was by climbing the stairs to bring them customers and furious at the profits which he accused them of taking out of his pocket. It was a secret warfare, into which the young ladies themselves entered with equal fierceness; and in their mutual weariness, always on foot and worked to death, all difference of sex disappeared and nothing remained but their contending interests, irritated by the fever of business.

"So there's no one here to serve?" asked Hutin.

But he suddenly caught sight of Denise. She had been kept folding all the morning, only allowed to serve a few doubtful customers, to whom moreover she had not sold anything. When Hutin recognised her, occupied in clearing an enormous heap of garments off the counters, he ran up to her.

"Look here, mademoiselle! serve these ladies who are waiting."

Thereupon he quickly slipped Madame Marty's purchases into her arms, tired as he was of carrying them about. His smile returned to him but it was instinct with the secret maliciousness of the experienced salesman, who shrewdly guessed into what an awkward position he had just thrown both the ladies and the young girl. The latter, however, remained quite perturbed by the prospect of this unhoped-for sale which suddenly presented itself. For the second time Hutin appeared to her as an unknown friend, fraternal and tender-hearted, always ready to spring out of the darkness to save her. Her eyes glistened with gratitude; she followed him with a lingering look, whilst he began elbowing his way as fast as possible towards his department.

"I want a mantle," said Madame Marty.

Then Denise questioned her. What style of mantle? But the lady had no idea, she wished to see what the house had got. And the young girl, already very tired, bewildered by the crowd, quite lost her head; she had never served any but the rare customers who came to Cornaille's, at Valognes; she did not even know the number of the models, nor their places in the cupboards. And so she was hardly able to reply to the ladies, who were beginning to lose patience, when Madame Aurélie perceived Madame Desforges, of whose connection with Mouret she was no doubt aware, for she hastened up and asked with a smile:

"Are these ladies being served?"

"Yes, that young person over there is attending to us," replied Henriette. "But she does not appear to be very well up to her work; she can't find anything."

At this, the first-hand completely paralyzed Denise by stepping up to her and saying in a whisper: "You see very well you know nothing. Don't interfere any more, please." Then turning round she called out: "Mademoiselle Vadon, these ladies require a mantle!"

She remained looking on whilst Marguerite showed the models. This girl assumed a dry polite voice with customers, the disagreeable manner of a young person robed in silk, accustomed to rub against elegance in every form, and full, unknown to herself, of jealousy and rancour. When she heard Madame Marty say that she did not wish to pay more than two hundred francs, she made a grimace of pity. Oh! madame would certainly give more, for it would be impossible to find anything at all suitable for two hundred francs. Then she threw some of the common mantles on a counter with a gesture which signified: "Just see, aren't they pitiful?" Madame Marty dared not think them nice after that; but bent over to murmur in Madame Desforges's ear: "Don't you prefer to be served by men? One feels more comfortable?"

At last Marguerite brought a silk mantle trimmed with jet, which she treated with respect. And thereupon Madame Aurélie abruptly called Denise.

"Come, do something at all events. Just put that on your shoulders."

Denise, wounded to the heart, despairing of ever succeeding, had remained motionless, her hands dangling by her side. No doubt she would be sent away, and the children would be without food. All the tumult of the crowd buzzed in her head, her legs were tottering and her arms bruised by the handling of so many garments, a porter's work which she had never done before. However, she was obliged to obey and allow Marguerite to put the mantle on her, as on a dummy.

"Stand upright," said Madame Aurélie.

But a moment afterwards Denise was forgotten. Mouret had just come in with Vallagnosc and Bourdoncle; and he bowed to the ladies, who complimented him on his magnificent exhibition of winter novelties. Of course they went into raptures over the oriental saloon. Vallagnosc, who was finishing his walk through the departments, displayed more surprise than admiration; for, after all, thought he, with his pessimist nonchalance, it was nothing more than an immense collection of drapery. Bourdoncle, however, forgetting that he himself belonged to the establishment, likewise congratulated the governor in order to make him forget his anxious doubts and persecutions of the earlier part of the day.

"Yes, yes; things are going on very well, I'm quite satisfied," repeated Mouret, radiant, replying with a smile to Madame Desforges's loving looks. "But I must not interrupt you, ladies."

Then all eyes were again turned on Denise. She placed herself entirely in the hands of Marguerite, who was making her turn round.

"What do you think of it—eh?" asked Madame Marty of Madame Desforges.

The latter gave her opinion, like a supreme umpire of fashion. "It isn't bad, the cut is original, but it doesn't seem to me very graceful about the waist."

"Oh!" interrupted Madame Aurélie, "it must be seen on the lady herself. You can understand, it does not have much effect on this young person, who is so slim. Hold up your head, mademoiselle, give the mantle all its importance."

They smiled. Denise had turned very pale. She felt ashamed at being thus turned into a machine, which they examined and joked about so freely.

Madame Desforges, yielding to the natural antipathy of a contrary nature, annoyed by the girl's gentle face, maliciously added: "No doubt it would set better if the young person's gown were not so loose-fitting."

Thereupon she cast at Mouret the mocking glance of a Parisienne amused by the ridiculous rig of a country girl. He felt the amorous caress of this glance, the triumph of a woman proud of her beauty and her art. And so out of pure gratitude, the gratitude of a man who knew himself to be adored, he felt obliged to joke in his turn, despite his good-will towards Denise of whose secret charm he was conscious.

"Besides, her hair should be combed," he murmured.

This was the last straw. The director deigned to laugh so all the young ladies ventured to do the same. Marguerite risked a slight chuckle, like a well-behaved girl who restrains herself; but Clara left a customer so as to enjoy the fun at her ease; and even some saleswomen of the under-clothing department came in, attracted by the talking. As for the lady customers they took it more quietly, with an air of well-bred enjoyment. Madame Aurélie was the only one who did not smile; it was as if Denise's splendid wild-looking hair and slender virginal shoulders had dishonoured her, compromised the good reputation of her department. Denise herself had turned paler still, amidst all these people who were laughing at her. She felt herself violated, exposed to all their hostile glances, without defence. What had she done that they should thus attack her spare figure, and her too luxuriant hair? But she was especially wounded by Madame Desforges's and Mouret's laughter, instinctively divining their connection and her heart sinking with an unknown grief. That lady was surely very ill-natured to attack a poor girl who had said nothing; and as for Mouret, he most decidedly filled her with a freezing fear, in which all her other sentiments disappeared. And, totally abandoned, assailed in her most cherished feelings of modesty,

ÉMILE ZOLA

indignant at such injustice, she was obliged to stifle the sobs which were rising in her throat.

"I should think so; let her comb her hair to-morrow," said the terrible Bourdoncle to Madame Aurélie. Full of scorn for Denise's small limbs he had condemned her the first time he had seen her.

At last the first-hand came and took the mantle off Denise's shoulders, saying to her in a low tone: "Well! mademoiselle, here's a fine start. Really, if this is the way you show your capabilities—It is impossible to be more stupid!"

Fearing that her tears might gush from her eyes Denise hastened back to the heap of garments, which she began sorting on the counter. There at least she was lost in the crowd. Fatigue prevented her from thinking. But all at once near by she perceived the saleswoman of the under-clothing department, who had already defended her that morning. The latter had followed the scene, and murmured in her ear:

"My poor child, you mustn't be so sensitive. Keep that to yourself, or they'll go on worse and worse. I come from Chartres. Yes, Pauline Cugnot is my name; and my parents are millers. Well! the girls here would have devoured me during the first few days if I had not stood up firm. Come, be brave! give me your hand, we'll have a talk together whenever you like."

This outstretched hand redoubled Denise's confusion; she shook it furtively and hastened to take up a load of cloaks, fearing lest she might again be accused of a transgression and receive a scolding if it were known she had a friend.

However, Madame Aurélie herself, had just put the mantle on Madame Marty, and they all exclaimed: "Oh! how nice! delightful!" It at once looked quite different. Madame Desforges decided that it would be impossible to improve on it. A good deal of bowing ensued, Mouret took his leave, whilst Vallagnosc, who had perceived Madame de Boves and her daughter in the lace department, hastened to offer his arm to the former. Marguerite, standing before one of the pay-desks, was already calling out the different purchases made by Madame Marty, who settled for them and ordered the parcel to be taken to her cab. Madame Desforges had found her articles at pay-desk No. 10. Then the ladies met once more in the oriental saloon. They were leaving, but it was amidst a loquacious outburst of admiration. Even Madame Guibal became enthusiastic.

"Oh! delicious! it makes you think you are in the East; doesn't it?"

"A real harem, and not at all dear!"

"And the Smyrnas! oh, the Smyrnas! what tones, what delicacy!"

"And that Kurdestan! Just look, a real Delacroix!"

The crowd was thinning. The bell, at an hour's interval, had already announced the first two dinners; the third was about to be served, and in the departments there now only remained a few lingering customers, whose fever for spending money had made them forget the time. Outside nothing was heard but the rolling of the last cabs breaking upon the husky voice of Paris, a snort like that of a satiated ogre digesting all the linens and cloths, silks and laces with which he had been gorged since the morning. Within, beneath the flaming gas-jets, which, burning in the twilight, had illumined the last supreme efforts of the sale, everything looked like a field of battle still warm with the massacre of the materials. The salesmen, harassed and fatigued, camped amidst the contents of their shelves and counters, which appeared to have been thrown into confusion by the furious blast of a hurricane. It was with difficulty that you traversed the galleries on the ground floor, obstructed by straggling chairs. In the glove department it was necessary to step over a pile of cases heaped up around Mignot; through the woollens there was no means of passing at all, Liénard was dozing on an ocean of bales, in which certain pieces standing on end, though half destroyed, seemed like houses which an overflowing river was carrying away; and, further on, the linen department appeared like a heavy fall of snow, and you stumbled against icebergs of napkins, and walked through flakes of handkerchiefs.

The same disorder prevailed upstairs, in the departments of the first floor: the furs were scattered over the flooring, the mantles were heaped up like the great-coats of soldiers *hors-de-combat*, the laces and the under-linen, unfolded, crumpled, thrown about everywhere, made you think of a nation of women who had disrobed themselves there; whilst down below, in the depths of the establishment, the delivery department, now in full activity, was still and ever disgorging the parcels which filled it to suffocation and which were carried off by the vans, in a last effort of the overheated machine. But it was on the silk department especially that the customers had flung themselves with the greatest ardour. There they had cleared off everything, there was abundant room to pass, the hall was bare; the whole of the colossal stock of Paris Delight had been cut up and carried away, as if by a swarm of devouring locusts. And in the midst of this great void, Hutin and Favier were running through the counterfoils of their debit-notes, calculating their commission, and still short of breath from the struggle. Favier, it turned out, had made fifteen francs while Hutin had only managed to make thirteen; he had been thoroughly beaten that day, and was enraged at his bad luck. The eyes of both sparkled with the passion for gain. And all around them other shopmen were likewise adding up figures, glowing with the same fever, in the brutal gaiety which follows victorious carnage.

"Well, Bourdoncle!" cried out Mouret, "are you trembling still?"

He had returned to his favourite position against the balustrade, at the top of the stairs, and, in presence of the massacre of stuffs spread out below him, he indulged in a victorious laugh. His fears of the morning, that moment of unpardonable weakness which nobody would ever know of, inspired him with a greater desire to triumph. The battle was definitely won, the small tradespeople of the neighbourhood were done for, and Baron Hartmann was conquered, with his millions and his building sites. Whilst Mouret gazed at the cashiers bending over their ledgers, adding up long columns of figures, whilst he listened to the sound of the gold, falling from their fingers into the metal bowls, he already beheld The Ladies' Paradise growing and growing, enlarging its hall and prolonging its galleries as far as the Rue du Dix-Décembre.

"And now," he resumed, "are you not convinced, Bourdoncle, that the house is really too small? We could have sold twice as much."

Bourdoncle humbled himself, enraptured, moreover, to find himself in the wrong. But another spectacle rendered them grave. As was the custom every evening, Lhomme, the chief sales' cashier, had just collected the receipts from each pay-desk; and after adding them up, he wrote the total amount on a paper which he displayed by hanging it on the iron claw with which the stump of his mutilated arm, severed at the elbow, was provided. And then he took the receipts up to the chief cash office, some in a leather case and some in bags, according to the nature of the specie. On this occasion the gold and silver predominated, and he slowly walked upstairs carrying three enormous bags, which he clasped with his one arm against his breast, holding one of them with his chin in order to prevent it from slipping. His heavy breathing could be heard at a distance as he passed along, staggering and superb, amidst the respectful shopmen.

"How much, Lhomme?" asked Mouret.

"Eighty thousand seven hundred and forty-two francs ten centimes," replied the cashier.

A joyous laugh stirred up The Ladies' Paradise. The amount ran through the establishment. It was the highest figure ever attained in one day's sales by a draper's shop.

That evening, when Denise went up to bed, she felt so faint that she was obliged to lean against the partition in the corridor under the zinc roof. And when she was inside her room, with the door closed, she fell down on the bed; her feet pained her so much. For a long time she continued gazing with a stupid air at the dressing-table, the wardrobe, all the lodginghouse-like bareness. This, then, was where she was going to live; and her first day—an abominable, endless day—filled her with sore distress. She would never have the courage to go through such another. Then she perceived that she was dressed in silk; and this uniform depressed her. She was childish enough, before unpacking her box, to put on her old woollen gown, which hung over the back of a chair. But when she had once more donned this poor garment a painful emotion choked her; the sobs which she had kept back all day suddenly found vent in a flood of hot tears. She fell back on the bed, weeping at the thought of the two children, and she wept on and on, without even the strength to take off her boots, so completely was she overcome with fatigue and grief.

ÉMILE ZOLA

# V

The next day Denise had scarcely been downstairs half an hour, when Madame Aurélie said to her in her sharp voice: "You are wanted at the director's office, mademoiselle."

The girl found Mouret alone, in his spacious room hung with green rep. He had suddenly remembered that "unkempt girl," as Bourdoncle called her; and he, who usually detested the part of fault-finder, had thought of sending for her and stirring her up a bit, if she were still dressed in the style of a country wench. On the previous day, despite his jocularity, he had experienced a feeling of wounded pride, on seeing the elegance of one of his saleswomen questioned in Madame Desforges's presence. He harboured a mixed sentiment with regard to Denise, a commingling, as it were, of sympathy and anger.

"We engaged you, mademoiselle," he commenced, "out of regard for your uncle, and you must not put us under the sad necessity—"

But all at once he stopped. On the other side of his table stood Denise, upright, serious, and pale. Her silk gown was no longer too big for her, but fitted tightly to her pretty figure, displayed the pure lines of her virgin shoulders; and if her hair, knotted in thick tresses, still appeared somewhat wild, she had at least tried to keep it in order. After falling asleep with her clothes on, her eyes red with weeping, she had, on waking at about four o'clock, felt ashamed of her nervous sensibility, and had immediately set about taking-in her dress; besides spending an hour before the tiny looking-glass, combing her hair, which she was unable to reduce as much as she would have liked to.

"Ah! thank heavens!" said Mouret, "you look better this morning. But there's still that dreadful hair!" With these words he rose from his seat and stepped up to her to try and smooth her rebellious tresses in the same familiar way as Madame Aurélie on the previous day. "There! Just tuck that in behind your ear," he said, "The chignon is too high."

She did not speak, but let him arrange her hair. In spite of her vow to be strong and brave she had reached the office full of misgivings, feeling certain that she had been summoned to be informed of her dismissal. And Mouret's evident kindliness did not reassure her; she was still afraid of him, feeling whenever near him that uneasiness which she attributed to natural anxiety in the presence of a powerful man on whom her future depended. And when he saw her thus trembling under his hands, which were grazing her neck, he began to regret his good-natured impulse, for he feared above all to lose his authority.

"In short, mademoiselle," he resumed, once more placing the table between himself and her, "try and look to your appearance. You are no longer at Valognes; study our Parisian young ladies. If your uncle's name has sufficed to gain you admittance to our house, I at least trust that you will seek to justify the good opinion I formed of you from your appearance. Unfortunately, everybody here is not of the same opinion as myself. Let this be a warning to you. Don't make me tell a falsehood."

He treated her like a child, with more pity than kindness, his curiosity simply awakened by the troublous, womanly charm which he divined was springing up in this poor awkward girl. And she, whilst he was lecturing her, having suddenly perceived the portrait of Madame Hédouin, whose handsome regular face was smiling gravely in its gold frame—felt herself shivering again, despite the encouraging words he addressed to her. That was the dead lady, she whom people accused him of having killed, in order to found the house with the blood of her limbs.

Mouret was still speaking. "Now you may go," he said at last, sitting down and taking up his pen. And thereupon she went off, heaving a deep sigh of relief.

From that day onward, Denise put forth all her courage. Beneath her attacks of sensitiveness, a strong sense of reason was constantly working, quite a feeling of bravery at finding herself weak and alone, with a cheerful determination to carry out her self-imposed task. She made very little stir but went straight ahead to her goal, overcoming all obstacles, and that simply and naturally, for her nature was one of unconquerable sweetness.

At first she had to surmount the terrible fatigues of her work in the department. The piles of garments strained her arms to such a degree that during the first six weeks she cried with pain when she turned over at night, her back aching and her shoulders bruised. But she suffered still more from her shoes, heavy shoes which she had brought from Valognes; lack of money preventing her from replacing them by light boots. Always on her legs, trotting about from morning to night, scolded if she were seen leaning for a moment against a partition, her feet, small like those of a child, became swollen by prolonged imprisonment in those torturing bluchers; the heels throbbed with fever and the soles were covered with blisters, the skin of which chafed off and stuck to her stockings. She experienced, too, a shattering of her whole frame;

the constant weariness of her legs painfully affected her system and her face was ever pale. And yet she, so spare and frail, resisted courageously, whilst a great many other saleswomen, attacked by special maladies, were obliged to quit the business. Her readiness to suffer, her valiant stubbornness sustained her, smiling and upright, however, even when she felt ready to give way, thoroughly worn out by labour to which many men would have succumbed.

Another torment was to have the whole department against her. To physical martyrdom was added the secret persecutions of her comrades. Two months of patience and gentleness had not disarmed them. She was constantly exposed to offensive remarks, cruel inventions, a series of slights which cut her to the heart, in her longing for affection. For a long time the others joked over her unfortunate first appearance; and such nicknames as "clogs" and "numbskull" were bestowed on her. Then those who missed a sale were advised to go to Valognes; in short, she passed for the fool of the place. And afterwards when she revealed herself to be a remarkably clever saleswoman, well up in the mechanism of the house, the others conspired to deprive her of all good customers. Marguerite and Clara pursued her with instinctive hatred, allying themselves together in order that they might not be swallowed up by this new-comer, whom they really feared in spite of their affected disdain. As for Madame Aurélie, she was hurt by the proud reserve displayed by Denise, who did not hover round her skirts with an air of caressing admiration; and she therefore abandoned her to the rancour of her favourites, the preferred ones of her court, who were always on their knees, feeding her with the continual flattery which could alone impart any amiability to her proud domineering nature. For a while, the second-hand, Madame Frédéric, appeared not to enter into the conspiracy, but this must have been by inadvertence, for she showed herself equally harsh directly she saw to what annoyances her good-nature was likely to expose her. Then the abandonment became complete, they all made a butt of the "unkempt girl," who lived on in an hourly struggle, only managing by dint of the greatest courage to hold her own in the department.

Such then was her life now. She had to smile, look brave and gracious in a silk gown which did not belong to her, and she was ever suffering from fatigue, badly treated, under the continual menace of a brutal dismissal. Her room was her only refuge, the only spot where she could indulge in the luxury of a cry, when she had suffered too much during the day. But a terrible coldness fell from the zinc roof, now covered with the December snow; she was obliged to nestle in her iron bedstead, pile all her clothes over her, and weep under the counterpane to prevent the frost from chapping her face. Mouret never spoke to her now; when she noticed Bourdoncle's severe looks during business hours she trembled, for she divined in him a born enemy who would not forgive her the slightest fault. And amidst this general hostility, inspector Jouve's strange friendliness astonished her. If he met her in any out-of-the-way corner he smiled at her and made some amiable remark; twice, too, he had saved her from being reprimanded without any show of gratitude on her part, for she was more troubled than touched by his protecting airs.

One evening, after dinner, while the young ladies were setting the cupboards in order, Joseph came to inform Denise that a young man wanted her below. She went down, feeling very anxious.

"Hallo!" said Clara, "the 'unkempt girl' has got a follower then."

"He must be hard up for a sweetheart," declared Marguerite.

Meantime, downstairs at the door, Denise found her brother Jean. She had formally prohibited him from coming to the shop in this way, as it looked so bad. But she did not dare to scold him, so excited did he appear, bareheaded, out of breath through running all the way from the Faubourg du Temple.

"Have you got ten francs?" he stammered. "Give me ten francs, or I'm a lost man."

With his flowing locks and handsome girlish face the young rascal looked so comical, whilst launching out this melodramatic phrase, that she could have smiled had it not been for the anguish which his application for money caused her.

"What! ten francs?" she murmured. "Whatever's the matter?"

Thereupon he blushed, and explained that he had met a friend's sister. Denise stopped him, feeling embarrassed and not wishing to know any more about it. Twice already had he rushed in to obtain similar loans, but on the first occasion it had only been a matter of twenty-five sous, and on the next of thirty. He was, however, always getting into bad company.

"I can't give you ten francs," she resumed. "Pépé's board isn't paid yet, and I've only just the money for it. I shall have hardly enough to buy a pair of boots, which I want very badly. You are really not reasonable, Jean. It's too bad of you."

"Well, I'm lost," he repeated, with a tragical gesture. "Just listen, little sister; she's a tall, dark girl; we went to the café with her brother. I never thought the drinks would—"

She had to interrupt him again, and as tears were coming into his eyes, she took out her purse and slipped a ten-franc piece into his hand. He at once set up a laugh.

"I was sure of it!—But on my honour! never again! A fellow would have to be a regular scamp."

And thereupon he ran off, after kissing his sister, like a madman. The assistants in the shop seemed quite astonished.

That night Denise did not sleep much. Since her entry into The Ladies' Paradise, money had been her cruel anxiety. She was still a probationer, without a salary; the other girls in her department frequently prevented her from selling, and she only just managed to pay Pépé's board and lodging, thanks to the unimportant customers they were good enough to leave her. It was a time of black misery—misery in a silk dress. She was often obliged to spend the night in repairing her small stock of clothes, darning her linen, mending her chemises as if they had been lace; without mentioning the patches that she put on her shoes, as cleverly as any bootmaker could have done. She even risked washing things in her hand basin. But her old woollen dress was an especial source of anxiety to her; she had no other, and was forced to put it on every evening when she quitted the uniform silk, and this wore it terribly; a stain on it gave her quite a fever, the least rent was a catastrophe. And she had nothing, not a sou, not even enough to buy the trifling articles which a woman always wants; she had even been obliged to wait a fortnight to renew her stock of needles and cotton. Thus it was a real disaster when Jean, with his love affairs, suddenly swooped down and pillaged her purse. A franc-piece taken out of it left an abyss which she did not know how to fill up. As for finding ten francs on the morrow it was not to be thought of for a moment. All that night she was haunted by nightmare in which she saw Pépé thrown into the street, whilst she turned the paving stones over with her bruised fingers to see if there might not be some money underneath them.

It happened that the next day she had to play the part of the well-dressed girl. Some well-known customers came in, and Madame Aurélie summoned her several times in order that she might show off the new styles. And whilst she was posing there, with the stereotyped graces of a fashion-plate, she thought all the time of Pépé's board and lodging, which she had promised to pay that evening. She would contrive to do without any boots for another month; but even on adding the thirty francs left her of Pépé's money to the four francs which she had saved up sou by sou, there would never be more than thirty-four francs, and where was she to find six francs to complete the sum she required? It was an anguish in which her heart failed her.

"You will notice that the shoulders are quite free," Madame Aurélie was saying. "It's very fashionable and very convenient. The young person can fold her arms."

"Oh! easily," replied Denise, who continued to smile amiably. "One can't feel it. I am sure you will like it, madame."

She was now blaming herself for having gone to fetch Pépé from Madame Gras' on the previous Sunday, to take him for a walk in the Champs-Elysées. The poor child so seldom went out with her! But she had been obliged to buy him some gingerbread and a little spade, and then take him to see Punch and Judy, and all that had cost twenty-nine sous. Really Jean could not think much about the little one, or he would not be so foolish. Everything fell upon her shoulders.

"Of course, if it does not suit you, madame—" resumed the first-hand. "Just put this other cloak on, mademoiselle, so that the lady may judge."

And Denise then walked slowly round, wearing the cloak and saying: "This is warmer. It's this year's fashion."

And beneath her professional graces she continued worrying and worrying until the evening, at a loss as to where she might find this money. The young ladies, who were very busy, left her an important sale; but it was only Tuesday, and she must wait four days before drawing any cash. After dinner she decided to postpone her visit to Madame Gras till the morrow. She would excuse herself, say she had been detained, and before then she would perhaps have obtained the six francs. As Denise avoided the slightest expense, she went to bed early. What could she do out-of-doors, penniless and wild, and still frightened by the big city in which she only knew the streets around the shop? After venturing as far as the Palais-Royal for the sake of a little fresh air, she would quickly return, lock herself in her room and set about sewing or washing.

Along the corridor conducting to the bed-rooms reigned a barrack-like promiscuity—the girls, who were often not very tidy, would gossip there over dirty water and dirty linen, break into frequent quarrels and patch up continual reconciliations. They were prohibited from going up to their rooms in the day-time; they did not live there, but merely slept there at night, climbing the stairs only at the last minute, and coming

ÉMILE ZOLA

down again in the morning when still half asleep, hardly awakened by a rapid wash; and this hurry-skurry which night and morning swept through the corridor, the fatigue of thirteen hours' work which threw them all on their beds thoroughly worn out, made the upper part of the house like an inn traversed by tired and illtempered travellers. Denise had no friend. Of all the young ladies, one alone, Pauline Cugnot, showed her a little affection; and the mantle and under-clothing departments being close to one another, and in open war, the sympathy between the two saleswomen had hitherto been confined to a few rare words hastily exchanged. Pauline certainly occupied a neighbouring room, to the right of Denise's; but as she disappeared immediately after dinner and only returned at eleven o'clock, the latter simply heard her get into bed, and never met her after business hours.

That evening, Denise had made up her mind to play the part of bootmaker once more. She was holding her shoes, turning them about and wondering how she could make them last another month. At last she decided to take a strong needle and sew on the soles, which were threatening to leave the uppers. Meantime a collar and a pair of cuffs were soaking in a basinful of soapsuds.

Every evening she heard the same sounds, the girls coming up one by one, brief whispered conversations, bursts of laughter and sometimes disputes which they stifled as much as possible. Then the beds creaked, the tired occupants yawned, and fell into heavy slumber. Denise's left hand neighbour often talked in her sleep, which at first frightened her very much. Perhaps others, like herself, stopped up to mend their things, in spite of the regulations; but if so they probably took the same precautions as she did, moving with prudent care, and avoiding the least noise, for a quivering silence prevailed behind the closed doors.

It had struck eleven some ten minutes previously when a sound of footsteps made Denise raise her head. Another young lady late, thought she. And she realised that it was Pauline, by hearing the door next to her own open.

But she was astonished when Pauline quietly came back into the passage and knocked at her door.

"Make haste, it's me!"

The saleswomen were forbidden to visit each other in their rooms, and Denise quickly unlocked her door, in order that her neighbour might not be caught by Madame Cabin, who was supposed to see this regulation strictly carried out.

"Was she there?" asked Denise, when the other had entered.

"Who? Madame Cabin?" replied Pauline. "Oh, I'm not afraid of her, she's easily settled with a five-franc piece!" And then she added: "I've wanted to have a talk with you for a long time past. But it's impossible to do so downstairs. Besides, you looked so down-hearted to-night at table."

Denise thanked her, and, touched by her good-natured air invited her to sit down. But in the bewilderment, caused by this unexpected visit she had not laid down the shoe she was mending, and Pauline at once perceived it. She shook her head, looked round and espied the collar and cuffs in the basin.

"My poor child, I thought as much," resumed she. "Ah, I know what it is! When I first came up from Chartres, and old Cugnot didn't send me a sou, I many a time washed my own chemises! Yes, yes, my chemises! I had only two, and there was always one in soak."

She sat down, still out of breath from running. Her broad face, with small bright eyes, and big tender mouth, possessed a certain grace, notwithstanding its rather coarse features. And, without any transition, all of a sudden, she began to relate her story; her childhood at the mill; old Cugnot ruined by a law-suit; she sent to Paris to make her fortune with twenty francs in her pocket; then her start as a saleswoman in a shop at Batignolles, then at The Ladies' Paradise—a terrible start, every suffering and privation imaginable; and at last her present life, the two hundred francs she earned each month, the pleasures she indulged in, the carelessness in which she allowed her days to glide away. Some jewellery, a brooch, and watch-chain, glistened on her close-fitting gown of dark-blue cloth; and she smiled from under a velvet toque ornamented with a large grey feather.

Denise had turned very red, worried with reference to her shoe; and began to stammer out an explanation.

"But the same thing happened to me," repeated Pauline. "Come, come, I'm older than you, I'm over twenty-six, though I don't look it. Just tell me your little troubles."

Thereupon Denise yielded to this friendship so frankly offered. She sat down in her petticoat, with an old shawl over her shoulders, near Pauline in full dress; and an interesting gossip ensued.

It was freezing in the room, the cold seemed to run down the bare prison-like walls; but they were so fully taken up by their conversation that they did not notice that their fingers were almost frost-bitten.

ÉMILE ZOLA

Little by little, Denise opened her heart entirely, spoke of Jean and Pépé, and of how grievously the money question tortured her; which led them both to abuse the young ladies in the mantle department. Pauline relieved her mind. "Oh, the hussies!" said she, "if they treated you in a proper way, you might make more than a hundred francs a month."

"Everybody is down on me, and I'm sure I don't know why," answered Denise, beginning to cry. "Look at Monsieur Bourdoncle, he's always watching me, trying to find me in fault just as if I were in his way. Old Jouve is about the only one—"

The other interrupted her. "What, that old ape of an inspector! Ah! my dear, don't you trust him. He may display his decoration as much as he likes, but there's a story about something that happened to him in our department. But what a child you are to grieve like this! What a misfortune it is to be so sensitive! Of course, what is happening to you happens to every one; they are making you pay your footing."

Then carried away by her good heart she caught hold of Denise's hands and kissed her. The money-question was a graver one. Certainly a poor girl could not support her two brothers, pay the little one's board and lodging, and stand treat for the big one's sweethearts with the few paltry sous she picked up from the others' cast-off customers; for it was to be feared that she would not get any salary until business improved in March.

"Listen to me, it's impossible for you to live in this way any longer. If I were you—" said Pauline.

But a noise in the corridor stopped her. It was probably Marguerite, who was accused of prowling about at night to spy upon the others. Pauline, who was still pressing her friend's hand, looked at her for a moment in silence, listening. Then, with an air of affectionate conviction, she began to whisper to her.

Denise did not understand at first, and when she did, she withdrew her hands, looking very confused by what her friend had told her. "Oh! no," she replied simply.

"Then," continued Pauline, "you'll never manage, I tell you so, plainly. Here are the figures: forty francs for the little one, a five-franc piece now and again for the big one; and then there's yourself, you can't always go about dressed like a pauper, with shoes that make the other girls laugh at you; yes, really, your shoes do you a deal of harm. It would be much better to do as I tell you."

"No, no," repeated Denise.

"Well! you are very foolish. It's inevitable, my dear, we all come to it sooner or later. Look at me, I was a probationer, like you, without a sou. We are boarded and lodged, it's true; but there's our dress; besides, it's impossible to go without a copper in one's pocket and shut oneself up in one's room, watching the flies. So you see girls forcibly drift into it."

She then spoke of her first admirer, a lawyer's clerk whom she had met at a party at Meudon. After him, had come a post-office clerk. And, finally, ever since the autumn, she had been keeping company with a salesman at the Bon Marché, a very nice tall fellow. However, her advice had no effect whatever upon Denise.

"No," the latter replied in a tone of decision; and a fresh silence fell. In the small cold room they were smiling at each other, greatly affected by this whispered conversation. "Besides, one must have affection for some one," she resumed, her cheeks quite scarlet.

Pauline was astonished. She set up a laugh, and embraced her a second time exclaiming: "But, my darling, when you meet and like each other! You are really droll! Look here, would you like Baugé to take us somewhere in the country on Sunday? He'll bring one of his friends."

"No," again said Denise in her gently obstinate way.

Then Pauline insisted no further. Each was free to act as she pleased. What she had said was out of pure kindness of heart, for she felt really grieved to see a comrade so miserable. And as it was nearly midnight, she got up to leave. But before doing so she forced Denise to accept the six francs she wanted to make up Pépé's board-money, begging her not to trouble about the matter, but to repay her the amount whenever she earned more.

"Now," she added, "blow your candle out, so that they may not see which door opens; you can light it again immediately afterwards."

The candle having been extinguished, they shook hands; and then Pauline ran off to her room, giving no sign of her passage through the darkness save the vague rustling of her petticoats amidst the deep slumber that had fallen on the occupants of the other little rooms.

Before going to bed Denise wished to finish her boot and do her washing. The cold became sharper still as the night advanced; but she did not feel it, the conversation had stirred her heart's blood. She was not shocked; it seemed to her that every woman had a right to arrange her life as she liked, when she was alone and free in the world. For her own part, however, she had never given way to such ideas; her sense of right and her healthy nature naturally maintained her in the respectability in which she had always lived. At last, towards one o'clock she went to bed. No, she thought, she did not love any one. So what was the use of upsetting her life, the maternal devotion which she had vowed for her two brothers? However, she did not sleep; insomnia gained upon her and a crowd of indistinct forms flitted before her closed eyes, then vanished in the darkness.

From that time forward Denise took an interest in the love-stories of the department. During slack times the girls were constantly occupied with their amatory affairs. Gossiping tales flew about, stories of adventures which amused them all for a week. Clara was a scandal and merely remained at the shop under pretence of leading a respectable life in order to shield herself from her family; for she was mortally afraid of old Prunaire, who had threatened to come to Paris and break her arms and legs with his clogs. Marguerite, on the contrary, behaved very well, and was not known to have any lover; which caused some surprise, for all knew of the circumstances which had led to her arrival in Paris. The young women also joked about Madame Frédéric, declaring that she was discreetly connected with certain great personages; but the truth was they knew nothing of her love-affairs; for she disappeared every evening, stiff as starch with her widow's sulkiness, and apparently always in a great hurry, though nobody knew whither she hastened so eagerly. As for the tittle-tattle about Madame Aurélie this was certainly false; mere invention, spread abroad by discontented saleswomen just for fun. Perhaps she had formerly displayed rather more than a motherly feeling for one of her son's friends, but she now occupied too high a position in the business to indulge in such childishness. Then there was the flock, the crowd of the girls going off in the evening, nine out of every ten having young men waiting for them at the door. On the Place Gaillon, along the Rue de la Michodière, and the Rue Neuve-Saint-Augustin, there was always a troop of motionless sentries watching for the girls' departure; and, when the *défilé* began, each gave his arm to his lady and walked away. It was like the stage-door exit of some theatre where figurantes predominate.

What most troubled Denise, however, was that she had discovered Colomban's secret. He was continually to be seen on the other side of the street, on the threshold of The Old Elbeuf, his eyes raised and never quitting the young ladies of the jacket and mantle department. When he espied Denise watching him he blushed and turned away his head, as if afraid that she might betray him to Geneviève, although there had been no further connection between the Baudus and their niece since her engagement at The Ladies' Paradise. At first, on seeing his despairing airs, she had fancied that he was in love with Marguerite, for Marguerite, being very well-conducted, and sleeping in the house, was not easy to approach. But great was her astonishment to find that Colomban's ardent glances were intended for Clara. For months past he had been devoured by passion in this way, remaining on the other side of the street and lacking the courage to declare himself; and this for a girl who was perfectly free, who lived in the Rue Louis-le-Grand, and whom he could have spoken to any evening! Clara herself appeared to have no idea of her conquest. Denise's discovery filled her with painful emotion. Was love so idiotic then? What! this fellow, who had real happiness within his reach, was ruining his life for the sake of that good-for-nothing girl whom he adored as reverently as if she had been a saint! From that day forward she felt a heart pang each time she espied Geneviève's pale suffering face behind the greeny panes of The Old Elbeuf.

In the evening, Denise could not help thinking a great deal, on seeing the young ladies march off with their sweethearts. She was sometimes obliged to reply by a smile to a friendly nod from Pauline, for whom Baugé waited regularly every evening at half-past eight, beside the fountain on the Place Gaillon. Then, after going out the last and taking a furtive walk, always alone, she was invariably the first to return, going upstairs to work, or to sleep, her head full of dreams, inquisitive as to the outdoor life of the others, of which she knew nothing. She certainly did not envy them, she was happy in her solitude, in the unsociableness in which she shut herself up, as in a hiding-place; but all the same her imagination carried her away, she would try to guess things, picture the pleasures constantly described before her, the cafés, the restaurants, the theatres, the Sundays spent on the river and in the country taverns. Quite a weariness of mind, a desire mingled with lassitude resulted from these imaginings; and she seemed to have already had her fill of amusements which she had never tasted.

However, there was but little room for dangerous dreams in her daily working life. During the thirteen hours of hard toil in the shop, there was no time for any display of affection between the salesmen and the saleswomen. If the continual fight for money had not abolished all sexual difference, the unceasing press of business which occupied their minds and fatigued their bodies would have sufficed to stifle desire. But very few love-affairs had been known in the establishment amidst the various hostilities and friendships between the men and the women, the constant elbowing from department to department. They were all nothing but pieces of mechanism forced to contribute of the working of the immense machine, abdicating all individuality and simply contributing their strength to the total, commonplace, phalansterian power. It was only outside the shop that they resumed their individual lives, with a sudden flaming of awakened passion.

Denise, however, one day saw Albert Lhomme slip a note into the hand of a young lady in the under-clothing department, after several times passing by with an air of indifference. The dead season, which lasts from December to February, was commencing; and she now had periods of rest, hours spent on her feet with her eyes wandering all over the shop whilst waiting for customers. The young ladies of her department were especially friendly with the salesmen who served the lace, but their intimacy never seemed to go any further than whispered banter. In the lace department there was a second-hand, a gay young spark who pursued Clara with all sorts of suggestive stories, simply by way of a joke—for he really cared so little for her that he made no effort to meet her out of doors; and thus it was from counter to counter, the gentlemen and the young ladies would exchange winks, nods, and remarks, which they alone understood. At times with their backs half turned and a dreamy look on their faces in order to put the terrible Bourdoncle off the scent, they would indulge in some sly gossip. As for Deloche, he long contented himself with smiling at Denise when he met her; but, getting bolder, he at last occasionally murmured a friendly word. On the day she had noticed Madame Aurélie's son giving a note to the young lady in the under-linen department, it precisely happened that Deloche was asking her if she had enjoyed her lunch, feeling a desire to say something, and unable to think of anything more amiable. He also saw the billet pass; and as he glanced at the young girl, they both blushed at thought of this intrigue carried on under their eyes.

But despite all these occurrences which gradually awoke the woman in her, Denise still retained her infantile peace of mind. The one thing that stirred her heart was to meet Hutin. But even this was only gratitude in her eyes; she simply thought herself touched by the young man's politeness. He could not bring a customer to the department without making her feel quite confused. Several times, on returning from a pay-desk, she found herself making a *détour*, and traversing the silk hall though she had no business there, her bosom heaving the while with emotion. One afternoon she met Mouret there and he seemed to follow her with a smile. He paid scarcely any attention to her now, only addressing a few words to her from time to time, to give her a few hints about her toilet, and to joke with her, as an impossible girl, a little savage, almost a boy, whom he would never manage to transform into a coquette, notwithstanding all his knowledge of women. Sometimes indeed he even ventured to laugh at her and tease her, without caring to acknowledge to himself the troublous feeling, the charm which this little saleswoman, with such a comical head of hair, inspired in him. And that afternoon at sight of his mute smile, Denise trembled, as if she were in fault. Did he know why she was crossing the silk department, when she could not herself have explained what had impelled her to make such a *détour*?

Hutin, moreover, did not seem to be at all aware of the young girl's grateful looks. The shop-girls were not his style, he affected to despise them, boasting more than ever of his pretended adventures with the lady customers.

One day a baroness had beamed on him, he would relate, and on another occasion he had fascinated the wife of an eminent architect. But as a matter of fact his only conquests were among girls at cafés and music-halls. Like all young men in the drapery line, he had a mania for spending, battling throughout the week with a miser's greediness, with the sole object of squandering his money on Sundays on the race-courses or in the restaurants and dancing-saloons. He never thought of saving a penny, but spent his salary as soon as he drew it, absolutely indifferent about the future. Favier did not join him in these pleasure parties. Hutin and he, so friendly in the shop, bowed to each other at the door, where all further intercourse between them ceased. A great many of the shopmen, always side by side indoors, became perfect strangers, ignorant of each other's lives, as soon as they set foot in the streets. However, Hutin, had an intimate—Liénard of the woollen department. Both lived in the same lodging-house, the Hôtel de Smyrne, in the Rue Sainte-Anne, a murky building entirely inhabited by shop assistants. In the morning they arrived at the Paradise together; and in the evening, the first who found himself free, after the folding was done, waited for the other at the Café Saint-Roch, in the Rue Saint-Roch, a little place where many employees of The Ladies' Paradise met, brawling, drinking, and playing cards amidst the smoke of their pipes. They often stopped there till one in the morning, until indeed the tired landlord turned them out. For the last month, however, they had been spending three evenings a week at a free-and-easy at Montmartre; whither they would take their friends in order to fan the success of Mademoiselle Laure, a music-hall singer, Hutin's latest conquest, whose talent they applauded with such violent rapping of their walking-sticks and such clamorous shouts that on two occasions the police had been obliged to interfere.

The winter passed in this way, and at last Denise obtained a fixed salary of three hundred francs a-year. It was quite time she did so for her shoes were completely worn out. For the last month she had avoided going out, for fear of bursting them altogether.

"What a noise you make with your shoes, mademoiselle!" Madame Aurélie very often remarked, with an irritated look. "It's intolerable. What's the matter with your feet?"

On the day when Denise came down wearing a pair of cloth boots, which had cost her five francs, Marguerite and Clara expressed their astonishment in a kind of half whisper, so as to be heard. "Hullo! the unkempt one, has given up her goloshes," said the former.

"Ah," retorted the other, "she must have cried over them. They were her mother's."

In point of fact, there was a general uprising against Denise. The girls of her department had discovered her friendship with Pauline, and thought they detected a certain bravado in this display of affection for a saleswoman of a rival counter. They spoke of treason, accused her of going and repeating their slightest words to their enemies. The war between the two departments became more violent than ever, it had never waxed so warm; angry words were exchanged like cannon shots, and a slap even was given one evening behind some boxes of chemises. Possibly this long-standing quarrel arose from the fact that the young ladies in the under-linen department wore woollen gowns, whilst those of the mantles wore silk. In any case, the former spoke of their neighbours with the shocked air of respectable women; and facts proved that they were right, for it had been remarked that the silk dresses appeared to lead to dissolute habits among the young ladies who wore them. Clara was taunted with her troop of lovers; even Marguerite had her child thrown in her teeth, as it were; whilst Madame Frédéric was accused of all sorts of secret passions. And all this solely on account of Denise!

"Now, young ladies, no ugly words; behave yourselves!" Madame Aurélie would say with her imperial air, amidst the rising passions of her little kingdom. "Show who you are."

At heart she preferred to remain neutral. As she confessed one day, when talking to Mouret, these girls were all about the same, one was no better than another. But she suddenly became impassioned when she learnt from Bourdoncle that he had just caught her son downstairs kissing a young girl belonging to the under-linen department, the saleswoman to whom he had passed several letters. It was abominable, and she roundly accused the under-linen department of having laid a trap for Albert. Yes, it was a got-up affair against herself, they were trying to dishonour her by ruining an inexperienced boy, after finding it impossible to attack her department. Her only object however in making such a noise was to complicate the business, for she was well aware of her son's character and knew him to be capable of all sorts of stupid things. For a time the matter threatened to assume a serious aspect; Mignot, the glove salesman, was mixed up in it. He was a great friend of Albert's, and the rumour circulated that he favoured the girls whom Albert sent him and who rummaged in his boxes for hours together. There was also a story about some Suède kid gloves given to the saleswoman of the under-linen department, which was never properly cleared up. At last the scandal was stifled out of regard for Madame Aurélie, whom Mouret himself treated with deference. Bourdoncle contented himself a week later with dismissing, for some slight offence, the girl who had allowed herself to be kissed. At all events if the managers closed their eyes to the terrible doings of their employees out of doors, they did not tolerate the least nonsense in the house.

And it was Denise who suffered for all this. Madame Aurélie, although perfectly well aware of what was going on, nourished a secret rancour against her; and seeing her laughing one evening with Pauline she also took it for bravado, concluding that they were gossiping over her son's love-affairs. And she thereupon sought to increase the girl's isolation in the department. For some time she had been thinking of inviting the young ladies to spend a Sunday at Les Rigolles near Rambouillet where she had bought a country house with the first hundred thousand francs she had saved; and she suddenly decided to do so; it would be a means of punishing Denise, of putting her openly on one side. She was the only one not invited. For a fortnight in advance, nothing was talked of but this pleasure party; the girls kept their eyes on the sky already warmed by the May sunshine, and mapped out the whole day, looking forward to all sorts of pleasures: donkey-riding, milk and brown bread. And they were to be all women, which was more amusing still! As a rule, Madame Aurélie killed her holidays like this, in going out with lady friends; for she was so little accustomed to being at home, she always felt so uncomfortable, so out of her element on the rare occasions when she could dine with her husband and son, that she preferred even not to avail herself of the opportunity but to go and dine at a restaurant. Lhomme went his own way, enraptured to resume his bachelor existence, and Albert, greatly relieved, hastened off to his beauties; so that, unaccustomed to home-life, feeling they were in each other's way, bored to death whenever they were together on a Sunday, they paid nothing more than flying visits to the house, as to some common hotel where people take a bed for the night. With respect to the excursion to Rambouillet, Madame Aurélie simply declared that considerations of propriety would not allow Albert to join them, and that the father himself would display great tact by refusing to come; a declaration which enchanted both men. However, the happy day was drawing near, and the girls chattered away more than ever, relating their preparations in the way of dress, just as if they were going on a six months' tour, whilst Denise had to listen to them, pale and silent in her abandonment.

"Ah, they make you wild, don't they?" said Pauline to her one morning. "If I were you I would just catch them nicely! They are going to enjoy themselves. I would enjoy myself too. Come with us on Sunday, Baugé is going to take me to Joinville."

"No, thanks," said the girl with her quiet obstinacy.

"But why not? Are you still afraid of being made love to?"

And thereupon Pauline laughed heartily. Denise also smiled. She knew how such things came about; it was always during some similar excursions that the young ladies had made the acquaintance of their lovers.

"Come," resumed Pauline, "I assure you that Baugé won't bring any one. We shall be all by ourselves. As you don't want me to, I won't go and marry you off, of course."

Denise hesitated, tormented by such a strong desire to go that the blood rushed to her cheeks. Since the girls had been talking about their country pleasures she had felt stifled, overcome by a longing for fresh air, dreaming of tall grass into which she might sink to the neck, and of giant trees whose shadows would flow over her like so much cooling water. Her childhood, spent amidst the rich verdure of Le Cotentin, was awakening with a regret for sun and air.

"Well! yes," said she at last.

Then everything was soon arranged. Baugé was to come and fetch them at eight o'clock, on the Place Gaillon; whence they would take a cab to the Vincennes Station. Denise, whose twenty-five francs a month was quickly exhausted by the children, had only been able to do up her old black woollen dress by trimming it with some strips of check poplin; but she had made herself a bonnet, by covering a shape with some silk and ornamenting it with blue ribbon. In this quiet attire she looked very young, like an overgrown girl, displaying all the cleanliness of careful poverty, and somewhat shamefaced, and embarrassed by her luxuriant hair, which waved round the bareness of her bonnet. Pauline, on the contrary, displayed a pretty spring costume in silk, striped white and violet, a feathered bonnet, with bows matching the dress, and jewels about her neck and rings on her fingers, which gave her the appearance of a well-to-do tradesman's wife. It was like a Sunday revenge on the woollen gown which she was obliged to wear throughout the week in the shop; whereas Denise, who wore her uniform silk from Monday to Saturday, resumed, on Sundays, her thin woollen dress of poverty-stricken aspect.

"There's Baugé," said Pauline, pointing to a tall young man standing near the fountain.

And thereupon she introduced her lover, and Denise felt at her ease at once, he seemed such a nice fellow. Big, and strong as an ox, with a long Flemish face, in which his expressionless eyes twinkled with infantile puerility, Baugé was the younger son of a grocer of Dunkerque and had come to Paris, almost driven from home by his father and brother, who thought him a fearful dunce. However, he now made three thousand five hundred francs a year at the Bon Marché. Certainly in some things he was rather stupid, but he proved a very good hand in the linen department.

"And the cab?" asked Pauline.

They had to go on foot as far as the Boulevard. The sun was already warming the streets and the glorious May morning seemed to be smiling on the pavements. There was not a cloud in the sky; all was gay in the blue air, transparent as crystal. An involuntary smile played about Denise's lips; she breathed freely; it seemed to her that her bosom was throwing off a stifling fit of six months duration. At last she no longer felt the stuffy air and the heavy stones of The Ladies' Paradise weighing her down! She had the prospect of a long day in the country before her! and it was like a new lease of life, an infinite delight, into which she entered with all the glee of a little child. However, when they were in the cab, she turned her eyes away, feeling ill at ease as Pauline bent over to kiss her lover.

"Oh, look!" said she, her head still at the window, "there's Monsieur Lhomme. How he does walk!"

"He's got his French horn," added Pauline, leaning out. "What an old fool he is! One would think he was running off to meet his girl!"

Lhomme, with his nose in the air, and his instrument under his arm, was spinning along past the Gymnase Theatre, laughing with delight at the thought of the treat in store for him. He was about to spend the day with a friend, a flautist at a petty theatre, in whose rooms a few amateurs indulged in a little chamber-music on Sundays as soon as breakfast was over.

"At eight o'clock! what a madman!" resumed Pauline. "And you know that Madame Aurélie and her clique must have taken the Rambouillet train that left at half-past six. It's very certain the husband and wife won't come across each other to-day."

Both then began talking of the Rambouillet excursion. They did not wish it to be rainy for the others, because they themselves might suffer as well; still, if a cloud could only burst over there without a drop falling at Joinville, it would be funny all the same. Then they attacked Clara, who hardly knew how to spend the money she made by her vices. Hadn't she bought three pairs of boots all at the same time, and thrown them away the next day, after slashing them with her scissors, on account of her feet, which were covered with corns? In fact, the young ladies were just as bad as the young men, they squandered everything, never saving a sou, but wasting two or three hundred francs a month on dress and dainties.

"But he's only got one arm," all of a sudden said Baugé, who had kept his eyes on Lhomme. "How does he manage to play the French horn?"

Pauline, who sometimes amused herself by playing on her lover's stupidity, thereupon told him that the cashier kept the instrument up by leaning it against a wall. He thoroughly believed her, and thought it very ingenious. And when, stricken with remorse, she explained to him that Lhomme had adapted to his stump a system of claws which he made use of as fingers, he shook his head, full of doubt and declaring that they wouldn't make him swallow that.

"You are really too stupid!" she retorted, laughing. "Never mind, I love you all the same."

They reached the station of the Vincennes line just in time for a train. Baugé paid; but Denise had previously declared that she wished to defray her share of the expenses; they would settle up in the evening. They took second-class tickets, and found the train full of a gay, noisy throng. At Nogent, a wedding-party got out, amidst a storm of laughter. Then, at last they arrived at Joinville, and went straight to the island to order lunch; and afterwards lingered there, strolling along, under the tall poplars beside the Marne. It was rather cold in the shade, a sharp breeze was blowing in the sunshine, gathering strength as it swept from the distance over a plain dotted with cultivated fields, on the other side of the river. Denise lingered behind Pauline and her lover, who walked along with their arms round each other's waists. She had picked a handful of buttercups, and was watching the flow of the river, happy, but her heart beating and her head drooping, each time that Baugé leant over to kiss his sweetheart. Her eyes filled with tears. And yet she was not suffering. What could be the matter with her that she experienced this feeling of suffocation? Why did this vast landscape, amidst which she had looked forward to so much enjoyment, fill her with a vague regret that she could not explain? However, at lunch, Pauline's noisy laughter bewildered her. That young woman, who loved the suburbs with the passion of an actress living in the gas-light, in the heavy atmosphere of a crowd, wanted to lunch in an arbour, notwithstanding the sharp wind. She made merry over the sudden gusts which blew up the table-cloth, and thought the arbour very funny in its bareness, with its freshly-painted trellis-work which cast a reflection on the cloth. She ate ravenously, devouring everything with the voracity of one who, being badly fed at the shop, made up for it out of doors by giving herself an indigestion of all the things she liked. This was indeed her vice, she spent most of her money on cakes and indigestible dainties, tit-bits of all kinds, which she hastily nibbled in leisure moments. Now, however, as Denise seemed to have had enough with the eggs, fried fish, and stewed chicken, she restrained herself, not daring to order any strawberries which were still very dear, for fear of running the bill up too high.

"Now, what are we going to do?" asked Baugé, when the coffee was served.

As a rule Pauline and he returned to Paris to dine, and finish their outing in some theatre. But at Denise's request, they decided to remain at Joinville all day: it would be droll, they would take a fill of the country. So they wandered about the fields all the afternoon. They spoke for a moment of going for a row, but abandoned the idea as Baugé was not a good waterman. However, their strolls along the pathways ended by bringing them back to the banks of the Marne, all the same, and they became interested in all the river life, the squadrons of yawls and skiffs, and the young men who formed the crews. The sun was setting and they were returning towards Joinville, when they saw two boats coming down stream at a racing speed, their crews meantime exchanging volleys of insults, in which the repeated cries of "Sawbones!" and "Counter-jumpers!" predominated.

"Hallo!" said Pauline, "it's Monsieur Hutin."

"Yes," replied Baugé, shading his face with his hand, "I recognise his mahogany boat. The other one is manned by students, no doubt."

Thereupon he explained the deadly hatred existing between the students and the shopmen. Denise, on hearing Hutin's name mentioned, had suddenly stopped, and with fixed eyes followed the frail skiff. She tried to distinguish the young man among the rowers, but could only manage to make out the white dresses of two women, one of whom, who was steering, wore a red hat. Then the voices of the disputants died away amidst the loud flow of the river.

"Pitch 'em in, the sawbones!"

"Duck 'em, the counter-jumpers!"

In the evening they returned to the restaurant on the island. But it had turned very chilly and they were obliged to dine in one of the closed rooms, where the table-cloths were still damp from the humidity of winter. At six o'clock the tables were already crowded, yet the excursionists still hurried in, looking for vacant corners; and the waiters continued bringing in more chairs and forms, putting the plates closer and closer together and crowding the people up. Cold as it had been before, the atmosphere now became stifling and they had to open the windows. Out of doors, the day was waning, a greenish twilight fell from the poplars so quickly that the landlord, unprepared for these repasts under cover, and having no lamps, was obliged to put a candle on each table. What with the laughter, the calls and the clatter of plates and dishes the uproar became deafening; the candles flared and guttered in the draught from the open windows, whilst moths fluttered about in the air warmed by the odour of the food, and traversed by sudden cold gusts of wind.

"What fun they're having, eh?" said Pauline, very busy with a plate of stewed eels, which she declared extraordinary. And she leant over to add: "Didn't you see Monsieur Albert over there?"

It was really young Lhomme, in the midst of three questionable women. Already intoxicated, he was knocking his glass on the table, and talking of drubbing the waiter if he did not bring some *liqueurs* immediately.

"Well!" resumed Pauline, "there's a family for you! the mother is at Rambouillet, the father in Paris, and the son at Joinville; they won't tread on one another's toes to-day!"

Denise, though she detested noise, was smiling and tasting the delight of being unable to think, amid such uproar. But all at once they heard a commotion in the other room, a burst of voices which drowned all others. Men were yelling, and must have come to blows, for one could hear a scuffle, chairs falling, quite a struggle indeed, amid which the river-cries again resounded:

"Duck 'em, the counter-jumpers!"

"Pitch 'em in, the sawbones!"

And when the landlord's loud voice had calmed this tempest, Hutin, wearing a red jersey, and with a little cap at the back of his head, suddenly made his appearance, having on his arm the tall, fair girl, who had been steering his boat and who by way of wearing the crew's colours, had planted a bunch of poppies behind her ear. Clamorous applause greeted their entry; and Hutin, his face beaming with pride at thus being remarked, threw his chest forward and assumed a nautical rolling gait, displaying the while a bruised cheek, quite blue from a blow he had received. Behind him and his companion followed the crew. They took a table by storm, and the uproar became deafening.

"It appears," explained Baugé, after listening to the conversation behind him, "it appears that the students recognised the woman with Hutin as an old friend from their neighbourhood, who now sings in a music-hall at Montmartre. So they were kicking up a row about her."

"In any case," said Pauline, stiffly, "she's precious ugly, with her carroty hair. Really, I don't know where Monsieur Hutin picks them up, but they're an ugly, dirty lot."

Denise had turned pale, and felt an icy coldness, as if her heart's blood were flowing away, drop by drop. Already, on seeing the boats from the bank she had felt a shiver; but now she no longer had any doubt at seeing that girl with Hutin. With trembling hands, and a choking sensation in her throat, she suddenly ceased to eat.

"What's the matter?" asked her friend.

"Nothing," she stammered, "but it's rather warm here."

However Hutin's table was close to theirs, and when Hutin perceived Baugé, whom he knew, he commenced a conversation in a shrill voice, in order to attract further attention.

"I say," he cried, "are you as virtuous as ever at the Bon Marché?"

"Not so much as all that," replied Baugé, turning very red.

"That won't do! You know there's a confessional box at your place for the salesmen who venture to look at the young ladies there. No, no! A house where they insist on their employees marrying, that won't do for me!"

The other fellows began to laugh, and Liénard who was one of Hutin's crew added some jocular remark about the Louvre establishment at which Pauline herself burst into a merry peal.

Baugé, however, was annoyed by the joke about the staid propriety and innocence of his establishment, and all at once he retorted: "Oh, you needn't talk, you are not so well off at The Ladies' Paradise. Sacked for the slightest thing! And a governor too who is always smirking round his lady customers."

Hutin no longer listened to him, but began to praise the Place Clichy establishment. He knew a girl there who was so inexpressibly dignified that customers dared not speak to her for fear of humiliating her. Then, drawing up closer, he related that he had made a hundred and fifteen francs that week; oh! a capital week. Favier had been left behind with merely fifty-two francs, in fact the whole lot had been floored. And it could be seen that he was telling the truth. He was squandering his cash as fast as possible and did not mean to go to bed till he had rid himself of the hundred and fifteen francs. Then, as he gradually became intoxicated, he fell foul of Robineau, that fool of a second-hand who affected to keep himself apart, to such a point that he refused to walk down the street with one of his salesmen.

"Shut up," said Liénard; "you talk too much, old man."

The heat had yet increased, the candles were guttering down on to the wine-stained table-cloths; and through the open windows, whenever the noise within ceased for an instant, there came a distant prolonged murmur, the voice of the river, and of the lofty poplars falling asleep in the calm night. Baugé had just called for the bill, seeing that Denise was no better; indeed she was now quite white, choking from the tears she withheld; however, the waiter did not appear, and she had to submit to more of Hutin's loud talk. He was now boasting of being much superior to Liénard, because Liénard simply squandered his father's money, whereas he, Hutin, spent his own earnings, the fruit of his intelligence. At last Baugé paid, and the two girls went out.

Denise heaved a sigh of relief. For a moment she had thought she was going to die in that suffocating heat, amidst all those cries; and she still attributed her faintness to want of air. At present she could breathe freely in the freshness of the starry night.

As the two young women were leaving the garden of the restaurant, a timid voice murmured in the shade: "Good evening, ladies."

It was Deloche. They had not seen him at the further end of the front room, where he had been dining alone, after coming from Paris on foot, for the pleasure of the walk. On recognising his friendly voice, Denise, suffering as she was, yielded mechanically to the need of some support.

"Monsieur Deloche," said she, "are you coming back with us? Give me your arm."

Pauline and Baugé had already gone on in front. They were astonished, never thinking it would turn out like that, and with that fellow above all. However, as there was still an hour before the train started, they went to the end of the island, following the bank, under the tall poplars; and, from time to time, they turned round, murmuring: "But where have they got to? Ah, there they are. It's rather funny, all the same."

At first Denise and Deloche remained silent. The uproar from the restaurant was slowly dying away, changing into a musical sweetness in the calmness of the night; and still feverish from that furnace, whose lights were disappearing one by one behind the foliage, they went further in amidst the coolness of the trees. Opposite them there was a sort of shadowy wall, a mass of shadow so dense that they could not even distinguish any trace of the path. However, they went forward quietly, without fear. Then, their eyes getting more accustomed to the darkness, they saw on the right hand the trunks of the poplar trees, resembling sombre columns upholding the domes of their branches, between which gleamed the stars; whilst the water occasionally shone like a mirror. The wind was falling and they no longer heard anything but the loud flow of the stream.

"I am very pleased to have met you," stammered Deloche at last, making up his mind to speak first. "You can't think how happy you render me in consenting to walk with me."

And, aided by the darkness, after many awkward attempts, he ventured to tell her that he loved her. He had long wanted to write to her and tell her so; but perhaps she would never have known it had it not been for that lovely night coming to his assistance, that water which murmured so softly, and those trees which screened them with their shade. However, she did not reply; she continued to walk by his side with the same suffering air. And he was trying to gaze into her face, when all at once he heard a sob.

"Oh! good heavens!" he exclaimed, "you are crying, mademoiselle, you are crying! Have I offended you?"

"No, no," she murmured.

She strove to keep back her tears, but could not do so. Even whilst she was at table, she had thought that her heart was about to burst. And now in the darkness she surrendered herself to her sensibility, stifled by her sobs and thinking that if Hutin had been in Deloche's place and had said such tender things to her, she would have been unable to say nay. But this self-confession suddenly filled her with confusion, and a burning flush of shame suffused her face.

"I didn't mean to offend you," continued Deloche, almost crying also.

"No, but listen," she replied, her voice still trembling; "I am not at all angry with you. But never speak to me again as you have just done. Oh! you're a good fellow, and I'm quite willing to be your friend, but nothing more. You understand—your friend."

He quivered, and after a few steps taken in silence, he stammered: "In fact, you don't love me?"

And then as she spared him the pain of a brutal "no," he resumed in a soft, heart-broken voice: "Oh, I was prepared for it. I have never had any luck, I know I can never be happy. At home, they used to beat me. In Paris, I've always been a drudge. You see, when a chap doesn't know how to rob other fellows of their sweethearts, and is too awkward to earn as much as the others, why the best thing he can do is to go into some corner and die. Never fear, I shan't torment you any more. As for loving you, you can't prevent me, can you? I shall love you like a dog. There, everything escapes me, that's my luck in life."

And then he, too, burst into tears. She tried to console him, and in their friendly effusion they found they belonged to the same part of the country—she to Valognes, he to Briquebec, eight miles from each other, and this proved a fresh tie. His father, a poor, needy process-server, sickly jealous, had been wont to drub him, exasperated by his long pale face and tow-like hair, which, said he, did not belong to the family. Then they got to talking of the vast Cotentin pastures, surrounded with quick-set hedges, of the shady paths and lanes winding beneath elm trees, and of the grass grown roads, like alleys in a park. Around them the night was yet paling and they could distinguish the rushes on the banks, and the lacework of the foliage, black against the twinkling stars; and a peacefulness came over them, they forgot their troubles, brought closer together, to a cordial feeling of friendship, by their ill-luck.

"Well?" asked Pauline of Denise, taking her aside when they reached the station.

The young girl, who understood her friend's meaning by her smile and stare of tender curiosity, turned very red and answered: "Oh! no, my dear. Remember what I told you. But he belongs to my part of the country. We were talking about Valognes."

Pauline and Baugé were perplexed, put out in their ideas, not knowing what to think. Deloche left them on the Place de la Bastille; like all young probationers, he slept in the house, and had to be back by eleven o'clock. Not wishing to go in with him, Denise, who had obtained what was called "theatre leave" which allowed her to remain out till past midnight, accepted Baugé's invitation to accompany Pauline to his home in the Rue Saint-Roch. They took a cab, and on the way Denise was stupefied to learn that her friend would not return to The Paradise till the morrow, having squared matters with Madame Cabin by giving her a five-franc piece. Baugé, who did the honours of his room, which was furnished with some old Empire furniture, given him by his father, got angry when Denise spoke of settling up, but at last accepted the fifteen francs twelve sous which she had laid on the chest of drawers; however, he insisted on making her a cup of tea, and after struggling with a spirit-lamp and saucepan, was obliged to go and fetch some sugar. Midnight struck as he was pouring out the tea.

"I must be off," said Denise.

"Presently," replied Pauline. "The theatres don't close so early."

Denise however felt uncomfortable in that bachelor's room and a quarter of an hour later she contrived to slip away.

The private door which conducted to Mouret's apartments and to the assistants' bedrooms was in the Rue Neuve-Saint-Augustin. Madame Cabin opened it by pulling a string and then gave a glance in order to see who was returning. A night-light was burning dimly in the hall, and Denise on finding herself in this uncertain glimmer, hesitated, and was seized with fear, for a moment previously, on turning the corner of the street, she had seen the door close on the shadowy figure of a man.

It must have been the governor coming home from a party; and the idea that he was there in the dark possibly waiting for her, caused her one of those strange fears with which he still inspired her, without any reasonable cause. Some one was certainly moving about on the first-floor, for she heard a creaking of boots, whereupon quite losing her head, she opened a door which led into the shop, and which was always left unlocked for the night-watch to make his rounds. On entering she found herself in the printed cotton department.

"Good heavens! what shall I do?" she stammered, in her emotion.

Then the idea occurred to her that there was another door upstairs leading to the bedrooms; but to reach it she would have to go right across the shop. She preferred this, however, notwithstanding the darkness reigning in the galleries. Not a gas-jet was burning there; only a few lighted oil-lamps hung here and there from the branches of the chandeliers; and these scattered lights, like yellow specks fading away in the gloom, resembled the lanterns hung up in mines. Big shadows loomed before her; she could hardly distinguish the piles of goods, which assumed all sorts of threatening aspects—now they looked like fallen columns, now like squatting beasts, and now like lurking thieves. The heavy silence, broken by distant breathing, moreover increased the darkness. However, she found her way. From the linen department on her left came a paler gleam, bluey, like a house front under a summer sky at night; then she wished to cross the central hall, but on running up against some piles of printed calico, she thought it safer to traverse the hosiery department, and then the woollen one. There she was frightened by a loud noise of snoring. It was Joseph, the messenger, sleeping behind some mourning articles. She then quickly ran into the hall where the skylight cast a sort of crepuscular light, which made it appear larger, and, with its motionless shelves, and the shadows of its yard-measures describing reversed crosses, lent it the awe-inspiring aspect of a church at night. And she, indeed full of fear, now fairly fled. In the mercery and glove departments she nearly trod on some more assistants, and only felt safe when she at last found herself on the staircase. But up above, just outside the mantle department, she was again seized with terror on perceiving a lantern twinkling in the darkness and moving forward. It was the patrol of two firemen, marking their passage on the faces of the indicators. She stood still for a moment failing to understand their business, and watched them passing from among the shawls to the furniture, and then on to the under-linen department, terrified the while by their strange manœuvres, by the grating of their keys and the closing of the iron doors which shut with a resounding clang. When they approached, she took refuge in the lace department, but suddenly heard herself called by name and thereupon ran off to the door conducting to the private stairs. She had recognised Deloche's voice. He slept in his department, on a little iron bedstead which he set up himself every evening; and he was not asleep yet, but with open eyes was rememorating aloud the pleasant hours he had spent that evening.

"What! it's you, mademoiselle?" said Mouret, whom Denise despite all her manœuvring found before her on the staircase, a small pocket-candleholder in his hand.

She stammered, and tried to explain that she had been to look for something. But he was not angry. He gazed at her with his paternal, and at the same time inquisitive, air.

"You had permission to go to the theatre, then?"

"Yes, sir."

"And have you enjoyed yourself? What theatre did you go to?"

"I have been in the country, sir."

This made him laugh. Then laying a certain stress on his words, he added: "All alone?"

"No, sir; with a lady friend," she replied, her cheeks burning, shocked as she was by the suspicion which his words implied.

He said no more; but he was still looking at her in her simple black dress and bonnet trimmed with a strip of blue ribbon. Was this little savage going to turn out a pretty girl? She looked all the better for her day in the open air, quite charming indeed with her splendid hair waving over her forehead. And he, who during the last six months had treated her like a child, sometimes giving her advice, yielding to a desire to inform himself, to a wicked wish to know how a woman grew up and became lost in Paris, no longer laughed, but experienced a feeling of surprise and fear mingled with tenderness. No doubt it was a lover who was improving her like this. At this thought he felt as if pecked to the heart by a favourite bird, with which he had been playing.

"Good night, sir," murmured Denise, continuing on her way without waiting.

He did not answer, but remained watching her till she had disappeared. And then he entered his own apartments.

ÉMILE ZOLA

# VI

When the dead summer season arrived, quite a hurricane of panic swept through The Ladies' Paradise. The reign of terror—terror of dismissal—commenced; many employees were sent away on leave, and others were dismissed in dozens by the principals, bent on clearing the shop, as no customers appeared there during the July and August heat. Mouret, on making his daily round with Bourdoncle, would call aside the managers, whom he had prompted during the winter to engage more men than were really necessary, in order that the business might not suffer; but it was now a question of reducing expenses and this was effected by casting quite a third of the shop people—the weak ones who allowed themselves to be swallowed up by the strong ones—on to the pavements again.

"Come," he would say, "you must have some who don't suit you. We can't keep them all this time doing nothing."

And if the manager hesitated, hardly knowing whom to sacrifice, he would continue: "Make your own arrangements, six salesmen must suffice; you can take on others in October, there are always plenty to be had!"

Moreover Bourdoncle undertook the executions. He had a terrible way of saying: "Go and be paid!" which fell on the poor devil he had singled out like a blow from an axe. Anything served him as a pretext for clearing off the superfluous staff. He invented misdeeds, speculating on the slightest negligence. "You were sitting down, sir; go and get paid!" "You dare to answer me; go and get paid!" "Your shoes have not been blackened; go and get paid!" And even the bravest trembled in presence of the massacre which he left behind him. Then, this system not working quickly enough, he invented a trap by which in a few days and without fatigue, he got rid of the number of salesmen condemned beforehand. At eight o'clock, he took his stand at the door, watch in hand; and at three minutes past the hour, the breathless young people who arrived were greeted with his implacable "Go and get paid!" This was a quick and cleanly manner of doing the work.

"You've an ugly mug," he ended by saying one day to a poor devil whose nose, all on one side, annoyed him, "go and get paid!"

The favoured ones obtained a fortnight's holiday without pay, which was a more humane way of lessening the expenses. Moreover the salesmen quietly accepted their precarious situation, obliged to do so by necessity and habit. Since their arrival in Paris, they had roamed about, commencing their apprenticeship here, finishing it there, getting dismissed or they themselves resigning all at once, just as interest dictated. When business slackened the workmen lost their daily bread; and this went on amidst the subdued working of the machine, the useless gear was quietly thrown aside, like so much old plant. There was no gratitude shown for services rendered. So much the worse for those who did not know how to look after themselves!

Nothing else was now talked of in the various departments. Fresh stories circulated every day. The dismissed salesmen were named, in the same way as one counts the dead in time of cholera. The shawl and the woollen departments suffered especially; seven employees disappeared from them in one week. Then quite a drama threw the under-linen department into confusion: a customer, nearly fainting away, accused the young person who had served her of eating garlic; and the latter was dismissed at once, although, badly fed and dying of hunger, she had simply been finishing a collection of bread-crusts at the counter. However, the authorities showed themselves pitiless at the least complaint from customers; no excuse was admitted, the employee was always wrong, and had to disappear like a defective instrument, which interfered with the proper working of the business; and the others bowed their heads, not even attempting any defence. In the panic which was raging, each trembled for himself. Mignot, going out one day with a parcel under his coat, notwithstanding the regulations, was nearly caught, and really thought himself lost. Liénard, celebrated for his idleness, was simply indebted to his father's position in the drapery trade for not being turned away one afternoon when Bourdoncle found him dozing between two piles of English velvets. But the Lhommes were especially anxious, each day expecting to see their son Albert sent away, as the principals were very dissatisfied with his conduct at his pay-desk. He frequently had women there who diverted his attention from his work; and twice already Madame Aurélie had been obliged to plead for him.

Denise was so menaced amid this general clearance, that she lived in constant expectation of a catastrophe. It was in vain that she summoned up her courage, struggling with all her gaiety and all her reason in the endeavour not to yield to the misgivings of her tender nature; she burst into blinding tears as soon as she had closed the door of her bedroom, in desolation at the thought of finding herself in the street, on bad terms with her uncle, not knowing where to go, without a copper saved, and with the two children to look after. The sensations she had experienced during the first few weeks again returned, she fancied herself a grain of seed under a powerful millstone; and utter discouragement came over her at the thought of what a small atom she was in this great machine, which would certainly crush her with its quiet indifference. There was no illusion possible; if they dismissed any one from her department it would certainly be herself. During the Rambouillet excursion no doubt the other young ladies had incensed Madame Aurélie against her, for since then that lady had treated her with an air of severity into which entered a certain rancour. Besides, they could not forgive her for going to Joinville, regarding it as a sign of revolt, a means of setting the whole department at defiance, by exhibiting herself out of doors with a young lady from a rival counter. Never had Denise suffered so much in the department, and she now gave up all hope of conquering it.

"Let them alone!" repeated Pauline, "a lot of stuck-up things, as stupid as geese!"

But it was just these fine-lady airs which intimidated Denise. Nearly all the saleswomen, by their daily contact with rich customers, acquired certain graces, and finished by forming a vague nameless class—something between a work-girl and a middle-class lady. But beneath their art in dress, and the manners and phrases they had learnt by rote, there was often only a false, superficial education, the fruit of reading worthless papers, attending cheap theatres and music-halls, and picking up all the current stupidities of Paris.

"You know the 'unkempt one' has got a child?" said Clara one morning, on arriving in the department. And, as the others seemed astonished, she continued: "Yes, I saw her yesterday myself taking the child out for a walk! She's got it stowed away in the neighbourhood, somewhere."

Two days later, Marguerite came up after dinner with another piece of news. "A nice thing, I've just seen the unkempt one's sweetheart—a workman, just fancy! Yes, a dirty little workman, with yellow hair, who was watching her through the windows."

From that moment it became an accepted fact: Denise had a workman for a lover, and an infant concealed somewhere in the neighbourhood. They overwhelmed her with spiteful allusions. The first time she understood them she turned quite pale at the monstrosity of their suppositions. It was abominable; she tried to explain, and stammered out: "But they are my brothers!"

"Oh! oh! her brothers!" said Clara in a bantering tone.

Madame Aurélie was obliged to interfere. "Be quiet! young ladies. You had better go on changing those tickets. Mademoiselle Baudu is quite free to misbehave herself out of doors, if only she worked a bit when she is here."

This curt defence was a condemnation. The poor girl, suffocating as if they had accused her of a crime, vainly endeavoured to explain the facts. They laughed and shrugged their shoulders, and she felt wounded to the heart. On hearing the rumours Deloche was so indignant that he wanted to slap the faces of the young ladies in Denise's department; and was only restrained from doing so by the fear of compromising her. Since the evening at Joinville, he had harboured a submissive love, an almost religious friendship for her, which he proved by his faithful doglike looks. He was careful not to show his affection before the others, for they would have laughed at him, still that did not prevent him dreaming of the avenging blow he would deal if ever any one should attack her in his presence.

Denise finished by not answering the insults. It was all too odious, nobody would believe it. When any of her companions ventured a fresh allusion, she contented herself with looking at her with a sad, calm air. Besides, she had other troubles, material anxieties which took up her attention. Jean went on as badly as ever, always worrying her for money. Hardly a week passed that she did not receive some fresh story from him, four pages long; and when the house postman brought her these letters, in a big, passionate handwriting, she hastened to hide them in her pocket, for the saleswomen affected to laugh, and hummed snatches of some doubtful ditties. Then, after inventing some pretext to enable her to go to the other end of the establishment and read these letters, she became full of fear; poor Jean seemed to be lost. All his fibs succeeded with her, she believed in all his extraordinary love adventures, her complete ignorance of such things making her exaggerate his dangers. Sometimes it was a two-franc piece he wanted to enable him to escape some woman's jealousy, at other times five francs, six francs, to get some poor girl out of a scrape as her father would otherwise kill her. And so, as her salary and commission did not suffice, Denise conceived the idea of looking for a little work after business hours. She spoke about it to Robineau, who had shown a certain sympathy for her since their first meeting at Vinçard's, and he procured her the making of some neckties at five sous a dozen. At night, between nine and one o'clock, she could sew six dozen of these which represented thirty sous, out of which she had to deduct four sous for a candle. And as this sum kept Jean going she did not complain of the want of sleep, and would have thought herself very happy had not another catastrophe once more upset her budgetary calculations. At the end of the second fortnight, when she went to the necktie-dealer's, she found the door closed; the woman had failed, become bankrupt, thus carrying off her eighteen francs six sous, a considerable sum on which she had been relying for the last week. All the annoyances she experienced in the department disappeared before this disaster.

"You seem worried," said Pauline, meeting her one day in the furniture gallery, looking very pale. "Are you in want of anything?"

But as Denise already owed her friend twelve francs, she tried to smile and replied: "No, thanks. I've not slept well, that's all."

It was the twentieth of July, and the panic caused by the dismissals was at its height. Out of the four hundred employees, Bourdoncle had already sacked fifty, and there were rumours of fresh executions. She, however, thought but little of the menaces which were flying about, entirely absorbed as she was by the anguish caused her by one of Jean's adventures, an adventure yet more terrifying than any previous one. That very day he wanted fifteen francs, which sum alone could save him from somebody's vengeance. On the previous evening she had received the first letter opening the drama; then, one after the other had come two more; and in the last, the perusal of which she was finishing when Pauline met her, Jean had announced his death for that evening, if she did not send the money. She was in agony. She couldn't take the sum out of Pépé's board money as this she had paid away two days before. Every sort of bad luck was pursuing her, for she had hoped to get her eighteen francs six sous through Robineau, who might perhaps be able to find the necktie-dealer; but Robineau, having got a fortnight's holiday, had not returned on the previous night though expected to do so.

However, Pauline still questioned her in a friendly way. Whenever they met, in an out-of-the-way department, they would thus converse for a few minutes, keeping a sharp look-out the while. And suddenly, Pauline made a move as if to run off, having observed the white tie of an inspector coming out of the shawl department.

"Ah! it's only old Jouve!" she murmured in a relieved tone. "I can't think what makes the old man grin as he does when he sees us together. In your place I should beware, for he's too kind to you. He's an old humbug, as spiteful as a cat, and thinks he's still got his troopers to talk to."

This was quite true; Jouve was detested by all the salespeople for his severity. More than half the dismissals were the result of his reports; and, rakish ex-captain that he was, with a big red nose, he only shewed himself lenient in the departments served by women. Thus though he must have perceived Denise and Pauline he went away, pretending not to see them; and they heard him dropping on a salesman of the lace department, guilty of watching a fallen horse in the Rue Neuve-Saint-Augustin.

"By the way," resumed Pauline, "weren't you looking for Monsieur Robineau yesterday? He's come back."

At this Denise thought herself saved. "Thanks," said she, "I'll go round the other way then, and pass through the silk department. So much the worse! They sent me upstairs to the work-room to fetch a bodkin."

And thereupon they separated. The young girl, with a busy look, as if she were running from pay-desk to pay-desk in search of something, reached the stairs and went down into the hall. It was a quarter to ten, the first lunch-bell had rung. A warm sun was playing on the windows, and in spite of the grey linen blinds, the heat penetrated the stagnant air. Now and then a refreshing breath arose from the floor, which some assistants were gently watering. A somnolence, a summer siesta reigned in all the vacant spaces around the counters, you might have thought yourself in a church wrapt in sleeping shadow after the last mass. Some salesmen were standing about listlessly, and a few rare customers crossed the galleries and the hall, with the indolent step of women annoyed by the sun.

Just as Denise went down, Favier was measuring a dress length of light silk, with pink spots, for Madame Boutarel, who had arrived in Paris from the South on the previous day. Since the commencement of the month, the provinces had been sending up their detachments; you saw nothing but queerly-dressed dames in yellow shawls, green skirts, and flaring bonnets. But the shopmen were even too indolent to laugh at them. Favier accompanied Madame Boutarel to the mercery department, and on returning, remarked to Hutin:

"Yesterday they were all Auvergnat women, to-day they're all Provençales. I'm sick of them."

But just then Hutin rushed forward, for it was his turn, and he had recognised "the pretty lady," the lovely blonde thus nicknamed by the department which knew nothing about her, not even her name. They all smiled at her, not a week passed without her coming to The Ladies' Paradise, hitherto always alone. This time, however, she had a little boy of four or five with her, and this gave rise to various comments.

"She's married, then?" asked Favier, when Hutin returned from the pay-desk, where he had debited her with thirty yards of Duchess satin.

"Possibly," replied he, "although the youngster proves nothing. Perhaps he belongs to a lady friend. What's certain is, that she must have been weeping. She was awfully melancholy, and her eyes were so red!"

A silence ensued. The two salesmen gazed vaguely into the depths of the shop. Then Favier resumed in a low voice: "If she's married, perhaps her husband's smacked her face."

"Possibly," repeated Hutin, "unless a lover has played her false." And after a fresh silence, he added: "Any way, I don't care a hang!"

At this moment Denise crossed the silk department, slackening her steps and looking around her, in search of Robineau. She could not see him, so she went into the linen department, then passed through again. The two salesmen had noticed her movements.

"There's that bag of bones again," murmured Hutin.

"She's looking for Robineau," said Favier. "I can't think what they get up to together. Oh! nothing wrong. But they say Robineau has procured her a little work, some neckties. What a spec, eh?"

Hutin was meditating something spiteful; and when Denise passed near him, he stopped her, saying: "Is it me you're looking for?"

She turned very red. Since the Joinville excursion, she had not dared to read her heart, full of confused sensations. She was constantly recalling his appearance with that red-haired girl, and if she still trembled before him, it was doubtless from uneasiness. Had she ever loved him? Did she love him still? She hardly liked to stir up these things, which were painful to her.

"No, sir," she replied, embarrassed.

Hutin thereupon began to laugh at her uneasy manner. "Would you like us to serve him to you? Favier, just serve Robineau to this young lady."

She looked at him fixedly, with the sad calm look with which she had met the wounding remarks made by the girls, her companions. Ah! so he was spiteful, he attacked her as well as the others! And she felt a sort of supreme anguish, the breaking of a last tie. Her face expressed such real suffering, that Favier, although not of a very tender nature, came to her assistance.

"Monsieur Robineau has gone out to match some goods," said he. "No doubt he will be back for lunch. You'll find him here this afternoon, if you want to speak to him."

Denise thanked him, and went up to her department, where Madame Aurélie was waiting for her in a terrible rage. What! she had been gone half an hour! Where had she just sprung from? Not from the workroom, that was quite certain! The poor girl hung her head, thinking of this avalanche of misfortunes. All would be over if Robineau should not come in. However, she resolved to go down again, later on.

In the silk department, Robineau's return had provoked quite a revolution. The salesmen had hoped that, disgusted with the annoyances they were incessantly causing him, he would not return to the establishment; and, in fact, there was a moment, when pressed by Vinçard to take over his business, he had almost decided to do so. Hutin's secret labour, the mine which he had been laying under the second-hand's feet for months past, was about to explode. During Robineau's holidays, he had temporarily taken his place and had done his best to injure him in the minds of the principals, and secure possession of his situation by excess of zeal; he discovered and reported all sorts of trifling irregularities, suggested improvements, and invented new designs. There was, however, nothing exceptional in all this. Everybody in the department—from the unpaid probationer, longing to become a salesman, to the first salesman who coveted the situation of manager—had but one fixed idea, and that was to dislodge the comrade above them, to ascend another rung of the ladder, by knocking him over if necessary; and this battle of appetites, this constant hurtling, even contributed to the better working of the machine, inspiriting the sales and fanning the flame of success which was astonishing Paris. Behind Hutin, there was Favier; and behind Favier came the others, in a long line. You heard a loud noise as of jaws working. Robineau was condemned, and each was grabbing for one of his bones. So when the second-hand returned from his holiday there was a general grumbling. The matter had to be settled at once, the salesmen's attitude appearing so menacing that the head of the department had sent Robineau out to match some goods at the dépôts of manufacturers in order to give the authorities an opportunity to come to a decision.

"We would sooner all leave, if he is to be kept," declared Hutin.

The affair greatly bothered Bouthemont, whose gaiety ill-accorded with such worries. He was pained to see nothing but scowling faces around him. Nevertheless he desired to be just.

"Come, leave him alone, he doesn't hurt you," he said.

But they protested energetically. "What! doesn't hurt us! An insupportable being who is always irritable and so proud that he would walk over one rather than not pass."

This was the great grievance of the department. Robineau, nervous as a woman, was intolerably stiff and susceptible. They related scores of stories about him; one poor little fellow had fallen ill through his treatment, and even lady customers had been humiliated by his curt remarks.

"Well, gentlemen, I won't take anything on myself," said Bouthemont. "I've notified the position to the directors, and am going to speak about it shortly."

The second lunch was being rung; the clang of a bell came up from the basement with a distant muffled sound in the close air of the shop. Hutin and Favier went down. From all the counters, came salesmen one by one, hastening, helter-skelter, through the narrow entrance to the kitchen passage down below, a damp passage always lighted by gas. The flock pushed forward, without a laugh or a word, amidst an increasing clatter of crockery and a strong odour of food. Then at the far end of the passage there was a sudden halt, before a wicket. Flanked by piles of plates, and armed with forks and spoons, which he plunged into copper-pans, a cook was distributing the portions. And when he stood aside, the flaring kitchen could be seen beyond his white-covered belly.

"Of course!" muttered Hutin, consulting the bill of fare, written on a black-board above the wicket. "Boiled beef and pungent sauce, or skate. Never any roast meat in this rotten shop! Their boiled beef and fish don't do a fellow a bit of good!"

Moreover, the fish was universally neglected, for the pan was quite full. Favier, however, took some skate. Behind him, Hutin stooped down, saying: "Beef and sauce."

With a mechanical movement of his fork, the cook picked up a piece of meat; then poured a spoonful of sauce over it, and Hutin, suffocated by the hot air from the kitchen, had hardly secured his portion, before the words, "Beef, pungent sauce; beef, pungent sauce," followed each other like a litany; whilst the cook continued to pick up the meat and pour the sauce over it with the rapid rhythmical movement of a well-regulated clock.

"But the skate's cold," declared Favier, whose hand felt no warmth from the plate.

They were now all hurrying along, with arms extended and plates held straight, for fear of running against one another. Ten steps further was the bar, another wicket with a shiny zinc counter, on which were ranged the shares of wine, small bottles, without corks and still damp from rinsing. And each took one of these bottles in his empty hand as he passed, and then, completely laden, made for his table with a serious air, careful not to spill anything.

Hutin, however, grumbled between his teeth. "This is a fine dance, with all this crockery!"

The table at which he and Favier sat, was at the end of the corridor, in the last dining-room. The rooms were all alike, old cellars twelve feet by fifteen, which had been cemented over and fitted up as refectories; but the damp came through the paint-work, the yellow walls were covered with greenish spots; and, from the narrow windows, opening on the street, on a level with the pavement, there fell a livid light, incessantly traversed by the vague shadows of passers-by. In July as in December, you stifled in the warm air, laden with nauseous smells, which came from the kitchen near by.

Hutin went in first. On the table, which was fixed at one end to the wall, and covered with American cloth, there were only the glasses, knives, and forks, marking the places. A pile of clean plates stood at each end; whilst in the middle was a big loaf, a knife sticking in it, with the handle in the air. Hutin rid himself of his bottle and laid down his plate; then, after taking his napkin from the bottom of a set of pigeon-holes, the sole ornament on the walls, he heaved a sigh and sat down.

"And I'm fearfully hungry, too!" he murmured.

"It's always like that," replied Favier, seating himself on the left. "Nothing to eat when one is starving."

The table was rapidly filling. It contained twenty-two places. At first nothing was heard but a loud clattering of knives and forks, the gormandizing of big fellows whom thirteen hours' daily work incessantly rendered hungry. Formerly the employees had been allowed an hour for meals, which had enabled them to go to a café and take their coffee; and they would then despatch their dinner in twenty minutes, anxious to get into the street. But this excited them too much, they came back careless, their minds bent on other things than business; and so the managers had decided that they should not go out, but pay an extra three halfpence for a cup of coffee, if they wanted one. So now they were in no hurry, but prolonged the meal, being in no wise anxious to go back to work before time. Between their big mouthfuls a great many read newspapers which they had folded and placed against their bottles. Others, their first hunger satisfied, talked noisily, always returning to the eternal grievance of the bad food, to the money they had earned, to what they had done on the previous Sunday, and what they were going to do on the next one.

"I say, what about your Robineau?" a salesman suddenly asked Hutin.

The struggle between the men of the silk department and their second-hand occupied all the counters. The question was discussed every evening at the Café Saint-Roch until midnight. Hutin, who was busy with his piece of beef, contented himself with replying:

"Well! he's come back." Then, suddenly getting angry, he resumed: "But confound it! I really believe they've given me a slice of donkey! It's become disgusting, my word of honour!"

"You needn't grumble!" said Favier. "I was flat enough to ask for skate. It's putrid."

They were all speaking at once, some complaining and some joking. At a corner of the table, against the wall, sat Deloche silently eating. He was afflicted with a ravenous appetite, which he had never been able to satisfy, and not earning enough to afford any extras, he cut himself huge chunks of bread, and bolted even the least savoury platefuls, with a gormandizing air. They all laughed at him, crying: "Favier, pass your skate to Deloche. He likes it like that. And your meat, Hutin; Deloche wants it for his dessert."

The poor fellow shrugged his shoulders, and did not even reply. It wasn't his fault if he was dying of hunger. Besides, the others might abuse the food as much as they liked, they swallowed it all the same.

But a low whistle stopped their talk; Mouret and Bourdoncle were in the corridor. For some time the complaints had become so frequent that the principals pretended to come and judge the quality of the food themselves. They gave thirty sous a head per day to the chief cook, who had to pay for everything, provisions, coal, gas, and staff, and they displayed a naive astonishment when the food was not good. That very morning even, each department had deputed a spokesman. Mignot and Liénard had undertaken to speak for their comrades. And so, in the sudden silence which fell, all ears were cocked to catch the conversation going on in the next room, which Mouret and Bourdoncle had just entered. The latter declared the beef excellent; and Mignot, astounded by this quiet assertion, was repeating, "But chew it, and see;" whilst

Liénard, attacking the skate, gently remarked, "But it stinks, sir!" Mouret thereupon launched into a cordial speech; he would do everything for his employees' welfare, he was their father, and would rather eat dry bread himself than see them badly fed.

"I promise you to look into the matter," he said in conclusion, raising his voice so that they might all hear it from one end of the passage to the other.

The inquiry being finished, the noise of the knives and forks commenced once more. "Yes, reckon on that, and drink water!" Hutin muttered. "Ah, they're not stingy of fine words. You want some promises, there you are! But all the while they continue feeding you on old boot-leather, and chuck you out like dogs!"

The salesman who had already questioned him thereupon repeated: "You say that Robineau—"

But a clatter of heavy crockery-ware drowned his voice. The men changed their plates themselves, and the piles at both ends were diminishing. When a kitchen-help brought in some large tin dishes, Hutin cried out: "Baked rice! this is a finisher!"

"Good for a penn'orth of gum!" said Favier, serving himself.

Some liked it but others thought it too sticky. Those who were plunged in the fiction of their newspaper, not even knowing what they were eating, remained silent. All, however, mopped their foreheads, and the narrow cellar-like apartment filled with a ruddy vapour whilst the shadows of the passers-by continually passed like black bars over the littered tables.

"Pass Deloche the bread," cried one of the wags.

Each one cut a piece, and then again dug the knife into the loaf up to the handle; and the bread still went round.

"Who'll take my rice for a dessert?" all at once asked Hutin; and when he had concluded his bargain with a short, thin young fellow, he attempted to sell his wine also; but no one would take it as it was known to be detestable.

"As I was telling you, Robineau is back," he continued, amid the cross-fire of laughter and conversation that went on. "Oh! his affair is serious. Just fancy, he has been leading the saleswomen astray! Yes, and he gets them cravats to make!"

"Silence!" muttered Favier. "They're just judging him."

And with a wink he called attention to Bouthemont, who was walking up and down the passage between Mouret and Bourdoncle, all three absorbed in an animated conversation, carried on in a low tone. The dining-room of the managers and second-hands happened to be just opposite. And so on seeing Mouret pass, Bouthemont, having finished his meal, had got up to relate the affair and explain the awkward position he was in. The other two listened, still refusing to sacrifice Robineau, a first-class salesman, who dated from Madame Hédouin's time. But when Bouthemont came to the story of the neckties, Bourdoncle got angry. Was this fellow mad to interfere with the saleswomen and procure them extra work? The house paid dearly enough for the women's time; if they worked on their own account at night they must work less during the daytime in the shop, that was certain; therefore it was a robbery, they were risking their health which did not belong to them. No, the night was intended for sleep; they must all sleep, or they would be sent to the right-about!

"Things are getting rather warm!" remarked Hutin.

Each time the three principals passed the dining-room, the shopmen watched them, commenting on their slightest gestures. The baked rice, in which a cashier had just found a brace-button, was momentarily forgotten.

"I just heard the word 'cravat,'" said Favier. "And you saw how Bourdoncle's face turned pale all at once."

Mouret shared his partner's indignation. That a saleswoman should be reduced to work at night, seemed to him an attack on the very organization of The Ladies' Paradise. Who was the stupid that couldn't earn enough in the business? But when Bouthemont named Denise he softened down, and invented excuses. Ah! yes, that poor little girl; she wasn't very sharp, and had others dependent on her, it was said. Bourdoncle interrupted him to declare they ought to send her packing immediately. They would never do anything with such an ugly creature, he had always said so; and he seemed to be indulging a spiteful feeling. Thereupon Mouret, in embarrassment, affected to laugh. Dear me! what a severe man! couldn't they forgive her for once? They could call in the culprit and give her a scolding. In short, Robineau was the one to blame, for he ought to have dissuaded her, he, an old hand, knowing the ways of the house.

"Well! there's the governor laughing now!" resumed Favier, in astonishment, as the group again passed the door.

"Ah, by Jove!" exclaimed Hutin, "if they persist in shoving Robineau on our shoulders, we'll make it lively for them!"

Bourdoncle looked straight at Mouret and then simply made a gesture of disdain, to intimate that he saw how it was, and thought it idiotic. Bouthemont meantime resumed his complaints; the salesmen threatened to leave, and there were some very good men amongst them. However, what appeared to have most effect on these gentlemen, was the rumour of Robineau's friendly relations with Gaujean; the latter, it was said, was urging the former to set up for himself in the neighbourhood, offering him any amount of credit, to run in opposition to The Ladies' Paradise. There was a pause. Ah! Robineau thought of showing fight, did he! Mouret had become serious, though he affected a certain scorn, and avoided coming to a decision, as if it were matter of no importance. They would see, they would speak to him. And he immediately began to joke with Bouthemont, whose father, arriving from his little shop at Montpellier two days previously, had almost choked with stupefaction and rage on seeing the immense hall in which his son reigned. Everyone was still laughing about the old man, who, recovering his Southern assurance, had immediately begun to run everything down, pretending that the drapery business would soon go to the dogs.

"Ah! precisely, here's Robineau," said Bouthemont. "I sent him to attend to some matching so as to avoid any unpleasant occurrence. Excuse me if I insist, but things have come to such a pass that something must really be done."

Robineau, who had just come in, passed by the group with a bow, on his way to the table. Mouret simply repeated: "All right, we'll see about it."

Then all three went off. Hutin and Favier were still watching for them, but on seeing that they did not return began to relieve their feelings. Did the governor mean to come down like that at every meal, to count their mouthfuls? A nice thing it would be if they could not even eat in peace! The truth was, they had just seen Robineau come in, and the governor's good-humour made them anxious about the result of the struggle they were engaged in. They lowered their voices, trying to find fresh subjects for grumbling.

"But I'm dying of hunger!" continued Hutin, aloud. "One is hungrier than ever on rising from table!" And yet he had eaten two portions of jam, his own and the one which he had secured in exchange for his plate of rice. All at once he cried out: "Hang it, I'm going in for an extra! Victor, give me another jam!"

The waiter was finishing the serving of the desserts. He then brought in the coffee, and those who took it gave him their three sous there and then. A few had gone away, dawdling along the corridor and looking for a dark corner where they might smoke a cigarette. The others remained at table before the greasy plates, rolling pellets of bread-crumbs and recounting the same old stories, amidst the sickly odour of victuals, which they could no longer smell, and the sweltering heat which was reddening their ears. The walls reeked with moisture, a slow asphyxia fell from the mouldy vaulted ceiling. Leaning against the wall was Deloche, stuffed with bread and digesting in silence, his eyes on the window. His daily recreation, after luncheon was to watch the feet of the passers-by spinning along the street, a continual procession of living feet in big shoes, elegant boots, and ladies' tiny boots, without either head or body. On rainy days all were very dirty.

"What! Already?" suddenly exclaimed Hutin.

A bell had begun to ring at the end of the passage and they had to make way for the third lunch. The waiters came in with pails of warm water and big sponges to clean the American cloth. Gradually the rooms emptied and the salesmen returned to their departments, loitering as they went up the stairs. In the kitchen, the head cook had resumed his place at the wicket, between the pans of skate, beef, and sauce, again armed with his forks and spoons and ready to fill the plates anew with the rhythmical movement of a well-regulated clock. As Hutin and Favier slowly withdrew, they saw Denise coming down.

"Monsieur Robineau is back, mademoiselle," said the former with sneering politeness.

"He is still at table," added the other. "But if you are in a very great hurry you can go in."

Denise continued on her way without replying or turning round; but when she passed the dining-room of the managers and second-hands, she could not help just looking in, and saw that Robineau was really there. She resolved that she would try to speak to him in the afternoon, and continued her journey along the corridor to her own dining-room, which was at the other end.

The women took their meals apart, in two special rooms. Denise entered the first one. This also was an old cellar, transformed into a refectory; but it had been fitted up with more comfort. On the oval table, in the middle of the apartment, the fifteen places were set further apart and the wine was in decanters, a dish of skate and a dish of beef with pungent sauce occupying the two ends of the table. Waiters in white aprons moreover attended to the young ladies, and spared them the trouble of fetching their portions from the wicket. The manager had thought this arrangement more seemly.

"You went round, then?" asked Pauline, already seated and cutting herself some bread.

"Yes," replied Denise, blushing, "I was accompanying a customer."

But this was a fib. Clara nudged her neighbour. What was the matter with the unkempt girl? She was quite strange in her ways that day. One after the other she had received two letters from her lover and then went running all over the shop like a madwoman, pretending she was going to the work-room, where she did not even put in an appearance. There was something up, that was certain. Then Clara, eating her skate without any show of disgust, with the indifference of a girl who had been used to nothing better than rancid bacon, began speaking of a frightful drama, accounts of which filled the newspapers.

"You've read about that man cutting his mistress's throat with a razor, haven't you?"

"Well!" said a little, quiet, delicate-looking girl belonging to the under-linen department, "she was unfaithful to him. Serve her right!"

But Pauline protested. What! just because you had ceased to love a man, he was to be allowed to cut your throat? Ah! no, never! And stopping all at once, she turned round to the waiter, saying: "Pierre, I can't get through this beef. Just tell them to do me an extra, an omelet, nice and soft, if possible."

Then to while away the time, she took out some chocolate which she began eating with her bread, for she always had her pockets full of sweetmeats.

"It certainly isn't very amusing," resumed Clara. "And some people are fearfully jealous, you know! Only the other day there was a workman who pitched his wife into a well."

She kept her eyes on Denise, thinking she had guessed her trouble on seeing her turn pale. Evidently that little prude was afraid of being beaten by her lover, whom she no doubt deceived. It would be a lark if he should come into the shop after her, as she seemed to fear he would. But the conversation took another turn, for one of the girls was giving a recipe for cleaning velvet. Then they went on to speak of a piece at the Gaiety, in which some lovely little children danced better than any grown-up persons. Pauline, saddened for a moment at the sight of her omelet, which was overdone, recovered her spirits on finding that it tasted fairly well.

"Pass the wine," said she to Denise. "You should take an omelet."

"Oh! the beef is enough for me," replied the young girl, who, in order to avoid expense, contented herself with the food provided by the house, no matter how repugnant it might be.

When the waiter brought in the baked rice, the other young ladies protested. They had refused it the previous week, and had hoped it would not appear again. Denise, inattentive, worrying the more about Jean after Clara's stories, was the only one to eat it; and all the others looked at her with disgust. There was a great demand for extras, they gorged themselves with jam. Moreover this was a sort of elegance, they considered it aristocratic to feed themselves at their own expense.

"You know that the gentlemen have complained," said the delicate little girl from the under-linen department, "and the management has promised—"

But the others interrupted her with a burst of laughter, and began to rail at the management. Coffee was taken by all excepting Denise, who couldn't bear it, she said. And they lingered there before their cups, the young ladies from the under-linen department all middle-class simplicity in their woollen dresses, and the young ladies from the mantle department arrayed in silk, their napkins tucked under their chins, in order not to stain their gowns, like ladies who might have come down to the servants' hall to dine with their chamber-maids. Having opened the glazed sash of the air-hole to change the stifling poisoned air, they were speedily obliged to close it for the cab-wheels seemed to be passing over the table.

"Hush!" whispered Pauline; "here's that old beast!"

It was inspector Jouve, who was rather fond of prowling about at meal times, when the young ladies were there. He was supposed, in fact, to look after their dining-rooms. With a smiling face he would come in and walk round the tables; sometimes he would even indulge in a little gossip, and inquire if they had made a good lunch. But as he annoyed them and made them feel uncomfortable, they all hastened to get away. Although the bell had not rung, Clara was the first to disappear; the others followed her, and soon only Denise and Pauline remained. The latter, after drinking her coffee, was finishing her chocolate drops. But all at once she got up, saying: "I'm going to send a messenger for some oranges. Are you coming?"

"Presently," replied Denise, who was nibbling at a crust, determined to wait till the last, so that she might be able to see Robineau on her way upstairs.

However, when she found herself alone with Jouve she felt uneasy and annoyed, and quitted the table; but as she was going towards the door he stopped her saying: "Mademoiselle Baudu—"

Erect before her, he was smiling with a paternal air. His thick grey moustache and short cropped hair gave him a respectable military appearance; and he threw out his chest, on which was displayed the red ribbon of his decoration.

"What is it, Monsieur Jouve?" asked she, feeling reassured.

"I caught you again this morning talking upstairs behind the carpet department. You know it is not allowed, and if I reported you—She must be very fond of you, your friend Pauline." His moustache quivered, and his huge nose seemed all aflame. "What makes you so fond of each other, eh?"

Denise had again been seized with an uneasy feeling. He was getting too close, and was speaking in her face.

"It's true we were talking, Monsieur Jouve," she stammered, "but there's no harm in talking a bit. You are very kind to me, and I'm very much obliged to you."

"I ought not to be kind," said he. "Justice, and nothing more, is my motto. But when it's a pretty girl—"

And thereupon he came closer still, and she felt really afraid. Pauline's words returned to her memory and she recalled the stories which were told of old Jouve's goings-on.

"Leave me alone," she murmured drawing back.

"Come," said he, "you are not going to play the savage with me, who always treat you so well. Be amiable, come and take a cup of tea and a slice of bread-and-butter with me this evening. You are very welcome."

She was struggling now. "No! no!" she exclaimed.

The dining-room remained empty, the waiter had not come back. Jouve, listening for the sound of any footsteps, cast a rapid glance around him; and then, very excited, losing all control over himself, he attempted to kiss her on the neck.

"What a spiteful, stupid little girl you are!" he said.

But she was quite shocked and terrified by the approach of his burning face, and all at once she gave him so rough a push that he staggered and nearly fell upon the table. Fortunately, a chair saved him; but in the shock, some wine left in a glass spurted on to his white necktie, and soaked his decoration. And he remained there, without wiping himself, choked with anger at such brutality.

"Ah, you will be sorry for this, on my word of honour!" he growled between his teeth.

Denise ran away. Just at that moment the bell rang; but sorely perturbed, still shuddering, she forgot Robineau, and went straight up to her counter. And she did not dare to go down again. As the sun fell on the frontage of the Place Gaillon of an afternoon, they were soon all stifling in the first-floor rooms, notwithstanding the grey linen blinds. A few customers came, put the young ladies into perspiration, and went away without buying anything. Every one was yawning even under Madame Aurélie's big sleepy eyes. At last towards three o'clock, Denise, seeing the first-hand falling asleep, quietly slipped off, and resumed her journey across the shop, with a busy air. To put the curious ones, who might be watching her, off the scent, she did not go straight to the silk department; pretending that she wanted something among the laces, she went up to Deloche, and asked him a question; and then, on reaching the ground-floor, she passed through the printed cottons department, and was just going into the cravat gallery, when she stopped short, startled and surprised. Jean was before her.

"What! it's you?" she murmured, quite pale.

He was wearing his working blouse, and was bare-headed, with his hair in disorder, its curls falling over his girlish face. Standing before a show-case of narrow black neckties, he appeared to be thinking deeply.

"What are you doing here?" resumed Denise.

"What do you think?" replied he. "I was waiting for you. You won't let me come. So I came in all the same but haven't said anything to anybody. You may be quite easy. Pretend not to know me, if you like."

Some salesmen were already looking at them in astonishment. Jean lowered his voice. "She wanted to come with me, you know. Yes, she is close by, opposite the fountain. Give me the fifteen francs quick, or we are done for as sure as the sun is shining on us!"

Denise then lost her head. The lookers-on were grinning, listening to this adventure. And as behind the cravat department there was a staircase leading to the basement, she hastily pushed her brother, and made him go down. Once below he resumed his story, embarrassed, inventing his facts as he went on, and fearing that he might not be believed.

"The money is not for her. She is too respectable for that. And as for her husband, he does not care a straw for fifteen francs. No, it's for a low fellow, one of her friends, who saw me kissing her, and if I don't give him this money this evening—"

"Be quiet," murmured Denise. "Presently, do get along."

They were now in the parcels office. The dead season had steeped the vast basement in a sort of torpor, in the pale light falling from the air-holes. It was cool as well, and a silence fell from the ceiling. However, there was a porter collecting from one of the compartments a few parcels for the neighbourhood of the Madeleine; and, on the large sorting-table, sat Campion, the chief clerk, his legs dangling, and his eyes wandering.

Jean began again: "The husband, who has a big knife—"

"Get along!" repeated Denise, still pushing him forward.

They followed one of the narrow passages, where the gas was always kept burning. In the dark vaults to the right and the left were the reserve goods, shadowy behind the gratings. At last she stopped opposite one of these. Nobody was likely to pass that way; but the assistants were not allowed there, and she shuddered.

"If this rascal says anything," resumed Jean, "the husband, who has a big knife—"

"But where do you expect me to find fifteen francs?" exclaimed Denise in despair. "Can't you be more careful? You're always getting into some stupid scrape!"

He struck his chest. Amidst all his romantic inventions he had almost forgotten the exact truth. He dramatized his pecuniary wants, but there was always some immediate necessity behind his display. "By all that's sacred, it's really true this time," said he.

She stopped him again, and lost her temper, tortured and completely at a loss. "I don't want to know," she replied. "Keep your wicked conduct to yourself. It's too bad, you ought to know better! You're always tormenting me. I'm killing myself to keep you in money. Yes, I have to stay up all night at work. Not only that, but you are taking the bread out of your little brother's mouth."

Jean stood there with his mouth agape, and his face paling. What! it was wicked? And he could not understand; from infancy he had always treated his sister like a comrade, and thought it quite a natural thing to open his heart to her. But what upset him above all else was to learn that she stopped up all night. The idea that he was killing her, and taking Pépé's share as well, affected him so much that he began to cry.

"You're right; I'm a scamp," he exclaimed. "Really now, I am quite furious with myself! I could slap my face!" He had taken her hands, and was kissing them and inundating them with tears. "Give me the fifteen francs, and this shall be the last time, I swear it to you. Or rather—no!—

don't give me anything. I prefer to die. If the husband murders me it will be a good riddance for you." And as she was now crying as well, he became stricken with remorse. "I say that, but of course I'm not sure. Perhaps he doesn't want to kill any one. We'll manage. I promise you that, little sister. Good-bye, I'm off."

However, a sound of footsteps at the end of the passage suddenly frightened them. She quickly drew him close to the grating, in a dark corner. For an instant they heard nothing but the hissing of a gas-burner near them. Then the footsteps drew nearer; and, on stretching out her neck, she recognised inspector Jouve, who had just entered the corridor, with his stiff military walk. Was he there by chance, or had some one at the door warned him of Jean's presence? She was seized with such fright that she quite lost her head; and, pushing Jean out of the dark spot where they were concealed, drove him before her, stammering out: "Be off! Be off!"

Both galloped along, hearing Jouve behind them, for he also had began to run. And again they crossed the parcels office, and reached the foot of the stairs leading out into the Rue de la Michodière.

"Be off!" repeated Denise, "be off! If I can, I'll send you the fifteen francs all the same."

Jean, bewildered, scampered away. The inspector, who came up panting, out of breath, could only distinguish a corner of his white blouse, and his locks of fair hair flying in the wind. For a moment Jouve remained trying to get his breath back and resume his dignified demeanour. He now wore a brand-new white necktie which he had purchased in the linen department and the large bow of which glistened like snow.

"Well! this is nice behaviour, mademoiselle!" said he, his lips trembling. "Yes, it's nice, very nice! If you think I'm going to stand this sort of thing you're mistaken."

And with this remark he pursued her whilst she was returning to the shop, overcome with emotion and unable to find a word of defence. She was sorry now that she had run away. Why hadn't she explained the matter, and brought her brother forward? They would now imagine all sorts of villanies, and, say what she might, they would never believe her. Once more she forgot Robineau, and went back to her counter, while Jouve repaired to the manager's office to report the matter. But the messenger on duty told him that Monsieur Mouret was with Monsieur Bourdoncle and Monsieur Robineau; they had been talking together for the last quarter of an hour. In fact, the door was half-open, and he could hear Mouret gaily asking Robineau if he had spent a pleasant holiday; there was not the least question of a dismissal—on the contrary, the conversation fell on certain things to be done in the silk department.

"Do you want anything, Monsieur Jouve?" exclaimed Mouret. "Come in."

But a sudden instinct warned the inspector. As Bourdoncle had come out, he preferred to relate everything to him; and they slowly passed through the shawl department, walking side by side, the one leaning over and talking in a low tone, the other listening without a muscle of his severe face betraying his impressions.

"All right," he said at last.

And as they had arrived at the mantle department, he went in. Just at that moment Madame Aurélie was scolding Denise. Where had she come from again? This time she couldn't say that she had been to the work-room. Really, these continual absences could not be tolerated any longer.

"Madame Aurélie!" cried Bourdoncle.

He had decided on a bold stroke, not wishing to consult Mouret, for fear of some weakness. The first-hand came up, and the story was once more related in a low voice. All the girls were waiting in the expectation of some catastrophe. At last, Madame Aurélie turned round with a solemn air.

"Mademoiselle Baudu!" she called, and her puffy Cæsarian countenance assumed the inexorable sternness of sovereign power: "Go and get paid!"

The terrible phrase rang out loudly in the empty department. Denise stood there pale as a ghost, without saying a word. At last she was able to ask in broken sentences:

"Me! me! What for? What have I done?"

Bourdoncle harshly replied that she knew very well, that she had better not provoke any explanation; and he spoke of the cravats, and added that it would be a fine thing if all the young ladies were to receive men down in the basement.

"But it was my brother!" she cried with the grievous anger of an outraged virgin.

Marguerite and Clara began to laugh. Madame Frédéric, usually so discreet, shook her head with an incredulous air. Always her brother! Really it was very stupid! Denise looked round at all of them: at Bourdoncle, who had taken a dislike to her from the first; Jouve, who had stopped to serve as a witness, and from whom she expected no justice; and then at those girls whom she had not been able to soften by nine months of smiling courage, who were happy, in fact, to help in turning her out of doors. What was the use of struggling? what was the use of trying to impose herself on them when none of them liked her? And she went away without a word, not even casting another look at the room where she had so long battled. But as soon as she was alone, before the hall staircase, a deeper sense of suffering filled her heart. No one cared for her, and the sudden thought of Mouret had just deprived her of all resignation. No! no! she could not accept such a dismissal. Perhaps he would believe that villanous story of a rendezvous with a man down in the cellars. At this thought, a feeling of shame tortured her, an anguish with which she had never before been afflicted. She wished to go and see him to explain the matter to him, simply in order to let him know the truth; for she was quite ready to go away as soon as he should know it. And her old fear, the shiver which chilled her whenever she was in his presence, suddenly developed into an ardent desire to see him, not to leave the house in fact without telling him that she had never belonged to another.

It was nearly five o'clock, and the shop was waking into life again in the cool evening air. She quickly started off for Mouret's office. But when she reached the door, a hopeless, melancholy feeling again took possession of her. Her tongue refused its office, the intolerable burden of existence again fell on her shoulders. He would not believe her, he would laugh like the others, she thought; and this idea made her almost faint away. All was over, she would be better alone, out of the way, dead! And thereupon, without informing either Pauline or Deloche, she at once went for her money.

"You have twenty-two days, mademoiselle," said the clerk, "that makes eighteen francs and fourteen sous; to which must be added seven francs for commission. That's right, isn't it?"

"Yes, sir. Thanks."

And Denise was about to go off with her money, when she at last met Robineau. He had already heard of her dismissal, and promised to find the necktie-dealer. Then in a lower tone he tried to console her, but lost his temper: what an existence, to be at the continual mercy of a whim! to be thrown on to the pavement at an hour's notice, without even being able to claim a full month's salary. Denise went up to inform Madame Cabin that she would endeavour to send for her box during the evening. It was just striking five when she found herself on the pavement of the Place Gaillon, bewildered, in the midst of the crowd of people and vehicles.

That same evening when Robineau got home he received a letter from the management informing him, in a few lines, that for certain reasons relating to internal arrangements they were obliged to deprive themselves of his services. He had been at The Paradise for seven years, and only that afternoon had been talking to the principals. Thus it was a heavy blow for him. Hutin and Favier, however, were crowing in the silk department, as loudly as Clara and Marguerite in the other one. A jolly good riddance! Such clean sweeps made room for others! Deloche and Pauline were the only ones who when they met amidst the crush of the galleries exchanged distressful words, in their regret at the departure of Denise, so virtuous and gentle.

"Ah," said the young man, "if ever she succeeds anywhere else, I should like to see her come back here, and trample on all those good-for-nothing creatures!"

It was Bourdoncle who in this affair had to bear the brunt of Mouret's anger. When the latter heard of Denise's dismissal, he was exceedingly annoyed. As a rule he never interfered with the staff; but this time he affected to see an encroachment on his attributions, an attempt to over-ride his authority. Was he no longer master in the place, that they dared to give orders? Everything must pass through his hands, absolutely everything; and he would immediately crush any one who should resist. Then, after making personal inquiries, all the while in a nervous torment which he could not conceal, he again lost his temper. The poor girl had not lied; it was really her brother. Campion had fully recognised him. Why had she been sent away, then? He even spoke of taking her back.

However, Bourdoncle, strong is his passive resistance, bent before the storm. He studied Mouret, and one day when he saw him a little calmer he ventured to say in a meaning voice: "It's better for everybody that she's gone."

Mouret stood there looking very awkward, the blood rushing to his face. "Well!" he replied laughing, "perhaps you're right. Let's go and take a turn downstairs. Things are looking better, the receipts rose to nearly a hundred thousand francs yesterday."

ÉMILE ZOLA

# VII

For a moment Denise stood bewildered on the pavement, in the sun which still shone fiercely at five o'clock. The July heat warmed the gutters, Paris was blazing with that white chalky light of summer-time, whose reverberations are so blinding. And the catastrophe had fallen on her so suddenly, they had turned her out so roughly, that she stood there turning her money over in her pocket in a mechanical way, while she wondered where she could go, and what she could do.

A long line of cabs prevented her from quitting the pavement alongside The Ladies' Paradise. When she at last ventured amongst the wheels she crossed the Place Gaillon, as if intending to take the Rue Louis-le-Grand; then altering her mind, she walked towards the Rue Saint-Roch. But she still had no plan, for she stopped at the corner of the Rue Neuve-des-Petits-Champs, into which she finally turned, after looking around her with an undecided air. The Passage Choiseul opening before her, she passed through it and found herself in the Rue Monsigny, without knowing how, and ultimately came into the Rue Neuve-Saint-Augustin again. Her head was full of a fearful buzzing, she thought of her box on seeing a commissionaire; but where could she have it sent and why all this trouble, when but an hour ago she had still had a bed in which to sleep that night?

Then with her eyes fixed on the houses, she began examining the windows. There were any number of bills announcing, "Apartments to Let." But repeatedly overcome by the emotion which was agitating her whole being she saw them confusedly. Was it possible? Thrown into solitude so suddenly, lost in this immense city in which she was a stranger, without support, without resources! She must contrive to eat and sleep, however. The streets succeeded one another, after the Rue des Moulins came the Rue Sainte-Anne. She wandered about the neighbourhood, frequently retracing her steps, indeed always coming back to the only spot she knew really well. And suddenly she felt quite astonished for she was again standing before The Ladies' Paradise. To escape this obsession she hurried into the Rue de la Michodière. Fortunately Baudu was not at his door. The Old Elbeuf appeared lifeless, behind its murky windows. She would never have dared to show herself at her uncle's, for he now always pretended not to recognise her, and she did not wish to become a burden to him, in the misfortune which he had predicted to her. However, on the other side of the street, a yellow bill attracted her attention. "Furnished room to let." It was the first that did not frighten her, so poor was the aspect of the house. She soon recognised it, with its two low storeys, and rusty-coloured front, squeezed between The Ladies' Paradise and the old Hôtel Duvillard. On the threshold of the umbrella shop, old Bourras, hairy and bearded like a prophet, and with spectacles on his nose, stood studying the ivory handle of a walking-stick. Tenanting the whole house, he under-let the two upper floors furnished, in order to lighten the rent.

"You have a room to let, sir?" said Denise, approaching him in obedience to an instinctive impulse.

He raised his big bushy eyes, surprised to see her, for he knew all the young persons at The Ladies' Paradise. And after noticing her clean little gown and respectable appearance, he replied: "It won't suit you."

"How much is it, then?" replied Denise.

"Fifteen francs a month."

She asked to see it. Then on entering the narrow shop, and observing that he still eyed her with an astonished air, she told him of her departure from the Paradise and of her desire not to trouble her uncle. The old man thereupon fetched a key from a shelf in the back-shop, a small dark room, where he did his cooking and had his bed; beyond it, through a dirty window, you could espy a back-yard about six feet square.

"I'll walk in front to prevent you from falling," said Bourras, entering the damp corridor on one side of the shop.

He stumbled against a stair, and then commenced the ascent, reiterating his warning to be careful. The rail, said he, was close against the wall, there was a hole at the corner, sometimes the lodgers left their dust-boxes there. So complete was the obscurity that Denise could distinguish nothing, but simply felt how chilly the old damp plaster was. On the first floor, however, a small window overlooking the yard enabled her to obtain a vague glimpse of the rotten staircase, the walls black with dirt and the cracked, discoloured doors.

"If only one of these rooms were vacant," resumed Bourras. "You would be very comfortable there. But they are always occupied."

On the second floor the light increased, illumining with a raw pallor the distressful aspect of the house. A journeyman-baker occupied the first room, and it was the other, the further one, that was vacant. When Bourras had opened the door he was obliged to remain on the landing in order that Denise might enter with ease. The bed, placed in the corner nearest the door, left just sufficient room for one person to pass. At the other end there was a small walnut-wood chest of drawers, a deal table stained black, and two chairs. Such lodgers as did any cooking were obliged to kneel before the fire-place, where there was an earthenware stove.

"Oh! it's not luxurious," said the old man, "but the view from the window is gay. You can see the people passing in the street." And, as Denise gazed with surprise at the ceiling just above the bed, where a chance lady-lodger had written her name—Ernestine—by drawing the flame of a candle over the plaster, he added with a smile: "If I did a lot of repairs, I should never make both ends meet. There you are; it's all I have to offer."

"I shall be very well here," declared the young girl.

She paid a month in advance, asked for the linen—a pair of sheets and two towels, and made her bed without delay, happy and relieved to know where she would sleep that night. An hour later she had sent a commissionaire to fetch her box, and was quite at home.

During the first two months she had a terribly hard time of it. Being unable to pay for Pépé's board, she had taken him away, and slept him on an old couch lent by Bourras. She could not do with less than thirty sous a day, including the rent, even by living on dry bread herself, in order to procure a bit of meat for the little one. During the first fortnight she got on fairly well, having begun her housekeeping with about ten francs; and then too she was fortunate enough to find the cravat-dealer, who paid her the eighteen francs six sous which were due to her. But after that she became completely destitute. In vain did she apply to the various large shops, the Place Clichy, the Bon Marché, and the Louvre: the dead season had stopped business everywhere and she was told to apply again in the autumn. More than five thousand drapery employees, dismissed like herself, were wandering about Paris in want of situations. She then tried to obtain work elsewhere; but in her ignorance of Paris she did not know where to apply, and often accepted most ungrateful tasks, sometimes not even getting paid. On certain evenings she merely gave Pépé his dinner, a plate of soup, telling him that she had dined out; and she would go to bed with her head in a whirl, nourished by the fever which was burning her hands. When Jean suddenly dropped into the midst of this poverty, he called himself a scoundrel with such despairing violence that she was obliged to tell some falsehood to reassure him; and she even occasionally found the means to slip a two-franc piece into his hand, by way of proving that she still had money. She never wept before the children. On Sundays, when she was able to cook a piece of veal in the stove, on her knees before the fire, the tiny room re-echoed with the gaiety of children, careless about existence. Then, when Jean had returned to his master's and Pépé was asleep, she spent a frightful night, in anguish how to provide for the coming day.

Other fears kept her awake. Two women lodging on the first floor received visitors; and sometimes these visitors mistook the floor and came banging at Denise's door. Bourras having quietly told her not to answer, she buried her face under her pillow to escape hearing their oaths. Then, too, her neighbour, the baker, who never came home till morning, had shown a disposition to annoy her. But she suffered still more from the annoyances of the street, the continual persecution of passers-by. She could not go downstairs to buy a candle, in those streets swarming with debauchees, without feeling a man's hot breath behind her, and hearing crude, insulting remarks; and some individuals pursued her to the very end of the dark passage, encouraged by the sordid appearance of the house. Why had she no lover? It astonished people and seemed ridiculous. She herself could not have explained why she resisted, menaced as she was by hunger, and perturbed by all the sexuality in the air around her.

One evening when Denise had not even any bread for Pépé's soup, a well-dressed man, wearing a decoration, commenced to follow her. On reaching the passage he became brutal, and it was with loathing and revolt that she banged the door in his face. Then, once more upstairs, she sat down, with her hands trembling. The little one was sleeping. What should she say if he woke up and asked her for bread? And yet had she chosen her misery would have ceased, she could have had money, dresses, and a fine room. It was very simple, every one came to that, it was said; for a woman alone in Paris could not live by her labour. But her whole being rose up in protest, against the disgrace of the thing. She considered life a matter of logic, good conduct, and courage.

Denise frequently questioned herself in this way. An old love story floated in her memory, the story of a sailor's betrothed whom her love guarded from all perils. At Valognes she had often hummed this sentimental ballad whilst gazing into the deserted street. Had she likewise some tender affection in her heart that she proved so brave? She still thought of Hutin, full of uneasiness. Morning and evening she saw him pass under her window. Now that he was second-hand he walked by himself, saluted with respect by the mere salesmen. He never raised his head, and she thought she suffered from his vanity. Still she watched him without fear of being discovered; whereas, as soon as she saw Mouret, who also passed every day, she began to tremble, and quickly concealed herself, her bosom heaving. He had no need to know where she was lodging. And then she would feel ashamed of the house, and suffer at the idea of what he must think of her, although perhaps they would never meet again.

Denise still lived amidst all the hubbub of The Ladies' Paradise. A mere wall separated her room from her old department; and, from early morning, she lived her old days afresh, divining and hearing the arrival of the crowd and the increasing bustle of business. The slightest noise shook the old hovel which clung to the side of the colossus, and shared in its pulsations. Moreover, she could not avoid certain meetings. She twice had found herself face to face with Pauline, who had offered her services, grieved to see her so unfortunate; and she had even been obliged to tell a falsehood to avoid receiving her friend or paying her a visit, one Sunday, at Baugé's. But it was more difficult still for her to defend herself against Deloche's desperate affection; aware of all her troubles, he watched her, waited for her in the doorways. One day he wanted to lend her thirty francs, a brother's savings, he said, with a blush. And these meetings made her regret the shop, and continually brought her back to thoughts of the life the others led there, as if she herself had not quitted it.

No one had ever called upon her till one afternoon when she was surprised by a knock. It was Colomban. She received him standing. For his part he seemed greatly embarrassed and began stammering, asking how she was getting on, and speaking of The Old Elbeuf. Perhaps, thought she, it was Uncle Baudu who had sent him, regretting his rigour; for he continued to pass her without taking any notice of her, although he was well aware of her miserable position. However, when she plainly questioned her visitor, he appeared more embarrassed than ever. No, no, it was not the governor who had sent him; and he finished by naming Clara—he simply wanted to talk about Clara. Then little by little he grew bolder, and asked Denise's advice, imagining no doubt that she might be willing to play the part of a go-between. And it was in vain that she tried to dishearten him, by reproaching him with the pain he was causing Geneviève for such a heartless girl. He came up another day, indeed got into the habit of coming to see her. This seemed to suffice for his timid passion; he continually began the same conversation afresh, unable to resist the impulse and trembling with joy at finding himself with one who had approached Clara. And all this caused Denise to live more than ever at The Ladies' Paradise.

Towards the end of September the poor girl experienced the blackest misery. Pépé had fallen ill, having caught a severe cold. He ought to have had plenty of good broth, and she had not even a piece of bread to give him. One evening, completely conquered, she was sobbing, in one of those despairing straits which drive women on to the streets, or into the Seine, when old Bourras gently knocked at the door. He had brought with him a loaf, and a milk-can full of broth.

"There! there's something for the youngster," said he in his abrupt way. "Don't cry like that; it annoys my lodgers." And as she thanked him with a fresh outburst of tears, he resumed: "Do keep quiet! Come and see me to-morrow. I've some work for you."

Since the terrible blow which The Ladies' Paradise had dealt him by opening an umbrella department, Bourras had ceased to employ any workwomen. In order to save expenses he did everything himself, cleaning, mending, and sewing. His trade moreover was diminishing to such a point that he sometimes remained without work. And so he was obliged to invent some occupation on the following day when he installed Denise in a corner of his shop. He felt, however, that he could not allow any one to die of hunger in his house.

"You'll have two francs a day," said he. "When you find something better, you can leave me."

She was afraid of him, and did the work so quickly that he was embarrassed to find her more. He had given her some silk to stitch, some lace to repair. During the first few days she did not dare to raise her head, uneasy at feeling him near her, with his lion-like mane, hooked nose, and piercing eyes, shaded by bushy brows. His voice was harsh, his gestures were extravagant, and the mothers of the neighbourhood often frightened their youngsters by threatening to send for him, as they would for a policeman. However, the boys never passed his door without calling out some insulting words, which he did not even seem to hear. All his maniacal anger was directed against the scoundrels who dishonoured his trade by selling cheap trashy articles, which dogs, said he, would not consent to use.

Denise trembled whenever he burst out thus: "Art is done for, I tell you! There's not a single respectable handle made nowadays. They make sticks, but as for handles, it's all up! Bring me a proper handle, and I'll give you twenty francs!"

He had a real artist's pride; not a workman in Paris was capable of turning out a handle like his, as light and as strong. He carved the knobs with charming ingenuity, continually inventing fresh designs, flowers, fruit, animals, and heads, all executed in a free and life-like style. A little pocket-knife sufficed him and, with his spectacles on his nose he would spend whole days in chipping bits of boxwood and ebony.

"A pack of ignorant beggars," said he, "who are satisfied with sticking a certain quantity of silk on so much whalebone! They buy their handles by the gross, handles ready-made. And they sell just what they like! I tell you, art is done for!"

At last Denise began to feel easier. He had desired that Pépé should come down into the shop to play, for he was wonderfully fond of children. When the little one was crawling about on all-fours, neither of them had room to move. She sat in her corner doing the mending, he near the window, carving away with his little knife. Every day now brought round the same work and the same conversation. Whilst working, he would continually assail The Ladies' Paradise; never weary of explaining how affairs stood in the terrible duel between that bazaar and himself. He had occupied his house since 1845, and had a thirty years' lease of it at a rent of eighteen hundred francs a year; and, as he made a thousand francs out of his four furnished rooms, he only paid eight hundred for the shop. It was a mere trifle, he had no expenses, and could thus hold out for a long time still. To hear him, there was no doubt about his eventual triumph; he would certainly swallow up the monster. Then suddenly he would break off to ask:

"Have they got any dog's heads like that?"

And he would blink his eyes behind his glasses, whilst judging the dog's head which he was carving, with its lip turned up and its fangs displayed, in a life-like growl. Pépé delighted with the dog, would thereupon get up, resting his two little arms on the old man's knee.

"As long as I make both ends meet I don't care a hang about the rest," the latter resumed, whilst delicately shaping the dog's tongue with the point of his knife. "The scoundrels have taken away my profits; but if I'm making nothing I'm not losing anything yet, or at least only a trifle. And, you see, I'm ready to sacrifice everything rather than yield."

Thereupon he would brandish his knife, and his white hair would blow about in a storm of anger.

"But if they made you a reasonable offer," Denise would mildly observe, without raising her eyes from her needle, "it would be wiser to accept it."

This suggestion, however, only produced an outburst of ferocious obstinacy. "Never! If my head were under the knife I should still say no, by heavens I would! I've another ten years' lease, and they shan't have the house before then, even if I should have to die of hunger within the four bare walls. Twice already they've tried to get over me. They offered me twelve thousand francs for my good-will, and eighteen thousand francs for the last ten years of my lease; in all thirty thousand. But no, no—not for fifty thousand even! I have them in my power, and intend to see them licking the dust before me!"

"Thirty thousand francs! it's a good sum," thereupon resumed Denise. "You could go and establish yourself elsewhere. And suppose they were to buy the house?"

Bourras, now putting the finishing touches to his dog's tongue, appeared absorbed for a moment, a childish laugh pervading his venerable, prophet's face. Then he continued: "The house, no fear! They spoke of buying it last year, and offered eighty thousand francs, twice as much as it's worth. But the landlord, a retired fruiterer, as big a scoundrel as they, wanted to make them shell out more. Besides, they are suspicious about me; they know I should then be even less inclined to give way. No! no! here I am, and here I intend to stay. The emperor with all his cannon could not turn me out."

Denise did not dare to say any more, but went on with her work, whilst the old man continued to vent short sentences, between two cuts of his knife; now muttering something to the effect that the game had hardly begun; and then that they would see wonderful things later on, for he had certain plans which would sweep their umbrella counter away; and, deeply blended with his obstinacy, you detected the personal revolt of the skilled manufacturer against the growing invasion of commonplace rubbish. Pépé, however, at last climbed on his knees, and impatiently stretched out his hands towards the dog's head.

"Give it me, sir."

"Presently, youngster," the old man replied in a voice that suddenly became softer. "He hasn't any eyes as yet; we must make his eyes now." And whilst carving the eyes he continued talking to Denise. "Do you hear them? Isn't there a roar next door? That's what exasperates me more than anything, my word of honour! to have them always on my back like this with their infernal locomotive-like noise."

It made his little table tremble, he asserted. The whole shop was shaken, and he would spend the entire afternoon without a customer of his own but amidst all the trepidation of the jostling multitude in The Ladies' Paradise. From morning to night this was a subject for eternal grumbling. Another good day's work; they were knocking against the wall, the silk department must have cleared ten thousand francs; or else he made merry, not a sound came from behind the wall, a showery day had killed the receipts. And the slightest stir, the faintest vibration, thus furnished him with matter for endless comment.

"Did you hear? some one has slipped down! Ah, if they could only all fall and break their backs!—That, my dear, is a dispute between some ladies. So much the better! So much the better!—Ah! you hear the parcels falling into the basement? What a row they make. It's disgusting!"

It did not do for Denise to discuss his remarks, for he bitterly retorted by reminding her of the shameful way in which she had been dismissed. For the hundredth time she was obliged to relate her life in the jacket and mantle department, the hardships she had at first endured, the small unhealthy bedrooms, the bad food, and the continual battle between the salesmen; and thus they would talk about the shop from morning to night, absorbing it hourly in the very air they breathed.

But with eager, outstretched hands Pépé repeated: "Give it me, sir, give it me!"

The dog's head was finished and Bourras held it at a distance, then examined it closely with noisy glee. "Take care, it will bite you!" he said, "there, go and play, and don't break it, if you can help it." Then speedily reverting to his fixed idea, he shook his fist at the wall. "You may do all you can to knock the house down," he exclaimed. "You shan't have it, even if you invade the whole street!"

Denise now had something to eat each day, and she was extremely grateful to the old umbrella-dealer, realizing that he had a good heart beneath his strange, violent ways. Nevertheless she felt a strong desire to find some work elsewhere, for she often saw him inventing some trifle for her to do and fully understood that he did not require a workwoman in the present collapse of his business, and was merely employing her out of charity. Six months had passed thus, and the dull winter season having again returned, she was despairing of finding a situation before March, when, one evening in January, Deloche, who was watching for her in a doorway, gave her a bit of advice. Why did she not call on Robineau; perhaps he might want some one?

During the previous September, Robineau, though fearing to jeopardize his wife's sixty thousand francs, had made up his mind to buy

Vinçard's silk-business. He had paid forty thousand for the good-will and stock, and was starting with the remaining twenty thousand. It was not much, but he had Gaujean behind him to back him up with any amount of credit. Gaujean ever since his quarrel with The Ladies' Paradise had been longing to stir up competitors against the colossus; and he thought victory certain, by creating special shops in the neighbourhood, where the public would find a large and varied choice of articles. Only the very rich Lyons manufacturers, such as Dumonteil, could accept the big shops' terms, satisfied to keep their looms going with them, and seeking their profits in their sales to less important establishments. But Gaujean was far from having the solidity and staying power possessed by Dumonteil. For a long time a mere commission agent, it was only during the last five or six years that he had possessed looms of his own, and he still had a lot of his work done by piece-workers, furnishing them with the raw material and paying them by the yard. It was precisely this system which, increasing his manufacturing expenses, had prevented him from competing with Dumonteil for the supply of the Paris Delight. This had filled him with rancour, and he saw in Robineau the instrument of a decisive battle with those drapery bazaars which he accused of ruining French manufactures.

When Denise called she found Madame Robineau alone. Daughter of an overseer in the Highways and Bridges Service, entirely ignorant of business matters, the young wife still retained the charming awkwardness of a girl educated in a convent. She was dark, very pretty, with a gentle, cheerful manner, which made her extremely charming. Moreover she adored her husband, living solely by his love. Just as Denise was about to leave her name Robineau himself came in, and at once engaged her, one of his two saleswomen having left him on the previous day to go to The Ladies' Paradise.

"They don't leave us a single good hand," said he. "However, I shall feel quite easy with you, for you are like me, you can't be very fond of them. Come to-morrow."

In the evening Denise hardly knew how to announce her departure to Bourras. In fact, he called her an ungrateful girl, and lost his temper. And when, with tears in her eyes, she tried to defend herself by intimating that she could see through his charitable conduct, he softened down, stammered that he had plenty of work, that she was leaving him indeed just as he was about to bring out a new umbrella of his invention.

"And Pépé?" he asked.

This was Denise's great trouble; she dared not take him back to Madame Gras, and could not leave him alone in the bedroom, shut up from morning to night.

"Very good, I'll keep him," said the old man; "he'll be all right in my shop. We'll do the cooking together." And then as she refused the offer fearing that it might inconvenience him, he thundered out: "Great heavens! have you no confidence in me? I shan't eat your child!"

Denise was much happier at Robineau's. He only paid her sixty francs a month, with her board, without giving her any commission on the sales, that not being the rule in the old-fashioned houses; but she was treated with great kindness, especially by Madame Robineau who was always smiling at her counter. He, nervous and worried, was sometimes rather abrupt. At the expiration of the first month, Denise had become quite one of the family, like the other saleswoman, a silent, consumptive, little body. The Robineaus were not at all particular before them, but freely talked of the business whilst at table in the back-shop, which looked on to a large yard. And it was there they decided one evening to start the campaign against The Ladies' Paradise. Gaujean had come to dinner and, after the roast leg of mutton, had broached the subject in his Lyonese voice, thickened by the Rhône fogs.

"It's getting unbearable," said he. "They go to Dumonteil, purchase the sole right to a design, and take three hundred pieces straight off, insisting on a reduction of half a franc a yard; and, as they pay ready money, they also secure the profit of eighteen per cent. discount. Very often Dumonteil barely makes four sous a yard out of it. He simply works to keep his looms going, for a loom that stands still is a dead loss. Under these circumstances how can you expect that we, with our limited plant, and our piece-workers, can keep up the struggle?"

Robineau, pensive, forgot his dinner. "Three hundred pieces!" he murmured. "I tremble when I take a dozen, and at ninety days too. They can sell at a franc or two francs cheaper than we can. I have calculated that their catalogued articles are offered at fifteen per cent. less than our own prices. That's what kills the small Houses."

He was passing through a period of discouragement. His wife, full of anxiety, looked at him with a loving air. She understood very little about the business, all these figures confused her; she could not understand why people worried over things so much, when it was so easy to be gay and love one another. However, it sufficed that her husband desired to conquer, and she became as impassioned as he himself, and would have stood to her counter till death.

"But why don't all the manufacturers come to an understanding together?" resumed Robineau, violently. "They could then lay down the law, instead of submitting to it."

Gaujean, who had asked for another slice of mutton, was slowly chewing. "Ah! why, why? The looms must be kept going, I tell you. When you have weavers a little bit everywhere, in the neighbourhood of Lyons, in the Gard, in the Isère, you can't stand still a day without an enormous loss. Then we who sometimes employ piece-workers with ten or fifteen looms of their own are better able to control our output, whereas the big manufacturers are obliged to have continual outlets, the quickest and most extensive possible. And so they are on their knees before the big shops. I know three or four who out-bid each other, and who would sooner work at a loss than not obtain the orders. But they make up for it with the small establishments like yours. Yes, if they manage to live through the big places, they make their profit out of you little fellows. Heaven knows how the crisis will end!"

"It's odious!" exclaimed Robineau, relieved by this cry of anger.

Denise was quietly listening. With her instinctive love of logic and life she was secretly in favour of the big shops.

They had relapsed into silence, and were eating some preserved French beans, when at last she ventured to remark in a cheerful tone: "The public does not complain."

At this Madame Robineau could not restrain a little laugh, which annoyed both her husband and Gaujean. No doubt the customer was satisfied, for, in the end, it was the customer who profited by the fall in prices. But everybody must live; where would they all be if, under the pretext of conducing to the general welfare, the consumer was fattened at the expense of the producer? And then began a long discussion. Denise affected to be joking, though all the while producing solid arguments. By the new system the middle-men disappeared, and this greatly contributed to cheapen the articles; besides, the manufacturers could no longer live without the big shops, for as soon as one of them lost their custom, failure became a certainty; in short, it was a natural commercial evolution. It would be impossible to prevent things from going on as they ought to, when everybody was working towards that result, whether they liked it or not.

"So you are for those who turned you out into the street?" thereupon asked Gaujean.

Denise became very red. She herself was surprised at the vivacity of her defence. What had she at heart, that such a flame should have risen in her breast?

"Dear me, no!" she replied. "Perhaps I'm wrong, for you are more competent to judge than I. I simply express my opinion. The prices, instead of being settled by fifty houses as they formerly used to be, are now fixed by four or five, which have lowered them, thanks to the power of their capital, and the strength of their immense custom. So much the better for the public, that's all!"

Robineau was not angry, but had become grave, and had fixed his eyes on the table-cloth. He had often felt the force of the new style of business, the evolution which the young girl spoke about; and in his clear, quiet moments he would ask himself why he should try to resist such a powerful current, which must carry everything before it. Madame Robineau herself, on seeing her husband deep in thought, glanced with approval at Denise, who had modestly resumed her silent attitude.

"Come," resumed Gaujean, to cut short the argument, "all that is simply theory. Let's talk of our matter."

After the cheese, the servant brought in some jam and some pears. He took some jam, and ate it with a spoon, with the unconscious greediness of a big man very fond sweet things.

"This is it," he resumed, "you must attack their Paris Delight, which has been their success of the year. I have come to an understanding with several of my brother manufacturers at Lyons, and have brought you an exceptional offer—a black silk, a faille which you can sell at five francs fifty centimes a mètre. They sell theirs at five francs sixty, don't they? Well! this will be two sous cheaper, and that will suffice to upset them."

At this Robineau's eyes lighted up again. In his continual nervous torment, he often skipped like this from despair to hope. "Have you got a sample?" he asked. And when Gaujean drew from his pocket-book a little square of silk, he went into raptures, exclaiming: "Why, this is a handsomer silk than the Paris Delight! At all events it produces a better effect, the grain is coarser. You are right, we must make the attempt. Ah! I'll bring them to my feet or give up for good!"

Madame Robineau, sharing the enthusiasm, declared the silk superb, and even Denise herself thought they might succeed. The latter part of the dinner thus proved very gay. They talked in a loud tone; it seemed as if The Ladies' Paradise was at its last gasp. Gaujean, who was finishing the pot of jam, explained what enormous sacrifices he and his colleagues would be obliged to make to deliver an article of such quality at so low a price; but they would ruin themselves rather than yield; they had sworn to kill the big shops. As the coffee came in the gaiety was still further increased by the arrival of Vinçard who called, on his way past, just to see how his successor was getting on.

"Famous!" he cried, feeling the silk. "You'll floor them, I stake my life! Ah! you owe me a rare good thing; I told you that this was a golden affair!"

He had just taken a restaurant at Vincennes. It was an old, cherished idea of his, slyly nurtured while he was struggling with his silk business, trembling with fear lest he should not sell it before the crash came, and vowing that he would afterwards put his money into some undertaking where he could rob folks at his ease. The idea of a restaurant had struck him at the wedding of a cousin, who had been made to pay ten francs for a tureen of dish water, in which floated some Italian paste. And, in presence of the Robineaus, the joy he felt at having saddled them with an unremunerative business, which he had despaired of getting rid of, made his face with its round eyes and large loyal-looking mouth, a face beaming with health, expand as it had never done before.

"And your pains?" asked Madame Robineau, good-naturedly.

"My pains?" he murmured, in astonishment.

"Yes, those rheumatic pains which tormented you so much when you were here."

He then recollected the fibs he had told and slightly coloured. "Oh! I suffer from them still!" said he. "But the country air, you know, has done me a deal of good. Never mind, on your side you've done a good stroke of business. Had it not been for my rheumatics, I could soon have retired with ten thousand francs a year. Yes, on my word of honour!"

A fortnight later, the battle between Robineau and The Ladies' Paradise began. It became celebrated, and for a time occupied the whole Parisian market. Robineau, using his adversary's weapons, had advertised extensively in the newspapers. Besides that, he made a fine display, piling huge bales of the famous silk in his windows and displaying immense white tickets, on which the price, five francs and a half per mêtre, appeared in gigantic figures. It was this price that caused a revolution among the women; it was two sous less than that charged at

The Ladies' Paradise, and the silk appeared more substantial. From the first day a crowd of customers flocked in. Madame Marty bought a dress she did not need, pretending it to be a bargain; Madame Bourdelais also thought the silk very fine, but preferred waiting, guessing no doubt what would happen. And, indeed during the following week, Mouret boldly reduced the price of The Paris Delight by four sous, after a lively discussion with Bourdoncle and the other managers, in which he had succeeded in convincing them that they must accept the challenge, even at a sacrifice; for these four sous represented a dead loss, the silk being already sold at strict cost price. It was a heavy blow to Robineau, who had not imagined that his rival would lower his price; for this suicidal style of competition, this practice of selling at a loss, was then unknown. However, the tide of customers, attracted by Mouret's cheapness, had immediately flown back towards the Rue Neuve-Saint-Augustin, whilst the shop in the Rue Neuve-des-Petits-Champs gradually emptied.

Gaujean then hastened from Lyons; there were hurried confabulations, and they finished by coming to a heroic resolution; the silk should be lowered in price, they would sell it at five francs six sous, and lower than that no one could go, without acting madly. But the next day Mouret marked his material at five francs four sous. Then the struggle became rageful. Robineau replied by five francs three sous, whereupon Mouret at once ticketed The Paris Delight at five francs and two sous. Neither lowered more than a sou at a time now, for both lost considerable sums as often as they made this present to the public. The customers laughed, delighted with this duel, quite stirred by the terrible thrusts which the rivals dealt one another in order to please them. At last Mouret ventured as low as five francs; and his staff paled and shuddered at such a challenge to fortune. Robineau, utterly beaten, out of breath, also stopped at five francs, not having the courage to go any lower. And thus they rested on their positions, face to face, with the massacre of their goods around them.

But if honour was saved on both sides, the situation was becoming fatal for Robineau. The Ladies' Paradise had money at its disposal and a patronage which enabled it to balance its profits; whereas he, sustained by Gaujean alone, unable to recoup his losses by gaining on other articles, found himself nearing the end of his tether, slipping further and further down the slope toward bankruptcy. He was dying from his hardihood, despite the numerous customers whom the hazards of the struggle had brought him. One of his secret worries was to see these customers slowly quitting him, returning to The Ladies' Paradise, after all the money he had lost in the efforts he had made to secure them.

One day he quite lost patience. A customer, Madame de Boves, had called at his shop for some mantles, for he had added a ready-made department to his business. She would not come to a decision, however, but complained of the quality of the material, and at last exclaimed: "Their Paris Delight is a great deal stronger."

Robineau restrained himself, assuring her that she was mistaken with a tradesman's politeness, all the more respectful, moreover, as he feared to reveal his inward revolt.

"But just look at the silk of this cloak!" she resumed, "one would really take it for so much cobweb. You may say what you like, sir, but their silk at five francs is like leather compared with this."

He did not reply; with the blood rushing to his face, he kept his lips tightly closed. In point of fact he had ingeniously thought of buying some of his rival's silk for these mantles; so that it was Mouret, not he, who lost on the material. And to conceal his practice he simply cut off the selvage.

"Really," he murmured at last, "you think the Paris Delight thicker?"

"Oh! a hundred times!" said Madame de Boves. "There's no comparison."

This injustice on her part, this fixed determination to run down the goods in spite of all evidence filled him with indignation. And, as she was still turning the mantle over with a disgusted air, a little bit of the blue and silver selvage, which through carelessness had not been cut off, appeared under the lining. Thereupon he could not restrain himself any longer; but confessed the truth at all hazards.

"Well, madame, this is Paris Delight. I bought it myself! Look at the selvage."

Madame de Boves went away greatly annoyed, and a number of customers quitted him, for the affair became known. And he, amid this ruin, when fear for the future came upon him, only trembled for his wife, who had been brought up in a happy, peaceful home, and would never be able to endure a life of poverty. What would become of her if a catastrophe should throw them into the street, with a load of debts? It was his fault, he ought never to have touched her money. She was obliged to comfort him. Wasn't the money as much his as hers? He loved her dearly, and she wanted nothing more; she gave him everything, her heart and her life. They could be heard embracing one another in the back shop. Then, little by little, the affairs of the house got into a regular groove; each month the losses increased, but with a slowness which postponed the fatal issue. A tenacious hope sustained them, and they still predicted the approaching discomfiture of The Ladies' Paradise.

"Pooh!" he would say, "we are young yet. The future is ours."

"And besides, what matters, if you have done what you wanted to do?" she resumed. "As long as you are satisfied, I am as well, darling."

Denise's affection for them increased on seeing their tenderness. She trembled, divining their inevitable fall; however, she dared not interfere. And it was here that she ended by fully understanding the power of the new system of business, and became impassioned for this force which was transforming Paris. Her ideas were ripening, a woman's grace was being evolved from the wildness of a child freshly arrived from Valognes. Her life too was a pretty pleasant one, notwithstanding its fatigue and the little money she earned. When she had spent all the day on her feet, she had to go straight home, and look after Pépé, whom old Bourras fortunately insisted on feeding; but there was still a lot to do; a shirt to wash, a blouse to mend; without mentioning the noise made by the youngster, which made her head ache fit to split. She never went to bed before midnight. Sunday was her hardest day: for she then cleaned her room, and mended her own things, so busy that it was often five o'clock before she could comb her hair. However, she sometimes went out for health's sake, taking the little one for a long walk, out towards Neuilly; and their treat over there was to drink a cup of milk at a dairyman's, who allowed them to sit down in his yard. Jean disdained these excursions; he put in an appearance now and again on week-day evenings and then disappeared, pretending he had other visits to pay. He asked for no more money, but he arrived with such a melancholy countenance, that his anxious sister always managed to keep a five-franc piece for him. That was her sole luxury.

"Five francs!" he would exclaim each time. "My stars! you're too good! It just happens, there's the—"

"Not another word," Denise would say; "I don't want to know."

Three months passed away, spring was coming back. However Denise refused to return to Joinville with Pauline and Baugé. She sometimes met them in the Rue Saint-Roch, on leaving the shop in the evening. Pauline, on one occasion when she was alone, confided to her that she was perhaps going to marry her lover; it was she who was hesitating, for they did not care for married saleswomen at The Ladies' Paradise. This idea of marriage surprised Denise and she did not dare to advise her friend. Then one day, just as Colomban had stopped her near the fountain to talk about Clara, the latter tripped across the road; and Denise was obliged to run away, for he implored her to ask her old comrade if she would marry him. What was the matter with them all? why were they tormenting themselves like this? She thought herself very fortunate not to be in love with anybody.

"You've heard the news?" the umbrella dealer said to her one evening on her return from business.

"No, Monsieur Bourras."

"Well! the scoundrels have bought the Hôtel Duvillard. I'm hemmed in on all sides!" He was waving his long arms about, in a burst of fury which made his white mane stand up on end. "A regular underhand affair," he resumed. "But it seems that the hotel belonged to the Crédit Immobilier, whose president, Baron Hartmann, has just sold it to our famous Mouret. And now they've got me on the right, on the left, and at the back, just in the way that I'm holding the knob of this stick in my hand!"

It was true, the sale must have been concluded on the previous day. Bourras's small house, hemmed in between The Ladies' Paradise and the Hôtel Duvillard, clinging there like a swallow's nest in a crack of a wall, seemed certain to be crushed, as soon as the shop galleries should invade the hôtel. And the time had now arrived, the colossus had outflanked the feeble obstacle, and was investing it with its piles of goods, threatening to swallow it up, absorb it by the sole force of its giant aspiratory powers. Bourras could well feel the close embrace which was making his shop creak. He thought he could see the place getting smaller; he was afraid of being absorbed himself, of being carried off into kingdom come with his sticks and umbrellas, so loudly was the terrible machine now roaring.

"Do you hear them?" he asked. "One would think they were eating the very walls! And in my cellar and in the attic, everywhere, there's the same noise—like that of a saw cutting through the plaster. But never mind! They won't flatten me as easily as they might a sheet of paper. I shall stick here, even if they blow up my roof, and the rain falls in bucketfuls on my bed!"

It was just at this moment that Mouret caused fresh proposals to be made to Bourras; they would increase the figure of their offer, they would give him fifty thousand francs for his good-will and the remainder of his lease. But this offer redoubled the old man's anger; he refused in an insulting manner. How those scoundrels must rob people to be able to pay fifty thousand francs for a thing which wasn't worth ten thousand! And he defended his shop as a young girl defends her virtue, for honour's sake.

Denise noticed that Bourras was pre-occupied during the next fortnight. He wandered about in a feverish manner, measuring the walls of his house, surveying it from the middle of the street with the air of an architect. Then one morning some workmen arrived. This was the decisive blow. He had conceived the bold idea of beating The Ladies' Paradise on its own ground by making certain concessions to modern luxury. Customers, who had often reproached him for the darkness of his shop, would certainly come back to it again, when they saw it all bright and new. In the first place, the workmen stopped up the crevices and whitewashed the frontage, then they painted the woodwork a light green, and even carried the splendour so far as to gild the sign-board. A sum of three thousand francs, held in reserve by Bourras as a last resource, was swallowed up in this way. Moreover, the whole neighbourhood was revolutionized by it all, people came to look at him losing his head amid all these riches, and no longer able to find the things he was accustomed to. He did not seem to be at home in that bright frame, that tender setting; he looked quite scared, with his long beard and white hair. On the opposite side of the street passers-by lingered in astonishment at seeing him waving his arms about while he carved his handles. And he was in a state of fever, perpetually afraid of dirtying his shop, more and more at sea amidst this luxury which he did not at all understand.

Meantime, as at Robineau's, so at Bourras's was the campaign against The Ladies' Paradise carried on. Bourras had just brought out his invention, the automatic umbrella, which later on was to become popular. But The Paradise people immediately improved on the invention, and a struggle of prices began. Bourras had an article at one franc and nineteen sous, in zanella, with a steel mounting, an everlasting article said the ticket. But he was especially anxious to vanquish his competitors with his handles of bamboo, dogwood, olive, myrtle, rattan, indeed every imaginable sort of handle. The Paradise people, less artistic, paid more attention to the material, extolling their alpacas and mohairs, twills and sarcenets. And they came out victorious. Bourras, in despair, repeated that art was done for, that he was reduced to carving his handles for the pleasure of doing so, without any hope of selling them.

"It's my fault!" he cried to Denise. "I never ought to have kept a lot of rotten articles, at one franc nineteen sous! That's where these new notions lead one to. I wanted to follow the example of those brigands; so much the better if I'm ruined by it!"

The month of July proved very warm, and Denise suffered greatly in her tiny room under the roof. So, after leaving the shop, she sometimes went to fetch Pépé, and instead of going up-stairs at once, took a stroll in the Tuileries Gardens until the gates closed. One evening as she was walking towards the chestnut-trees she suddenly stopped short with surprise: for a few yards off, coming straight towards her, she fancied she recognised Hutin. But her heart commenced to beat violently. It was Mouret, who had dined on the other side of the river and was hurrying along on foot to call on Madame Desforges. At the abrupt movement which she made to escape him, he caught sight of her. The night was coming on, but still he recognised her clearly.

"Ah, it's you, mademoiselle!" he said.

She did not reply, astonished that he should deign to stop. He, smiling, concealed his constraint beneath an air of amiable protection. "You are still in Paris?" he inquired.

"Yes, sir," said she at last.

She was slowly drawing back, desirous of making a bow and continuing her walk. But he abruptly turned and followed her under the dark shadows of the chestnut-trees. The air was getting cooler, some children were laughing in the distance, while trundling their hoops.

"This is your brother, is it not?" he resumed, looking at Pépé.

The little boy, frightened by the unusual presence of a gentleman, was walking gravely by his sister's side, holding her tightly by the hand.

"Yes, sir," she replied once more; and as she did so she blushed, thinking of the abominable inventions circulated by Marguerite and Clara.

No doubt Mouret understood why she was blushing, for he quickly added: "Listen, mademoiselle, I have to apologize to you. Yes, I should have been happy to have told you sooner how much I regret the error that was made. You were accused too lightly of a fault. However, the evil is done. I simply wanted to assure you that every one in our establishment now knows of your affection for your brothers." Then he went on speaking with a respectful politeness to which the saleswomen of The Ladies' Paradise were little accustomed. Denise's confusion had increased; but her heart was full of joy. He knew, then, that she had ever remained virtuous! Both remained silent; he still lingered beside her, regulating his walk to the child's short steps; and the distant murmurs of the city died away under the black shadows of the spreading chestnut-trees. "I have only one reparation to offer you," he resumed. "Naturally, if you would like to come back to us—"

But she interrupted him, refusing his offer with a feverish haste. "No, sir, I cannot. Thank you all the same, but I have found another situation."

He knew it, they had informed him she was with Robineau; and leisurely, putting himself on a footing of amiable equality, he spoke of the latter, rendering him full justice. He was a very intelligent fellow, no doubt, but too nervous. He would certainly come to grief: Gaujean had burdened him with a very heavy business, in which they would both suffer. Thereupon Denise, subjugated by this familiarity, opened her mind further, and allowed it to be seen that she was on the side of the big shops in the war between them and the small traders. She grew animated, citing examples, showing herself well up in the question and even expressing new and enlightened ideas. He, quite charmed, listened to her in surprise; and turned round, trying to distinguish her features in the growing darkness. She appeared to be still the same with her simple dress and sweet face; but from amidst her modest bashfulness, there seemed to ascend a penetrating perfume, of which he felt the powerful influence. Doubtless this little girl had got used to the atmosphere of Paris, she was becoming quite a woman, and was really perturbing, with her sound common-sense and her beautiful sweet-scented hair.

"As you are on our side," said he, laughing, "why do you stay with our adversaries? I was told too that you lodged with Bourras."

"A very worthy man," she murmured. "No, not a bit of it! he's an old idiot, a madman who will force me to ruin him, though I should be glad to get rid of him with a fortune! Besides, your place is not in his house, which has a bad reputation. He lets to certain women—" But realizing that the young girl was confused, he hastened to add: "Oh! one can be respectable anywhere, and there's even more merit in remaining so when one is so poor."

They took a few steps in silence. Pépé seemed to be listening with the attentive air of a precocious child. Now and again he raised his eyes to his sister, whose burning hand, quivering with sudden starts, astonished him.

"Look here!" resumed Mouret, gaily, "will you be my ambassador? I intended increasing my offer to-morrow—of proposing eighty thousand francs to Bourras. Will you speak to him first about it? Tell him he's cutting his own throat. Perhaps he'll listen to you, as he has a liking for you, and you'll be doing him a real service."

"Very well!" said Denise, smiling also, "I will deliver your message, but I am afraid I shall not succeed."

Then a fresh silence ensued, neither of them having anything more to say. For a moment he attempted to talk of her uncle Baudu; but had to give it up on seeing how uncomfortable this made the girl. Nevertheless, they continued walking side by side, and at last found themselves near the Rue de Rivoli, in a path where it was still light. On emerging from the darkness of the trees this was like a sudden awakening. He understood that he could not detain her any longer.

"Good night, mademoiselle," he said.

"Good night, sir."

Nevertheless he did not go away. On raising his eyes he had perceived in front of him, at the corner of the Rue d'Alger, the lighted windows of Madame Desforges's flat whither he was bound. And looking at Denise, whom he could now see, in the pale twilight, she appeared to him very puny compared to Henriette. Why was it then that she touched his heart in this manner? It was a stupid caprice.

"This little man is getting tired," he resumed, by way of saying something. "Remember, mind, that our house will always be open to you; you've only to knock, and I'll give you every compensation possible. Good night, mademoiselle."

"Good night, sir."

When Mouret had quitted her, Denise went back under the chestnut-trees, into the black gloom. For a long time she walked on at random, between the huge trunks, her face burning, her head in a whirl of confused ideas. Pépé still held her hand and was stretching out his short legs to keep pace with her. She had forgotten him. But at last he said: "You go too quick, little mother."

At this she sat down on a bench; and as he was tired, the child went to sleep on her lap. She held him there, pressing him to her virgin bosom, her eyes wandering far away into the darkness. When, an hour later, they slowly returned to the Rue de la Michodière, she had regained her usual quiet, sensible expression.

"Hell and thunder!" shouted Bourras, when he saw her coming, "the blow is struck. That rascal of a Mouret has just bought my house." He was half mad, and was striking himself in the middle of the shop with such outrageous gestures that he almost broke the windows. "Ah! the scoundrel! It's the fruiterer who's written to tell me of it. And how much do you think the rogue, has got for the house? One hundred and fifty thousand francs, four times its value! There's another thief, if you like! Just fancy, he has taken advantage of my embellishments, making capital out of the fact that the house has been done up. How much longer are they going to make a fool of me?"

The thought that his money spent on paint and whitewash had brought the fruiterer a profit exasperated him. And now Mouret would be his landlord; he would have to pay him! It was beneath this detested competitor's roof that he must in future live! Such a thought raised his fury to the highest pitch.

"Ah! I could hear them digging a hole through the wall. At this moment, they are here, eating out of my very plate, so to say!"

And the shop shook under his heavy fist as he banged it on the counter, making the umbrellas and the parasols dance again.

Denise, bewildered, could not get in a word. She stood there, motionless, waiting for the end of this fit; whilst Pépé, very tired, fell asleep again, this time on a chair. At last, when Bourras became a little calmer, she resolved to deliver Mouret's message. No doubt the old man was irritated, but the excess even of his anger, the blind alley, as it were, in which he found himself, might determine an abrupt acceptance on his part.

"I've just met some one," she commenced. "Yes, a person from The Paradise, who is very well informed. It appears that they are going to offer you eighty thousand francs to-morrow."

"Eighty thousand francs!" he interrupted, in a terrible voice; "eighty thousand francs! Not for a million now!"

She tried to reason with him. But at that moment the shop door opened, and she suddenly drew back, pale and silent. It was her uncle Baudu, with his yellow face and aged look. Bourras caught his neighbour by the buttonhole, and without allowing him to say a word, as if goaded on by his presence, roared in his face: "What do you think they have the cheek to offer me? Eighty thousand francs! They've got to that point, the brigands! they think I'm going to sell myself like a prostitute. Ah! they've bought the house, and think they've got me now! Well! it's all over, they shan't have it! I might have given way, perhaps; but now it belongs to them, let them try to take it!"

"So the news is true?" said Baudu, in his slow voice. "I had heard of it, and came over to know if it was so."

"Eighty thousand francs!" repeated Bourras. "Why not a hundred thousand at once? It's this immense sum of money that makes me so indignant. Do they think they can make me commit a knavish trick with their money! They shan't have it, by heavens! Never, never, you hear me?"

Then Denise broke her silence to remark, in her calm, quiet way: "They'll have it in nine years' time, when your lease expires."

And, notwithstanding her uncle's presence, she begged the old man to accept. The struggle was becoming impossible, he was fighting against a superior force; it would be madness to refuse the fortune offered him. But he still replied no. In nine years' time he hoped to be dead, so as not to see it.

"You hear, Monsieur Baudu," he resumed, "your niece is on their side, it's she whom they have commissioned to corrupt me. She's with the brigands, my word of honour!"

Baudu, who had so far appeared not to notice Denise, now raised his head, with the surly movement that he affected when standing at his shop door, every time she passed. But, slowly, he turned round and looked at her, and his thick lips trembled.

"I know it," he replied in an undertone, and he continued looking at her.

Denise, affected almost to tears, thought him greatly changed by worry. Perhaps too he was stricken with remorse at not having assisted her during the time of misery through which she had lately passed. Then the sight of Pépé sleeping on the chair, amidst the hubbub of the discussion, seemed to suddenly inspire him with compassion.

"Denise," said he simply, "come to-morrow and have dinner with us, and bring the little one. My wife and Geneviève asked me to invite you if I met you."

She turned very red, went up to him and kissed him. And as he was going away, Bourras, delighted at this reconciliation, again cried out to him: "Just give her a lecture, she isn't a bad sort. As for me, the house may fall, I shall be found in the ruins."

"Our houses are already falling, neighbour," said Baudu with a gloomy air. "We shall all of us be crushed under them."

ÉMILE ZOLA

# VIII

At this time the whole neighbourhood was talking of the great thoroughfare which was to be opened between the Bourse and the new Opera House, under the name of the Rue du Dix-Décembre.[1] The expropriation judgments had been delivered, and two gangs of demolishers were already beginning operations at either end, the first pulling down the old mansions in the Rue Louis-le-Grand, and the other destroying the thin walls of the old Vaudeville. You could hear the picks getting closer, and the Rue de Choiseul and the Rue de la Michodière waxing quite excited over their condemned houses. Before a fortnight passed, the opening would leave in both these streets a great gap full of sunlight and uproar.

But what stirred up the district still more, was the work undertaken at The Ladies' Paradise. People talked of considerable enlargements, of gigantic shops with frontages on the Rue de la Michodière, the Rue Neuve-Saint-Augustin, and the Rue Monsigny. Mouret, it was said, had made arrangements with Baron Hartmann, the chairman of the Crédit Immobilier, and would occupy the whole block, excepting the future frontage in the Rue du Dix-Décembre, where the baron wished to erect a rival establishment to the Grand Hôtel. The Paradise people were buying up leases on all sides, shops were closing, and tenants moving; and in the empty buildings an army of workmen was commencing the various alterations amidst a cloud of plaster. And alone in all this disorder, old Bourras's narrow hovel remained intact, still obstinately clinging between the high walls covered with masons.

When on the following day, Denise went with Pépé to her uncle Baudu's, the street was blocked up by a line of carts discharging bricks outside the Hôtel Duvillard. Baudu was standing at his shop door looking on with a gloomy air. In proportion as The Ladies' Paradise became larger, The Old Elbeuf seemed to grow smaller. The young girl thought that the windows looked blacker than ever, lower and lower still beneath the first storey, with its rounded prison-like windows. The damp, moreover, had still further discoloured the old green sign-board;

---

1. This is at the present day the Rue du Quatre Septembre. Napoleon III. gave as the name of the new thoroughfare the date of his coronation (Dec. 10); and after Sedan the Republican government ironically retorted by altering the name to the date of his downfall (Sept. 4).

woefulness appeared on the whole frontage, livid in hue, and, as it were, shrunken.

"Here you are, then!" said Baudu. "Take care! they would run right over you."

Inside the shop, Denise experienced the same heart pang; she found it darker, steeped more deeply than ever in the somnolence of approaching ruin. Empty corners formed dark cavities, dust was covering the counters and filling the drawers, whilst a cellar-like odour of saltpetre rose from the bales of cloth that were no longer moved about. At the desk Madame Baudu and Geneviève stood mute and motionless, as in some solitary spot, where no one would come to disturb them. The mother was hemming some dusters. The daughter, her hands resting on her knees, was gazing at the emptiness before her.

"Good evening, aunt," said Denise; "I'm delighted to see you again, and if I have hurt your feelings, I hope you will forgive me."

Madame Baudu kissed her, greatly affected. "My poor child," said she, "if I had no other troubles, you would see me gayer than this."

"Good evening, cousin," resumed Denise, kissing Geneviève on the cheeks.

The latter woke with a sort of start, and returned her kisses but without finding a word to say. Then the two women took up Pépé, who was holding out his little arms, and the reconciliation was complete.

"Well! it's six o'clock, let's go to dinner," said Baudu. "Why haven't you brought Jean?"

"Well, he was to have come," murmured Denise, in embarrassment. "I saw him this morning, and he faithfully promised me. Oh! we must not wait for him; his master has kept him, I dare say." In reality she suspected some extraordinary adventure, and wished to apologize for him in advance.

"In that case, we will commence," said her uncle and turning towards the dim depths of the shop, he added:

"You may as well dine with us, Colomban. No one will come."

Denise had not noticed the assistant. Her aunt explained to her that they had been obliged to get rid of the other salesman and the young lady. Business was getting so bad that Colomban sufficed; and even he spent many idle hours, drowsy, falling asleep with his eyes open.

The gas was burning in the dining-room, although they were now in the long days of summer. Denise shivered slightly as she went in, chilled by the dampness oozing from the walls. She once more beheld the round table, the places laid on the American cloth, the window deriving its air and light from the dark and fetid back-yard. And all these things appeared to her to be gloomier than ever, and tearful like the shop.

"Father," said Geneviève, uncomfortable for Denise's sake, "shall I close the window? there's rather a bad smell."

He himself smelt nothing, and seemed surprised. "Shut the window if you like," he replied at last. "But we shan't get any air then."

And indeed they were almost stifled. It was a very simple family dinner. After the soup, as soon as the servant had served the boiled beef, the old man as usual began talking about the people opposite. At first he showed himself very tolerant, allowing his niece to have a different opinion.

"Dear me!" said he, "you are quite free to support those big tricky shows. Each person has his ideas, my girl. If you were not disgusted at being so disgracefully chucked out you must have strong reasons for liking them; and even if you went back again, I should think none the worse of you. No one here would be offended, would they?"

"Oh, no!" murmured Madame Baudu.

Thereupon Denise quietly gave her reasons for her preference, just as she had at Robineau's: explaining the logical evolution in business, the necessities of modern times, the greatness of these new creations, in short, the growing well-being of the public. Baudu, his eyes dilated, and his mouth clammy, listened with a visible mental strain. Then, when she had finished, he shook his head.

"That's all phantasmagoria, you know. Business is business, there's no getting over that. Oh! I own that they succeed, but that's all. For a long time I thought they would smash up; yes, I expected that, waiting patiently—you remember? Well, no, it appears that nowadays thieves make fortunes, whilst honest people die of hunger. That's what we've come to. I'm obliged to bow to facts. And I do bow, on my word, I do bow to them!" A deep anger was gradually rising within him. All at once he flourished his fork. "But The Old Elbeuf will never give way! I said as much to Bourras, you know, 'Neighbour,' said I 'you're going over to the cheapjacks; your paint and your varnish are a disgrace to you.'"

"Eat your dinner!" interrupted Madame Baudu, feeling anxious, on seeing him so excited.

"Wait a bit, I want my niece thoroughly to understand my motto. Just listen, my girl: I'm like this decanter, I don't budge. They succeed, so much the worse for them! As for me, I protest—that's all!"

The servant brought in a piece of roast veal. He cut it up with trembling hands; and no longer showed his accurate glance, his deft skill in weighing the portions. The consciousness of his defeat deprived him of the confidence he had formerly possessed as a respected employer. Pépé had thought that his uncle was getting angry, and they had to pacify him, by giving him some dessert, some biscuits which were near his plate. Then Baudu, lowering his voice, tried to talk of something else. For a moment he spoke of the demolitions going on, approving of the Rue du Dix-Décembre, the piercing of which would certainly increase the business of the neighbourhood. But then he again returned to The Ladies' Paradise; everything brought him back to it, as to a chronic complaint. They were being covered with plaster, and business had quite ceased since the builders' carts had commenced to block up the street. Moreover the place would soon be really ridiculous, in its immensity; the customers would lose themselves in it. Why not have the Central Markets at once? And, in spite of his wife's supplicating looks, notwithstanding his own effort, he went on from the works to the amount of business done in the big shop. Was it not inconceivable? In less than four years they had increased their figures five-fold: the annual receipts, formerly some eight million francs, now attained the sum of forty millions, according to the last balance-sheet. In fact it was a piece of folly, a thing that had never been seen before, and against which it was perfectly useless to struggle. They were always swelling and growing; they now had a thousand employees and twenty-eight departments. Those twenty-eight departments enraged him more than anything else. No doubt they had duplicated a few, but others were quite new; for instance a furniture department, and a department for fancy goods. The idea! Fancy goods! Really those people had no pride whatever, they would even end by selling fish. Then Baudu, though still affecting to respect Denise's opinions, attempted to convert her.

"Frankly, you can't defend them. What would you say if I were to add an ironmongery department to my cloth business? You would say I was mad, eh? Confess, at least, that you don't esteem them."

And as the young girl simply smiled, feeling uncomfortable and realizing how futile the best of reasons would be, he resumed: "In short, you are on their side. We won't talk about it any more, for it's useless to let that part us again. That would be the climax—to see them come between me and my family! Go back with them, if you like; but pray don't worry me with any more of their stories!"

ÉMILE ZOLA

A silence ensued. His previous violence fell to this feverish resignation. As they were suffocating in the narrow room, heated by the gas-burner, the servant had to open the window again; and the damp, pestilential air from the yard blew into the apartment. A dish of *sauté* potatoes had appeared, and they helped themselves slowly, without a word.

"Look at those two," began Baudu again, pointing with his knife to Geneviève and Colomban. "Ask them if they like your Ladies' Paradise."

Side by side in the places where they had found themselves twice a-day for the last twelve years, Colomban and Geneviève were eating slowly, without uttering a word. He, exaggerating the coarse good-nature of his face, seemed to be concealing, behind his drooping eyelashes, the inward flame which was consuming him; whilst she, her head bowed lower beneath her heavy hair, appeared to be giving way entirely, as if a prey to some secret grief.

"Last year was very disastrous," explained Baudu, "and we have been obliged to postpone the marriage. Just to please them, ask them what they think of your friends."

In order to pacify him, Denise interrogated the young people.

"Naturally I can't be very fond of them, cousin," replied Geneviève. "But never fear, every one doesn't detest them."

And so speaking she looked at Colomban, who was rolling up some bread-crumbs with an absorbed air. But when he felt that the young girl's gaze was turned upon him, he broke out into a series of violent exclamations: "A rotten shop! A lot of rogues, every man-jack of them! In fact a regular pest in the neighbourhood!"

"You hear him! You hear him!" exclaimed Baudu, delighted. "There's one whom they'll never get hold of! Ah! my boy, you're the last of the old stock, we shan't see any more!"

But Geneviève, with her severe and suffering look, did not take her eyes off Colomban, but dived into the depths of his heart. And he felt troubled, and again launched out into invective. Madame Baudu was watching them in silence with an anxious air, as if she foresaw another misfortune in this direction. For some time past her daughter's sadness had frightened her, she felt her to be dying.

"The shop is left to take care of itself," she said at last, rising from table, in order to put an end to the scene. "Go and see, Colomban; I fancy I heard some one."

They had finished, and got up. Baudu and Colomban went to speak to a traveller, who had come for orders. Madame Baudu carried Pépé off to show him some pictures. The servant had quickly cleared the table, and Denise was lingering by the window, looking curiously into the little back-yard, when on turning round she saw Geneviève still in her place, her eyes fixed on the American cloth, which was still damp from the sponge that had been passed over it.

"Are you suffering, cousin?" she asked.

The young girl did not reply but seemed to be obstinately studying a rent in the cloth, though really absorbed in the reflections passing through her mind. But after a while she raised her head with difficulty, and looked at the sympathizing face bent over hers. The others had gone, then? What was she doing on that chair? And suddenly sobs stifled her, her head fell forward on the edge of the table. She wept on, wetting her sleeve with her tears.

"Good heavens! what's the matter with you?" cried Denise in dismay. "Shall I call some one?"

But Geneviève nervously caught her by the arm, and held her back, stammering: "No, no, stay here. Don't let mamma know! With you I don't mind; but not the others—not the others! It's not my fault, I assure you. It was on finding myself all alone. Wait a bit; I'm better, I'm not crying now."

Nevertheless sudden attacks kept on seizing her, sending shudders through her frail body. It seemed as though her pile of hair was weighing down her neck. While she was rolling her head on her folded arms, a hair-pin slipped out, and then her hair fell over her neck, burying it beneath gloomy tresses. Denise, as quietly as possible for fear of attracting attention, sought to console her. She undid her dress, and was heart-rent on seeing how fearfully thin she had become. The poor girl's bosom was as hollow as a child's. Then Denise took hold of her hair by the handful, that superb hair, which seemed to be absorbing all her life, and twisted it up tightly to clear her neck, and make her cooler.

"Thanks, you are very kind," said Geneviève. "Ah! I'm not stout, am I? I used to be stouter, but it's all gone away. Do up my dress or mamma might see my shoulders. I hide them as much as I can. Good heavens! I'm not at all well, I'm not at all well."

However, the attack passed away, and she sat there completely exhausted and looking fixedly at her cousin. After a pause she abruptly inquired: "Tell me the truth: does he love her?"

Denise felt a blush rising to her cheeks. She was perfectly well aware that Geneviève referred to Colomban and Clara; but she pretended to be surprised. "Who, dear?"

Geneviève shook her head with an incredulous air. "Don't tell falsehoods, I beg of you. Do me the favour of setting my doubts at rest. You must know, I feel it. Yes, you were that girl's comrade, and I've seen Colomban run after you, and talk to you in a low voice. He was giving you messages for her, wasn't he? Oh! for pity's sake, tell me the truth; I assure you it will do me good."

Never before had Denise been in such an awkward position. She lowered her eyes before this girl, who was ever silent and yet guessed all. However, she had the strength to deceive her still. "But it's you he loves!" she said.

Geneviève made a gesture of despair. "Very well, you won't tell me anything. However, I don't care, I've seen them. He's continually going outside to look at her. She, upstairs, laughs like a bad woman. Of course they meet out of doors."

"As for that, no, I assure you!" exclaimed Denise, forgetting herself and carried away by the desire to give her cousin at least that consolation.

Geneviève drew a long breath, and smiled feebly. Then in the weak voice of a convalescent she said, "I should like a glass of water. Excuse me if I trouble you. Look, over there in the sideboard."

When she got hold of the bottle, she drank a large glassful right off, keeping Denise away with one hand. The young saleswoman was afraid that she might do herself harm.

"No, no," said she, "let me be; I'm always thirsty. In the night I get up to drink."

Silence again fell. Then Geneviève once more began in a gentle voice. "If you only knew, I've been accustomed to the idea of this marriage for the last ten years. I was still wearing short dresses, when Colomban began courting me. I can hardly remember how things came about. By always living together, shut up here together, without any other distractions between us, I must have ended by believing him to be my husband before he really was. I didn't know whether I loved him, I was his wife, that was all. And now he wants to go off with another girl! Oh, heavens! my heart is breaking! You see, it's a grief that I never felt before. It hurts me in the bosom, and in the head; then it spreads everywhere, it's killing me."

Her eyes filled with tears. Denise, whose eyelids were also moistening with pity, asked her: "Does my aunt suspect anything?"

"Yes, mamma has her suspicions, I think. As for papa, he is too much worried, and does not know the pain he is causing me by postponing the marriage. Mamma has questioned me several times, greatly alarmed to see me pining away. She has never been very strong herself, and has often said to me: 'My poor child, you're like myself, by no means strong. Besides, one doesn't grow much in these shops. But she must find me getting really too thin now. Look at my arms; would you believe it?"

Then with a trembling hand she again took up the water bottle. Her cousin tried to prevent her from drinking.

"But I'm so thirsty," said she, "let me drink."

They could hear Baudu talking in a loud voice. Then suddenly yielding to an inspiration of her heart, Denise knelt down before Geneviève and throwing her sisterly arms round her neck, kissed her, and assured her that everything would yet turn out all right, that she would marry Colomban, would get well, and live happily. And then she got up quickly for her uncle was calling her.

"Jean is here. Come along."

It was indeed Jean, who, looking rather scared, had just arrived for dinner. When they told him it was striking eight, he seemed amazed. Impossible! He had only just left his master's. They chaffed him. No doubt he had come by way of the Bois de Vincennes. But as soon as he could get near his sister, he whispered to her: "It's all the fault of a little laundry-girl. I've got a cab outside by the hour. Give me five francs."

He went out for a minute, and then returned to dinner, for Madame Baudu would not hear of his going away without taking, at least, a plate of soup. Geneviève had returned to the shop in her usual silent and retiring manner. Colomban was now half asleep behind the counter; and the evening passed away, slow and melancholy, only animated by Baudu's tramp, as he walked from one end of the empty shop to the other. A single gas-burner was alight—the shadows of the low ceiling fell in large masses, like black earth from a ditch.

Several months passed away. Denise came in nearly every evening to cheer up Geneviève a bit, but the Baudus' home became more melancholy than ever. The works opposite were a continual torment, which made them feel their bad luck more and more keenly. Even when they had an hour of hope—some unexpected joy—the uproar of a tumbrel-load of bricks, the sound of a stone-cutter's saw or the simple call of a mason would at once suffice to mar their pleasure. In fact, the whole neighbourhood was stirred by it all. From behind the hoarding edging and obstructing the three streets, there issued a movement of feverish activity. Although the architect was utilizing the existing buildings, he was opening them in various ways to adapt them to their new uses; and right in the centre of the vacant space supplied by the court-yards, he was building a central gallery as vast as a church, which would be reached by a grand entrance in the Rue Neuve-Saint-Augustin in the very middle of the frontage. They had, at first, experienced great difficulty in laying the foundations, for they had come upon sewer deposits and loose earth, full of human bones; besides which the boring of the well—a well three hundred feet deep—destined to yield two hundred gallons a minute had made the neighbours very anxious. They had now got the walls up to the first storey; and the entire block was surrounded by scaffoldings, regular towers of timber. There was an incessant noise from the grinding of the windlasses hoisting up the free-stone, the abrupt unloading of iron bars, the clamour of the army of workmen, accompanied by the noise of picks and hammers. But above all else, what most deafened you was the sound of the machinery. Everything went by steam, screeching whistles rent the air; and then too, at the slightest gust of wind, clouds of plaster flew about and covered the neighbouring roofs like a fall of snow. The despairing Baudus looked on at this implacable dust penetrating everywhere—filtering through the closest woodwork, soiling the goods in their shop, even gliding into their beds; and the idea that they must continue to breathe it—that it would end by killing them—empoisoned their existence.

The situation, however, was destined to become worse still, for in September, the architect, afraid of not being ready in time, decided to carry on the work at night also. Powerful electric lamps were established, and then the uproar became continuous. Gangs of men relieved each other; the hammers never stopped, the engines whistled night and day; and again the everlasting clamour seemed to raise and scatter the white dust. The exasperated Baudus now had to give up the idea of sleeping even; they were shaken in their alcove; the noises changed into nightmare whenever they managed to doze off. Then, if they got up to calm their fever, and went, with bare feet, to pull back the curtains and look out of the window, they were frightened by the vision of The Ladies' Paradise flaring in the darkness like a colossal forge, where their ruin was being forged. Along the half-built walls, pierced with empty bays, the electric lamps threw broad bluey rays, of blinding intensity. Two o'clock struck—then three, then four; and during the painful sleep of the neighbourhood, the works, expanding in the lunar-like brightness, became colossal and fantastic, swarming with black shadows, noisy workmen, whose silhouettes gesticulated against the crude whiteness of the new walls.

Baudu had spoken correctly. The small traders of the adjacent streets were receiving another mortal blow. Every time The Ladies' Paradise created new departments there were fresh failures among the shopkeepers of the district. The disaster spread, one could hear the oldest houses cracking. Mademoiselle Tatin, of the under-linen shop in the Passage Choiseul, had just been declared bankrupt; Quinette, the glover, could hardly hold out another six months; the furriers, Vanpouille, were obliged to sub-let a part of their premises; and if the Bédorés, brother and sister, still kept on as hosiers, in the Rue Gaillon, they were evidently living on the money they had formerly saved. And now more smashes were on the point of being added to those long since foreseen; the fancy goods department threatened a dealer in the Rue Saint-Roch, Deslignières, a big, full-blooded man; whilst the furniture department was injuring Messrs. Piot and Rivoire, whose shops slumbered in the gloom of the Passage Sainte-Anne. It was even feared that an attack of apoplexy would carry off Deslignières, who had been in a terrible rage ever since The Ladies' Paradise had marked up purses at thirty per cent. reduction. The furniture dealers, who were much calmer, affected to joke at these counter-jumpers who wanted to meddle with such articles as chairs and tables; but customers were already leaving them, and the success of Mouret's department threatened to be a formidable one. It was all over, they must bow their heads. After these, others would be swept off in their turn and there was no reason why every business should not be driven away. Some day The Ladies' Paradise alone would cover the neighbourhood with its roof.

At present, when the thousand employees went in and came out morning and evening, they formed such a long procession on the Place Gaillon that people stopped to look at them as they might at a passing regiment. For ten minutes they blocked up all the streets; and the shopkeepers standing at their doors thought bitterly of their one assistant, whom they hardly knew how to find food for. The last balance-sheet of the big bazaar, the turn-over of forty millions, had also revolutionized the neighbourhood. The figure passed from house to house amid cries of surprise and anger. Forty millions! Think of that! No doubt the net profit did not exceed more than four per cent., given the heavy general expenses, and the system of low prices; but sixteen hundred thousand francs was still a handsome sum; one could well be satisfied with four per cent., when one operated on such a scale as that. It was said that Mouret's starting capital of five hundred thousand francs, each year increased by the total profits of the house—a capital which must at that moment have amounted to four millions—had in one twelvemonth passed ten times over the counters in the form of goods. Robineau, when he made this calculation in Denise's presence one evening, after dinner, was quite overcome for a moment, and remained staring at his empty plate. She was right, it was this incessant renewal of capital that constituted the invincible power of the new system of business. Bourras alone denied the facts, refusing to understand, superb and stupid as a milestone. To him the Paradise people were a pack of thieves and nothing more! A lying set! Cheap-jacks who would be picked out of the gutter some fine morning!

The Baudus, however, despite their determination not to change anything in the system of The Old Elbeuf, tried to sustain the competition. Customers no longer coming to them, they sought to reach the customers through the agency of travellers. There was at that time, in the Paris market, a traveller connected with all the leading tailors, who saved the little cloth and flannel houses when he condescended to represent them. Naturally they all tried to get hold of him; he was quite a personage; and Baudu, having haggled with him, had the misfortune to see him come to terms with the Matignons, of the Rue Croix-des-Petits-Champs. Then one after the other, two other travellers robbed him; a third, an honest man, did no business. It was a slow death, exempt from shocks, a continual decrease of business, customers falling away one by one. A day came when the bills to be met fell on the Baudus very heavily. Until that time they had lived on their former savings; but now they began to contract debts. In December, Baudu, terrified by the amount of his acceptances, resigned himself to a most cruel sacrifice: he sold his country-house at Rambouillet, a house which cost him a lot of money in continual repairs, and whose tenants had not even paid the rent when he decided to get rid of it. This sale killed the sole dream of his life, his heart bled as for the loss of some dear one. And for seventy thousand francs he had to part with what had cost him more than two hundred thousand, considering himself fortunate even in meeting the Lhommes, his neighbours, who were desirous of adding to their property. Those seventy thousand francs would keep the business going a little longer; for in spite of all the repulses the idea of struggling on ever sprang up again; perhaps with great care they might conquer even now.

On the Sunday on which the Lhommes paid the money, they condescended to dine at The Old Elbeuf. Madame Aurélie was the first to arrive; they had to wait for the cashier, who came late, scared by a whole afternoon's music: as for young Albert, he had accepted the invitation, but did not put in an appearance. It was, moreover, a painful evening. The Baudus, living without air in their tiny dining-room, suffered from the breeze which the Lhommes, with their lack of family ties and their taste for a free life, brought in with them. Geneviève, wounded by Madame Aurélie's imperial airs, did not open her mouth; but Colomban admired her with a shiver, on reflecting that she reigned over Clara. Later on, when Madame Baudu was already in bed, her husband remained for a long time walking about the room. It was a mild night—damp, thawing weather—and in spite of the closed windows, and drawn curtains, one could hear the engines snorting on the opposite side of the way.

"Do you know what I'm thinking of, Elisabeth?" said Baudu at last. "Well! those Lhommes may earn as much money as they like, I'd rather be in my shoes than theirs. They get on well, it's true. The wife said, didn't she? that she had made nearly twenty thousand francs this year, and that had enabled her to take my poor house. Never mind! I've no longer got the house, but I don't go playing music in one direction, whilst you are gadding about in the other. No, look you, they can't be happy."

He was still keenly fretting over the sacrifice he had been compelled to make, full of rancour against those people who had bought up his darling dream. When ever he came near the bed, he leant over his wife and gesticulated, then, returning to the window, he stood silent for a minute, listening to the noise of the works. And again he vented his old accusations, his despairing complaints about the new times; nobody had ever seen such things, shop-assistants now earned more than tradesmen, cashiers bought up employers' property. So no wonder that everything was going to the dogs; family ties no longer existed, people lived at hotels instead of eating their meals at home in a respectable manner. At last he ended by prophesying that young Albert would swallow up the Rambouillet property later on with a lot of actresses.

Madame Baudu listened to him, her head flat on the pillow, and so pale that her face seemed the colour of the sheets. "They've paid you," she at length said softly.

At this Baudu became dumb. He walked about for an instant with his eyes on the ground. Then he resumed: "They've paid me, 'tis true;

and, after all, their money is as good as another's. It would be funny if we revived the business with this money. Ah! if I were not so old and worn out!"

A long silence ensued. The draper was full of vague projects. Suddenly, without moving her head, her eyes fixed on the ceiling, his wife spoke again: "Have you noticed your daughter lately?"

"No," he replied.

"Well! she makes me rather anxious. She's getting pale, she seems to be pining away."

He stood before the bed, full of surprise. "Really! whatever for? If she's ill she should say so. To-morrow we must send for the doctor."

Madame Baudu still remained motionless; but after a time, she declared, with her meditative air: "I think it would be better to get this marriage with Colomban over."

He looked at her and then began walking about again. Certain things came back to his mind. Was it possible that his daughter was falling ill over the shopman? Did she love him so much that she could not wait? Here was another misfortune! It worried him all the more from the circumstance that he himself had fixed ideas about this marriage. He could never consent to it in the present state of affairs. However, his anxiety softened him.

"Very good," said he at last, "I'll speak to Colomban."

And without adding another word he continued his walk. Soon afterwards his wife fell asleep still looking quite white, as if dead; while he still kept on tramping about. Before getting into bed he drew aside the curtains and glanced outside; across the street through the gaping windows of the old Hôtel Duvillard the workmen could be seen stirring in the dazzling glare of the electric light.

On the following morning Baudu took Colomban to the further end of the store-room on the upper floor, having made up his mind over night as to what he would say to him. "My boy," he began, "you know I've sold my property at Rambouillet. That will enable us to show some fight. But I should first of all like to have a talk with you."

The young man, who seemed to dread the interview, waited with an awkward air. His small eyes twinkled in his broad face, and he stood there with his mouth open—with him a sign of profound agitation.

"Just listen to me," resumed the draper. "When old Hauchecorne left me The Old Elbeuf, the house was prosperous; he himself had received it from old Finet in a satisfactory state. You know my ideas; I should consider it wrong if I passed this family trust over to my children in a diminished state; and that's why I've always postponed your marriage with Geneviève. Yes, I was obstinate; I hoped to bring back our former prosperity; I wanted to hand you the books, saying: 'Look here! the year I commenced we sold so much cloth, and this year, the year I retire, we have sold ten thousand or twenty thousand francs' worth more.' In short, you understand, it was a vow I made to myself, the very natural desire I had to prove that the house had not declined in my hands. Otherwise it would seem to me that I was robbing you." His voice became husky with emotion. He blew his nose to recover himself a bit, and then asked, "You don't say anything?"

But Colomban had nothing to say. He shook his head, and waited, feeling more and more perturbed, and fancying that he could guess what the governor was aiming at. It was the marriage without further delay. How could he refuse? He would never have the strength to do so. And yet there was that other girl, of whom he dreamed at night, devoured by insensate passion.

"Now," continued Baudu, "a sum of money has come in that may save us. The situation becomes worse every day, but perhaps by making a supreme effort.—In short, I thought it right to warn you. We are going to venture our last stake. If we are beaten, why that will entirely ruin us! Only, my poor boy, your marriage must again be postponed, for I don't wish to throw you two all alone into the struggle. That would be too cowardly, wouldn't it?"

Colomban, greatly relieved, had seated himself on a pile of molleton. His legs were still trembling. He was afraid of showing his delight, so he held down his head whilst rolling his fingers on his knees.

"You don't say anything?" repeated Baudu.

No, he said nothing, he could find nothing to say. Thereupon the draper slowly resumed: "I was sure this would grieve you. You must muster up courage. Pull yourself together a bit, don't let yourself be crushed in this way. Above all, understand my position. Can I hang such a weight about your neck? Instead of leaving you a good business, I should leave you a bankruptcy perhaps. No, only scoundrels play such tricks as that! No doubt, I desire nothing but your happiness, but nobody shall ever make me go against my conscience."

And he went on for a long time in this way, meandering through a maze of contradictory sentences, like a man who would have liked to be understood at the first word but finds himself obliged to explain everything. As he had promised his daughter and the shop, strict probity forced him to deliver both in good condition, without defects or debts. But he was weary, the burden seemed to be too much for him, and entreaty almost pierced though his stammering accents. At last he got more entangled than ever, awaiting some sudden impulse from Colomban, some heartfelt cry, which did not come.

"I know," he murmured, "that old men are wanting in ardour. With young ones, things light up. They are full of fire, it's only natural. But, no, no, I can't, my word of honour! If I gave it up to you, you would blame me later on."

He stopped, trembling, and as the young man still kept his head down, he asked him for the third time, after a painful silence: "You don't say anything?" Then, at last, without venturing to look at him, Colomban replied: "There's nothing to say. You are the master, you know better than all of us. As you wish it we'll wait, we'll try and be reasonable."

It was all over. Baudu still hoped he was going to throw himself into his arms, exclaiming: "Father, do you take a rest, we'll fight in our turn; give us the shop as it is, so that we may work a miracle and save it!" Then, however, he looked at him, and felt full of shame, reproaching himself for having wished to dupe his children. His deep-rooted maniacal commercial honesty was awakened in him; it was this prudent fellow who was right, for there is no such thing as sentiment in business, which is only a question of figures.

"Embrace me, my boy," he said in conclusion. "It's settled; we won't speak about the marriage for another year. One must think of the business before everything."

That evening, in their room, when Madame Baudu questioned her husband as to the result of the conversation, the draper had regained his obstinate resolve to fight on in person to the bitter end. He gave Colomban high praise, calling him a solid fellow, firm in his ideas, brought up in the best principles, incapable, for instance, of joking with the customers like those puppies at The Paradise. No, he was honest, he belonged to the family, he didn't speculate on the business as though he were a stock-jobber.

"Well, then, when's the marriage to take place?" asked Madame Baudu.

"Later on," he replied, "when I am able to keep my promises."

She made no gestures but simply remarked: "It will be our daughter's death."

Baudu restrained himself though hot with anger. He was the one whom it would kill, if they continually upset him like this! Was it his fault? He loved his daughter—would lay down his life for her; but he could not make the business prosper when it obstinately refused to do so. Geneviève ought to have a little more sense, and wait patiently for a better balance. The deuce! Colomban would always be there, no one would run away with him!

"It's incredible!" he repeated; "such a well-trained girl!"

Madame Baudu said no more. She had doubtless guessed Geneviève's jealous agony; but she did not dare to inform her husband of it. A singular womanly modesty always prevented her from approaching certain tender, delicate subjects with him. When he saw her so silent, he turned his anger against the people opposite, stretching out his fists towards the works, where they were that night setting up some large iron girders, with a great noise of hammers.

Denise had now decided to return to The Ladies' Paradise, having understood that the Robineaus, obliged to cut down their staff, were at a loss how to dismiss her. To maintain their position they were now obliged to do everything themselves. Gaujean, still obstinate in his rancour, renewed their bills and even promised to find them funds; but they were frightened, they wanted to try the effect of economy and order. During a whole fortnight Denise had felt that they were embarrassed about her, and it was she who spoke the first, saying that she had found a situation elsewhere. This came as a great relief. Madame Robineau embraced her, deeply affected, and declaring that she should always miss her. Then when, in answer to a question, the young girl acknowledged that she was going back to Mouret's, Robineau turned pale.

"You are right!" he exclaimed violently.

It was not so easy to tell the news to old Bourras however. Still, Denise had to give him notice, and she trembled at the thought, for she felt full of gratitude towards him. Bourras was at this time in a rage from morn till night, for he more than any other suffered from the uproar of the adjacent works. The builder's carts blocked up his doorway; the picks tapped on his walls; umbrellas and sticks, everything in his place, danced about to the noise of the hammers. It seemed as if the hovel, obstinately remaining in the midst of these demolitions, would suddenly split to pieces. But the worst was that the architect, in order to connect the existing shops with those about to be opened in the

Hôtel Duvillard, had conceived the idea of tunnelling a passage under the little house that separated them. This house now belonged to the firm of Mouret & Co., and as the lease stipulated that the tenant should submit to all necessary repairs, the workmen one morning appeared on the scene. At this Bourras nearly went into a fit. Wasn't it enough that they should grip him on all sides, on the right, the left, and behind, without attacking him underfoot as well, taking the very ground from under him! And he drove the masons away, and went to law. Repairs, yes! but this was a work of embellishment. The neighbourhood thought he would win the day, without, however, being sure of anything. The case, at any rate, threatened to be a long one, and people became quite impassioned over this interminable duel.

On the day when Denise at last resolved to give him notice, Bourras had just returned from his lawyer's. "Would you believe it!" he exclaimed, "they now say that the house is not solid; they pretend that the foundations must be strengthened. Confound it! they have shaken it up so much with their infernal machines, that it isn't astonishing if it gives way!"

Then, when the girl announced she was going to leave, and was returning to The Ladies' Paradise at a salary of a thousand francs, he became so amazed that he could only raise his trembling hands in the air. Emotion made him drop upon a chair.

"You! you!" he stammered. "Ah, I'm the only one—I'm the only one left!" And after a pause, he asked: "And the youngster?"

"He'll go back to Madame Gras's," replied Denise. "She was very fond of him."

They again became silent. She would have rather seen him furious, swearing and banging the counter with his fist; the sight of this old man, suffocating and crushed, made her heart bleed. But he gradually recovered, and began shouting out once more. "A thousand francs! that isn't to be refused. You'll all go. Go, then, leave me here alone. Yes, alone—you understand! One at all events will never bow his head. And tell them I'll win my lawsuit, if I have to sell my last shirt for it!"

Denise was not to leave Robineau's till the end of the month. She had seen Mouret again and everything had been settled. One evening as she was going up to her room, Deloche, who was watching for her in a doorway, stopped her. He was delighted, having just heard the good news; they were all talking about it in the shop, said he. And he gaily told her of all the gossip at the counters.

"The young ladies in the mantle department are pulling fearfully long faces, you know." And then breaking off, he added: "By the way, you remember Clara Prunaire? Well, it appears the governor has taken a fancy to her."

He had turned quite red. She, very pale, exclaimed:

"What! Monsieur Mouret!"

"Funny taste—eh?" he resumed. "A woman who looks like a horse. However, that's his business."

Once upstairs, Denise almost fainted away. It was surely through coming up too quickly. Leaning out of the window she had a sudden vision of Valognes, the deserted street and grassy pavement, which she had seen from her room as a child; and she was seized with a desire to go and live there once more—to seek refuge in the peace and forgetfulness of the country. Paris irritated her, she hated The Ladies' Paradise, she no longer knew why she had consented to go back. She would certainly suffer there as much as formerly; she was already suffering from an unknown uneasiness since Deloche's stories. And then all at once a flood of tears forced her to leave the window. She continued weeping on for some time, but at last found a little courage to live on still.

The next day at lunch time, as Robineau had sent her on an errand, and she was passing The Old Elbeuf, she opened the door on seeing Colomban alone in the shop. The Baudus were having their meal; she could hear the clatter of the knives and forks in the little dining-room.

"You can come in," said the shopman. "They are at table."

But she motioned him to be silent, and drew him into a corner. Then, lowering her voice, she said: "It's you I want to speak to. Have you no heart? Can't you see that Geneviève loves you, and that it's killing her."

She was trembling, her fever of the previous night had taken possession of her again. He, frightened and surprised by this sudden attack, stood looking at her, without a word.

"Do you hear?" she continued. "Geneviève knows you love another. She told me so. She wept like a child. Ah, poor girl! she isn't very strong now, I can tell you! If you had seen her thin arms! It's heart-breaking. You can't leave her to die like this!"

At last he spoke, quite overcome. "But she isn't ill—you exaggerate! I don't see anything myself. Besides, it's her father who is postponing the marriage."

Denise sharply corrected this falsehood, certain as she was that the least insistence on the young man's part would have decided her uncle.

As for Colomban's surprise, however, it was not feigned; he had really never noticed Geneviève's slow agony. For him it was a very disagreeable revelation; for while he remained ignorant of it, he had no great blame to tax himself with.

"And who for indeed?" resumed Denise. "For an utterly worthless girl! You can't know whom you are loving! So far I have not wished to hurt your feelings, I have often avoided answering your continual questions. Well! she goes about with everybody, she laughs at you, and will never marry you."

He listened to her, turning very pale; and at each of the sentences she threw in his face, his lips quivered. She, in a cruel fit, yielded to a transport of anger of which she had no consciousness. "In short," she said, in a final cry, "she's Monsieur Mouret's mistress if you want to know!"

As she spoke her voice died away in her throat and she turned even paler than Colomban himself. Both stood looking at each other. Then he stammered out: "I love her!"

Denise felt ashamed of herself. Why was she talking in this fashion to this young fellow? Why was she getting so excited? She stood there mute, the simple reply which he had just given her resounded in her heart like the distant but deafening clang of a bell. "I love her, I love her!" and it seemed to spread. He was right, he could not marry another woman.

And as she turned round, she observed Geneviève on the threshold of the dining-room. "Be quiet!" she said rapidly.

But it was too late, Geneviève must have heard, for her face was white and bloodless. Just at that moment a customer opened the door— Madame Bourdelais, one of the last faithful customers of The Old Elbeuf, where she found substantial goods for her money. For a long time past Madame de Boves had followed the fashion, and gone over to The Ladies' Paradise; Madame Marty also no longer came, being entirely subjugated by the fascinations of the display opposite. And Geneviève was forced to come forward, and inquire in her weak voice:

"What do you desire, madame?"

Madame Bourdelais wished to see some flannel. Colomban took down a roll from a shelf. Geneviève showed the stuff; and once again the young people found themselves close together behind the counter. Meanwhile Baudu came out of the dining-room, behind his wife, who went to seat herself at the pay-desk. At first he did not meddle with the sale, but after smiling at Denise stood there, looking at Madame Bourdelais.

"It is not good enough," said the latter. "Show me the thickest you have."

Colomban took down another bundle. There was a silence. Madame Bourdelais examined the stuff.

"How much?" she asked.

"Six francs, madame," replied Geneviève.

The lady made an abrupt gesture. "Six francs!" said she. "But they have the same opposite at five francs."

A slight contraction passed over Baudu's face. He could not help interfering politely. No doubt madame made a mistake, indeed the stuff ought to have been sold at six francs and a half; it was impossible to sell it at five francs. It must be another quality that she was referring to.

"No, no," she repeated, with the obstinacy of a house-wife who prided herself on her knowledge of such matters. "The quality is the same. The other may even be a little thicker."

And the discussion ended by becoming quite bitter. Baudu with his bile rising to his face had to make an effort to continue smiling. His rancour against The Ladies' Paradise was bursting in his throat.

"Really," said Madame Bourdelais at last, "you must treat me better for otherwise I shall go opposite, like the others."

Thereupon he lost his head, and, shaking with all the passion he had restrained, cried out: "Well! go opposite then!"

At this she got up, greatly wounded, and went off without turning round, but saying: "That's just what I am going to do, sir."

A general stupor ensued. The governor's violence had frightened all of them. He was himself scared, and trembled at what he had just said. The phrase had escaped him against his will in an explosion of long pent-up rancour. And the Baudus now stood there motionless, their arms hanging by their sides as they watched Madame Bourdelais cross the street. She seemed to be carrying off their fortune. When with a tranquil step she passed through the lofty portal of The Ladies' Paradise and they saw her disappear in the crowd, they felt a sort of sudden wrench.

"There's another they've taken from us!" murmured the draper. And turning towards Denise, of whose re-engagement he was aware, he said: "You as well, they've taken you back. Oh, I don't blame you for it. As they've got the money, they are naturally the strongest."

Just then, Denise, still hoping that Geneviève had not overheard Colomban, was saying to her: "He loves you. Try and cheer up."

But in a very low and heart-broken voice the girl replied: "Why do you tell me a falsehood? Look! he can't help it, he's glancing up there again. I know very well that they've stolen him from me, just as they've robbed us of everything else."

Then she went to sit down at the desk beside her mother. The latter had doubtless guessed the fresh blow which her daughter had received, for her anxious eyes wandered from her to Colomban, and then to The Paradise. It was true, they had stolen everything from them: from the father, his fortune; from the mother, her dying child; from the daughter, the husband, for whom she had waited ten long years. In presence of this condemned family, Denise, whose heart was overflowing with pity, felt for an instant afraid that she might be wicked. For was she not going to assist that machine which was crushing the poor? However, she was carried away, as it were, by an invisible force, and felt that she could be doing no wrong.

"Bah!" resumed Baudu, to give himself courage; "we shan't die of it, after all. For one customer lost we shall find two others. You hear, Denise, I've got over seventy thousand francs there, which will certainly make your Mouret spend some sleepless nights. Come, come, you others, don't look so glum!"

But he could not enliven them. He himself relapsed into a pale consternation; and they all remained with their eyes fixed on the monster, attracted, possessed, glutting themselves with thoughts of their misfortune. The work was now nearly finished, the scaffoldings had been removed from the front, a whole side of the colossal edifice appeared, with its white walls and large light windows. Beside the footway, where traffic had at last been resumed, stood eight delivery vans which the messengers were loading one after the other outside the parcels-office. In the sunshine, a ray of which enfiladed the street, the vehicles' green panels, picked out with red and yellow, sparkled like so many mirrors, and cast blinding reflections even into the depths of The Old Elbeuf. The drivers, clad in black and dignified in manner, held the horses well in—superb horses they were, champing silvered bits. And each time a van was loaded, there came a sonorous roll over the paving stones which made all the little neighbouring shops tremble. And then in presence of this triumphal procession, the sight of which they must needs endure twice a day, the Baudus' hearts broke. The father half fainted away, asking himself where this continual stream of goods could go to; whilst the mother, sickening at thought of her daughter's torture, continued gazing blankly into the street, her eyes blurred by big tears.

# IX

It was on a Monday, the 14th of March, that The Ladies' Paradise inaugurated its new buildings by a great exhibition of summer novelties, which was to last three days. Outside, a sharp north wind was blowing and the passers-by, surprised by this return of winter, hurried along buttoning up their overcoats. In the neighbouring shops, however, all was fermentation; and against the windows one could see the pale faces of the petty tradesmen, counting the first carriages which stopped before the new grand entrance in the Rue Neuve-Saint-Augustin. This doorway, lofty and deep like a church porch, and surmounted by an emblematical group of Industry and Commerce hand-in-hand amidst a variety of symbols—was sheltered by a vast glazed *marquise*, the fresh gilding of which seemed to light up the pavement with a ray of sunshine. To the right and left the shop fronts, of a blinding whiteness, stretched along the Rue Monsigny and the Rue de la Michodière, occupying the whole block, except on the Rue du Dix-Décembre side, where the Crédit Immobilier intended to build. And along these barrack-like frontages, the petty tradesmen, whenever they raised their heads, could see the piles of goods through the large plate-glass windows which, from the ground floor to the second storey, opened the house to the light of day. And this enormous cube, this colossal bazaar which concealed the sky from them, seemed in some degree the cause of the cold which made them shiver behind their frozen counters.

As early as six o'clock, Mouret was on the spot, giving his final orders. In the centre, starting from the grand entrance, a large gallery ran from end to end, flanked right and left by two narrower ones, the Monsigny Gallery and the Michodière Gallery. Glass roofings covered the court-yards turned into huge halls, iron staircases ascended from the ground floor, on both upper floors iron bridges were thrown from one end to the other of the establishment. The architect, who happened to be a young man of talent, with modern ideas, had only used stone for the basement and corner work, employing iron for all the rest of the huge carcass— columns upholding all the assemblage of beams and joists. The vaulting of the ceilings, like the partitions, was of brick. Space had been gained everywhere; light and air entered freely, and the public circulated with the greatest ease under the bold flights of the far-stretching girders. It was the cathedral of modern commerce, light but strong, the very thing for a nation of customers. Below, in the central gallery, after the door bargains, came the cravat, glove, and silk departments; the Monsigny Gallery was occupied by the linen and Rouen goods; and the Michodière Gallery by the mercery, hosiery, drapery, and woollens. Then, on the first floor came the mantle, under-linen, shawl, lace, and various new departments, whilst the bedding, the carpets, the furnishing materials, all the cumbersome articles difficult to handle, had been relegated to the second floor. In all there were now thirty-nine departments with eighteen hundred employees, two hundred of whom were women. Quite a little world abode there, amidst the sonorous life of the high metallic naves.

Mouret's unique passion was to conquer woman. He wished her to be queen in his house, and had built this temple that he might there hold her completely at his mercy. His sole aim was to intoxicate her with gallant attentions, traffic on her desires, profit by her fever. Night and day he racked his brain to invent fresh attractions. He had already introduced two velvet-padded lifts, in order to spare delicate ladies the trouble of climbing the stairs to the upper floors. Then, too, he had just opened a bar where the customers could find gratuitous light refreshments, syrups and biscuits, and a reading-room, a monumental gallery decorated with excessive luxury, in which he had even ventured on an exhibition of pictures. But his deepest scheme was to conquer the mother through her child, when unable to do so through her own coquetry; and to attain this object there was no means that he neglected. He speculated on every sentiment, created special departments for little boys and girls, and waylaid the passing mothers with distributions of chromo-lithographs and air-balls for the children. There was real genius in his idea of presenting each buyer with a red air-ball made of fine gutta-percha and bearing in large letters the name of the establishment. Held by a string it floated in the air and sailed along every street like a living advertisement.

But the greatest power of all was the advertising. Mouret now spent three hundred thousand francs a year in catalogues, advertisements, and bills.[1] For his summer sale he had launched forth two hundred thousand catalogues, fifty thousand of which went abroad, translated into every language. He now had them illustrated with engravings,

---

1. After all, this is only £12,000 or about a quarter of the amount which a single English firm of soap-manufacturers spends in advertising every year.

and embellished with samples, gummed to the leaves. There was an overflowing display; the name of The Ladies' Paradise met the eye all over the world, it invaded the walls and hoardings, the newspapers, and even the curtains of the theatres. He claimed that woman was powerless against advertising, that she was bound to be attracted by uproar. Analyzing her moreover like a great moralist he laid still more enticing traps for her. Thus he had discovered that she could not resist a bargain, that she bought without necessity whenever she thought she saw a thing cheap, and on this observation he based his system of reductions, progressively lowering the price of unsold articles, and preferring to sell them at a loss rather than keep them by him, given his principle of constantly renewing his goods. And he had penetrated still further into the heart of woman, and had just planned the system of "returns", a masterpiece of Jesuitical seduction. "Take whatever you like, madame; you can return it if you find you don't like it." And the woman who hesitated, herein found a last excuse, the possibility of repairing an act of folly were it deemed too extravagant: she took the article with an easy conscience. And now the returns and reduction of prices system formed part of the everyday working of the new style of business.

But where Mouret revealed himself as an unrivalled master was in the interior arrangement of his shops. He laid it down as a law that not a corner of The Ladies' Paradise ought to remain deserted; he required a noise, a crowd, evidence of life everywhere; for life, said he, attracts life, increases and multiplies it. And this principle he applied in a variety of ways. In the first place, there ought always to be a crush at the entrance, so that the people in the street should mistake it for a riot; and he obtained this crush by placing a lot of bargains at the doors, shelves and baskets overflowing with low-priced articles; and so the common people crowded there, stopping up the doorway and making the shop look as if it were crammed with customers, when it was often only half full. Then, in the galleries, he found a means of concealing the departments where business occasionally became slack; for instance, he surrounded the shawl department in summer, and the printed calico department in winter, with other busy departments, steeping them in continual uproar. It was he alone who had thought of reserving the second-floor for the carpet and furniture galleries; for customers were less numerous in such departments which if placed on the ground floor would have often presented a chilly void. If he could only have managed it, he would have let the street run through his shop.

ÉMILE ZOLA

Just at that moment, Mouret was absorbed in another wonderful inspiration. On the Saturday evening, whilst giving a last look at the preparations for the Monday's great sale, he had been struck with the idea that the arrangement of the departments adopted by him was idiotic; and yet it seemed a perfectly logical one: the stuffs on one side, the made-up articles on the other, an intelligent order of things which would enable customers to find their way about by themselves. He had dreamt of some such orderly arrangement in the old days of Madame Hédouin's narrow shop; but now, just as he had carried out his idea, he felt his faith shaken. And he suddenly cried out that they would "have to alter all that." They had forty-eight hours before them, and half of what had been done had to be changed. The staff, utterly bewildered, had been obliged to work two nights and all day on Sunday, amidst frightful disorder. On the Monday morning even, an hour before the opening, there were still some goods remaining to be placed. Decidedly the governor was going mad, no one understood the meaning of it all, and general consternation prevailed.

"Come, look sharp!" cried Mouret, with the quiet assurance of genius. "There are some more costumes to be taken upstairs. And the Japan goods, are they placed on the central landing? A last effort, my boys, you'll see the sale by-and-by."

Bourdoncle had also been there since daybreak. He did not understand the alterations any more than the others did and followed the governor's movements with an anxious eye. He hardly dared to ask him any questions, knowing how Mouret received people in these critical moments. However, he at last made up his mind, and gently inquired: "Was it really necessary to upset everything like that, on the eve of our sale?"

At first Mouret shrugged his shoulders without replying. Then as the other persisted, he burst out: "So that all the customers should heap themselves into one corner—eh? A nice idea of mine! I should never have got over it! Don't you see that it would have localised the crowd. A woman would have come in, gone straight to the department she wanted, passed from the petticoat to the dress counter, from the dress to the mantle gallery, and then have retired, without even losing herself for a moment! Not one would have thoroughly seen the establishment!"

"But, now that you have disarranged everything, and thrown the goods all over the place," remarked Bourdoncle, "the employees will wear out their legs in guiding the customers from department to department."

Mouret made a gesture of superb contempt. "I don't care a fig for that! They're young, it'll make them grow! So much the better if they do walk about! They'll appear more numerous, and increase the crowd. The greater the crush the better; all will go well!" He laughed, and then deigned to explain his idea, lowering his voice: "Look here, Bourdoncle, this is what the result will be. First, this continual circulation of customers will disperse them all over the shop, multiply them, and make them lose their heads; secondly, as they must be conducted from one end of the establishment to the other, if, for instance, they require a lining after purchasing a dress, these journeys in every direction will triple the size of the house in their eyes; thirdly, they will be forced to traverse departments where they would never have set foot otherwise, temptations will present themselves on their passage, and they will succumb; fourthly—" But Bourdoncle was now laughing with him. At this Mouret, delighted, stopped to call out to the messengers: "Very good, my boys! now for a sweep, and it'll be splendid!"

However, on turning round he perceived Denise. He and Bourdoncle were standing opposite the ready-made departments, which he had just dismembered by sending the dresses and costumes up to the second-floor at the other end of the building. Denise, the first down, was opening her eyes with astonishment, quite bewildered by the new arrangements.

"What is it?" she murmured; "are we going to move?"

This surprise appeared to amuse Mouret, who adored these sensational effects. Early in February Denise had returned to The Ladies' Paradise, where she had been agreeably surprised to find the staff polite, almost respectful. Madame Aurélie especially proved very kind; Marguerite and Clara seemed resigned; whilst old Jouve bowed his head, with an awkward, embarrassed air, as if desirous of effacing all disagreeable memories of the past. It had sufficed for Mouret to say a few words and everybody was whispering and following her with their eyes. And in this general amiability, the only things that hurt her were Deloche's singularly melancholy glances and Pauline's inexplicable smiles.

However, Mouret was still looking at her in his delighted way.

"What is it you want, mademoiselle?" he asked at last.

Denise had not noticed him. She blushed slightly. Since her return she had received various marks of kindness from him which had greatly touched her. On the other hand Pauline—she knew not why—had given her a full account of the governor's and Clara's love affairs; and often returned to the subject, alluding at the same time to that Madame

Desforges, with whom the whole shop was well acquainted. Such stories stirred Denise's heart; and now, in Mouret's presence, she again felt all her former fears, an uneasiness in which her gratitude struggled against her anger.

"It's all this confusion going on in the place," she murmured.

Thereupon Mouret approached her and said in a lower voice: "Have the goodness to come to my office this evening after business. I wish to speak to you."

Greatly agitated, she bowed her head without replying a word; and went into the department where the other saleswomen were now arriving. Bourdoncle, however, had overheard Mouret, and looked at him with a smile. He even ventured to say when they were alone: "That girl again! Be careful; it will end by becoming serious!"

But Mouret hastily defended himself, concealing his emotion beneath an air of superior indifference. "Never fear, it's only a joke! The woman who'll catch me isn't born, my dear fellow!"

And then, as the shop was opening at last, he rushed off to give a final look at the various departments. Bourdoncle shook his head. That girl Denise, so simple and quiet, began to make him feel uneasy. The first time, he had conquered by a brutal dismissal. But she had returned, and he felt her power to be so much increased that he now treated her as a redoubtable adversary, remaining mute before her and again patiently waiting developments. When he overtook Mouret, he found him downstairs, in the Saint-Augustin Hall, opposite the entrance door, where he was shouting:

"Are you playing the fool with me? I ordered the blue parasols to be put as a border. Just pull all that down, and be quick about it!"

He would listen to nothing; a gang of messengers had to come and re-arrange the exhibition of parasols. Then seeing that customers were arriving, he even had the doors closed for a moment, declaring that he would rather keep the place shut than have the blue parasols in the centre. It ruined his composition. The renowned dressers of the Paradise, Hutin, Mignot, and others, came to look at the change he was carrying out, but they affected not to understand it, theirs being a different school.

At last the doors were again opened, and the crowd flowed in. From the outset, long before the shop was full, there was such a crush at the doorway that they were obliged to call the police to regulate the traffic on the foot pavement. Mouret had calculated correctly; all the housewives, a compact troop of middle-class women and work women, swarmed around the bargains and remnants displayed in the open street. They felt the "hung" goods at the entrance; calico at seven sous the mètre, wool and cotton grey stuff at nine sous, and, above all, some Orleans at seven sous and a half, which was fast emptying the poorer purses. Then there was feverish jostling and crushing around the shelves and baskets where articles at reduced prices, lace at two sous, ribbon at five, garters at three the pair, gloves, petticoats, cravats, cotton socks, and stockings, were quickly disappearing, as if swallowed up by the voracious crowd. In spite of the cold, the shopmen who were selling in the street could not serve fast enough. One woman cried out with pain in the crush and two little girls were nearly stifled.

All the morning this crush went on increasing. Towards one o'clock there was a crowd waiting to enter; the street was blocked as in a time of riot. Just at that moment, as Madame de Boves and her daughter Blanche stood hesitating on the pavement opposite, they were accosted by Madame Marty, also accompanied by her daughter Valentine.

"What a crowd—eh?" said the countess. "They're killing themselves inside. I ought not to have come, I was in bed, but got up to take a little fresh air."

"It's just like me," said the other. "I promised my husband to go and see his sister at Montmartre. Then just as I was passing, I thought of a piece of braid I wanted. I may as well buy it here as anywhere else, mayn't I? Oh, I shan't spend another sou! in fact I don't want anything."

However, seized, carried away as it were, by the force of the crowd, they did not take their eyes off the door.

"No, no, I'm not going in, I'm afraid," murmured Madame de Boves. "Blanche, let's go away, we should be crushed."

But her voice failed her, she was gradually yielding to a desire to follow the others; and her fears dissolved before the irresistible attractions of the crush. Madame Marty likewise was giving way, repeating the while: "Keep hold of my dress, Valentine. Ah, well! I've never seen such a thing before. I'm lifted off my feet. What will it be inside?"

Caught by the current the ladies could not now go back. Just as rivers attract the fugitive waters of a valley, so it seemed as if the stream of customers, flowing into the vestibule, was absorbing the passers-by, drinking in people from the four corners of Paris. They advanced but slowly, squeezed almost to death, and maintained upright by the shoulders around them; and their desires already derived enjoyment from this painful entrance which heightened their curiosity. It was a medley of ladies arrayed in silk, of poorly dressed middle-class women, and of bare-headed girls, all excited and carried away by the same passion. A few men, buried beneath the overflowing bosoms, were casting anxious glances around them. A nurse, in the thickest of the crowd, held her baby above her head, the youngster crowing with delight. The only one to get angry was a skinny woman who broke out into bad words, accusing her neighbour of digging right into her.

"I really think I shall lose my skirts in this crowd," remarked Madame de Boves.

Mute, her face still cool from the open air, Madame Marty was standing on tip-toe in her endeavour to catch a glimpse of the depths of the shop before the others. The pupils of her grey eyes were as contracted as those of a cat coming out of the broad daylight, and she had the restful feeling, and clear expression of a person just waking up.

"Ah, at last!" said she, heaving a sigh.

The ladies had just extricated themselves. They were in the Saint-Augustin Hall, which they were greatly surprised to find almost empty. But a feeling of comfort penetrated them, they seemed to be entering into spring after emerging from the winter of the street. Whilst the piercing wind, laden with rain and hail, was still blowing out of doors, the fine season was already budding forth in The Paradise galleries, with the light stuffs, soft flowery shades and rural gaiety of summer dresses and parasols.

"Do look there!" exclaimed Madame de Boves, standing motionless, her eyes in the air.

It was the exhibition of parasols. Wide-open and rounded like shields, they covered the whole hall, from the glazed roofing to the varnished oak mouldings below. They described festoons round the arches of the upper storeys; they descended in garlands down the slender columns; they ran in close lines along the balustrades of the galleries and the staircases; and everywhere ranged symmetrically, speckling the walls with red, green, and yellow, they looked like huge Venetian lanterns, lighted up for some colossal entertainment. In the corners were more complicated designs, stars composed of parasols at thirty-nine sous whose light shades, pale blue, cream-white, and blush rose, had the subdued glow of night-lights; whilst, up above, immense Japanese parasols, on which golden-coloured cranes soared in purple skies, blazed forth with fiery reflections.

Madame Marty endeavouring to find a phrase to express her rapture, exclaimed: "It's like fairyland!" And then trying to find out where she was she continued: "Let's see, the braid is in the mercery department. I shall buy my braid and be off."

"I will go with you," said Madame de Boves. "Eh? Blanche, we'll just go through the shop, nothing more."

But they had hardly left the door before they lost themselves. They turned to the left, and as the mercery department had been moved, they dropped into the one devoted to collarettes, cuffs, trimmings, etc. A hot-house heat, moist and close, laden with the insipid odour of the materials, and muffling the tramping of the crowd, prevailed in the galleries. Then they returned to the door, where an outward current was already established, an interminable *défilé* of women and children, above whom hovered a multitude of red air-balls. Forty thousand of these were ready; there were men specially placed for their distribution; and to see the customers on their way out, one might have imagined that a flight of enormous soap-bubbles, reflecting the fiery glare of the parasols, was hovering in the air. The whole place was illuminated by them.

"There's quite a world here!" declared Madame de Boves. "You hardly know where you are."

However, the ladies could not remain in the eddy of the door, right in the crush of the entrance and exit. Fortunately, inspector Jouve came to their assistance. He stood in the vestibule, grave and attentive, eyeing each woman as she passed. Specially charged with the indoor police service he was on the look-out for thieves and "lifters."

"The mercery department, ladies?" said he obligingly, "turn to the left; you see! just there behind the hosiery department."

Madame de Boves thanked him. But Madame Marty, on turning round, no longer saw her daughter Valentine beside her. She was beginning to feel frightened, when she caught sight of her, already a long way off, at the end of the Saint-Augustin Hall, deeply absorbed before a table covered with a heap of women's cravats at nineteen sous. Mouret practised the system of offering articles to the customers, hooking and plundering them as they passed; for he made use of every sort of advertisement, laughing at the discretion of certain fellow-tradesmen who thought their goods should be left to speak for themselves. Special salesmen, idle and smooth-tongued Parisians, in this way got rid of considerable quantities of small trashy things.

"Oh, mamma!" murmured Valentine, "just look at these cravats. They have a bird embroidered at one corner."

The shopman cracked up the article, swore that it was all silk, that the manufacturer had become bankrupt, and that they would never have such a bargain again.

"Nineteen sous—is it possible?" said Madame Marty, tempted like her daughter. "Well! I can take a couple, that won't ruin us."

Madame de Boves, however, disdained this style of thing; she detested to have things offered to her. A shopman calling her made her run away. Madame Marty, surprised, could not understand such nervous horror of commercial quackery, for she was of another nature; she was one of those women who delight in being thus caressed by a public offer, in plunging their hands into everything, and wasting their time in useless talk.

"Now," said she, "I'm going for my braid. I don't wish to see anything else."

However, as she crossed the scarf and glove departments, her heart once more failed her. Here in the diffuse light was a display made up of bright gay colours, of ravishing effect. The counters, symmetrically arranged, seemed like so many flower-borders, changing the hall into a French garden, where smiled a soft scale of blossoms. Lying now on the bare wood, now in open boxes, and now protruding from overflowing drawers was a quantity of silk handkerchiefs of every hue. You found the bright scarlet of the geranium, the creamy white of the petunia, the golden yellow of the chrysanthemum, the celestial azure of the verbena; and higher up, on brass rods, another florescence was entwined, a florescence of carelessly hung *fichus* and unrolled ribbons, quite a brilliant *cordon*, which extended on and on, climbing the columns and constantly multiplying in the mirrors. But what most attracted the throng was a Swiss chalet in the glove department, a chalet made entirely of gloves, Mignot's *chef d'œuvre* which it had taken him two days to arrange. In the first place, the ground-floor was composed of black gloves; and then in turn came straw-coloured, mignonette, and tan-coloured gloves, distributed over the decoration, bordering the windows, outlining the balconies, and taking the place of the tiles.

"What do you desire, madame?" asked Mignot, on seeing Madame Marty planted before the cottage. "Here are some Suède gloves at one franc seventy-five centimes the pair, first quality."

He offered his wares with furious energy, calling the passing customers to his counter and dunning them with his politeness. And as she shook her head in token of refusal he continued: "Tyrolian gloves, one franc twenty-five. Turin gloves for children, embroidered gloves in all colours."

"No, thanks; I don't want anything," declared Madame Marty.

But realising that her voice was softening, he attacked her with greater energy than ever, holding the embroidered gloves before her eyes; and she could not resist, she bought a pair. Then, as Madame de Boves looked at her with a smile, she blushed.

"Don't you think me childish—eh? If I don't make haste and get my braid and be off, I shall be done for."

Unfortunately, there was such a crush in the mercery department that she could not get served. They had both been waiting for over ten minutes, and were getting annoyed, when a sudden meeting with Madame Bourdelais and her three children diverted their attention. Madame Bourdelais explained, with her quiet practical air, that she had brought the little ones to see the show. Madeleine was ten, Edmond eight, and Lucien four years old; and they were laughing with joy, it was a cheap treat which they had long looked forward to.

"Those red parasols are really too comical; I must buy one," said Madame Marty all at once, stamping with impatience at doing nothing.

She choose one at fourteen francs and a half; whereupon Madame Bourdelais, after watching the purchase with a look of censure, said to her amicably: "You are wrong to be in such a hurry. In a month's time you could have had it for ten francs. They won't catch me like that."

And thereupon she developed quite a theory of careful housekeeping. Since the shops lowered their prices, it was simply a question of waiting. She did not wish to be taken in by them, she preferred to profit by their real bargains. She even showed some malice in the struggle, boasting that she had never left them a sou of profit.

"Come," said she at last, "I've promised my little ones to show them the pictures upstairs in the reading-room. Come up with us, you have plenty of time."

And thereupon the braid was forgotten. Madame Marty yielded at once, whilst Madame de Boves declined, preferring to take a turn on the ground-floor first of all. Besides, they were sure to meet again upstairs. Madame Bourdelais was looking for a staircase when she perceived one of the lifts; and thereupon she pushed her children into it, in order to cap their pleasure. Madame Marty and Valentine also entered the narrow cage, where they were very closely packed; however the mirrors, the velvet seats, and the polished brasswork took up so much of their attention that they reached the first floor without having felt the gentle ascent of the machine. Another pleasure was in store for them, in the first gallery. As they passed before the refreshment bar, Madame Bourdelais did not fail to gorge her little family with syrup. It was a square room with a large marble counter; at either end there were silvered filters from which trickled small streams of water; whilst rows of bottles stood on small shelves behind. Three waiters were continually engaged in wiping and filling the glasses. To restrain the thirsty crowd, they had been obliged to imitate the practice followed at theatres and railway-stations, by erecting a barrier draped with velvet. The crush was terrific. Some people, whom these gratuitous treats rendered altogether unscrupulous, really made themselves ill.

"Well! where are they?" exclaimed Madame Bourdelais, when she extricated herself from the crowd, after wiping the children's faces with her handkerchief.

But she caught sight of Madame Marty and Valentine at the further end of another gallery, a long way off. Buried beneath a heap of petticoats, they were still buying. There was no more restraint, mother and daughter vanished in the fever of expenditure which was carrying them away. When Madame Bourdelais at last reached the reading-room she installed Madeleine, Edmond, and Lucien before the large table; and taking some photographic albums from one of the book-cases she brought them to them. The ceiling of the long apartment was covered with gilding; at either end was a monumental chimney-piece; some pictures of no great merit but very richly framed, covered the walls; and between the columns, before each of the arched bays opening into the shop, were tall green plants in majolica vases. A silent throng surrounded the table, which was littered with reviews and newspapers, with here and there some ink-stands, boxes of stationery, and blotting-pads. Ladies took off their gloves, and wrote letters on the paper stamped with the name of the establishment, through which they ran their pens. A few gentlemen, lolling back in armchairs, were reading the newspapers. But a great many people sat there doing nothing: these were husbands waiting for their wives, who were roaming through the various departments, young women on the watch for their lovers, and old relations left there as in a cloak-room, to be taken away when it was time to leave. And all these people lounged and rested whilst glancing through the open bays into the depths of the galleries and the halls, whence a distant murmur ascended amidst the scratching of pens and the rustling of newspapers.

"What! you here!" said Madame Bourdelais all at once. "I didn't recognise you."

Near the children sat a lady, her face hidden by the open pages of a review. It was Madame Guibal. She seemed annoyed at the meeting; but quickly recovering herself, related that she had come to sit down for a moment in order to escape the crush. And as Madame Bourdelais asked her if she was going to make any purchases, she replied with her languorous air, veiling the egoistical greediness of her glance with her eyelids:

"Oh! no. On the contrary, I have come to return some goods. Yes, some door-curtains which I don't like. But there is such a crowd that I am waiting to get near the department."

Then she went on talking, saying how convenient this system of returns was; formerly she had never bought anything, but now she sometimes allowed herself to be tempted. In fact, she returned four articles out of every five, and was getting known at all the counters for the strange trafficking she carried on—a trafficking easily divined by the perpetual discontent which made her bring back her purchases one by one, after she had kept them several days. However, whilst speaking, she did not take her eyes off the doors of the reading-room; and she appeared greatly relieved when Madame Bourdelais rejoined her children, to explain the photographs to them. Almost at the same moment Monsieur de Boves and Paul de Vallagnosc came in. The count, who affected to be showing the young man through the new buildings, exchanged a quick glance with Madame Guibal; and she then plunged into her review again, as if she had not seen him.

"Hallo, Paul!" suddenly exclaimed a voice behind the two gentlemen.

It was Mouret taking a glance round the various departments. They shook hands, and he at once inquired:

"Has Madame de Boves done us the honour of coming?"

"Well, no," replied the husband, "and she very much regrets it. She's not very well. Oh! nothing dangerous, however!"

But he suddenly pretended to catch sight of Madame Guibal, and hastened off, approaching her bareheaded, whilst the others merely bowed to her from a distance. She also pretended to be surprised. Paul smiled; he now understood the affair, and he related to Mouret in a low voice how Boves, whom he had met in the Rue de Richelieu, had tried to get away from him, and had finished by dragging him into The Ladies' Paradise, under the pretext that he must show him the new buildings. For the last year the lady had drawn all the money she could from Boves, making constant appointments with him in public places, churches, museums, and shops.

"Just look at him," added the young man, "isn't he splendid, standing there before her with his dignified air? It's the old French gallantry, my dear fellow, the old French gallantry!"

"And your marriage?" asked Mouret.

Paul, without taking his eyes off the count, replied that they were still waiting for the death of the aunt. Then, with a triumphant air, he added: "There, did you see him? He stooped down, and slipped an address into her hand. She's now accepting the rendezvous with the most virtuous air. She's a terrible woman is that delicate red-haired creature with her careless ways. Well! some fine things go on in your place!"

"Oh!" replied Mouret, smiling, "these ladies are not in my house, they are at home here."

Then, still continuing his gossip, he carried his old comrade along to the threshold of the reading-room, opposite the grand central gallery, whose successive halls spread out below them. In the rear, the reading-room still retained its quietude, only disturbed by the scratching of pens and the rustling of newspapers. One old gentleman had gone to sleep over the *Moniteur*. Monsieur de Boves was looking at the pictures, with the evident intention of losing his future son-in-law in the crowd as soon as possible. And, alone, amid this calmness, Madame Bourdelais was amusing her children, talking very loudly, as in a conquered place.

"You see, they are quite at home," said Mouret, who pointed with a broad gesture to the multitude of women with which the departments were overflowing.

Just then Madame Desforges, after nearly having her mantle carried away in the crowd, at last effected an entrance and crossed the first hall. Then, on reaching the principal gallery, she raised her eyes. It was like a railway span, surrounded by the balustrades of the two storeys, intersected by hanging stairways and crossed by flying bridges. The iron staircases developed bold curves, which multiplied the landings; the bridges suspended in space, ran straight along at a great height; and in the white light from the windows all this iron work formed an excessively delicate architecture, an intricate lace-work through which the daylight penetrated, the modern realization of a dreamland palace, of a Babel with storeys piled one above the other, and spacious halls affording glimpses of other floors and other halls *ad infinitum*. In fact, iron reigned everywhere: the young architect had been honest and courageous enough not to disguise it under a coating of paint imitating stone or wood. Down below, in order not to outshine the goods, the decoration was sober, with large regular spaces in neutral tints; then as the metallic work ascended, the capitals of the columns became richer, the rivets formed ornaments, the shoulder-pieces and corbels were covered with sculptured work; and at last, up above, glistened painting, green and red, amidst a prodigality of gold, floods of gold, heaps of gold, even to the glazed-work, whose panes were enamelled and inlaid with gold. In the galleries, the bare brick-work of the arches was also decorated in bright colours. Mosaics and faience likewise formed part of the decoration, enlivening the friezes, and lighting up the severe *ensemble* with their fresh tints; whilst the stairs, with red-velvet covered hand-rails, were edged with bands of polished iron, which shone like the steel of armour.

Although Madame Desforges was already acquainted with the new establishment, she stopped short, struck by the ardent life which that day animated the immense nave. Below and around her continued the eddying of the crowd; the double current of those entering and those leaving, making itself felt as far as the silk department. It was still a crowd of very mixed elements, though the afternoon was bringing a greater number of ladies amongst the shopkeepers and house-wives. There were many women in mourning, with flowing veils; and there were always some wet nurses straying about and protecting their infantile charges with their outstretched arms. And this sea of faces, of many-coloured hats and bare heads, both dark and fair, rolled from one to the other end of the galleries, vague and discoloured amidst the glare of the stuffs. On all sides Madame Desforges saw large price-tickets bearing enormous figures and showing prominently against the bright printed cottons, the shining silks, and the sombre woollens. Piles of ribbons half hid the heads of the customers, a wall of flannel threw out a promontory; on all sides mirrors multiplied the departments, reflecting the displays and the groups of people, now showing faces reversed, and now halves of shoulders and arms; whilst to the right and to the left the lateral galleries opened up other vistas, the snowy depths of the linen department and the speckled depths of the hosiery counters—distant views which were illumined by rays of light from some glazed bay, and in which the crowd seemed but so much human dust. Then, when Madame Desforges raised her eyes, she beheld on the staircases and the flying bridges and behind the balustrades of each successive storey, a continual buzzing ascent, an entire population in the air, passing along behind the open work of this huge carcass of metal and showing blackly against the diffuse light from the enamelled glass. Large gilded lustres were suspended from the ceiling; decorations of rugs, embroidered silks and stuffs worked with gold, hung down, draping the balustrades as with gorgeous banners; and, from one to the other end were clouds of lace, palpitations of muslin, trophies of silks, fairy-like groups of half-dressed dummies; and right at the top, above all the confusion, the bedding department, hanging, as it were, in the air, displayed its little iron bedsteads provided with mattresses, and hung with curtains, the whole forming a sort of school dormitory asleep amidst the tramping of the customers, who became fewer and fewer as the departments ascended.

"Does madame require a cheap pair of garters?" asked a salesman of Madame Desforges on seeing her standing still. "All silk, at twenty-nine sous."

She did not condescend to answer. Things were being offered around her more feverishly than ever. She wanted, however, to find out where she was. Albert Lhomme's pay-desk was on her left; he knew her by sight and ventured to give her an amiable smile, not showing the least hurry amidst the heaps of bills by which he was besieged; though behind him, Joseph, struggling with the string-box, could not pack up the articles fast enough. She then saw where she was; the silk department must be in front of her. But it took her ten minutes to reach it, so dense was the crowd becoming. Up in the air, at the end of their invisible strings, the red air-balls had become more numerous than ever; they now formed clouds of purple, gently blowing towards the doors whence they continued scattering over Paris; and she had to bow her head beneath their flight whenever very young children held them with the string rolled round their little fingers.

"What! you have ventured here, madame?" exclaimed Bouthemont gaily, as soon as he caught sight of Madame Desforges.

The manager of the silk department, introduced to her by Mouret himself, now occasionally called on her at her five o'clock tea. She thought him common, but very amiable, of a fine sanguine temper, which surprised and amused her. Moreover some two days previously he had boldly told her of the intrigue between Mouret and Clara, He had not done this with any calculating motive but out of sheer stupidity, like a fellow who loves a joke. She, however, stung with jealousy, concealing her wounded feelings beneath an appearance of disdain, had that afternoon come to try and discover her rival, a young lady in the mantle department, so Bouthemont had told her, though declining to give the name.

"Do you require anything to-day?" he inquired.

"Of course, or I should not have come. Have you any *foulard* for morning gowns?"

She hoped to obtain the name of the young lady from him, for she was full of a desire to see her. He immediately called Favier; and then went on chatting whilst waiting for the salesman, who was just serving another customer. This happened to be "the pretty lady," that beautiful blonde of whom the whole department occasionally spoke, without knowing anything of her life or even her name. This time the pretty lady was in deep mourning. Whom could she have lost—her husband or her father? Not her father, for she would have appeared more melancholy. What had they all been saying then? She could not be a questionable character; she must have had a real husband—that is unless she were in mourning for her mother. For a few minutes, despite the press of business, the department exchanged these various speculations.

"Make haste! it's intolerable!" cried Hutin to Favier, when he returned from showing his customer to the pay-desk. "Whenever that lady is here you never seem to finish. She doesn't care a fig for you!"

"She cares a deuced sight more for me than I do for her!" replied the vexed salesman.

But Hutin threatened to report him to the directors if he did not show more respect for the customers. The second-hand was becoming terrible, of a morose severity ever since the department had conspired to get him Robineau's place. He even showed himself so intolerable, after all the promises of good-fellowship, with which he had formerly warmed his colleagues' zeal, that the latter were now secretly supporting Favier against him.

"Now, then, no back answers," replied Hutin sharply. "Monsieur Bouthemont wishes you to show some *foulards* of the lightest patterns."

In the middle of the department, an exhibition of summer silks illumined the hall with an aurora-like brilliancy, like the rising of a planet amidst the most delicate tints: pale rose, soft yellow, limpid blue, indeed the whole scarf of Iris. There were *foulards* of a cloudy fineness, surahs lighter than the down falling from trees, satined pekins as soft and supple as a Chinese beauty's skin. Then came Japanese pongees, Indian tussores and corahs, without counting the light French silks, the narrow stripes, the small checks and the flowered patterns, all the most fanciful designs, which made one think of ladies in furbelows, strolling in the sweet May mornings, under the spreading trees of some park.

"I'll take this, the Louis XIV, with figured roses," said Madame Desforges at last.

And whilst Favier was measuring it, she made a last attempt with Bouthemont, who had remained near her.

"I'm going up to the ready-made department to see if they have any travelling cloaks. Is she fair, the young lady you were talking about?"

The manager, who felt rather anxious on finding her so persistent, merely smiled. But, just at that moment, Denise passed by. She had just come from the merinoes which were in the charge of Liénard to whom she had escorted Madame Boutarel, that provincial lady who came to Paris twice a year, to scatter the money she saved out of her housekeeping all over the Ladies' Paradise. And thereupon, just as Favier was about to take up Madame Desforges's silk, Hutin, thinking to annoy him, interfered.

"It's quite unnecessary, Mademoiselle will have the kindness to conduct this lady."

Denise, quite confused, at once took charge of the parcel and the debit-note. She could never meet this young man face to face without experiencing a feeling of shame, as if he reminded her of some former fault; and yet she had only sinned in her dreams.

"But just tell me," said Madame Desforges, in a low tone, to Bouthemont, "isn't it this awkward girl? He has taken her back, I see? It must be she who is the heroine of the adventure!"

"Perhaps," replied the silk manager, still smiling, but fully decided not to tell the truth.

Madame Desforges then slowly ascended the staircase, preceded by Denise; but after every two or three steps she had to pause in order to avoid being carried away by the descending crowd. In the living vibration of the whole building, the iron supports seemed to sway under your feet as if quivering beneath the breath of the multitude. On each stair was a strongly fixed dummy, displaying some garment or other: a costume, cloak, or dressing-gown; and the whole was like a double row of soldiers at attention whilst some triumphal procession went past.

Madame Desforges was at last reaching the first storey, when a still greater surging of the crowd forced her to stop once more. Beneath her she now had the departments on the ground-floor, with the press of customers through which she had just passed. This was a new spectacle, a sea of fore-shortened heads, swarming with agitation like an ant-hill. The white price-tickets now seemed but so many narrow lines, the piles of ribbon became quite squat, the promontory of flannel was but a thin partition barring the gallery; whilst the carpets and the embroidered silks which decked the balustrades hung down like processional banners suspended from the gallery of a church. In the distance Madame Desforges could perceive some corners of the lateral galleries, just as from the top of a steeple one perceives the corners of neighbouring streets, with black specks of passers-by moving about. But what surprised her above all, in the weariness of her eyes blinded by the brilliant medley of colours, was, on lowering their lids, to realize the presence of the crowd more keenly than ever, by its dull roar like that of the rising tide, and the human warmth that it exhaled. A fine dust rose from the floor, laden with *odore di femina*, a penetrating perfume, which seemed like the incense of this temple raised for the worship of woman.

Meanwhile Mouret, still standing before the reading-room with Vallagnosc, was inhaling this odour, intoxicating himself with it, and repeating: "They are quite at home. I know some who spend the whole day here, eating cakes and writing letters. There's only one thing left me to do, and that is, to find them beds."

This joke made Paul smile, he who, in his pessimistic boredom considered the turbulence of this multitude running after a lot of gew-gaws to be idiotic. Whenever he came to give his old comrade a look-up, he went away almost vexed to find him so full of life amidst his people of coquettes. Would not one of them, with shallow brain and empty heart, some day make him realize the stupidity and uselessness of life? That very day Octave seemed to have lost some of his equilibrium; he who generally inspired his customers with a fever, with the tranquil grace of an operator, was as though caught by the passion which was gradually consuming the whole establishment. Since he had caught sight of Denise and Madame Desforges coming up the grand staircase, he had been talking louder, gesticulating against his will; and though he affected not to turn his face towards them, he grew more and more animated as he felt them drawing nearer. His face became flushed and in his eyes was a little of that bewildered rapture with which the eyes of his customers at last quivered.

"You must be fearfully robbed," murmured Vallagnosc, who thought that the crowd looked very criminal.

Mouret threw his arms out. "My dear fellow, it's beyond all imagination," said he.

And, nervously, delighted at having something to talk about, he gave a number of details, related cases, and classified the delinquents. In the first place, there were the professional thieves; these women did the least harm of all, for the police knew every one of them. Then came the kleptomaniacs, who stole from a perverse desire, a new form of nervous affection which a doctor had classed, showing it to be the result of the temptations of the big shops. And finally came the women who were *enceintes* and whose thefts were invariably thefts of some especially coveted article. For instance, at the house of one of them, the district commissary of police had found two hundred and forty-eight pairs of pink gloves stolen from well nigh every shop in Paris.

"That's what gives the women such funny eyes here, then," murmured Vallagnosc, "I've been watching them with their greedy, shameful looks, like mad creatures. A fine school for honesty!"

"Hang it!" replied Mouret, "though we make them quite at home, we can't let them take the goods away under their mantles. And sometimes they are very respectable people. Last week we caught the sister of a chemist, and the wife of a judge. Yes, the wife of a judge! However, we always try to settle these matters."

He paused to point out Jouve, who was just then looking sharply after a woman at the ribbon counter below. This woman, who appeared to be suffering a great deal from the jostling of the crowd, was accompanied by a friend, whose mission seemed to be to protect her against all hurt, and each time she stopped in a department, Jouve kept his eyes on her, whilst her friend near by ransacked the card-board boxes at her ease.

"Oh! he'll catch her!" resumed Mouret; "he knows all their tricks."

But his voice trembled and he laughed in an awkward manner. Denise and Henriette, whom he had ceased to watch, were at last passing behind him, after having had a great deal of trouble to get out of the crush. He turned round suddenly, and bowed to his customer with the discreet air of a friend who does not desire to compromise a woman by stopping her in a crowd of people. But Henriette, on the alert, had at once perceived the look with which he had first enveloped Denise. It must be this girl—thought she—yes, this was the rival she had been curious to come and see.

In the mantle department, the young ladies were fast losing their heads. Two of them had fallen ill, and Madame Frédéric, the second-hand, had quietly given notice the previous day, and repaired to the cashier's office to take her money, leaving The Ladies' Paradise at a minute's notice, just as The Ladies' Paradise itself discharged its employees. Ever since the morning, in spite of the feverish rush of business, every one had been talking of this affair. Clara, still kept in the department by Mouret's caprice, thought it grand. Marguerite related how exasperated Bourdoncle was; whilst Madame Aurélie, greatly vexed, declared that Madame Frédéric ought at least to have informed her, for such hypocrisy had never before been heard of.

Although Madame Frédéric had never confided in any one, she was suspected of having relinquished her position to marry the proprietor of some baths in the neighbourhood of the Halles.

"It's a travelling cloak that madame desires, I believe?" inquired Denise of Madame Desforges, after offering her a chair.

"Yes," curtly replied the latter, who had made up her mind to be impolite.

The new decorations of the department were of a rich severity: on all sides were high carved oak cupboards with mirrors filling the whole space of their panels, while a red carpet muffled the continued tramping of the customers. Whilst Denise went off to fetch the cloaks, Madame Desforges, who was looking round, perceived her face in a glass; and she continued contemplating herself. Was she getting old then that she should be cast aside for the first-comer? The glass reflected the entire department with all its commotion, but she only beheld her own pale face; she did not hear Clara behind her, relating to Marguerite a story of Madame Frédéric's mysterious goings-on, the manner in which she went out of her way night and morning so as to pass through the Passage Choiseul, and thus make people believe that she lived over the water.

"Here are our latest designs," said Denise. "We have them in several colours."

She laid out four or five cloaks. Madame Desforges looked at them with a scornful air, and became harsher at each fresh one that she examined. What was the reason of those pleats which made the garment look so scanty? And that other one, square across the shoulders, why, you might have thought it had been cut out with a hatchet! Though people went travelling they could not dress like sentry-boxes!

"Show me something else, mademoiselle."

Denise unfolded and refolded the garments without the slightest sign of ill temper. And it was just this calm, serene patience which exasperated Madame Desforges the more. Her glances continually returned to the glass in front of her. Now that she saw herself there, close to Denise she ventured on a comparison. Was it possible that he should prefer that insignificant creature to herself? She now remembered that this was the girl whom she had formerly seen cutting such a silly figure at the time of her début—as clumsy as any peasant wench freshly arrived from her village. No doubt she looked better now, stiff and correct in her silk gown. But how puny, how common-place she was!

"I will show you some other patterns, madame," said Denise, quietly.

When she returned, the scene began again. Then it was the cloth that was too heavy or of no good whatever. And Madame Desforges turned round, raising her voice, and endeavouring to attract Madame Aurélie's attention, in the hope of getting the girl a scolding. But Denise, since her return, had gradually conquered the department, and now felt quite at home in it; the first-hand had even recognised that she possessed some rare and valuable qualities as a saleswoman—a stubborn sweetness, a smiling force of conviction. And thus when Madame Aurélie heard Madame Desforges she simply shrugged her shoulders, taking care not to interfere.

"Would you kindly tell me the kind of garment you require, madame?" asked Denise, once more, with her polite persistence, which nothing could discourage.

"But you've got nothing!" exclaimed Madame Desforges.

She stopped short, surprised to feel a hand laid on her shoulder. It was the hand of Madame Marty, who was being carried through the establishment by her fever for spending. Since the cravats, the embroidered gloves, and the red parasol, her purchases had increased to such an extent that the last salesman had just decided to place them all on a chair, as to have carried them on his arm, might have broken it; and he walked in front of her, drawing along the chair, upon which petticoats, napkins, curtains, a lamp, and three straw hats were heaped together.

"Ah!" said she, "you are buying a travelling cloak."

"Oh! dear, no," replied Madame Desforges; "they are frightful."

However Madame Marty had just noticed a striped cloak which she rather liked. Her daughter Valentine was already examining it. So Denise called Marguerite to clear the article out of the department, it being one of the previous year's patterns, and Marguerite, at a glance from her comrade, presented it as an exceptional bargain. When she had sworn that they had twice lowered the price, that they had reduced it from a hundred and fifty francs, to a hundred and thirty, and that it was now ticketed at a hundred and ten, Madame Marty could not withstand the temptation of its cheapness. She bought it, and the salesman who accompanied her thereupon went off, leaving the chair and the parcels behind him with all the debit-notes attached to the goods.

Whilst Marguerite was debiting the cloak, Madame Marty turned her head, and on catching sight of Clara made a slight sign to Madame Desforges, then whispered to her: "Monsieur Mouret's caprice, you know!"

The other, in surprise, looked round at Clara; and then, after again turning her eyes on Denise, replied: "But it isn't the tall one; it's the little one!"

And as Madame Marty could not be sure which of the two it was, Madame Desforges resumed aloud, with the scorn of a lady for chambermaids: "Perhaps both!"

Denise had heard everything, and raised her large, pure eyes on this lady who was thus wounding her, and whom she did not know. No doubt it was the lady of whom people had spoken to her, the lady with whom Mouret's name was so often associated. In the glances that were exchanged between them, Denise displayed such melancholy dignity, such frank innocence, that Henriette felt quite uncomfortable.

"As you have nothing presentable to show me here, conduct me to the dress and costume department," she said all at once.

"I'll go with you as well," exclaimed Madame Marty, "I wanted to see a costume for Valentine."

Marguerite thereupon took the chair by its back, and dragged it along on its hind legs, which were getting rather worn by this species of locomotion. Denise on her side only carried the few yards of silk, bought by Madame Desforges. They had, however, quite a journey before them now that the robes and costumes were installed on the second floor, at the other end of the establishment.

And the long walk commenced along the crowded galleries. Marguerite went in front, drawing the chair along, like some little vehicle, and slowly opening a passage. As soon as she reached the under-linen department, Madame Desforges began to complain: wasn't it ridiculous, a shop where you were obliged to walk a couple of leagues to find the least thing! Madame Marty also declared that she was tired to death, yet she none the less enjoyed this fatigue, this slow exhaustion of strength, amidst the inexhaustible wealth of merchandise displayed on every side. Mouret's idea, full of genius, had absolutely subjugated her and she paused in each fresh department. She made a first halt before the trousseaux, tempted by some chemises which Pauline sold her; and Marguerite then found herself relieved of the burden of the chair, which Pauline had to take, with the debit-notes. Madame Desforges might have gone on her way, and thus have liberated Denise more speedily, but she seemed happy to feel her behind her, motionless and patient, whilst she also lingered, advising her friend. In the baby-linen department the ladies went into ecstasies, but, of course, without buying anything. Then Madame Marty's weaknesses began anew; she succumbed successively before a black silk corset, a pair of fur cuffs, sold at a reduction on account of the lateness of the season, and some Russian lace much in vogue at that time for trimming table-linen. All these things were heaped up on the chair, the number of parcels still increased, making the chair creak; and the salesmen who succeeded one another, found it more and more difficult to drag the improvised vehicle along as its load became heavier and heavier.

"This way, madame," said Denise without a murmur, after each halt.

"But it's absurd!" exclaimed Madame Desforges. "We shall never get there. Why did they not put the dresses and costumes near the mantles department? It *is* a mess!"

Madame Marty, whose eyes were sparkling, intoxicated by the succession of riches dancing before her, repeated in an undertone: "Oh, dear! What will my husband say? You are right, there is no order in this place. A person loses herself and commits all sorts of follies."

On the great central landing there was scarcely room for the chair to pass, as Mouret had just blocked the open space with a lot of fancy goods—cups mounted on gilt zinc, flash dressing-cases and liqueur stands—being of opinion that the crowd there was not sufficiently great, and that circulation was too easy. And he had also authorized one of his shopmen to exhibit on a small table there some Chinese and Japanese curiosities, low-priced knick-knacks which customers eagerly snatched up. It was an unexpected success, and he already thought of extending this branch of his business. Whilst two messengers carried the chair up to the second floor, Madame Marty purchased six ivory studs, some silk mice, and a lacquered match-box.

On the second floor the journey began afresh. Denise, who had been showing customers about in this way ever since the morning, was sinking with fatigue; but she still continued correct, gentle, and polite. She again had to wait for the ladies in the furnishing materials department, where a delightful cretonne had caught Madame Marty's eye. Then, in the furniture department, a work-table took her fancy. Her hands trembled, and with a laugh she was entreating Madame Desforges to prevent her from spending any more money, when a meeting with Madame Guibal furnished her with an excuse to continue her purchases. The meeting took place in the carpet department, whither Madame Guibal had gone to return some Oriental door-curtains which she had purchased five days previously. And she was standing there, talking to the salesman, a brawny fellow with sinewy arms, who from morning to night carried loads heavy enough to break a bullock's back. Naturally he was in consternation at this "return," which deprived him of his commission, and so did his best to embarrass his customer, suspecting some queer adventure, no doubt a ball given with these curtains, bought at The Ladies' Paradise, and then returned, to avoid the cost of hire at an upholsterer's. He knew indeed that this was frequently done by the economical middle-class people. In short, she must have some reason for returning them; if she did not like the designs or the colours, he would show her others, he had a most complete assortment. To all these insinuations, however, Madame Guibal with queenly assurance replied quietly that the curtains did not suit her; and she did not deign to add any explanation. She refused to look at any others, and he was obliged to give way, for the salesmen had orders to take the goods back even if they saw that they had been used.

As the three ladies went off together, and Madame Marty referred remorsefully to the work-table for which she had no earthly need, Madame Guibal said in her calm voice: "Well! you can return it. You saw it was quite easy. Meantime let them send it to your house. You can put it in your drawing-room, keep it for a time and then if you don't like it, return it."

"Ah! that's a good idea!" exclaimed Madame Marty. "If my husband makes too much fuss, I'll send everything back." This was for her the supreme excuse, she ceased calculating and went on buying, with the secret wish, however, to keep everything, for she was not one of those women who give things back.

At last they arrived in the dress and costume department. But as Denise was about to deliver to another young lady the silk which Madame Desforges had purchased the latter seemed to change her mind, and declared that she would decidedly take one of the travelling cloaks, the light grey one with the hood; and Denise then had to wait complacently till she was ready to return to the mantle department. The girl felt that she was being treated like a servant by this imperious, whimsical customer; but she had vowed to do her duty, and retained her calm demeanour, notwithstanding the rising of her heart and rebellion of her pride. Madame Desforges bought nothing in the dress and costume department.

"Oh! mamma," said Valentine, "if that little costume should only fit me!"

In a low tone, Madame Guibal was explaining her tactics to Madame Marty. When she saw a dress she liked in a shop, she had it sent home, took a pattern of it, and then sent it back. And thereupon Madame Marty bought the costume for her daughter remarking: "A good idea! You are very practical, my dear madame."

They had been obliged to abandon the chair. It had been left in distress, in the furniture department, beside the work-table, for its weight had become too great, and its hind legs threatened to break off. So it was arranged that all the purchases should be centralized at one pay-desk, and thence sent down to the delivery department. And then the ladies, still accompanied by Denise, began roaming all over the establishment, making a second appearance in nearly every department. They were ever on the stairs and in the galleries; and at each moment some fresh meeting brought them to a standstill. Thus, near the reading-room, they once more came across Madame Bourdelais and her three children. The youngsters were loaded with parcels: Madeleine had a dress for herself under her arm, Edmond was carrying a collection of little shoes, whilst the youngest, Lucien, was wearing a new cap.

"You as well!" said Madame Desforges, laughingly, to her old school-friend.

"Pray, don't speak of it!" exclaimed Madame Bourdelais. "I'm furious. They get hold of us by the little ones now! You know how little I spend on myself! But how can you expect me to resist the entreaties of these children, who want everything? I merely came to show them round, and here am I plundering the whole establishment!"

Mouret, who still happened to be there, with Vallagnosc and Monsieur de Boves, listened to her with a smile. She observed it, and complained gaily, though with an undercurrent of real irritation, of these traps laid for a mother's affection; the idea that she had just yielded to the force of puffery raised her indignation, and he, still smiling, bowed, fully enjoying his triumph. Monsieur de Boves meanwhile had manœuvred so as to get near Madame Guibal, whom he ultimately followed, for the second time trying to lose Vallagnosc; but the latter, weary of the crush, hastened to rejoin him. And now once more Denise was brought to a standstill, obliged to wait for the ladies. She turned her back, and Mouret himself affected not to see her. But from that moment Madame Desforges, with the delicate scent of a jealous woman, had no further doubt. Whilst he was complimenting her and walking beside her, like a gallant host, she became deeply absorbed in thought, wondering how she could convict him of his treason.

Meanwhile Monsieur de Boves and Vallagnosc, who had gone on in front with Madame Guibal, reached the lace department, a luxurious room, surrounded by nests of carved oak drawers, which were constantly being opened and shut. Around the columns, covered with red velvet, spirals of white lace ascended; and from one to the other end of the department hung festoons of guipure, whilst on the counters were quantities of large cards, wound round with Valenciennes, Malines, and hand-made point. At the further end two ladies were seated before a mauve silk *transparent*, on which Deloche was placing some pieces of Chantilly, the ladies meantime looking on in silence and without making up their minds.

"Hallo!" said Vallagnosc, quite surprised, "you said that Madame de Boves was unwell. But she is standing over there, near that counter, with Mademoiselle Blanche."

The count could not help starting back, and casting a side glance at Madame Guibal. "Dear me! so she is," said he.

It was very warm in this room. The half stifled customers had pale faces with glittering eyes. It seemed as if all the seductions of the shop converged to this supreme temptation, this secluded corner of perdition where the strongest must succumb. Women plunged their hands into the overflowing heaps, quivering with intoxication at the contact.

"I fancy those ladies are ruining you," resumed Vallagnosc, amused by the meeting.

Monsieur de Boves assumed the look of a husband who is perfectly sure of his wife's discretion, from the simple fact that he does not give her a copper to spend. The countess, after wandering through all the departments with her daughter, without buying anything, had just stranded in the lace department in a rage of unsated desire. Overcome with fatigue, she was leaning against the counter while her clammy

ÉMILE ZOLA

hands dived into a heap of lace whence a warmth rose to her shoulders. Then suddenly, just as her daughter turned her head and the salesman went away, it occurred to her to slip a piece of point d'Alençon under her mantle. But she shuddered, and dropped it, on hearing Vallagnosc gaily saying: "Ah! we've caught you, madame."

For several seconds she stood there speechless and very pale. Then she explained that, feeling much better, she had thought she would take a stroll. And on noticing that her husband was with Madame Guibal, she quite recovered herself, and looked at them with such a dignified air that the other lady felt obliged to say: "I was with Madame Desforges, these gentlemen just met us."

As it happened the other ladies came up just at that moment, accompanied by Mouret who again detained them to point out Jouve, who was still following the suspicious woman and her lady friend. It was very curious, said he, they could not form an idea of the number of thieves arrested in the lace department. Madame de Boves, who was listening, fancied herself between a couple of gendarmes, with her forty-five years, her luxury, and her husband's high position; however, she felt no remorse, but reflected that she ought to have slipped the lace up her sleeve. Jouve, however, had just decided to lay hold of the suspicious woman, despairing of catching her in the act, but fully suspecting that she had filled her pockets, by means of some sleight of hand which had escaped him. But when he had taken her aside and searched her, he was wild with confusion at finding nothing on her—not a cravat, not a button. Her friend had disappeared. All at once he understood: the woman he had searched had only been there as a blind; it was the friend who had done the trick.

This affair amused the ladies. Mouret, rather vexed, merely said: "Old Jouve has been floored this time but he'll have his revenge."

"Oh!" replied Vallagnosc, "I don't think he's equal to it. Besides, why do you display such a quantity of goods? It serves you right, if you are robbed. You ought not to tempt these poor, defenceless women so."

This was the last word, which sounded like the supreme note of the day, in the growing fever that reigned in the establishment. The ladies separated, crossing the crowded departments for the last time. It was four o'clock, the rays of the setting sun were darting obliquely through the large front windows and throwing a cross light on the glazed roofs of the halls; and in this red, fiery glow arose, like a golden vapour, the thick dust raised by the circulation of the crowd since early morning. A broad sheet of light streamed along the grand central gallery, showing up the staircases, the flying bridges, all the network of suspended iron. The mosaics and faiences of the friezes glittered, the green and red paint reflected the fire of the lavish gilding. The Paradise seemed like a red-hot furnace, in which the various displays—the palaces of gloves and cravats, the festoons of ribbons and laces, the lofty piles of linen and calico, the variegated parterres in which bloomed the light silks and foulards—were now burning. The exhibition of parasols, of shield-like roundness, threw forth metallic reflections. In the distance, beyond streaks of shadow, were counters sparkling and swarming with a throng, ablaze with sunshine.

And at this last moment, in this over-heated atmosphere, the women reigned supreme. They had taken the whole place by storm, they were camping there as in a conquered country, like an invading horde installed amidst all the disorder of the goods. The salesmen, deafened and exhausted, were now nothing but their slaves, of whom they disposed with sovereign tyranny. Fat women elbowed their way along; even the thinnest took up a deal of space, and became quite arrogant. They were all there, with heads erect and gestures abrupt, quite at home, not showing the slightest politeness to one another but making as much use of the house as they could, even to the point of carrying away the dust from its walls. Madame Bourdelais, desirous of making up for her expenditure had again taken her children to the refreshment bar: whither the crowd was now rushing with rageful thirst and appetite. Even the mothers were gorging themselves with Malaga; since the morning eighty quarts of syrup and seventy bottles of wine had been drunk. After purchasing her travelling cloak, Madame Desforges had secured some picture cards at the pay-desk; and she went away scheming how she might get Denise into her house, so as to humiliate her before Mouret himself, see their faces and arrive at a conclusion. And whilst Monsieur de Boves succeeded at last in plunging into the crowd and disappearing with Madame Guibal, Madame de Boves, followed by Blanche and Vallagnosc, had the fancy to ask for a red air-ball, although she had bought nothing. It would always be something, she would not go away empty-handed, she would make a friend of her doorkeeper's little girl with it. At the distributing counter they were just starting on the fortieth thousand: thirty nine thousand red air-balls had already taken flight in the warm atmosphere of the shop, a perfect cloud of red air-balls which were now floating from one end of Paris to the other, bearing upwards to the sky the name of The Ladies' Paradise!

ÉMILE ZOLA

Five o'clock struck. Of all the ladies, Madame Marty and her daughter were the only ones to remain, in the final throes of the day's sales. Although ready to drop with fatigue she could not tear herself away, being retained by so strong an attraction that although she needed nothing she continually retraced her steps, scouring the departments with insatiable curiosity. It was the moment in which the throng, goaded on by puffery, completely lost its head; the sixty thousand francs paid to the newspapers, the ten thousand bills posted on the walls, the two hundred thousand catalogues distributed all over the world, after emptying the women's purses, left their minds weakened by intoxication; and they still remained shaken by Mouret's inventions, the reduction of prices, the "returns," and the endless gallantries. Madame Marty lingered before the various "proposal" stalls, amidst the hoarse cries of the salesmen, the clink of the pay-desks, and the rolling of the parcels sent down to the basement; she again traversed the ground floor, the linen, silk, glove and woollen departments; she again went upstairs, yielding to the metallic vibrations of the hanging staircases and flying-bridges; she returned to the mantle, under-linen, and lace departments; she even ascended to the second floor, to the heights of the bedding and furniture galleries; and on all sides the employees, Hutin and Favier, Mignot and Liénard, Deloche, Pauline and Denise, nearly dead with fatigue, were making a final effort, snatching victories from the last fever of the customers. This fever had gradually increased since the morning, like the intoxication emanating from all the tumbled stuffs. The crowd flared under the fiery glare of the five o'clock sun. Madame Marty now had the animated nervous face of a child after drinking pure wine. Arriving with clear eyes and fresh skin from the cold of the street, she had slowly burnt both sight and complexion, by the contemplation of all that luxury, those violent colours, whose everlasting gallop irritated her passion. When she at last went away, after saying that she would pay at home, terrified as she was by the amount of her bill, her features were drawn, and her eyes dilated like those of a sick person. She was obliged to fight her way through the stubborn crush at the door, where people were almost killing each other, amidst the struggle for bargains. Then, when she got into the street, and again found her daughter, whom she had lost for a moment, the fresh air made her shiver, and she remained quite scared, her mind unhinged by the neurosis to which the great drapery establishments give birth.

In the evening, as Denise was returning from dinner, a messenger called her: "You are wanted at the director's office, mademoiselle."

She had forgotten the order which Mouret had given her in the morning, to go to his office when the sale was over. She found him standing, waiting for her. On going in she did not close the door, which remained wide open.

"We are very pleased with you, mademoiselle," said he, "and we have thought of proving our satisfaction. You know in what a shameful manner Madame Frédéric has left us. From to-morrow you will take her place as second-hand."

Denise listened to him motionless with surprise. Then she murmured in a trembling voice: "But there are saleswomen in the department who are much my seniors, sir."

"What does that matter?" he resumed. "You are the most capable, the most trustworthy. I select you; it's quite natural. Are you not satisfied?"

She blushed, feeling a delicious happiness and embarrassment, in which all her original fright vanished. Why had she, before aught else, thought of the suppositions with which this unhoped-for favour would be received? And she remained there full of confusion, despite her sudden burst of gratitude. With a smile he looked at her in her simple silk dress, without a single piece of jewellery, displaying only the luxury of her royal, blonde hair. She had become more refined, her skin was whiter, her manner delicate and grave. Her former puny insignificance was developing into a penetrating, gentle charm.

"You are very kind, sir," she stammered. "I don't know how to tell you—"

But she was cut short by the appearance of Lhomme on the threshold. In his hand he held a large leather bag, and with his mutilated arm he pressed an enormous note case to his chest; whilst, behind him came his son Albert weighed down by the load of bags he was carrying.

"Five hundred and eighty-seven thousand two hundred and ten francs thirty centimes!" exclaimed the cashier, whose flabby, worn face seemed to light up with a ray of sunshine, in the reflection of such a huge sum of money.

It was the day's receipts, the highest that The Ladies' Paradise had ever attained. In the distance, in the depths of the shop through which Lhomme had just slowly passed with the heavy gait of an overladen beast of burden, you could hear the uproar, the ripple of surprise and joy which this colossal sum had left behind it as it passed.

"Why, it's superb!" said Mouret, enchanted. "My good Lhomme, put it down there, and take a rest, for you look quite done up. I'll have the money taken to the central cashier's office. Yes, yes, put it all on my table, I want to see the heap."

He was full of a childish gaiety. The cashier and his son rid themselves of their burdens. The leather bag gave out a clear, golden ring, two of the other bags in bursting let a torrent of silver and copper escape, whilst from the note-case peeped the corners of bank notes. One end of the large table was entirely covered; it was like the tumbling of a fortune picked up in ten hours.

When Lhomme and Albert had retired, mopping their faces, Mouret remained for a moment motionless, dreamy, his eyes fixed on the money. But on raising his head, he perceived Denise, who had drawn back. Then he began to smile again, forced her to come forward, and finished by saying that he would make her a present of all the money she could take in her hand; and there was a sort of love bargain beneath his playfulness.

"Look! out of the bag. I bet it would be less than a thousand francs, your hand is so small!"

But she drew back again. He loved her, then? Suddenly she understood everything; she felt the growing flame of desire with which he had enveloped her ever since her return to the shop. What overcame her more than anything else was to feel her heart beating violently. Why did he wound her with the offer of all that money, when she was overflowing with gratitude? He was stepping nearer to her still, continuing to joke, when, to his great annoyance, Bourdoncle came in under the pretence of informing him of the enormous number of entries—no fewer than seventy thousand customers had entered The Ladies' Paradise that day. And thereupon Denise hastened off, after again expressing her thanks.

# X

On the first Sunday in August, the stock-taking, which had to be finished by the evening, took place. Early in the morning all the employees were at their posts, as on a week-day, and the work began with closed doors, not a customer was admitted.

Denise, however, had not come down with the other young ladies at eight o'clock. Confined to her room since the previous Thursday through having sprained her ankle whilst on her way up to the work-rooms, she was now much better; but, as Madame Aurélie treated her indulgently, she did not hurry down. Still after a deal of trouble she managed to put her boots on, having resolved that she would show herself in the department. The young ladies' bed-rooms now occupied the entire fifth storey of the new buildings in the Rue Monsigny; there were sixty of them, on either side of a corridor, and they were much more comfortable than formerly, although still furnished simply with an iron bedstead, large wardrobe, and little mahogany toilet-table. The private life of the saleswomen was now becoming more refined and elegant; they displayed a taste for scented soap and fine linen, quite a natural ascent towards middle-class ways as their positions improved, although high words and banging doors were still sometimes heard amidst the hotel-like gust that carried them away, morning and evening. Denise, being second-hand in her department, had one of the largest rooms with two attic windows looking into the street. Being now in much better circumstances she indulged in sundry little luxuries, a red eider-down bed quilt, covered with guipure, a small carpet in front of her wardrobe, a couple of blue-glass vases containing a few fading roses on her toilet table.

When she had succeeded in getting her boots on she tried to walk across the room; but was obliged to lean against the furniture, being still rather lame. However that would soon come right again, she thought. At the same time, she had been quite right in refusing an invitation to dine at uncle Baudu's that evening, and in asking her aunt to take Pépé out for a walk, for she had placed him with Madame Gras again. Jean, who had been to see her on the previous day, was also to dine at his uncle's. She was still slowly trying to walk, resolving, however, to go to bed early, in order to rest her ankle, when Madame Cabin, the housekeeper, knocked and gave her a letter, with an air of mystery.

The door closed. Denise, astonished by the woman's discreet smile, opened the letter. And at once she dropped on a chair; for it was a letter from Mouret, in which he expressed himself delighted at her recovery, and begged her to come down and dine with him that evening, since she could not go out. The tone of this note, at once familiar and paternal, was in no way offensive; but it was impossible for her to mistake its meaning. And thus her white cheeks slowly coloured with a flush.

With the letter lying on her lap and her heart beating violently she remained with her eyes fixed on the blinding light which came in by one of the windows. There was a confession which she had been obliged to make to herself in this very room, during her sleepless hours: if she still trembled when he passed, she now knew that it was not from fear; and her former uneasiness, her old terror, could have been only the frightened ignorance of love, the perturbation of passion springing up amidst her youthful wildness. She did not reason, she simply felt that she had always loved him, from the hour when she had shuddered and stammered before him. She had loved him when she had feared him as a pitiless master; she had loved him when her distracted heart was dreaming of Hutin, unconsciously yielding to a desire for affection. Yes, she had never loved any but this man, whose mere look terrified her. And all her past life came back to her, unfolding itself in the blinding light from the window: the hardships of her start, that sweet walk under the dark foliage of the Tuileries Gardens, and, lastly, the desires with which he had enveloped her ever since her return. The letter dropped on the floor and Denise was still gazing at the window, dazzled by the glare of the sun.

Suddenly there was a knock and she hastened to pick up the missive and conceal it in her pocket. It was Pauline, who, having slipped away from her department under some pretext or other, had come up for a little chat.

"How are you, my dear? We never meet now—"

As it was against the rules, however, to go up into the bed-rooms, and, above all, for two of the saleswomen to be shut in together, Denise took her friend to the end of the passage, to a saloon which Mouret had gallantly fitted up for the young ladies, who could spend their evenings there, chatting or sewing, till eleven o'clock. The apartment, decorated in white and gold, with the vulgar nudity of an hotel room, was furnished with a piano, a central table, and some arm-chairs and sofas protected by white covers. After spending a few evenings together there in the first novelty of the thing, the saleswomen now never entered the place without coming to high words at once. They required educating to it; so far their little circle lacked harmony. Meanwhile, almost the only girl that went there in the evening was the second-hand of the corset department, Miss Powell, who strummed away at Chopin on the piano, and whose envied talents were for much in driving the others away.

"You see my ankle's better now," said Denise, "I was just going down."

"Well!" exclaimed the other, "how zealous you are! I'd take it easy if I had the chance!"

They had both sat down on a sofa. Pauline's manner had changed since her friend had become second-hand in the mantle department. With her good-natured cordiality there mingled a touch of respect, a sort of surprise at realizing that the puny little saleswoman of former days was on the road to fortune. Denise, however, liked her very much, and amidst the continual gallop of the two hundred women that the firm now employed, confided in her alone.

"What's the matter?" asked Pauline, quickly, when she remarked her companion's troubled looks.

"Oh! nothing," replied Denise, with an awkward smile.

"Yes, yes; there's something the matter with you. Have you no faith in me, that you have given up telling me your worries?"

Thereupon Denise, in the emotion that was swelling her bosom—an emotion she could not control—abandoned herself to her feelings. She gave her friend the letter, stammering: "Look! he has just written to me."

Between themselves, they had never openly spoken of Mouret. But this very silence was like a confession of their secret thoughts. Pauline knew everything. After having read the letter, she clasped Denise in her arms, and softly murmured: "My dear, to speak frankly, I thought it had all happened long ago. Don't be shocked; I assure you the whole shop must think as I do. You see, he appointed you as second-hand so quickly, and then he's always looking at you. It's obvious!" She kissed her affectionately on the cheek and then asked her: "You will go this evening, of course?"

Denise looked at her without replying and all at once burst into tears, letting her head fall on Pauline's shoulder. The latter was quite astonished. "Come, try and calm yourself; there's nothing to upset you like this," she said.

"No, no; let me be," stammered Denise. "If you only knew what trouble I am in! Since I received that letter, I have felt beside myself. Let me have a good cry, that will relieve me."

Full of pity, though not understanding, Pauline endeavoured to console her, declaring that she must not worry, for it was quite certain that M. Mouret had ceased to pay any attention to Clara; whilst as for that other lady friend of his, Madame Desforges, it was probably all but so much gossip. Denise listened, and had she been ignorant of her love, she could no longer have doubted it after the suffering she felt at the allusions to those two women. She could again hear Clara's disagreeable voice, and see Madame Desforges dragging her about the different departments with all the scorn of a rich lady for a poor shop-girl.

Then the two friends went on conversing; and at last Denise in a sudden impulse exclaimed: "But when a man loves a girl he ought to marry her. Baugé is going to marry you."

This was true, Baugé, who had left the Bon Marché for The Ladies' Paradise, was going to marry her about the middle of the month. Bourdoncle did not like these married couples; however, they had managed to get the necessary permission, and even hoped to obtain a fortnight's holiday for their honeymoon.

On hearing Denise's remark Pauline laughed heartily. "But, my dear," said she. "Baugé is going to marry me because he is Baugé. He's my equal, that's natural. Whereas Monsieur Mouret! Do you think that Monsieur Mouret could marry one of his saleswomen?"

"Oh! no, oh! no," exclaimed Denise, shocked by the absurdity of the question, "and that's why he ought never to have written to me."

This argument seemed to astonish Pauline. Her coarse face, with small tender eyes, assumed quite an expression of maternal pity. Then she got up, opened the piano, and with one finger softly played the air of "King Dagobert," doubtless to enliven the situation. The noises of the street, the distant melopœia of a woman crying out green peas, ascended to the bare saloon, whose emptiness seemed increased by the white coverings of the furniture. Denise had thrown herself back on the sofa, her head against the woodwork and shaken by a fresh flood of sobs, which she stifled in her handkerchief.

"Again!" resumed Pauline, turning round. "Really you are not reasonable. Why did you bring me here? We ought to have stopped in your room."

She knelt down before her, and had begun lecturing her again, when a sound of footsteps was heard in the passage. And thereupon she ran to the door and looked out.

"Hush! Madame Aurélie!" she murmured. "I'm off, and just you dry your eyes. She need not know what's up."

When Denise was alone, she rose, and forced back her tears; and, her hands still trembling, fearful of being caught there weeping, she closed the piano, which her friend had left open. However, on hearing Madame Aurélie knocking at her door, she at once left the drawing-room.

"What! you are up!" exclaimed the first-hand. "It's very thoughtless of you, my dear child. I just came up to see how you were, and to tell you that we did not require you downstairs."

Denise assured her, however, that she felt much better and that it would do her good to have some occupation.

"I shan't tire myself, madame. You can put me on a chair, and I'll do some writing."

Both then went downstairs. Madame Aurélie, most attentive, insisted on Denise leaning on her shoulder. She must have noticed the young girl's red eyes, for she was stealthily examining her. No doubt she was aware of much that was going on.

Denise had gained an unexpected victory: she had at last conquered the department. Formerly she had struggled on for six months, amidst all the torments of drudgery, without disarming her comrades' ill-will, but now in a few weeks she had overcome them, and saw them submissive and respectful around her. Madame Aurélie's sudden affection had greatly assisted her in this ungrateful task of propitiating her companions. Indeed the first-hand had taken the young girl under her protection with such warmth that the latter must have been recommended to her in a very special manner. However, Denise had also brought her own charm into play in order to disarm her enemies. The task was all the more difficult from the fact that she had to obtain their forgiveness for her appointment to the situation of second-hand. The other young ladies spoke of this at first as an injustice, and even added a lot of abominable accusations. But in spite of their revolt, the title of second-hand influenced them, and Denise with her promotion assumed a certain air of authority which astonished and overawed even the most hostile spirits. Soon afterwards she actually found flatterers amongst the new hands; and her sweetness and modesty completed the conquest. Marguerite came over to her side; and Clara was the only one to continue her ill-natured ways, still venturing to allude to Denise as the "unkempt one," an insult in which nobody now saw any fun. During the short time that she had engaged Mouret's attention Clara had profited by the caprice to neglect her work, being of a wonderfully idle, gossiping nature unfitted for any responsible duty. Nevertheless she considered that Denise had robbed her of Madame Frédéric's place. She would never have accepted it, on account of the worry; but she was vexed that no attention had been paid to her claims.

Nine o'clock struck as Denise came down, leaning on Madame Aurélie's arm. Out of doors an ardent blue sky was warming the streets, cabs were rolling towards the railway stations, the whole population of Paris rigged out in Sunday attire was streaming towards the suburban woods. Inside the Paradise, which the large open bays flooded with sunshine, the imprisoned staff had just commenced stock-taking. They had closed the doors and people halted on the pavement, looking through the windows in astonishment that the shop should be shut when such extraordinary activity prevailed inside. From one end of the galleries to the other, from the top to the bottom floor, there was a continual tramping of employees; arms were ever being raised and parcels were flying about above their heads; and all this amidst a tempest of shouts and calling out of figures, ascending in confusion and becoming a deafening roar. Each of the thirty-nine departments did its work apart, without troubling about its neighbour. At this early hour the shelves had hardly been touched, there were only a few bales of goods on the floors. They must get up a good deal more steam if they were to finish that evening.

"Why have you come down?" asked Marguerite of Denise, good-naturedly. "You'll only make yourself worse, and we are quite numerous enough to do the work."

"That's what I told her," declared Madame Aurélie, "but she insisted on coming down to help us."

All the young ladies flocked round Denise. The work was even interrupted for a time. They complimented her, listening with all sorts of exclamations to the story of her sprained ankle. At last Madame Aurélie made her sit down at a table; and it was understood that she should merely write down the articles as they were called out. On such a day as this they requisitioned all the employees who were capable of holding a pen: the inspectors, the cashiers, the clerks, even the shop messengers; and each department annexed some of these assistants of a day in order to get the work over more quickly. It was thus that Denise found herself installed near Lhomme the cashier and Joseph the messenger, both of whom were bending over large sheets of paper.

"Five mantles, cloth, fur trimming, third size, at two hundred and forty francs!" called Marguerite. "Four ditto, first size, at two hundred and twenty!"

The work once more commenced. Behind Marguerite three saleswomen were emptying the cupboards, classifying the articles, and giving them to her in bundles; and, when she had called them out, she threw them on the table, where they were gradually accumulating in huge piles. Lhomme jotted down the articles whilst Joseph checked him by keeping another list. Whilst this was going on, Madame Aurélie herself, assisted by three other saleswomen, was counting out the silk garments, which Denise entered on the sheets of paper given to her. Clara on her side was looking after the heaps, arranging them in such a manner that they should occupy the least possible space on the tables. But she was not paying much attention to her work, for many things were already tumbling down.

"I say," she asked of a little saleswoman who had joined that winter, "are they going to give you a rise? You know that the second-hand is to have two thousand francs, which, with her commission, will bring her in nearly seven thousand."

The little saleswoman, without ceasing to pass some cloaks down, replied that if they didn't give her eight hundred francs she would take her hook. The rises were always given on the day after the stock-taking; it was also then, as the amount of business done during the year became known, that the managers of the departments drew their commission on the increase of this amount, as compared with that of the preceding year. Thus, despite the bustle and uproar of the work, the impassioned gossiping went on everywhere. Between every two articles that were called out, they talked of nothing but money. The rumour ran that Madame Aurélie's gains would exceed twenty-five thousand francs; and this huge sum greatly excited the young ladies. Marguerite, the best saleswoman after Denise, had for her part made four thousand five hundred francs, that is fifteen hundred francs salary and about three thousand francs commission; whilst Clara had not made two thousand five hundred altogether.

"I don't care a button for their rises!" she resumed, still talking to the little saleswoman. "If papa were dead I would jolly soon clear out of this! Still it exasperates me to see seven thousand francs given to that strip of a girl! What do you say?"

Madame Aurélie, turning round with her imperial air, violently interrupted the conversation. "Be quiet, young ladies! We can't hear ourselves speak, my word of honour!"

Then she again went on calling out: "Seven mantles, old style, Sicilian, first size, at a hundred and thirty! Three pelisses, surah, second size, at a hundred and fifty! Have you got that down, Mademoiselle Baudu?"

"Yes, madame."

Clara then had to look after the armfuls of garments piled upon the tables. She pushed them about, and made some more room. But she soon left them again to reply to a salesman, who was looking for her. It was the glover, Mignot, who had escaped from his department. He whispered a request for twenty francs; he already owed her thirty, a loan effected on the day after some races when he had lost his week's money on a horse; this time he had squandered his commission, drawn overnight, and had not ten sous left him for his Sunday. Clara had only ten francs about her, and she lent them with a fairly good grace. And they then went on talking of a party of six, which they had formed part of, at a restaurant at Bougival, where the women had paid their shares. It was much better to do that, they all felt more at ease. Next, Mignot, who wanted his twenty francs, went and bent over Lhomme's shoulder. The latter, stopped in his writing, appeared greatly troubled. However, he dared not refuse, and was looking for a ten-franc piece in his purse, when Madame Aurélie, astonished at not hearing the voice of Marguerite who had been obliged to pause, perceived Mignot, and understood everything. She roughly sent him back to his department, saying that she didn't want any one to come and distract her young ladies' attention from their work. The truth was, she dreaded this young man, a bosom friend of Albert's, and his accomplice in all sorts of questionable pranks which she feared would some day turn out badly. Accordingly, when Mignot had got his ten francs, and run away, she could not help saying to her husband: "Is it possible! to let a fellow like that get over you!"

"But, my dear, I really couldn't refuse the young man."

She closed his mouth with a shrug of her substantial shoulders. Then, as the saleswomen were slyly grinning at this family explanation, she resumed severely: "Now, Mademoiselle Vadon, don't let us go to sleep."

"Twenty cloaks, cashmere extra, fourth size, at eighteen francs and a half," resumed Marguerite in her sing-song voice.

Lhomme, with his head bowed down, again began writing. They had gradually raised his salary to nine thousand francs a year; but he was very humble before Madame Aurélie, who still brought nearly three times as much into the family.

For a while the work was pushed forward. Figures were bandied about, garments rained thick and fast on the tables. But Clara had invented another amusement: she was teasing the messenger, Joseph, about a passion which he was said to nourish for a young lady in the pattern-room. This young lady, already twenty-eight years old, and thin and pale, was a *protégée* of Madame Desforges, who had wanted Mouret to engage her as a saleswoman, backing up her recommendation with a touching story: An orphan, the last of the Fontenailles, an old and noble family of Poitou, had been thrown on to the streets of Paris with a drunken father; still she had remained virtuous amidst this misfortune which was the greater as her education was altogether too limited to enable her to secure employment as governess or music-mistress. Mouret generally got angry when any one recommended these broken-down gentlewomen to him; there were no more incapable, more insupportable, more narrow-minded creatures than these gentlewomen, said he; and, besides, a saleswoman could not be improvised, she must serve an apprenticeship, it was an intricate and delicate business. However, he took Madame Desforges's *protégée* placing her in the pattern-room, in the same way as (to oblige friends) he had already found places for two countesses and a baroness in the advertising department, where they addressed wrappers and envelopes. Mademoiselle de Fontenailles earned three francs a day, which just enabled her to live in her modest room, in the Rue d'Argenteuil. It was on seeing her with her sad look and shabby attire, that Joseph's heart, very tender despite his rough soldierly manner, had been touched. He did not confess, but blushed, when the young ladies of the mantle department chaffed him; for the pattern-room was not far off, and they had often observed him prowling about the doorway.

"Joseph is somewhat absent-minded," murmured Clara. "His nose is always turning towards the under-linen department."

They had requisitioned Mademoiselle de Fontenailles there, and she was assisting at the trousseau counter. As the messenger continually glanced in that direction, the saleswomen began to laugh; whereupon he became very confused, and plunged into his accounts, whilst Marguerite, in order to arrest the burst of gaiety which was tickling her throat, cried out louder still: "Fourteen jackets, English cloth, second size, at fifteen francs!"

At this, Madame Aurélie, who was calling out some cloaks, could not make herself heard. She interfered with a wounded air, and a majestic slowness of manner. "A little softer, mademoiselle. We are not in a market. And you are all of you very unreasonable, to be amusing yourselves with such childish matters, when our time is so precious."

Just at that moment, as Clara was not paying any attention to the packages, a catastrophe took place. Several mantles tumbled down, and all the heaps on the tables, carried with them, toppled over one after the other, so that the carpet was quite strewn with them.

"There! what did I say!" cried the first-hand, beside herself. "Pray be more careful, Mademoiselle Prunaire; it's altogether intolerable."

But a hum ran along: Mouret and Bourdoncle, making their round of inspection, had just appeared. The voices began calling again and the pens sputtered, whilst Clara hastened to pick up the garments. The governor did not interrupt the work. He stood there for several minutes, mute and smiling, with the gay victorious face of stock-taking days; and it was only on his lips that a slight feverish quiver could be detected. When he perceived Denise, he nearly gave way to a gesture of astonishment. She had come down, then? His eyes met Madame Aurélie's. Then, after a moment's hesitation, he went away into the under-linen department.

However, Denise, warned by the slight noise, had raised her head. And, having recognised Mouret, she had immediately bent over her work again. Since she had been writing in this mechanical way, amidst the calling-out of the goods, a peaceful feeling had stolen over her. She had always yielded thus to the first outburst of her sensitiveness: tears suffocated her, and passion increased her torments: but then she regained her self-command, a grand, calm courage, a quiet but inexorable strength of will. And now, with her limpid eyes, and pale complexion, she was free from all agitation, entirely absorbed in her work, resolved to silence her heart and to do nothing but her will.

Ten o'clock struck, the uproar of the stock-taking was increasing; and amidst the incessant shouts which rose and flew about on all sides the same news circulated with surprising rapidity: every salesman knew that Mouret had written that morning inviting Denise to dinner. The indiscretion came from Pauline. On going downstairs, still greatly excited, she had met Deloche in the lace department, and, without noticing that Liénard was talking to the young man, had immediately relieved her mind of the secret. "It's all over, my dear fellow. She's just received a letter. He has invited her to dinner for this evening."

Deloche turned very pale. He had understood, for he often questioned Pauline; each day they spoke of their common friend, and Mouret's passion for her. Moreover, she frequently scolded him for his secret love for Denise, with whom he would never succeed, and shrugged her shoulders when he expressed his approval of the girl's conduct with reference to their employer.

"Her foot's better, she's coming down," continued Pauline. "Pray don't put on that funeral face. There's no reason to cry." And thereupon she hastened back to her department.

"Ah! good!" murmured Liénard, who had heard everything, "you're talking about the young girl with the sprain. You were quite right to make haste in defending her last night at the café!"

Then he also ran off; but before he had returned to the woollen department, he had already related the story to four or five fellows. In less than ten minutes, it had gone the round of the whole shop.

Liénard's last remark to Deloche referred to a scene which had occurred on the previous evening, at the Café Saint-Roch. Deloche and he were now constantly together. The former had taken Hutin's room at the Hôtel de Smyrne, when that gentleman, on being appointed second-hand, had hired a suite of three rooms; and the two salesmen came to The Ladies' Paradise together in the morning, and waited for each other in the evening in order to go away together. Their rooms, which adjoined one another, overlooked a black yard, a narrow well, the stench from which pervaded the hotel. They got on very well together, notwithstanding their difference of character, the one carelessly squandering the money which he drew from his father, and the other penniless, perpetually tormented by ideas of thrift; both having, however, one point in common, their unskilfulness as salesmen, which kept them vegetating at their counters, without any increase of salary. After leaving the shop, they spent the greater part of their time at the Café Saint-Roch. Void of customers during the day, this café filled at about half-past eight with an overflowing crowd of employees, the stream of shopmen which rolled into the street from the great doorway in the Place Gaillon. Then a deafening uproar of dominoes, laughter and yelping voices burst forth amidst dense tobacco smoke. Beer and coffee were in great demand. Seated in the left-hand corner, Liénard would order the most expensive beverages, whilst Deloche contented himself with a glass of beer, which he would take four hours to drink. It was here that the latter had heard Favier relating, at a neighbouring table, some abominable things about the way in which Denise had "hooked" the governor. He had with difficulty restrained himself from striking him. However, as the other went on adding still viler and viler stories of the girl, he had at last called him a liar, feeling mad with rage.

"What a blackguard!" he had shouted. "It's a lie, it's a lie, I tell you!" And in the emotion agitating him, he had added a confession, entirely opening his heart in a stammering voice. "I know her, and it isn't true. She has never had any affection except for one man; yes, for Monsieur Hutin, and even he has never noticed it!"

The report of this quarrel, exaggerated and distorted, was already affording amusement to the whole shop when the story of Mouret's letter ran round. In fact, it was to a salesman in the silk department that Liénard first confided the news. With the silk-vendors the stock-taking was going on rapidly. Favier and two shopmen, mounted on stools, were emptying the shelves and passing the pieces of stuff to Hutin who, standing on a table, called out the figures, after consulting the tickets; and he then dropped the pieces on to the floor over which they spread, rising slowly like an autumn tide. Other employees were writing, Albert Lhomme being among the helpers, his face pale and heavy after a night spent in a low show at La Chapelle. A sheet of light fell from the glazed roof of the hall, through which could be seen the intense blue of the sky.

"Draw those blinds!" cried out Bouthemont who was very busy superintending the work. "That sun is unbearable!"

Favier, on tiptoe, trying to reach a piece of silk, then grumbled under his breath: "A nice thing to shut people up on a lovely day like this! No fear of it raining on stock-taking day! And they keep us under lock and key, like convicts, when all Paris is out of doors!"

He passed the silk to Hutin. On the ticket was the measurement, diminished at each sale by the quantity sold; which greatly simplified the work. The second-hand cried out: "Fancy silk, small check, twenty-one yards, at six francs and a half."

And then the piece went to increase the heap already on the floor. Whilst waiting for another he resumed a conversation previously begun, by saying to Favier: "So he wanted to fight you?"

"Yes, I was quietly drinking my glass of beer. It was hardly worth his while to contradict me, for she has just received a letter from the governor inviting her to dinner. The whole shop is talking about it."

"What! hadn't she dined with him before!"

Favier handed him another piece of silk.

"No, it seems not; though my opinion was all the other way."

The whole department was now joking about the affair, without, however, allowing the work to suffer. The young girl's name passed from mouth to mouth and the salesmen arched their backs and winked.

Bouthemont himself, who took a rare delight in all such stories, could not help adding his joke. Just then, however, Mignot came down, with the twenty francs which he had just borrowed, and he stopped to slip ten francs into Albert's hand, making an appointment with him for the evening: a projected spree, hampered by lack of money, but still possible, notwithstanding the smallness of the sum secured. However, when Mignot heard about the famous letter, he made such an abominable remark, that Bouthemont was obliged to interfere. "That's enough, gentlemen. It isn't any of our business. Go on, Monsieur Hutin."

"Fancy silk, small check, thirty-two yards, at six francs and a half," cried out the latter.

The pens started off again, the pieces fell; the flood of material still increased, as if the water of a river had emptied itself there. And there was no end to the calling out of the fancy silks. Favier, in an undertone thereupon remarked that the stock in hand would form a nice total; the governors would be enchanted; that big fool of a Bouthemont might be the best buyer in Paris, but as a salesman he was not worth his salt. Hutin smiled, delighted, and giving the other a friendly look of approval; for after having himself introduced Bouthemont to The Ladies' Paradise, in order to get rid of Robineau, he was now undermining him also, with the firm intention of depriving him of his berth. It was the same war as formerly—treacherous insinuations whispered in the partners' ears, excessive zeal to push one's self forward, a regular campaign carried on with affable cunning. Hutin was again displaying some condescension towards Favier, but the latter, thin and frigid with a bilious look, gave him a sly glance as if to count how many mouthfuls this short, little fellow would make, and to imply that he was waiting till he had swallowed up Bouthemont, in order to eat him afterwards. He, Favier, hoped to get the second-hand's place, should his friend be appointed manager. And after that they would see. Consumed by the fever which was raging from one to the other end of the shop, both of them began talking of the probable increases of salary, without however ceasing to call out the stock of fancy silks; they felt sure that Bouthemont would secure thirty thousand francs that year; Hutin for his part would exceed ten thousand whilst Favier estimated his pay and commission at five thousand five hundred. The amount of business in the department was increasing yearly, the salesmen secured promotion and increase of pay, like officers in time of war.

"Won't those fancy silks soon be finished?" asked Bouthemont suddenly, with an expression of annoyance. "But it was a miserable spring, always raining! People bought nothing but black silks."

His fat, jovial face became cloudy as he gazed at the growing heap on the floor, whilst Hutin called out louder still, in a sonorous voice tinged with an accent of triumph—"Fancy silks, small check, twenty-eight yards, at six francs and a half."

There was still another shelf-full. Favier whose arms were getting tired, was now progressing but slowly. As he handed Hutin the last pieces he resumed in a low tone—"Oh! I say, I forgot. Have you heard that the second-hand in the mantle department once had a regular fancy for you?"

Hutin seemed greatly surprised. "What! How do you mean?"

"Yes, that great booby Deloche let it out to us. But I remember her casting sheep's eyes at you some time back."

Since his appointment as second-hand Hutin had thrown up his music-hall singers. Flattered at heart by Favier's words he nevertheless replied with a scornful air, "I don't care for such scraggy creatures." And then he called out:

"White Poult, thirty-five yards, at eight francs seventy-five."

"Oh! at last!" murmured Bouthemont, greatly relieved.

But a bell rang, that for the second table, to which Favier belonged. He jumped off the stool where another salesman took his place, and he was obliged to climb over the mountain of materials with which the floor was littered. Similar heaps were scattered about in every department; the shelves, the boxes, the cupboards were being gradually emptied, whilst the goods overflowed on all sides, under-foot, between the counters and the tables, in ever rising piles. In the linen department you heard heavy bales of calico falling; in the mercery department there was a clicking of boxes; whilst distant rumbling sounds came from amongst the furniture. Every sort of voice was heard too, shrill, full, deep, and husky, figures whizzed through the air and a rustling clamour reigned in the immense nave—the clamour of forests in January when the wind whistles through the branches.

Favier at last got clear and went up the dining-room staircase. Since the enlargement of The Ladies' Paradise the refectories had been shifted to the fourth storey of the new buildings. As he hurried up he overtook Deloche and Liénard who had gone on before him, so he fell back on Mignot who was following at his heels.

"The deuce!" said he, in the corridor leading to the kitchen, on reaching the black-board on which the bill of fare was inscribed, "you can see it's stock-taking day. A regular feast! Chicken, or leg of mutton, and artichokes! Their mutton won't be much of a success!"

Mignot sniggered, murmuring, "Is there a poultry epidemic on, then?"

However, Deloche and Liénard had taken their portions and gone away. Favier thereupon leant over the wicket and called out—"Chicken!"

But he had to wait; one of the kitchen helps had cut his finger in carving, and this caused some confusion. Favier stood there with his face to the opening, gazing into the kitchen with its giant appliances. There was a central range, over which, by a system of chains and pullies, a couple of rails fixed to the ceiling brought colossal cauldrons which four men could not have lifted. Several cooks, quite white in the ruddy glow of the cast-iron, were attending to the evening soup mounted on metal ladders and armed with skimmers fixed to long handles. Then against the wall were grills large enough for the roasting of martyrs, saucepans big enough for the stewing of entire sheep, a monumental plate-warmer, and a marble basin filled by a continual stream of water. To the left could be seen a scullery with stone sinks as large as ponds; whilst on the other side, to the right, was a huge meat-safe, where a glimpse was caught of numerous joints of red meat hanging from steel hooks. A machine for peeling potatoes was working with the tic-tac of a mill; and two small trucks laden with freshly-picked salad were being wheeled by some kitchen helps into a cool spot under a gigantic filter.

"Chicken," repeated Favier, getting impatient. Then, turning round, he added in a lower tone, "One fellow has cut himself. It's disgusting, his blood's running over the food."

Mignot wanted to see. Quite a string of shopmen had now arrived; there was a deal of laughing and pushing. The two young men, their heads at the wicket, exchanged remarks about this phalansterian kitchen, in which the least important utensils, even the spits and larding pins, assumed gigantic proportions. Two thousand luncheons and two thousand dinners had to be served, and the number of employees was increasing every week. It was quite an abyss, into which something like forty-five bushels of potatoes, one hundred and twenty pounds of butter, and sixteen hundred pounds of meat were cast every day; and at each meal they had to broach three casks of wine, over a hundred and fifty gallons being served out at the wine counter.

"Ah! at last!" murmured Favier when the cook reappeared with a large pan, out of which he handed him the leg of a fowl.

"Chicken," said Mignot behind him.

And with their plates in their hands they both entered the refectory, after taking their wine at the "bar;" whilst behind them the word "Chicken" was repeated without cessation, and one could hear the cook picking up the portions with his fork with a rapid rhythmical sound.

The men's dining-room was now an immense apartment, supplying ample room for five hundred people at each repast. The places were laid at long mahogany tables, placed parallel across the room, and at either end were similar tables reserved for the managers of departments and the inspectors; whilst in the centre was a counter for the "extras." Right and left large windows admitted a white light to the gallery, whose ceiling, although over twelve feet from the floor, seemed very low, owing to the development of the other proportions. The sole ornaments on the walls, painted a light yellow, were the napkin cupboards. Beyond this first refectory came that of the messengers and carmen, where the meals were served irregularly, according to the needs of the moment.

"What! you've got a leg as well, Mignot?" said Favier, as he took his place at one of the tables opposite his companion.

Other young men now sat down around them. There was no tablecloth, the plates clattered on the bare mahogany, and in this particular corner everybody was raising exclamations, for the number of legs distributed was really prodigious.

"These chickens are all legs!" remarked Mignot.

"Yes, they're real centipedes," retorted another salesman.

Those who had merely secured pieces of carcase were greatly discontented. However, the food had been of much better quality since the late improvements. Mouret no longer treated with a contractor at a fixed rate; he had taken the kitchen into his own hands, organizing it like one of the departments, with a head-cook, under-cooks and an inspector; and if he spent more money he got on the other hand more work out of the staff—a practical humanitarian calculation which had long terrified Bourdoncle.

"Mine is pretty tender, all the same," said Mignot. "Pass the bread!"

The big loaf was sent round, and after cutting a slice for himself he dug the knife into the crust. A few dilatory ones now hurried in, taking their places; a ferocious appetite, increased by the morning's work, burst forth from one to the other end of the immense tables. There was an increasing clatter of forks, a gurgling sound of bottles being emptied, a noise of glasses laid down too violently amidst the grinding rumble of five hundred pairs of powerful jaws chewing with wondrous energy. And the talk, still infrequent, seemed to be hampered by the fullness of the mouths.

Deloche, however, seated between Baugé and Liénard, found himself nearly opposite Favier. They had glanced at each other with a rancorous look. Some neighbours, aware of their quarrel on the previous day, began whispering together. Then there was a laugh at poor Deloche's ill-luck. Although always famished he invariably fell on the worst piece at table, by a sort of cruel fatality. This time he had come in for the neck of a chicken and some bits of carcase. Without saying a word, however, he let them joke away, swallowing large mouthfuls of bread, and picking the neck with the infinite art of a fellow who entertains great respect for meat.

"Why don't you complain?" asked Baugé.

But he shrugged his shoulders. What would be the use of that? It was always the same. When he did venture to complain things went worse than ever.

"You know the Bobbinards have got their club now?" said Mignot, all at once. "Yes, my boy, the 'Bobbin Club.' It's held at a wine shop in the Rue Saint-Honoré, where they hire a room on Saturdays."

He was speaking of the mercery salesmen. The whole table began to joke. Between two mouthfuls, with his voice still thick, each made some remark, adding a detail; and only the obstinate readers remained mute, with their noses buried in their newspapers. It could not be denied that shopmen were gradually assuming a better style; nearly half of them now spoke English or German. It was no longer considered good form to go and kick up a row at Bullier or prowl about the music-halls for the pleasure of hissing ugly singers. No; a score of them got together and formed a club.

"Have they a piano like the linen-men?" asked Liénard.

"I should rather think they had!" exclaimed Mignot. "And they play, my boy, and sing! There's even one of them, little Bavoux, who recites verses."

The gaiety redoubled and they chaffed little Bavoux; nevertheless beneath their laughter lay a great respect. Then they spoke of a piece at the Vaudeville, in which a counter-jumper played a nasty part, which annoyed several of them, whilst others began anxiously wondering at what time they would get away that evening, having invitations to pass the evening at friends' houses. And from all points came similar

ÉMILE ZOLA

conversations amidst an increasing rattle of crockery. To drive away the odour of the food—the warm steam which rose from the five hundred plates—they had opened the windows, whose lowered blinds were scorching in the heavy August sun. Burning gusts came in from the street, golden reflections yellowed the ceiling, steeping the perspiring eaters in a reddish light.

"A nice thing to shut people up on such a fine Sunday as this!" repeated Favier.

This remark brought them back to the stock-taking. It had been a splendid year. And they went on to speak of the salaries—the rises—the eternal subject, the stirring question which occupied them all. It was always thus on chicken days; a wonderful excitement declared itself, the noise at last became unbearable. When the waiters brought the artichokes you could not hear yourself speak. However, the inspector on duty had orders to be indulgent.

"By the way," cried Favier, "you've heard the news?"

But his voice was drowned by Mignot asking: "Who doesn't like artichoke; I'll sell my dessert for an artichoke."

No one replied. Everybody liked artichoke. That lunch would be counted amongst the good ones, for peaches were to be given for dessert.

"He has invited her to dinner, my dear fellow," said Favier to his right-hand neighbour, finishing his story. "What! you didn't know it?"

The whole table knew it, they were tired of talking about it since early morning. And the same poor jokes passed from mouth to mouth. Deloche was quivering again, and his eyes at last rested on Favier, who was persisting in his shameful remarks. But all at once the silk salesman ducked his head, for Deloche, yielding to an irresistible impulse, had thrown his last glass of wine into his face, stammering: "Take that, you infernal liar! I ought to have drenched you yesterday!"

This caused quite a scandal. A few drops had spurted on Favier's neighbours, whilst he himself only had his hair slightly wetted: the wine, thrown by an awkward hand, had fallen on the other side of the table. However, the others got angry, asking Deloche if the girl was his property that he defended her in this way? What a brute he was! he deserved a good drubbing to teach him better manners. However, their voices fell, for an inspector was observed coming along, and it was useless to let the management interfere in the quarrel. Favier contented himself with saying: "If it had caught me, you would have seen some sport!"

Then the affair wound up in jeers. When Deloche, still trembling, wished to drink by way of hiding his confusion, and mechanically caught hold of his empty glass, they all burst out laughing. He laid his glass down again awkwardly enough and commenced sucking the leaves of the artichoke which he had already eaten.

"Pass Deloche the water bottle," said Mignot, quietly; "he's thirsty."

The laughter increased. The young men took clean plates from the piles standing at equal distances on the table whilst the waiters handed round the dessert, which consisted of peaches, in baskets. And they all held their sides when Mignot added, with a grin: "Each man to his taste. Deloche takes wine with his peaches."

Deloche, however, sat motionless, with his head hanging down, as if deaf to the joking going on around him: he was full of despairing regret at thought of what he had just done. Those fellows were right—what right had he to defend her? They would now think all sorts of villainous things: he could have killed himself for having thus compromised her, in attempting to prove her innocence. Such was always his luck, he might just as well kill himself at once, for he could not even yield to the promptings of his heart without doing some stupid thing. And then tears came into his eyes. Was it not also his fault if the whole shop was talking of the letter written by the governor? He heard them grinning and making abominable remarks about this invitation, which Liénard alone had been informed of, and he reproached himself, he ought never to have let Pauline speak before that fellow; he was really responsible for the annoying indiscretion which had been committed.

"Why did you go and relate that?" he murmured at last in a sorrowful voice. "It's very wrong."

"I?" replied Liénard; "but I only told it to one or two persons, enjoining secrecy. One never knows how these things get about!"

When Deloche made up his mind to drink a glass of water everybody burst out laughing again. They had finished their meal and were lolling back on their chairs waiting for the bell to recall them to work. They had not asked for many extras at the great central counter, especially as on stock-taking day the firm treated them to coffee. The cups were steaming, perspiring faces shone under the light vapour, floating like bluey clouds from cigarettes. At the windows the blinds hung motionless, without the slightest flapping. One of them, on being drawn up, admitted a ray of sunshine which sped across the room and gilded the ceiling. The uproar of the voices beat upon the walls with such force that the bell was at first only heard by those at the tables near the door. Then they got up and for some time the corridors were full of the confusion of the departure. Deloche, however, remained behind to escape the malicious remarks that were still being made. Baugé even went out before him, and Baugé was, as a rule, the last to leave, taking a circuitous route so as to meet Pauline on he way to the ladies' dining-room; a manœuvre they had arranged between them—the only chance they had of seeing one another for a minute during business hours. That day, however, just as they were indulging in a loving kiss in a corner of the passage they were surprised by Denise, who was also going up to lunch. She was walking slowly on account of her foot.

"Oh! my dear," stammered Pauline, very red, "don't say anything, will you?"

Baugé, with his big limbs and giant stature, was trembling like a little boy. He muttered, "They'd precious soon pitch us out. Although our marriage may be announced, they don't allow any kissing, the brutes!"

Denise, greatly agitated, affected not to have seen them: and Baugé disappeared just as Deloche, also going the longest way round, in his turn appeared. He wished to apologize, stammering out phrases that Denise did not at first catch. Then, as he blamed Pauline for having spoken before Liénard, and she stood there looking very embarrassed, Denise at last understood the meaning of the whispers she had heard around her all the morning. It was the story of the letter circulating. And again was she shaken by the shiver with which this letter had agitated her.

"But I didn't know," repeated Pauline. "Besides, there's nothing bad in the letter. Let them gossip; they're jealous, of course!"

"My dear," said Denise at last, with her sensible air, "I don't blame you in any way! You've spoken nothing but the truth. I *have* received a letter, and it is my duty to answer it."

Deloche went off heart-broken, in the belief that the girl accepted the situation and would keep the appointment that evening. When the two saleswomen had lunched in a small room, adjoining the larger one where the women were served much more comfortably, Pauline had to assist Denise downstairs again as her sprain was getting more painful.

In the afternoon warmth below, the stock-taking was roaring more loudly than ever. The moment for the supreme effort had arrived, when, as the work had not made much progress during the morning, everybody put forth their strength in order that all might be finished that night. The voices grew louder still, you saw nothing but waving arms continually emptying the shelves and throwing the goods down; and it was impossible to get along for the tide of the bales and packages on the floor rose as high as the counters. A sea of heads, brandished fists, and flying limbs seemed to extend to the very depths of the departments, with the confused aspect of a distant riot. It was the last fever of the clearing, the machine seemed ready to burst; and past the plate-glass windows all round the closed shop there still went a few pedestrians, pale with the stifling boredom of a summer Sunday. On the pavement in the Rue Neuve-Saint-Augustin three tall girls, bareheaded and sluttish-looking, were impudently pressing their faces against the windows, trying to see the curious work going on inside.

When Denise returned to the mantle department Madame Aurélie told Marguerite to finish calling out the garments. There was still the checking to be done, and for this, being desirous of silence, she retired into the pattern-room, taking Denise with her.

"Come with me, we'll do the checking;" she said, "and then you can add up the figures."

However, as she wished to leave the door open, in order to keep an eye on her young ladies, the noise came in, and they could not hear themselves much better even in this pattern-room—a large, square apartment furnished merely with some chairs and three long tables. In one corner were the great machine knives, for cutting up the patterns. Entire pieces of stuff were consumed; every year they sent away more than sixty thousand francs' worth of material, cut up in strips. From morning to night, the knives were cutting silk, wool, and linen, with a scythe-like noise. Then, too, the books had to be got together, gummed or sewn. And between the two windows, there was also a little printing-press for the tickets.

"Not so loud, please!" cried Madame Aurélie every now and again, quite unable as she was to hear Denise reading out the articles.

Then, the checking of the first lists being completed, she left the young girl at one of the tables, absorbed in the adding-up; but came back almost immediately, and placed Mademoiselle de Fontenailles near her. The under-linen department not requiring Madame Desforges' *protégée* any longer, had placed her at her disposal. She could also do some adding-up, it would save time. But the appearance of the marchioness, as Clara ill-naturedly called the poor creature, had disturbed the department. They laughed and joked at poor Joseph, and their ferocious sallies were wafted into the pattern-room.

"Don't draw back, you are not at all in my way," said Denise, seized with pity. "My inkstand will suffice, we'll dip together."

Mademoiselle de Fontenailles, brutified by her unfortunate position, could not even find a word of gratitude. She looked like a woman who drank, her meagre face had a livid hue, and her hands alone, white and delicate, attested the distinction of her birth.

However, the laughter all at once ceased, and the work resumed its regular roar. Mouret was once more going through the departments. But he stopped and looked round for Denise, surprised at not seeing her there. Then he made a sign to Madame Aurélie; and both drew aside, and for a moment talked in a low tone. He must have been questioning her. She nodded towards the pattern-room and then seemed to be making a report. No doubt she was relating that the young girl had been weeping that morning.

"Very good!" said Mouret, aloud, coming nearer. "Show me the lists."

"This way, sir," said the first-hand. "We have run away from the noise."

He followed her into the next room. Clara was not duped by this manœuvre, but Marguerite threw her the garments at a quicker rate, in order to take up her attention and close her mouth. Wasn't the second-hand a good comrade? Her affairs did not concern them. The whole department was now aiding and abetting the intrigue, the young ladies grew more agitated than ever, Lhomme and Joseph affected not to see or hear anything. And inspector Jouve, who, in passing by, had remarked Madame Aurélie's tactics, began walking up and down before the pattern-room door, with the regular step of a sentry guarding the will and pleasure of a superior.

"Give Monsieur Mouret the lists," said the first-hand.

Denise handed them over, and sat there with her eyes raised. She had started slightly, but had promptly conquered herself, and retained a fine calm look, although her cheeks were pale. For a moment, Mouret appeared to be absorbed in the lists of articles, never giving the girl a glance. A silence reigned, then Madame Aurélie all at once stepped up to Mademoiselle de Fontenailles, who had not even turned her head, and, apparently dissatisfied with her counting, said to her in an undertone:

"Go and help with the parcels. You are not used to figures."

Mademoiselle de Fontenailles got up, and returned to the department, where she was greeted with whispering. Joseph, under the laughing eyes of these young minxes, was writing anyhow. Clara though delighted to have an assistant nevertheless treated her very roughly, hating her as she hated all the women in the shop. What an idiotic thing to yield to the love of a workman, when you were a marchioness! And yet she envied the poor creature this love.

"Very good!" repeated Mouret, still pretending to read.

However, Madame Aurélie hardly knew how to get away in her turn in a decent fashion. She turned about, went to look at the machine knives, furious with her husband for not inventing a pretext for calling her. But then he was never of any use in serious matters, he would have died of thirst close to a pond. It was Marguerite who proved intelligent enough to go and ask the first-hand a question.

"I'm coming," replied the latter.

And her dignity now being saved, having a pretext to join the young ladies who were watching her, she at last left Denise and Mouret alone together, coming out of the pattern-room with a majestic step and so noble an air, that the saleswomen did not even dare to smile.

Mouret had slowly laid the lists on the table, and stood looking at Denise, who had remained seated, pen in hand. She did not avert her gaze, but she had merely turned paler.

"You will come this evening?" asked he.

"No, sir, I cannot. My brothers are to be at my uncle's to-night, and I have promised to dine with them."

"But your foot! You walk with such difficulty."

"Oh, I can get so far very well. I feel much better since the morning."

In his turn he had turned pale on hearing this quiet refusal. A nervous revolt made his lips quiver. However, he restrained himself, and with the air of a good-natured master simply interesting himself in one of his young ladies resumed: "Come now, if I begged of you—You know what great esteem I have for you."

Denise retained her respectful attitude. "I am deeply touched, sir, by your kindness to me, and thank you for this invitation. But I repeat, I cannot; my brothers expect me this evening."

She persisted in not understanding. The door remained open, and she felt that the whole shop was urging her on to ruin. Pauline had amicably called her a great simpleton; the others would laugh at her if she refused the invitation; Madame Aurélie, who had gone away, Marguerite, whose rising voice she could hear, Lhomme, whom she could espy, sitting motionless and discreet, all these people were wishing for her fall. And the distant roar of the stock-taking, the millions of goods enumerated on all sides and thrown about in every direction, were like a warm breeze wafting the breath of passion towards her. There was a silence. Now and again, Mouret's voice was drowned by the noisy accompaniment, the formidable uproar of a kingly fortune gained in battle.

"When will you come, then?" he asked again. "To-morrow?"

This simple question troubled Denise. She lost her calmness for a moment, and stammered: "I don't know—I can't—"

He smiled, and tried to take her hand, which she withheld. "What are you afraid of?" he asked.

But she quickly raised her head, looked him straight in the face, and smiling, with her sweet, brave look replied: "I am afraid of nothing, sir. I can do as I like, can I not? I don't wish to, that's all!"

As she finished speaking, she was surprised to hear a creaking noise, and on turning round saw the door slowly closing. It was inspector Jouve, who had taken upon himself to pull it to. The doors were a part of his duty, none ought ever to remain open. And he gravely resumed his position as sentinel. No one appeared to have noticed that this door was being closed in such a simple manner. Clara alone risked a strong remark in the ear of Mademoiselle de Fontenailles, but the latter's face remained expressionless.

Denise, however, had risen. Mouret was saying to her in a low and trembling voice: "Listen, Denise, I love you. You have long known it, pray don't be so cruel as to play the ignorant. I love you, Denise!" She was standing there very pale, listening to him and still looking straight into his face. "Tell me," he went on. "Why do you refuse? Have you no wants? Your brothers are a heavy burden. Anything you might ask of me, anything you might require of me—"

But with a word, she stopped him: "Thanks, I now earn more than I need."

"But it's perfect liberty that I am offering you, an existence of pleasure and luxury. I will set you up in a home of your own. I will assure you a little fortune."

"No, thanks; I should soon get tired of doing nothing. I earned my own living before I was ten years old."

He made a wild gesture. This was the first one who did not yield. With the others he had merely had to stoop. His passion, long restrained, goaded on by resistance, became stronger than ever, and he pressed her more and more urgently.

But without faltering she each time replied "No—no."

Then at last he let this heart-cry escape him: "But don't you see that I am suffering! Yes, it's stupid, but I am suffering like a child!"

Tears came into his eyes. A fresh silence reigned. They could still hear the softened roar of the stock-taking behind the closed door. It was like a dying note of triumph, the accompaniment subsided into a lower key in presence of this defeat of the master.

"And yet if I liked—" he said in an ardent voice, seizing her hands.

She left them in his, her eyes turned pale, her whole strength was deserting her. A warmth came from this man's burning grasp, filling her with a delicious cowardice. Good heavens! how she loved him, and with what delight she could have hung on his neck and remained there!

But in his passionate excitement he grew brutal. She set up a low cry; the pain she felt at her wrists restored her courage. With an angry shake she freed herself. Then, very stiff, looking taller in her weakness: "No, leave me alone! I am not a Clara, to be thrown over in a day. Besides, you love another; yes, that lady who comes here. I do not accept half an affection!"

He remained motionless with surprise. What was she saying, and what did she want? The other girls had never asked to be loved. He ought to have laughed at such an idea; yet this attitude of tender pride completely conquered his heart.

"Now, sir, please open the door," she resumed. "It is not proper that we should be shut up together in this way."

He obeyed; and with his temples throbbing, hardly knowing how to conceal his anguish, he recalled Madame Aurélie, and broke out angrily about the stock of cloaks, saying that the prices must be lowered, until every one had been got rid of. Such was the rule of the house—a clean sweep was made every year, they sold at sixty per cent. loss rather than keep an old pattern or any stale material. At that moment, Bourdoncle, seeking Mouret, was waiting for him outside, having been stopped before the closed door by Jouve, who had whispered a word in his ear with a grave air. He got very impatient, without however, summoning up sufficient courage to interrupt the governor's *tête-à-tête*. Was it possible? on such a day too, and with that creature! And when Mouret at last came out Bourdoncle spoke to him about the fancy silks, of which the stock left on hand would be something enormous This was a relief for Mouret, as it gave him an opportunity for shouting. What the devil was Bouthemont thinking about? He went off declaring that he could not allow a buyer to display such lack of sense as to buy beyond the requirements of the business.

ÉMILE ZOLA

"What is the matter with him?" murmured Madame Aurélie, quite overcome by his reproaches; while the young ladies looked at each other in surprise.

At six o'clock the stock-taking was finished. The sun was still shining—a fair summer sun, whose golden reflections streamed through the glazed roofs of the halls. In the heavy air of the streets, tired families were already returning from the suburbs laden with bouquets and dragging their children along. One by one, the departments had become silent. In the depths of the galleries you now only heard the lingering calls of a few men clearing a last shelf. Then even these voices ceased, and of all the bustle of the day there only remained a quivering vibration, above the formidable piles of goods. The shelves, cupboards, boxes, and band-boxes, were now empty: not a yard of stuff, not an object of any sort had remained in its place. The vast establishment displayed but the carcase of its usual appearance, the woodwork was absolutely bare, as on the day of taking possession. This bareness was the visible proof of the complete, exact taking of the stock. And on the floor was sixteen million francs' worth of goods, a rising sea, which had finished by submerging the tables and counters. However, the shopmen, surrounded to the shoulders, began to put each article back into its place. They expected to finish by about ten o'clock.

When Madame Aurélie, who went to the first dinner, came back from the dining-room, she announced the amount of business done during the year, which the totals of the various departments had just enabled one to arrive at. The figure was eighty million francs, ten millions more than the previous year. The only real decrease had been on the fancy silks.

"If Monsieur Mouret is not satisfied, I should like to know what more he wants," added the first-hand. "See! he's fuming over there, at the top of the grand staircase."

The young ladies went to look at him. He was standing alone, with a sombre countenance, above the millions scattered at his feet.

"Madame," said Denise, at this moment, "would you kindly let me go away now? I can't do anything more on account of my foot, and as I am to dine at my uncle's with my brothers—"

They were all astonished. She had not yielded, then! Madame Aurélie hesitated, and speaking in a sharp and disagreeable voice, seemed inclined to forbid her going out; whilst Clara shrugged her shoulders, full of incredulity. When Pauline learnt the news, she was in the baby-linen department with Deloche, and the sudden joy exhibited by the young man made her very angry. As for Bourdoncle, who did not dare to approach Mouret in his savage isolation, he marched up and down amidst these rumours, in despair also, and full of anxiety. However, Denise went down. As she slowly reached the bottom of the left-hand staircase, leaning on the banister, she came upon a group of grinning salesmen. Her name was pronounced, and she realized that they were talking about her adventure. They had not noticed her descent.

"Oh! all that's put on, you know," Favier was saying. "She's full of vice! Yes, I know some one whom she set her eyes on."

And thereupon he glanced at Hutin, who, in order to preserve his dignity as second-hand, was standing a short distance away without joining in their conversation. However, he was so flattered by the envious air with which the others contemplated him, that he deigned to murmur: "She was a regular nuisance to me, was that girl!"

Denise, wounded to the heart, clung to the banister. They must have seen her, for they all disappeared, laughing. He was right, she thought, and she reproached herself for her former ignorance, when she had been wont to think of him. But what a coward he was, and how she scorned him now! A great trouble had come upon her; was it not strange that she should have found the strength just now to repulse a man whom she adored, when she had felt herself so feeble in bygone days before that worthless fellow, whom she had only dreamed of? Her sense of reason and her bravery foundered in these contradictions of her being, which she could not clearly read. Then she hastened to cross the hall but a sort of instinct prompted her to raise her head, whilst an inspector was opening the door, closed since the morning. And still at the top of the stairs, on the great central landing dominating the gallery, she perceived Mouret. He had quite forgotten the stock-taking, he no longer beheld his empire, that building bursting with riches. Everything had disappeared, his former uproarious victories, his future colossal fortune. With a desponding look he was watching Denise and when she had crossed the threshold everything disappeared, a darkness came over the house.

# XI

That day, Bouthemont was the first to arrive at Madame Desforges's four o'clock tea. Waiting alone in her large Louis XVI drawing-room, the brasses and brocatel of which shone with a clear gaiety, she rose with an air of impatience, saying, "Well?"

"Well," replied the young man, "when I told him that I should no doubt call on you he formally promised me to come."

"You made him thoroughly understand that I expected the baron to-day?"

"Certainly. That's what appeared to decide him."

They were speaking of Mouret, who, the year before, had suddenly taken such a liking to Bouthemont that he had admitted him to share his pleasures; and had even introduced him to Henriette, glad to have an agreeable fellow always at hand to enliven an acquaintanceship of which he was getting tired. It was thus that Bouthemont had ultimately become the confidant of his employer and the handsome widow; he did their little errands, talked of the one to the other, and sometimes reconciled them. Henriette, in her jealous fits, displayed a familiarity which sometimes surprised and embarrassed him, for she was losing the prudence of a woman of the world who employed all her art to save appearances.

"You ought to have brought him," she exclaimed violently. "I should have been sure then."

"Well," said he, with a good-natured laugh, "it isn't my fault if he escapes so frequently now. Oh! he's very fond of me, all the same. Were it not for him I should be in a bad way at the shop."

His situation at The Ladies' Paradise had really been menaced since the last stock-taking. It was in vain that he talked of the rainy season, they could not overlook the considerable stock of fancy silks left on hand; and as Hutin was improving the occasion—undermining him with the governors with an increase of sly ferocity—he could feel the ground giving way beneath him. Mouret had condemned him, weary already, no doubt, of this witness who prevented him from breaking off with Henriette and tired of an acquaintanceship which yielded no profit. But, in accordance with his usual tactics, he was pushing Bourdoncle forward: it was Bourdoncle and the other partners who insisted on Bouthemont's dismissal at each board meeting; whilst he according to his own account resisted then, defending his friend energetically, at the risk even of getting into serious trouble with the others.

"Well, I shall wait," resumed Madame Desforges. "You know that the girl is to be here at five o'clock. I want to see them face to face. I must discover their secret."

And thereupon she reverted to her long-meditated plan, mentioning in her agitation that she had requested Madame Aurélie to send her Denise to look at a mantle which fitted badly. When she should once have got the young girl in her room, she would find some reason for calling Mouret, and would then act. Bouthemont, who had sat down opposite to her, was gazing at her with his handsome laughing eyes, which he was endeavouring to keep serious. This jovial fellow, with coal-black beard, this dissipated blade whose warm Gascon blood empurpled his cheeks, was thinking that fine ladies were not of much account after all, and let out a nice lot of things when they ventured to open their hearts.

"Come," he made bold to say at last, "what can that matter to you since I assure you that there is nothing whatever between them?"

"Just so!" she cried, "it's because he loves her! I don't care a fig for the others, the chance acquaintances, the friends of a day!"

She spoke of Clara with disdain. She was well aware that Mouret, after Denise's rejection, had fallen back on that tall, red-haired girl, with the horse's head: and he had done this doubtless by calculation; for he maintained her in the department, loading her with presents. Moreover for the last three months he had been leading a terribly dissipated life, squandering his money in costly and stupid caprices, with a prodigality which caused many remarks.

"It's that creature's fault," repeated Henriette. "I feel sure he's ruining himself with others because she repulses him. Besides, what's his money to me? I should have preferred him poor. You know how fond I am of him, you who have become our friend."

She stopped short, half choking, ready to burst into tears; and, in her emotion, she held out her hands to him. It was true, she adored Mouret for his youth and his triumphs, never before had any man thus conquered her; but, at the thought of losing him, she also heard the knell of her fortieth year, and asked herself with terror how she should replace this great affection.

"I'll have my revenge," she murmured, "I'll have my revenge, if he behaves badly!"

Bouthemont continued to hold her hands in his. She was still handsome. But hers would be a troublesome acquaintance to keep up and he did not care for that style of woman. The matter, however, deserved thinking over; perhaps it would be worth his while to risk some annoyance.

"Why don't you set up on your own account?" she asked all at once, drawing her hands away.

For a moment he was astonished. Then he replied: "But it would require an immense sum. Last year I had such an idea in my head. I feel convinced that there are enough customers in Paris for one or two more big shops; but the district would have to be well chosen. The Bon Marché holds the left side of the river; the Louvre occupies the centre of the city; we monopolize, at The Paradise, the rich west-end district. There remains the north, where one might start a rival establishment to the Place Clichy. And I had discovered a splendid position, near the Opera House—"

"Well, why not?" she asked.

He set up a noisy laugh. "Just fancy," he replied, "I was stupid enough to go and talk to my father about it. Yes, I was simple enough to ask him to find me some shareholders at Toulouse."

And he gaily described the anger of the old man who remained buried in his little country shop, full of rage against the great Parisian bazaars. Bursting at the thought of the thirty thousand francs a year which his son earned, he had replied that he would sooner give his money and that of his friends to the hospitals than contribute a copper to one of those great establishments which were the pests of trade.

"Besides," the young man concluded, "it would require millions."

"Suppose they were found?" observed Madame Desforges, quietly.

He looked at her, becoming serious all at once. Was not this merely a jealous woman's remark? However, she did not give him time to question her, but added: "In short, you know what a great interest I take in you. We'll talk about it again."

The outer bell had just rung. She got up, and he, himself, drew back his chair with an instinctive movement, as if some one might have surprised them. Silence reigned in the drawing-room with its gay hangings, and decorated with such a profusion of green plants that there was like a small wood between the two windows. Henriette stood waiting, with her ear towards the door.

"It is he," she murmured.

The footman announced Monsieur Mouret and Monsieur de Vallagnosc. Henriette could not restrain a movement of anger. Why had he not come alone? He must have gone for his friend, fearful of a *tête-à-tête* with her. However, she smiled and shook hands with both men.

"What a stranger you are becoming! I say the same for you, Monsieur de Vallagnosc."

Her great grief was that she was getting stout, and she now squeezed herself into the tightest fitting black silk dresses, in order to conceal her increasing corpulency. Yet her pretty head, with its dark hair, preserved its pleasing shapeliness. And Mouret could familiarly tell her, as he enveloped her with a look: "It's useless to ask after your health. You are as fresh as a rose."

"Oh! I'm almost too well," she replied. "Besides, I might have died; you would have known nothing about it."

She was examining him also, and thought that he looked tired and nervous, his eyes heavy, his complexion livid.

"Well," she resumed, in a tone which she endeavoured to render agreeable, "I cannot return your compliment; you don't look at all well this evening."

"Overwork!" remarked Vallagnosc.

Mouret shrugged his shoulders, without replying. He had just caught sight of Bouthemont, and nodded to him in a friendly way. During their closer intimacy he himself had been wont to take him away from the department, and bring him to Henriette's during the busiest moments of the afternoon. But times had changed; and he now said to him in an undertone:

"You went away very early. They noticed your departure, and are furious about it."

He referred to Bourdoncle and the other persons who had an interest in the business, as if he were not himself the master.

"Ah!" murmured Bouthemont, anxiously.

"Yes, I want to talk to you. Wait for me, we'll leave together."

Henriette had now sat down again; and, while listening to Vallagnosc, who was announcing that Madame de Boves would probably pay her a visit, she did not take her eyes off Mouret. The latter, again silent, gazed at the furniture, and seemed to be looking for something on the ceiling. Then, as she laughingly complained that she now only had gentlemen at her four o'clock tea, he so far forgot himself as to blurt out:

"I expected to find Baron Hartmann here."

Henriette turned pale. No doubt she well knew that he merely came to her house to meet the baron; still he might have avoided throwing his indifference in her face like that. At that moment the door had opened and the footman was standing behind her. When she had interrogated him by a sign, the servant leant over and said in a very low tone:

"It's for that mantle. Madame wished me to let her know. The young woman is there."

Henriette at once raised her voice, so as to be heard; and all her jealous suffering found relief in these scornfully harsh words: "She can wait!"

"Shall I show her into madame's dressing-room?" asked the servant.

"No, no. Let her stay in the ante-room!"

And, when the servant had gone, she quietly resumed her conversation with Vallagnosc. Mouret, who had relapsed into his former lassitude, had listened in an absent-minded way, without understanding, while Bouthemont, worried by the adventure, remained buried in thought. Almost at that moment, however, the door was opened again, and two ladies were shown in.

"Just fancy," said Madame Marty, "I was alighting at the door, when I saw Madame de Boves coming along under the arcade."

"Yes," explained the latter, "it's a fine day, and my doctor says I must take walking exercise."

Then, after a general hand-shaking, she inquired of Henriette: "So you're engaging a new maid?"

"No," replied the other, astonished. "Why?"

"Because I've just seen a young woman in the ante-room."

Henriette interrupted her, laughing. "It's true; all those shop-girls look like ladies' maids, don't they? Yes, it's a young person come to alter a mantle."

Mouret gazed at her intently, a suspicion flashing across his mind. But she went on with a forced gaiety, explaining that she had bought the mantle in question at The Ladies' Paradise during the previous week.

"What!" asked Madame Marty, "have you deserted Sauveur, then?"

"No, my dear, but I wished to make an experiment. Besides, I was pretty well satisfied with a first purchase I made—a travelling cloak. But this time it has not succeeded at all. You may say what you like, one is horribly rigged out in the big shops. I speak out plainly, even before Monsieur Mouret. He will never know how to dress a woman who is in the least degree stylish."

Mouret did not defend his establishment, but still kept his eyes on her, consoling himself with the thought that she would never have dared to do what he had suspected. And it was Bouthemont who had to plead the cause of The Ladies' Paradise.

"If all the aristocratic ladies who patronize us were to proclaim it," he retorted gaily, "you would be astonished by the names of our customers. Order a garment to measure at our place, it will equal one from Sauveur's and cost you but half the money. But there, just because it's cheaper, it's not so good."

"So it doesn't fit, the mantle you speak of?" resumed Madame de Boves. "Ah! now I remember the young person. It's rather dark in your ante-room."

"Yes," added Madame Marty, "I was wondering where I had seen that figure before. Well! go, my dear, don't stand on ceremony with us."

Henriette assumed a look of disdainful unconcern. "Oh, presently, there is no hurry."

Then the ladies continued the discussion on the garments sold at the large establishments; and afterwards Madame de Boves spoke of her husband, who, said she, had gone to inspect the stud-farm at Saint-Lô; while at the same time Henriette related that, owing to the illness of an aunt, Madame Guibal had been suddenly called into Franche-Comté. Moreover, she did not reckon that day on seeing Madame Bourdelais either, for at the end of every month the latter shut herself up with a needlewoman to look over her young people's clothes. Madame Marty, meantime, seemed agitated by some secret trouble. Her husband's position at the Lycée Bonaparte was menaced, in consequence of the lessons which the poor man gave in certain private establishments where a regular trade was carried on in B.A. diplomas; he now feverishly earned money wherever he could, in order to meet the rage for spending which was pillaging his household; and his wife, on seeing him weeping one evening from fear of dismissal, had conceived the idea of asking her friend Henriette to speak to a director at the Ministry of Public Instruction with whom she was acquainted. Henriette finished by quieting her with a few words. Monsieur Marty, however, was coming himself that afternoon to learn his fate and thank her.

"You look unwell, Monsieur Mouret," all at once observed Madame de Boves.

"Overwork!" repeated Vallagnosc, with ironic apathy.

Mouret quickly rose as if ashamed of forgetting himself in this fashion. He took his accustomed place in the midst of the ladies, and recovered all his agreeable manners. He was now busy with the winter novelties, and spoke of a considerable arrival of lace, whereupon Madame de Boves questioned him as to the price of Alençon point: she felt inclined to buy some. She was, however, now obliged to be sparing of even thirty sous for a cab fare and would return home quite ill from the effects of stopping before the displays in the shop windows. Draped in a mantle which was already two years old, she tried, in imagination, on her queenly shoulders all the most expensive garments she saw; and it was as though they had been torn from off her when she awoke and found herself still wearing her patched-up dresses, without the slightest hope of ever satisfying her passion.

"Baron Hartmann," now announced the footman.

Henriette observed with what pleasure Mouret shook hands with the new arrival. The latter bowed to the ladies, and glanced at the young man with that subtle expression which sometimes illumined his big Alsatian face.

"Always plunged in dress!" he murmured, with a smile; and like a friend of the house, he ventured to add: "There's a charming young person in the ante-room. Who is she?"

"Oh! nobody," replied Madame Desforges, in her ill-natured voice. "Only a shop-girl waiting to see me."

The door had remained half-open as the servant was bringing in the tea. He went out, came in again, placed the china service on the table and then brought some plates of sandwiches and biscuits. In the spacious room, a bright light, softened by the green plants, illumined the brass-work, and bathed the silk hangings in a tender glow; and each time the door opened one could perceive a dim corner of the ante-room, which was only lighted by two ground-glass windows. There, in the gloom, appeared a sombre form, motionless and patient. Denise was standing; there was indeed a leather-covered bench there, but a feeling of pride prevented her from sitting down on it. She felt the insult intended her. She had been there for the last half-hour, without a sign, without a word. The ladies and the baron had taken stock of her in passing; she could now just hear the voices from the drawing-room; all the pleasant luxury wounded her with its indifference; and still she did not move. Suddenly, however, through the half-open doorway, she perceived Mouret; and he, on his side, had at last guessed it to be her.

"Is it one of your saleswomen?" asked Baron Hartmann.

Mouret had succeeded in concealing his great distress of mind; still his voice trembled somewhat with emotion: "No doubt; but I don't know which."

"It's the little fair girl from the mantle department," replied Madame Marty, obligingly, "the second-hand, I believe."

Henriette looked at Mouret in her turn.

"Ah!" said he, simply.

And then he tried to change the conversation, speaking of the fêtes that were being given to the King of Prussia who had arrived in Paris the day before. But the baron maliciously reverted to the young ladies in the big establishments. He pretended to be desirous of gaining information, and put several questions: Where did they come from in general? Was their conduct as bad as it was said to be? Quite a discussion ensued.

"Really," he repeated, "you think them well-behaved?"

Mouret defended their conduct with a conviction which made Vallagnosc smile. Bouthemont then interfered, to save his chief. Of course, there were some of all sorts, bad and good, though they were all improving. Formerly they had secured nothing but the refuse of the trade; a poor, doubtful class of girls who had drifted into the drapery business; whereas now respectable families in the Rue de Sèvres positively brought up their daughters for the Bon Marché. In short, when they liked to conduct themselves well, they could; for they were not, like the work-girls of Paris, obliged to board and lodge themselves; they had bed and board given them, their existence, though an extremely hard one, no doubt, was at all events provided for. The worst was their neutral, ill-defined position, something between the shopwoman and the lady. Thrown into the midst of luxury, often without any primary instruction, they formed a nameless class apart from all others. Their misfortunes and vices sprang from that.

"For myself," said Madame de Boves, "I don't know any creatures who are more disagreeable. Really, one could slap them at times."

And then the ladies vented their spite. Quite a battle was waged at the shop-counters, where woman was pitted against woman in a sharp rivalry of wealth and beauty. There was the sullen jealousy of the saleswomen towards the well-dressed customers, the ladies whose manners they tried to imitate, and there was a still stronger feeling on the part of the poorly-dressed customers, those of the lower middle-class, against the saleswomen, those girls arrayed in silk, from whom they would have liked to exact a servant's humility even in the serving of a half franc purchase.

"Don't speak of them," said Henriette, by way of conclusion, "they are a wretched lot as worthless as the goods they sell!"

Mouret had the strength to smile. The baron was looking at him, so touched by his graceful command over himself that he changed the conversation, returning to the fêtes that were being given to the King of Prussia: they would be superb, said he, the whole trade of Paris would profit by them. Henriette meanwhile remained silent and thoughtful, divided between the desire to let Denise remain forgotten in the ante-room, and the fear that Mouret, now aware of her presence, might go away. At last she rose from her chair.

"You will allow me?" said she.

"Certainly, my dear!" replied Madame Marty. "I will do the honours of the house for you."

She got up, took the teapot, and filled the cups. Henriette turned towards Baron Hartmann, saying: "You will stay a few minutes, won't you?"

"Yes; I want to speak to Monsieur Mouret. We are going to invade your little drawing-room."

She went out, and her black silk dress, in rustling against the door, made a noise like that of a snake wriggling through brushwood. The baron at once manœuvred to carry Mouret off, leaving the ladies to Bouthemont and Vallagnosc. Then they stood talking before the window of the other room in a low tone. A fresh affair was in question. For a long time past Mouret had cherished a desire to realize his former project, the invasion of the whole block of building from the Rue Monsigny to the Rue de la Michodière and from the Rue Neuve-Saint-Augustin to the Rue du Dix-Décembre, by The Ladies' Paradise. Of this enormous square there still remained a large plot of ground fronting the last named street, which he had not acquired; and this sufficed to spoil his triumph, he was tormented by a desire to complete his conquest, to erect there a sort of apotheosis, a monumental façade. As long as his principal entrance should remain in the Rue Neuve-Saint-Augustin, in a dark street of olden Paris, his work would be incomplete, deficient in logic. He wished to set it up face to face with new Paris, in one of those modern avenues through which the busy multitude of the end of the nineteenth century passed in the full glare of the sunlight. He could imagine it dominating, imposing itself as the giant palace of commerce, casting even a greater shadow over the city than the old Louvre itself. But hitherto he had been baulked by the obstinacy of the Crédit Immobilier, which still clung to its first idea of building a rival establishment to the Grand Hôtel on the site in question. The plans were ready, they were only waiting for the clearing of the Rue du Dix-Décembre to begin digging the foundations. At last, however, by a supreme effort, Mouret had almost convinced Baron Hartmann.

"Well!" the latter began, "we had a board-meeting yesterday, and I came to-day, thinking I should meet you, and wishing to keep you informed. They still resist."

The young man allowed a nervous gesture to escape him. "But it's ridiculous. What do they say?"

"Dear me! they say what I have said to you myself, and what I am still inclined to think. Your façade is only an ornament, the new buildings would only increase the area of your establishment by about a tenth, and it would be throwing away immense sums on a mere advertisement."

At this, Mouret burst out. "An advertisement! an advertisement! In any case this one would be in stone, and outlive all of us. Just consider that it would increase our business tenfold! We should see our money back in two years. How can ground be lost if it returns you an enormous interest! You will see what crowds we shall have when our customers are no longer obliged to struggle through the Rue Neuve-Saint-Augustin, but can pass freely down a thoroughfare broad enough for six carriages abreast."

"No doubt," replied the baron, laughing. "But you are a poet in your way, let me tell you once more. These gentlemen think it would be dangerous for you to extend your business further. They want to be prudent for you."

"How! prudent? I no longer understand. Don't the figures show the constant increase in our sales? At first, with a capital of five hundred thousand francs, I did business to the extent of two millions, turning over the capital four times every year. It then became four million francs, which, turned over ten times, produced business to the extent of forty millions. In short, after successive increases, I have just learnt, from the last stock-taking, that the business done now amounts to a total of eighty millions; the capital, which has only been slightly increased—for it does not exceed six millions—has passed over our counters, in the form of goods sold, more than twelve times in the year!"

He raised his voice and tapped the fingers of his right hand on the palm of his left, knocking down those millions as he might have cracked nuts. The baron interrupted him. "I know, I know. But you don't hope to keep on increasing in this way, do you?"

ÉMILE ZOLA

"Why not?" asked Mouret, ingenuously. "There's no reason why it should stop. The capital can be turned over as many as fifteen times, I predicted as much long ago. In certain departments it can even be turned over twenty-five or thirty times. And after? well! after, we'll find a means of turning it over still more."

"So you'll finish by swallowing up all the money in Paris, as you'd swallow a glass of water?"

"Most decidedly. Doesn't Paris belong to the women, and don't the women belong to us?"

The baron laid his hands on Mouret's shoulders, looking at him with a paternal air. "Listen, you're a fine fellow, and I like you. There's no resisting you. We'll go into the matter seriously, and I hope to make them listen to reason. So far, we are perfectly satisfied with you. Your dividends astonish the Bourse. You must be right; it will be better to put more money into your business, than to risk this competition with the Grand Hôtel, which is hazardous."

Mouret's excitement at once subsided and he thanked the baron, but without any of his usual enthusiasm; and the other saw him turn his eyes towards the door of the next room, again a prey to the secret anxiety which he was concealing. Meanwhile Vallagnosc had come up, on seeing that they had finished talking business. He stood close to them, listening to the baron, who, with the air of an old man who had seen life, was muttering: "I say, I fancy they're taking their revenge."

"Who?" asked Mouret in embarrassment.

"Why, the women. They're getting tired of belonging to you, and you now belong to them, my dear fellow: it's only just!"

Then he joked him, well aware as he was of the young man's notorious love affairs. The enormous sums squandered by Mouret in costly and stupid caprices, amused him as an excuse for the follies which he had formerly committed himself. His old experience rejoiced to think that men had in no wise changed.

"Really, I don't understand you," repeated Mouret.

"Oh! you understand well enough," answered the baron. "They always get the last word. In fact, I thought to myself: It isn't possible, he's boasting, he can't be so strong as that! And now there you are! So though you obtain all you can from woman and work her as you would a coal mine, it's simply in order that she may work you afterwards, and force you to refund! And take care, for she'll draw more money from you than you have ever drawn from her."

He laughed louder still, and Vallagnosc standing by also began to grin, without, however, saying a word.

"Dear me! one must have a taste of everything," confessed Mouret, pretending to laugh as well. "Money is worthless, if it isn't spent."

"As for that, I agree with you," resumed the baron. "Enjoy yourself, my dear fellow. I'll not be the one to preach to you, or to tremble for the great interests we have confided to your care. Every one must sow his wild oats, and his head is generally clearer afterwards. Besides, there's nothing unpleasant in ruining one's self when one feels capable of building up another fortune. But if money is nothing, there are certain sufferings—"

He stopped and his smile became sad; former sufferings doubtless returned to his mind amid the irony of his scepticism. He had watched the duel between Henriette and Mouret with the curiosity of a man who still felt greatly interested in other people's love battles; and he divined that the crisis had arrived, he guessed the pending drama, being well acquainted with the story of that girl Denise whom he had seen in the ante-room.

"Oh! as for suffering, that's not in my line," said Mouret, in a tone of bravado. "It's quite enough to have to pay."

The baron looked at him for a moment without speaking. And not wishing to insist on the subject he added, slowly—"Don't make yourself out to be worse than you are! You'll lose something else besides your money. Yes, you'll lose a part of yourself, my dear fellow."

Then he broke off again, laughing, to ask: "That often happens, does it not, Monsieur de Vallagnosc?"

"So they say, baron," the latter merely replied.

Just at this moment the door opened. Mouret, who was about to answer in his turn, started slightly, and both he and his companions turned round. It was Madame Desforges who, looking very gay, had put her head through the doorway to call, in a hurried voice—"Monsieur Mouret! Monsieur Mouret!" And then perceiving the others, she added, "Oh! you'll excuse me, won't you, gentlemen? I'm going to take Monsieur Mouret away for a minute. The least he can do, as he has sold me such a frightful mantle, is to give me the benefit of his experience. This girl is a stupid thing without an idea in her head. Come, come! I'm waiting for you."

He hesitated, undecided, flinching from the scene he could foresee. However, he had to obey.

ÉMILE ZOLA

"Go, my dear fellow, go, madame wants you," the baron said to him, with his air at once paternal and mocking.

Thereupon Mouret followed her. The door closed, and he thought he could hear Vallagnosc's laugh, muffled by the hangings. His courage was entirely exhausted. Since Henriette had quitted the drawing-room, and he had known Denise to be there in jealous hands, he had experienced a growing anxiety, a nervous torment, which made him listen from time to time, as if suddenly startled by a distant sound of weeping. What could that woman invent to torture her? And all his love, that love which surprised him even now, went forth to the girl like a support and a consolation. Never before had he loved like this, found such a powerful charm in suffering. His former affections, his love for Henriette herself—so delicate, so handsome, so flattering to his pride—had never been more than agreeable pastimes; whereas nowadays his heart beat with anguish, his life was taken, he could no longer even enjoy the forgetfulness of sleep. Denise was ever in his thoughts. Even at this moment she was the sole object of his anxiety, and he was telling himself that he preferred to be there to protect her, notwithstanding his fear of some regrettable scene with the one he was following.

At first, they both crossed the bed-room, silent and empty. Then Madame Desforges, pushing open a door, entered the dressing-room, with Mouret behind her. It was a rather large room, hung with red silk and furnished with a marble toilet table and a large wardrobe with three compartments and great glass doors. As the window overlooked the court-yard, it was already rather dark, and the two nickel-plated gas burners on either side of the wardrobe had been lighted.

"Now, let's see," said Henriette, "perhaps we shall get on better."

On entering, Mouret had found Denise standing upright, in the middle of the bright light. She was very pale, modestly dressed in a cashmere jacket, with a black hat on her head; and she was holding the mantle purchased at The Ladies' Paradise. When she saw the young man her hands slightly trembled.

"I wish Monsieur Mouret to judge," resumed Henriette. "Just help me, mademoiselle."

Then Denise, approaching, had to give her the mantle. She had already placed some pins on the shoulders, the part that did not fit. Henriette turned round to look at herself in the glass.

"Is it possible? Speak frankly," said she.

"It really is a failure, madame," replied Mouret, to cut the matter short. "It's very simple; the young lady will take your measure, and we will make you another."

"No, I want this one, I want it immediately," she resumed with vivacity. "But it's too narrow across the chest, and it forms a ruck at the back between the shoulders." Then, in her sharpest voice, she added: "It's no use for you to stand looking at me, mademoiselle, that won't make it any better! Try and find a remedy. It's your business."

Denise again commenced to place the pins, without saying a word. This went on for some time: she had to pass from one shoulder to the other, and was even obliged to go almost on her knees, in order to pull the mantle down in front. Above her, placing herself entirely in her hands, was Madame Desforges, imparting to her face the harsh expression of a mistress exceedingly difficult to please. Delighted to lower the young girl to this servant's work, she gave her curt orders, watching the while for the least sign of suffering on Mouret's face.

"Put a pin here! No! not there, here, near the sleeve. You don't seem to understand! That isn't it, there's the ruck showing again. Take care, you're pricking me now!"

Twice again did Mouret vainly attempt to interfere, in order to put an end to this scene. His heart was beating violently from this humiliation of his love; and he loved Denise more than ever, with a deep tenderness, in presence of her admirably silent and patient demeanour. If the girl's hands still trembled somewhat, at being treated in this way before his face, she nevertheless accepted the necessities of her position with the proud resignation of one who was courageous. When Madame Desforges found they were not likely to betray themselves, she tried another device: she began to smile on Mouret, treating him openly as a lover. The pins having run short, she said to him:

"Look, my dear, in the ivory box on the dressing-table. Really! it's empty? Well, kindly look on the chimney-piece in the bed-room; you know, just beside the looking-glass."

She spoke as if he were quite at home there, and knew where to find everything. And when he came back with a few pins, she took them one by one, and forced him to remain near her, looking at him the while and speaking low: "I don't fancy I'm hump-backed, eh? Give me your hand, feel my shoulders, just to please me. Am I really made like that?"

Denise slowly raised her eyes, paler than ever, and in silence set about placing the pins. Mouret could only see her heavy blonde tresses, twisted at the back of her delicate neck; but by the slight tremor which was raising them, he could imagine the uneasiness and shame of her face. Hereafter she would most certainly repulse him, and send him back to this woman who did not conceal her affection even before strangers. Brutal thoughts came into his head, he could have struck Henriette. How was he to stop her talk? How tell Denise that he adored her, that she alone existed for him at this moment, and that he was ready to sacrifice for her all his former caprices of a day? The worst of women would not have indulged in the equivocal familiarities of this well-born lady. At last he withdrew his hand, saying:

"You are wrong in being so obstinate, madame, since I myself consider the garment to be a failure."

One of the gas jets was hissing; and in the stuffy, moist air of the room, nothing else was heard but that ardent sibilant breath. On the red silk hangings the glass-doors of the wardrobe cast broad sheets of vivid light in which the shadows of the two women played. A bottle containing some essence of verbena, which had been left uncorked inadvertently, emitted a vague expiring odour of fading flowers.

"There, madame, that is all I can do," at last said Denise, rising up.

She felt thoroughly worn out. Twice had she run the pins into her fingers, as if blind, her eyes clouded. Was he in the plot? Had he sent for her, to avenge himself for her refusal by showing her that other women had affection for him? This thought chilled her; she could not remember having ever stood in need of so much courage, not even during the terrible hours of her life when she had lacked bread. It was comparatively nothing to be humiliated in this way, but to see him so unconstrained with that other woman was dreadful. Henriette looked at herself in the glass, and once more burst into harsh words.

"What nonsense, mademoiselle! It fits worse than ever. Just see how tight it is across the chest. I look like a wet nurse!"

Denise, losing all patience thereupon made a rather unfortunate remark: "You are rather stout, madame. We cannot make you thinner than you are."

"Stout! stout!" exclaimed Henriette, turning pale in her turn. "You're becoming insolent now, mademoiselle. Really, I should advise you to criticize others!"

They both stood looking at one another, face to face, and trembling. There was now neither lady nor shop-girl left. They were simply two women, made equal by their rivalry. The one had violently taken off the mantle and cast it on a chair, whilst the other was throwing on the dressing-table the few pins still remaining in her hands.

"What astonishes me," resumed Henriette, "is that Monsieur Mouret should tolerate such insolence. I thought, sir, that you were more particular about your employees."

Denise had again recovered her brave, calm manner. "If Monsieur Mouret keeps me in his employ," she gently replied, "it's because he has no fault to find. I am ready to apologize to you, if he desires it."

Mouret was listening, excited by this quarrel but unable to find a word to put a stop to it. He had a great horror of these explanations between women, whose asperity clashed with his perpetual desire for grace and refinement. Henriette was seeking to compel him to say something in condemnation of the girl; and, as he still remained mute and undecided, she stung him with a final insult:

"Very good, sir. It seems that I must suffer the insolence of your mistresses in my own house even! A creature you've picked out of some gutter!"

Two big tears gushed from Denise's eyes. She had been keeping them back for some time past; but beneath this last insult her whole being succumbed. And when he saw her weeping like that with a silent, despairing dignity, never making the slightest attempt at retaliation, Mouret no longer hesitated; his heart went forth to her full of immense affection. He took her hands in his and stammered: "Go away quickly, my child, and forget this house!"

Henriette, perfectly amazed, choking with anger, stood looking at them.

"Wait a minute," he continued, folding up the mantle himself, "take this garment away. Madame will purchase another one elsewhere. And pray don't cry any more. You know how greatly I esteem you."

He went with her to the door, which he closed behind her. She had not said a word; but a pink flame had coloured her cheeks, whilst her eyes moistened with fresh tears, tears of a delicious sweetness. Henriette, who was suffocating, had taken out her handkerchief and was crushing her lips with it. This was a total overthrow of her calculations; she herself had been caught in the trap she had laid. She was mortified with herself for having carried matters too far, and bitterly tortured by jealousy. To be abandoned for such a creature as that! To see herself disdained before her! Her pride suffered even more than her affection.

"So, it's that girl you love?" she said painfully, when they were alone.

Mouret did not at once reply; he was walking about from the window to the door, seeking to stifle his violent emotion. At last, however, he stopped, and very politely, in a voice which he tried to render frigid, he replied in all simplicity: "Yes, madame."

The gas jet was still hissing in the stuffy air of the dressing-room. But the reflections of the glass doors were no longer traversed by dancing shadows, the room seemed bare and full of profound sadness. And Henriette suddenly dropped upon a chair, twisting her handkerchief between her febrile fingers, and, repeating amid her sobs: "Good heavens! how wretched I am!"

He stood perfectly still, looking at her for several seconds, and then went quietly away. She, left all alone, wept on in the silence, before the pins scattered over the dressing-table and the floor.

When Mouret returned to the little drawing-room, he found Vallagnosc alone, the baron having gone back to the ladies. As he still felt very agitated, he sat down at the further end of the apartment, on a sofa; and his friend on seeing him so faint charitably came and stood before him, to conceal him from curious eyes. At first, they looked at each other without saying a word. Then, Vallagnosc, who seemed to be inwardly amused by Mouret's emotion, finished by asking in his bantering voice: "Are you enjoying yourself?"

Mouret did not appear to understand him at first. But when he remembered their former conversations on the empty stupidity and useless torture of life, he replied: "Of course, I've never before lived so much. Ah! my boy, don't you laugh, the hours that make one die of grief are by far the shortest!" Then he lowered his voice and continued gaily, beneath his half-dried tears: "Yes, you know all, don't you? Between them they have rent my heart. But yet the wounds they make are nice, almost as nice as kisses. I am thoroughly exhausted but, no matter, you can't think how I love life! Oh! I shall win her at last, that little girl who still says no!"

But Vallagnosc once more trotted out his pessimism. What was the good of working so much if money could not procure everything? He would precious soon have shut up shop and have given up work on the day he found that his millions could not even win him the woman he loved! Mouret, as he listened became grave. But all at once he protested violently, believing as he did in the all-powerfulness of his will.

"I love her, and I'll win her!" said he. "But even if she escapes me, you'll see what a place I shall build to cure myself. It will be splendid, all the same. You don't understand this language, old man, otherwise you would know that action contains its own recompense. To act, to create, to struggle against facts, to overcome them or be overthrown by them, all human health and joy consists in that!"

"A mere way of diverting one's self," murmured the other.

"Well! I prefer diverting myself. As one must die, I would rather die of passion than boredom!"

They both laughed, this reminded them of their old discussions at college. Then Vallagnosc, in an effeminate voice, began to parade his theories of the insipidity of things, making almost a boast of the immobility and emptiness of his existence. Yes, he would be as bored at the Ministry on the morrow as he had been on the day before. In three years he had had a rise of six hundred francs, he was now receiving three thousand six hundred, barely enough to pay for his cigars. Things were getting worse than ever, and if he did not kill himself, it was simply from idleness and a dislike of trouble. On Mouret speaking of his marriage with Mademoiselle de Boves, he replied that despite the obstinacy of the aunt in refusing to die, the matter was about to be concluded; at least, he thought so, the parents were agreed, and he affected to have no will of his own. What was the use of wishing or not wishing, since things never turned out as one desired?

And as an example of this he mentioned his future father-in-law, who had expected to find in Madame Guibal an indolent blonde, the caprice of an hour, but was now led by her with a whip, like an old horse on its last legs. Whilst they supposed him to be inspecting the stud at Saint-Lô, he was squandering his last resources with her in a little house at Versailles.

"He's happier than you," said Mouret, getting up.

"Oh! rather!" declared Vallagnosc. "Perhaps there's only wrong-doing that's at all amusing."

Mouret was now himself again. He was thinking about getting away; but not wishing his departure to resemble a flight he resolved to take a cup of tea, and therefore went into the big drawing-room with his friend, both of them in high spirits. When the ladies inquired if the mantle had been made to fit, Mouret carelessly replied that he had given it up as a bad job as far as he was concerned. At this the others seemed astonished, and whilst Madame Marty hastened to serve him, Madame de Boves accused the shops of never allowing enough material for their garments.

At last, he managed to sit down near Bouthemont, who had not stirred. The two were forgotten for a moment, and, in reply to the anxious questions of Bouthemont, who wished to know what he had to expect, Mouret did not hesitate any longer, but abruptly informed him that the board of directors had decided to deprive themselves of his services. He sipped his tea between each sentence he uttered, protesting all the while that he was in despair. Oh! a quarrel that he had not even yet got over, for he had left the meeting beside himself with rage. But then what could he do? he could not break with those gentlemen about a simple staff question. Bouthemont, very pale, had to thank him once more.

"What a terrible mantle," at last observed Madame Marty. "Henriette can't get over it."

And really the prolonged absence of the mistress of the house had begun to make every one feel awkward. But, at that very moment, Madame Desforges appeared.

"So you've given it up as well?" exclaimed Madame de Boves, gaily.

"How do you mean?"

"Why, Monsieur Mouret told us that you could do nothing with it."

Henriette affected the greatest surprise. "Monsieur Mouret was joking," said she. "The mantle will fit splendidly."

She appeared very calm and smiling. No doubt she had bathed her eyes, for they were quite fresh, without the slightest trace of redness. Whilst her whole being was still trembling and bleeding, she managed to conceal her torment beneath a mask of smiling, well-bred elegance. And she offered some sandwiches to Vallagnosc with her usual graceful smile. Only the baron who knew her so well, remarked the slight contraction of her lips and the sombre fire which she had not been able to extinguish in the depths of her eyes. He guessed the whole scene.

"Dear me! each one to her taste," said Madame de Boves, also accepting a sandwich. "I know some women who would never buy a ribbon except at the Louvre. Others swear by the Bon Marché. It's a question of temperament, no doubt."

"The Bon Marché is very provincial," murmured Madame Marty, "and one gets so crushed at the Louvre."

They had again returned to the big establishments. Mouret had to give his opinion; he came up to them and affected to be very impartial. The Bon Marché was an excellent house, solid and respectable; but the Louvre certainly had a more showy class of customers.

"In short, you prefer The Ladies' Paradise," said the baron, smiling.

"Yes," replied Mouret, quietly. "There we really love our customers."

All the women present were of his opinion. It was indeed just that; at The Ladies' Paradise, they found themselves as at a sort of private party, they felt a continual caress of flattery, an overflowing adoration which made the most dignified of them linger there. The vast success of the establishment sprang from that gallant fascination.

"By the way," asked Henriette, who wished to appear entirely at her ease, "what have you done with my protégée, Monsieur Mouret? You know—Mademoiselle de Fontenailles." And, turning towards Madame Marty, she explained, "A marchioness, my dear, a poor girl fallen into poverty."

"Oh," said Mouret, "she earns three francs a day by stitching pattern-books, and I fancy I shall be able to marry her to one of my messengers."

"Oh! fie! what a horror!" exclaimed Madame de Boves.

He looked at her, and replied in his calm voice: "Why so, madame? Isn't it better for her to marry an honest, hard-working messenger than to run the risk of being picked up by some good-for-nothing fellow outside?"

Vallagnosc wished to interfere, for the sake of a joke. "Don't push him too far, madame, or he'll tell you that all the old families of France ought to sell calico."

"Well," declared Mouret, "it would at least be an honourable end for a great many of them."

They set up a laugh, the paradox seemed far fetched. But he continued to sing the praises of what he called the aristocracy of work. A slight flush had coloured Madame de Boves's cheeks, she was wild at the shifts to which she was put by her poverty; whilst Madame Marty, on the contrary, approved what was said, stricken with remorse on thinking of her poor husband. Just then the footman ushered in the professor, who had called to take her home. In his thin, shiny frock-coat he looked more shrivelled than ever by all his hard toil. When he had thanked Madame Desforges for having spoken for him at the Ministry, he cast at Mouret the timid glance of a man encountering the evil that is to kill him. And he was quite confused when he heard the other ask him:

"Isn't it true, sir, that work leads to everything?"

"Work and thrift," replied he, with a slight shiver of his whole body. "Add thrift, sir."

Meanwhile, Bouthemont had not moved from his chair, Mouret's words were still ringing in his ears. But at last he got up, and approaching

Henriette said to her in a low tone: "Do you know, he's given me notice; oh! in the kindest possible manner. But may I be hanged if he shan't repent it! I've just found my sign, The Four Seasons, and shall plant myself close to the Opera House!"

She looked at him with a gloomy expression. "Reckon on me, I'm with you. Wait a minute," she said.

And forthwith she drew Baron Hartmann into the recess of a window, and boldly recommended Bouthemont to him, as a fellow who would in his turn revolutionize Paris, by setting up for himself. When she went on to speak of an advance of funds for her new protégé, the baron, though now never astonished at anything, could not restrain a gesture of bewilderment. This was the fourth fellow of genius that she had confided to him, and he was beginning to feel ridiculous. But he did not directly refuse, the idea of starting a competitor to The Ladies' Paradise even pleased him somewhat; for in banking matters he had already invented this sort of competition, to keep off others. Besides, the adventure amused him, and he promised to look into the matter.

"We must talk it over to-night," whispered Henriette on returning to Bouthemont. "Don't fail to call about nine o'clock. The baron is with us."

At this moment the spacious room was full of chatter. Mouret, still standing in the midst of the ladies, had recovered his elegant gracefulness; he was gaily defending himself from the charge of ruining them in dress and offering to prove by figures that he enabled them to save thirty per cent on their purchases. Baron Hartmann watched him, seized with a fraternal admiration. Come! the duel was finished, Henriette was decidedly beaten, she certainly was not the woman who was to avenge all the others. And he fancied he could again see the modest profile of the girl whom he had observed when passing through the ante-room. She stood there, waiting, alone redoubtable in her sweetness.

# XII

It was on the 25th of September that the building of the new façade of The Ladies' Paradise commenced. Baron Hartmann, according to his promise, had managed to settle the matter at the last general meeting of the Crédit Immobilier. And Mouret was at length approaching the realization of his dream: this façade, about to arise in the Rue du Dix-Décembre, was like the very blossoming of his fortune. He therefore desired to celebrate the laying of the foundation stone; and made it a ceremony, besides distributing gratuities amongst his employees, and giving them game and champagne for dinner in the evening. Every one noticed his wonderful good humour during the ceremony, his victorious gesture as he made the first stone fast with a flourish of the trowel. For weeks he had been anxious, agitated by a nervous torment that he did not always manage to conceal; and his triumph brought a respite, a distraction to his suffering. During the afternoon he seemed to have returned to his former healthy gaiety. But, at dinner-time, when he went through the refectory to drink a glass of champagne with his staff, he appeared feverish again, smiling with a painful look, his features drawn by the unconfessed suffering which was consuming him. He was once more mastered by it.

The next day, in the cloak and mantle department, Clara Prunaire tried to be disagreeable with Denise. She had noticed Colomban's lackadaisical passion, and took it into her head to joke about the Baudus. As Marguerite was sharpening her pencil while waiting for customers, she said to her, in a loud voice:

"You know my admirer opposite. It really grieves me to see him in that dark shop which no one ever enters."

"He's not so badly off," replied Marguerite, "he's going to marry the governor's daughter."

"Oh! oh!" resumed Clara, "it would be good fun to flirt with him then! I'll try the game, on my word of honour!"

And she continued in the same strain, happy to feel that Denise was shocked. The latter forgave her everything else; but the thought of her dying cousin Geneviève being finished off by such cruelty, exasperated her. As it happened, at that moment a customer came in, and as Madame Aurélie had just gone downstairs, she took the direction of the counter, and called Clara.

"Mademoiselle Prunaire, you had better attend to this lady instead of gossiping there."

"I wasn't gossiping."

"Have the kindness to hold your tongue, and attend to this lady immediately."

Clara gave in, conquered. When Denise showed her authority, without raising her voice, not one of them resisted. She had acquired this absolute authority by her very moderation. For a moment she walked up and down in silence, amidst the young ladies who had become serious again. Marguerite had resumed sharpening her pencil, the point of which was always breaking.

"What! you're getting angry?" all at once said a voice behind Denise.

It was Pauline, on her way across the department. She had noticed the scene, and spoke in a low tone, smiling.

"But I'm obliged to," replied Denise in the same tone, "I can't manage them otherwise."

Pauline shrugged her shoulders. "Nonsense, you can be queen over all of us whenever you like," she replied. She was still unable to understand her friend's refusal.

Since the end of August, Pauline had been married to Baugé; a most stupid affair, she would sometimes gaily remark. That terrible Bourdoncle treated her anyhow, now, considering her as lost for trade. Her great fear was that they might some fine day send her to love her husband elsewhere, for the managers had decreed love to be execrable and fatal to business. So great was her dread, that when she met Baugé in the galleries she often affected not to know him. She had just had a fright—old Jouve having nearly caught her talking to her husband behind a pile of dusters.

"See! he's followed me," she added, after hastily relating the adventure to Denise. "Just look at him sniffing for me with his big nose!"

Jouve, in fact, was just then coming from the lace department, correctly arrayed in a white tie, and with his nose on the scent for some delinquent. But when he saw Denise, his face relaxed and he passed by with an amiable smile.

"Saved!" murmured Pauline. "My dear, you made him swallow that! I say, if anything should happen to me, you would speak for me, wouldn't you? Yes, yes, don't put on that astonished air, we know that a word from you would revolutionize the house."

And thereupon she ran off to her counter. Denise had blushed, troubled by these friendly allusions. It was true, however. She had a vague sensation of her power from the flattery with which she was surrounded. When Madame Aurélie returned, and found the department quiet and busy under the surveillance of the second-hand, she smiled at her amicably. She threw over Mouret himself, and her amiability daily increased for the young person who might some fine morning desire her situation as first-hand. In a word Denise's reign was commencing.

Bourdoncle alone still stood out. In the secret warfare which he carried on against the young girl, there was in the first place a natural antipathy. He detested her for her gentleness and her charm. Then too he fought against her as against a fatal influence which would place the house in peril on the day when Mouret should succumb. The governor's commercial genius seemed certain to founder in this stupid affection: all that they had gained by women would be swallowed up by this one. None of them touched Bourdoncle's heart, he treated them all with the disdain of a passionless man whose business was to live by them, and whose last illusions had been dispelled by seeing them so closely amidst the worries of his trade. And what made him especially anxious in the presence of this little saleswoman, who had gradually become so redoubtable, was that he did not in the least believe in her disinterestedness, in the genuineness of her refusals. In his opinion she was playing a part, the most skilful of parts, rendering Mouret absolutely mad, capable of any folly.

Thus Bourdoncle could never now catch sight of her, with her clear eyes, sweet face, and simple attitude, without experiencing a real fear, as if he had before him some disguised female flesh-eater, the sombre enigma of woman, Death in the guise of a virgin. In what way could he possibly confound the tactics of this spurious novice? He was now only anxious to penetrate her artful ways, in the hope of exposing them to the light of day. She would certainly commit some fault at last; he would surprise her with one of her sweethearts, and she would again be dismissed. The house would then resume its regular working like a well-appointed machine.

"Keep a good look-out, Monsieur Jouve," Bourdoncle kept saying to the inspector. "I'll take care that you shall be rewarded."

But Jouve was somewhat lukewarm for he knew something about women, and asked himself whether he had not better take the part of this girl, who might be the sovereign mistress of the morrow. Though he did not now dare to touch her, he still thought her bewitchingly pretty. His colonel in bygone days had killed himself for a similar little thing, with an insignificant face, delicate and modest, one look from whom had ravaged all hearts.

"I'm watching," he replied. "But, on my word, I cannot discover anything."

And yet stories were circulating, there was quite a current of abominable tittle-tattle running beneath the flattery and respect which Denise felt arising around her. The whole house now declared that she had formerly had Hutin for a sweetheart; and they were suspected of still meeting from time to time. Deloche also was said to keep company with her; they were continually meeting in dark corners and talking for hours together. It was quite a scandal!

"So, there's nothing about the first-hand in the silk department, or about the young man in the lace one?" asked Bourdoncle.

"No, sir, nothing yet," replied the inspector.

It was with Deloche especially that Bourdoncle expected to surprise Denise, for one morning he himself had caught them laughing together downstairs. In the meantime, he treated her on a footing of perfect equality, for he no longer disdained her, feeling that she was strong enough to overthrow even himself notwithstanding his ten years' service, should he lose the game.

"Keep your eye on the young man in the lace department," he concluded each time. "They are always together. If you catch them, call me, and I'll manage the rest."

Mouret, meanwhile, was living in anguish. Was it possible that such a child could torture him in this manner? He could always recall her arrival at The Ladies' Paradise, with her heavy shoes, thin black dress, and wild look. She stammered, they all used to laugh at her, he himself had thought her ugly at first. Ugly! and now she could have brought him to his knees by a look, for he thought her nothing less than an angel! Then she had remained the last in the house, repulsed, joked at, treated by him as a curious specimen of humanity. For months he had wanted to see how a girl sprung up, and had amused himself with this experiment, not understanding that he was risking his heart. She, little by little had grown and become redoubtable. Perhaps he had loved her from the very first, even at the time when he had thought that he felt nothing but pity for her. And yet, he had only really begun to feel this love on the evening of their walk under the chestnut trees of the Tuileries. His life dated from then; he could still hear the laughter of a group of little girls, the distant fall of a jet of water, whilst in the warm shade she walked on beside him in silence. After that, he knew no more, his fever had increased hour by hour; all his blood, his whole being, in fact, had been given to her. And she, such a child—was it possible? When she passed by now, the slight gust from her dress seemed to him so powerful that he staggered.

For a long time he had struggled, and even now he frequently became indignant and endeavoured to free himself from this idiotic possession. What power was it she possessed that she should be able to bind him in this way? Had he not seen her without boots to her feet? Had she not been received almost out of charity? He could have understood had it been a question of one of those superb creatures who charm the multitude! but this little girl; this nobody! She had, in short, one of those insignificant faces which excite no remark. She could not even be very intelligent, for he remembered her bad beginning as a saleswoman. But, after every explosion of anger, he experienced a relapse of passion, a kind of sacred terror at having insulted his idol. She possessed everything a woman can have that is good—courage, gaiety, simplicity; and from her gentleness a charm of penetrating, perfume-like subtlety was exhaled. One might at first ignore her, or elbow her like any other girl; but the charm soon began to act with invincible force; and one belonged to her for ever, if she deigned to smile. Everything then beamed in her white face, her soft eyes, her cheeks and chin full of dimples; whilst her heavy blonde hair also seemed to light up with a royal and conquering beauty. He acknowledged himself vanquished; she was as intelligent as she was beautiful, her intelligence came from the best part of her being. Whilst in his eyes the other saleswomen only possessed a superficial education, the varnish which scales off from girls of that class, she, without any false elegance, retained her native grace, the savour of her origin. The broadest commercial ideas sprang up from her experience, behind her narrow forehead, whose pure lines clearly announced the presence of a firm will and love of order. And he could have clasped his hands to ask her pardon for blaspheming in his hours of revolt.

Why did she still refuse with such obstinacy? Twenty times had he entreated her, increasing his offers, offering money and more money. Then, thinking that she must be ambitious, he had promised to appoint her first-hand, as soon as there should be a vacancy. And she had refused, and still refused! For him it was a stupor, a struggle in which his desire became rageful.

All his days were now spent amidst the same grievous obsession. Denise's image rose with him. After he had dreamed of her all night, she followed him to the desk in his office, where he signed the bills and orders from nine to ten o'clock: a work which he accomplished mechanically, never ceasing to feel her present, still saying "no," with her quiet air. Then, at ten o'clock, came the board-meeting, quite a cabinet council composed of the twelve directors, at which he had to preside; they discussed matters affecting the in-door arrangements, examined the purchases, settled the window displays; and yet she was still there, he heard her soft voice amidst the figures, he saw her bright smile amidst the most complicated financial situations. After the board-meeting, she accompanied him on the daily inspection of the departments, and returning with him to his office in the afternoon, she remained close to his chair from two till four o'clock, whilst he received a crowd of important business men, the principal manufacturers of France, bankers and inventors: a continual coming-and-going of the wealth and intelligence of the land, a mad dance of millions, rapid interviews during which the biggest affairs of the Paris market were concluded. If he forgot her for a moment whilst he was deciding to ruin or support an industry, he found her again at a sudden twitch of his heart; his voice died away, and he asked himself what could be the use of this princely fortune since she still refused. At last, when five o'clock struck, he had to sign the day's correspondence, and the mechanical working of his hand began again, whilst she rose up before him more domineering than ever, seizing him entirely, to hold possession of him throughout the solitary and ardent hours of the night. And the morrows were the same days over again, days which were so active, so full of colossal labour but which the slight shadow of a child sufficed to ravage with anguish.

However, it was particularly during his daily inspection of the departments that he felt his misery. To have built up this giant machine, to reign over such a world of people, and yet to be dying of grief because a little girl would not accept him! He scorned himself, dragging the fever and shame of his pain about with him everywhere. On certain days he became disgusted with his power; from one end to the other of the galleries he felt nothing but nausea. At other times he would have wished to extend his empire, and make it so vast that she would perhaps have yielded out of sheer admiration and fear.

He would begin by stopping in the basement opposite the shoot. This was still in the Rue Neuve-Saint-Augustin; but it had been necessary to enlarge it, and it was now as wide as the bed of a river, down which the continual flood of goods rolled with the loud noise of rushing water. There was a succession of arrivals from all parts of the world, rows of waggons from every railway, a ceaseless unloading, a stream of packing-cases and bales flowing underground and absorbed by the insatiable establishment. He gazed at this torrent pouring into his house, he felt that he was one of the masters of the public fortune, that he held in his hands the fate of French manufactures, and yet was unable to buy a kiss from one of his saleswomen.

Then he passed on to the receiving department, which now occupied that part of the basement skirting the Rue Monsigny. Twenty tables were ranged there, in the pale light from the air-holes; quite a crowd of assistants was bustling about, emptying cases, checking goods, and marking them in plain figures, amidst the neighbouring roar of the shoot, which almost drowned their voices. Various managers of departments stopped him, he had to solve difficulties and confirm orders. The cellar filled with the soft glimmer of satin and the whiteness of linen, a prodigious unpacking in which furs were mingled with lace, French fancy goods with Eastern hangings. With a slow step he wended his way amidst all these riches thrown about in disorder, heaped up in their rough state. Up above, they would shine in the window displays, set money galloping through the departments, no sooner shown than carried off, in the furious rush of business which traversed the place. But he kept on thinking that he had offered Denise silks and velvets, anything she might like to take in no matter what quantity, from among these enormous heaps, and that she had refused his offer by a slight shake of her fair head.

After that, he went to the other end of the basement, to pay his usual visit to the delivery department. Interminable corridors ran along, lighted by gas; to the right and the left, the reserves, closed in with gratings, seemed like so many subterranean stores, a complete commercial district, with its haberdashery, underclothing, glove, toy and other shops, all sleeping in the gloom. Further on stood one of the three hot-air stoves; further still, was a post of firemen guarding the main gas-meter, enclosed in its iron cage. He found, in the delivery department, the sorting tables already littered with heaps of parcels, band-boxes, and cases which were continually arriving in large hampers; and Campion, the superintendent, gave him particulars about the current work, whilst the twenty men placed under his orders distributed the parcels among large compartments, each of which bore the name of a district of Paris, and whence the messengers took them up to the vans waiting beside the foot pavement. There was a succession of cries, names of streets and other instructions were shouted out, quite an uproar arose, all the bustle of a mail-boat about to leave her moorings. And he stood there for a moment, motionless, watching this emission of goods which he had just seen the house absorb at the opposite end of the basement: the huge current ended here; it was here that it discharged itself into the street again after filling the tills with gold. But his eyes became dim, this colossal business no longer had any importance for him; he had but one idea, that of going away to some distant land, and abandoning everything, should she persist in saying no.

Then he went upstairs, continuing his inspection, talking and bestirring himself more and more, but without finding any respite. On the second floor, he entered the forwarding department, seeking quarrels and secretly exasperated with the perfect regularity of the machine which he had himself built up. This department was the one that was daily assuming a more considerable importance: it now occupied two hundred employees—some of whom opened, read, and classified the letters coming from the provinces and abroad, whilst others collected in compartments the goods ordered by customers. And the number of letters was increasing to such an extent that they no longer counted them; they weighed them, receiving as much as a hundredweight a day. He feverishly went through the three offices, questioning Levasseur, the chief, as to the weight of the correspondence; now it was eighty, now ninety, sometimes, on a Monday, a hundred pounds. The figure increased daily, he ought to have been delighted. But he stood quivering amid the noise made by a neighbouring squad of packers nailing down the cases. It was in vain that he roamed about the building: his fixed idea remained fast in his mind, and as his power unfolded itself before him, as the mechanism of the business and the army of employees passed before his gaze, he felt more deeply than ever the taunt of his powerlessness. Orders from all Europe were flowing in, a special post-office van was required for his correspondence; and yet she said no, always no.

He returned downstairs and visited the central cashier's office, where four clerks guarded the two giant safes, through which eighty-eight million francs had passed during the previous year. He glanced at the clearing-house office which now occupied thirty-five clerks, chosen from amongst the most trustworthy. He went into the checking office, where twenty-five young men, junior clerks, checked the debit-notes and calculated the salesmen's commissions. He returned to the chief cashier's office, grew exasperated by the sight of the safes, wandered about amidst these millions, the uselessness of which was driving him mad. She said no, always no.

And it was always and ever no, in all the departments, in the galleries, the saloons, in every part of the establishment! He went from the silk to the drapery department, from the linen to the lace; he ascended to the upper floors, pausing on the hanging bridges, prolonging his inspection with a maniacal, grievous minuteness. The house had grown and spread beyond all bounds, he had created this department, then that other; he governed that fresh domain, he extended his empire into that industry, the last one conquered; and it was no, always no, in spite of everything. His staff would now have sufficed to people a small town: there were fifteen hundred salesmen, and a thousand other employees of every sort, including forty inspectors and seventy cashiers; the kitchens alone gave occupation to thirty-two men; ten clerks were set apart for the advertising service; there were three hundred and fifty shop messengers, all wearing livery, and twenty-four firemen living on the premises. And the stables, royal buildings situated in the Rue Monsigny, opposite the warehouses, accommodated one hundred and forty-five horses, a splendid set of animals already celebrated. The first four conveyances which had stirred up the whole neighbourhood formerly when the house occupied only the corner of the Place Gaillon, had gradually increased to sixty-two: small hand-trucks, one-horse vans, and heavy two-horse ones. They were continually scouring Paris, skilfully driven by coachmen clad in black, and bearing hither and thither the gold and purple sign of The Ladies' Paradise. They even went beyond the fortifications, and sped through the suburbs; they were to be met in the hollow roads of Bicêtre and along the banks of the Marne, along even the shady drives of the Forest of Saint-Germain. Sometimes one would emerge from the depths of some sunny avenue, where all was silent and deserted, the superb animals which drew it passing by at a trot, whilst it cast the glaring advertisement of its varnished panels upon the mysterious peacefulness of nature. Mouret was actually thinking of sending these vehicles further still, even into the neighbouring departments; he would have liked to hear them rolling along every road in France, from one frontier to the other. But he no longer even crossed the street to visit his horses, though he was passionately fond of them. Of what good was this conquest of the world, since it was no, always no?

Nowadays of an evening, when he arrived at Lhomme's desk, he still from force of habit glanced at the amount of the takings written on a card, which the cashier stuck up on an iron file beside him; this figure rarely fell below a hundred thousand francs, sometimes on big sale days it ran up to eight and nine hundred thousand; but the amount no longer sounded in Mouret's ears like a trumpet-blast, he regretted having looked at it, and bitterly went his way, full of hatred and scorn of money.

But his sufferings were destined to increase, for he became jealous. One morning, in the office, before the board-meeting began, Bourdoncle ventured to hint that the little girl in the mantle department was playing with him.

"How so?" he asked, turning very pale.

"Why yes! she has sweethearts in this very building."

Mouret found strength to smile. "I don't think any more about her, my dear fellow. You can speak freely. Who are they?"

"Hutin, they say, and then a salesman in the lace department—Deloche, that tall awkward fellow. I can't speak with certainty, never having seen them together. But it appears that it's notorious."

There was a silence. Mouret affected to arrange the papers on his table in order to conceal the trembling of his hands. At last, he observed, without raising his head: "One must have proofs, try and bring me some proofs. As for myself, I assure you I don't care in the least, for I'm quite sick of her. But we can't allow such things to go on here."

"Never fear," replied Bouthemont, "you shall have proofs one of these days. I'm keeping a good look-out."

This news deprived Mouret of all rest. He had not the courage to revert to the conversation, but lived in continual expectation of a catastrophe, in which his heart would be crushed. And this torment rendered him terrible; he made the whole house tremble. He now disdained to conceal himself behind Bourdoncle, and performed the executions in person, feeling a nervous desire for revenge, solacing himself by abuse of his power, that power which could do nothing for the contentment of his sole desire. Each of his inspections became a massacre; as soon as he was seen a shudder of panic sped from counter to counter. The dead winter season was just then approaching, and he made a clean sweep in each department, piling up victims and hustling them into the street. His first idea had been to dismiss Hutin and Deloche; but he had reflected that if he did not keep them, he would never discover anything; and the others suffered for them: the whole staff trembled. In the evening, when he found himself alone again, tears made his eyelids swell.

One day especially terror reigned supreme. An inspector had the idea that Mignot was stealing. There was always a number of strange-looking girls prowling around his counter; and one of them had lately been arrested, her hips and bosom padded with sixty pairs of gloves. From that moment a watch was kept, and the inspector caught Mignot in the act of facilitating the sleight of hand of a tall fair girl who had formerly been a saleswoman at the Louvre. His plan was very simple, he pretended to be trying some gloves on her, waited till she had padded herself, and then conducted her to the pay-desk, where she paid for a single pair only. Mouret happened to be there, just at that moment. As a rule, he preferred not to mix himself up in affairs of this sort, which were fairly frequent; for notwithstanding the regular machine-like working, great disorder reigned in certain departments of The Ladies' Paradise, and scarcely a week passed by without some employee being dismissed for theft. The management preferred to hush up such matters as far as possible, considering it undesirable to set the police at work, and thus expose one of the fatal plague-spots of these great bazaars. But, that day, Mouret felt a real need of venting his anger on some one, and treated handsome Mignot with such violence, that the latter stood there trembling with fear, his face pale and distorted.

"I ought to call a policeman," cried Mouret, before all the other salesmen. "But answer me! who is this woman? I swear I'll send for the police commissary, if you don't tell me the truth."

The woman had been taken away, and two saleswomen were searching her. "I don't know her, sir," Mignot stammered out: "She's the one who came—"

"Don't tell lies!" interrupted Mouret, more violently still. "And there's nobody here to warn us! You are all in the plot, on my word! We are robbed, pillaged, plundered. It's enough to make us have the pockets of each one searched before he leaves!"

Murmurs were heard. The three or four customers buying gloves stood looking on, frightened.

"Silence!" he resumed, furiously, "or I'll clear the whole place!"

However, Bourdoncle came running up, all anxiety at the idea of the scandal. He whispered a few words in Mouret's ear, the affair was assuming exceptional gravity; and he prevailed on him to take Mignot into the inspectors office, a room on the ground-floor near the entrance in the Rue Gaillon. The woman was there, quietly putting on her things again. She had just mentioned Albert Lhomme's name. Mignot, on again being questioned, lost his head, and began to sob; he wasn't in fault, it was Albert who sent him these girls; he had at first merely afforded them certain advantages, enabling them to profit by the bargains; and at last when they took to stealing, he was already too far compromised to report the matter. The principals now discovered a series of extraordinary robberies; goods taken away by girls who went into the luxurious lavatories, situated near the refreshment bar and surrounded by evergreen plants, to hide them under their skirts; purchases which a salesman neglected to call out at a pay-desk, when he accompanied a customer there and the price of which he divided with the cashier; and even false "returns," articles which employees said had been brought back in order that they might pocket the refunded money; without mentioning the common robberies of things which the salesmen took away under their coats in the evening, sometimes rolled round their bodies, and sometimes even hung down their legs. For the last fourteen months, thanks to Mignot and other salesmen, no doubt, whom they refused to name, this pilfering had been going on at Albert's desk—quite an impudent trafficking in articles representing a large amount of money which was never correctly ascertained.

Meanwhile the news had spread through the various departments, causing guilty consciences to tremble, whilst the most honest quaked at thought of the general sweep that seemed imminent. Albert had disappeared into the inspector's office. Next his father had passed by, half choking, his face red and showing signs of apoplexy. Then Madame Aurélie herself was called; and came down bearing the affront with head erect, her fat puffy countenance having the appearance of a wax mask. The explanation lasted for some time; no one knew the exact details, but it was said that the first-hand had slapped her son's face, whilst the worthy old father wept, and the governor, contrary to all his elegant habits, swore like a trooper, absolutely wanting to hand the offenders over to justice. However, the scandal was hushed up. Mignot was the only one dismissed there and then. Albert did not disappear till two days later; his mother had doubtless begged that the family might not be dishonoured by an immediate execution. Still the panic lasted several days longer, for after this scene Mouret wandered from one end of the establishment to the other, with a terrible expression, venting his anger on all those who dared even to raise their eyes.

"What are you doing there, sir, looking at the flies? Go and get paid!"

At last, the storm burst one day on the head of Hutin himself. Favier, now appointed second, was undermining the first-hand, in order to dislodge him from his position. This was always the way; he addressed crafty reports to the directors, taking advantage of every opportunity to have the first-hand caught doing something wrong. Thus, one morning, as Mouret was going through the silk department, he stopped short quite surprised to see Favier altering the price tickets of a stock of black velvet.

"Why are you lowering the prices?" he asked. "Who gave you the order to do so?"

The second-hand, who was making a great fuss over this work, as if he wished to attract the governor's attention and foresaw the result, replied with an innocent, astonished air: "Why, Monsieur Hutin told me, sir."

"Monsieur Hutin! Where is Monsieur Hutin?"

And when the latter came up from the receiving department where a salesman had been sent to fetch him, an animated explanation ensued. What! he undertook to lower the prices of his own accord now! What did that mean? But in his turn he appeared greatly astonished, having merely talked the matter over with Favier, without giving any positive orders. The latter then assumed the sorrowful air of an employee who finds himself obliged to contradict his superior. Yet he was quite willing to accept the blame, if it would get the latter out of a scrape. Things began to look very bad.

"Understand, Monsieur Hutin!" cried Mouret, "I have never tolerated these attempts at independence. We alone decide about the prices."

He went on speaking in a sharp voice, and with wounding intentions, which surprised the salesmen, for as a rule these discussions were carried on quietly, and the affair might really have been the result of a misunderstanding. One could divine, however, that he had some unavowed spite to satisfy. He had at last caught that Hutin in fault, that Hutin who was said to be Denise's sweetheart. He could now relieve himself, by making the other feel that he, Mouret, was the master! And he exaggerated matters, even insinuating that this reduction of price appeared to conceal very questionable intentions.

"Sir," repeated Hutin, "I meant to consult you about it. It is really necessary, as you know, for there has been no demand for these velvets."

Mouret cut him short with a final harsh remark. "Very good, sir; we will look into the matter. But don't do such a thing again, if you value your situation."

And then he walked off. Hutin, bewildered, furious, finding no one but Favier to confide in, swore that he would go and throw his resignation at the brute's head. But he soon left off talking of leaving, and began to stir up all the abominable accusations which were current amongst the salesmen against their chiefs. And Favier, his eyes sparkling, defended himself with a great show of sympathy. He was obliged to reply, wasn't he? Besides, could any one have foreseen such a row over so trifling a matter? What had come on the governor lately, that he should be so unbearable?

"We all know what's the matter with him," replied Hutin. "Is it my fault if that little jade in the mantle department is turning his head? My dear follow, you can see that the blow comes from there. He's aware that she fancied me, and he doesn't like it; or perhaps it's she herself who wants to get me dismissed because I'm in her way. But I swear she shall hear from me, if ever she crosses my path."

Two days later, as Hutin was going into the work-rooms upstairs, under the leads, to recommend a girl of his acquaintance, he started on perceiving Denise and Deloche leaning against a window at the end of a passage and plunged so deeply in private conversation that they did not even turn round. The idea of having them caught there suddenly occurred to him, when he perceived with astonishment that Deloche was weeping. He at once went off without making any noise; and meeting Bourdoncle and Jouve on the stairs, told them some story about one of the fire-extinguishers, the door of which seemed to have been torn away; in this manner they would go upstairs and drop on to the two others. Bourdoncle discovered them first. He stopped short, and told Jouve to go and fetch the governor, whilst he remained there. The inspector had to obey, though greatly annoyed at being forced to mix himself up in such a matter.

This was a lost corner of the vast world where the people of The Ladies' Paradise bestirred themselves. You reached it by an intricate network of stairs and passages. The work-rooms, situated in the attics, were low sloping chambers, lighted by large windows cut in the zinc roofing, and furnished solely with long tables and large cast-iron stoves; and all along was a crowd of work-girls engaged on the under-clothing, the lace, the upholstery and the dressmaking, and living winter and summer in a stifling heat, amidst the odour peculiar to the business. You had to skirt all these rooms, and turn to the right after passing the dressmakers, before coming to the solitary end of the corridor. The few customers, whom a salesman occasionally brought here for an order, gasped for breath, tired out and frightened, with the sensation of having turned round and round for hours, and of being a hundred leagues above the street.

Denise had often found Deloche waiting for her. As second-hand she had charge of the arrangements between her department and the work-room where only the models and alterations were attended to, and was always going up and down to give the necessary orders. The young man would watch for her and invent any pretext to run after her; and then affected to be surprised when he met her at the work-room door. She got to laugh about the matter and it became quite an understood thing. The corridor ran alongside one of the cisterns, an enormous iron tank containing twelve thousand gallons of water; and on the roof there was another one of equal size, reached by an iron ladder. For an instant, Deloche would stand talking, leaning one shoulder against the cistern in the continual abandonment of his long body, bent by fatigue. A singsong noise of water was heard, a mysterious noise, the musical vibration of which the iron tank ever retained. Despite the solitude, Denise would at times turn round anxiously, thinking, she had seen a shadow pass on the bare, pale yellow walls. But the window would soon attract them, they would lean against it, and forget themselves in a pleasant gossip, in endless souvenirs of their native place. Below them extended the immense glass roof of the central gallery, a lake of glass bounded by the distant housetops, as by a rocky coast. Beyond, they saw nothing but the sky, a sheet of sky, which cast in the sleeping water of the glass work a reflection of the flight of its clouds and its soft azure.

It so happened that Deloche was that day speaking of Valognes. "I was six years old; my mother used to take me to Valognes market in a cart," he said. "You know it's ten miles away; we had to leave Briquebec at five o'clock. It's a fine country down our way. Do you know it?"

"Yes, yes," replied Denise, slowly, her glances wandering far away. "I was there once, but was very little then. Roads with grass on each side, eh? and now and again sheep browsing in couples, dragging their clog along by the rope." She stopped, then resumed with a vague smile: "Our roads run for miles as straight as arrows between rows of trees which afford some shade. We have meadows surrounded by hedges taller than I am, where there are horses and cows grazing. We have a little river too, and the water is very cold, under the brushwood, in a spot I well know."

"It is the same with us, exactly!" cried Deloche, delighted.

"There's grass everywhere, each one encloses his plot with thorns and elms, and is at once at home; and it's quite green, a green far different to what we see in Paris. Dear me! how I've played in the hollow road, on the left, coming down from the mill!"

Their voices died away, they remained with their eyes fixed, lost on the sunny lake of the glass work. A mirage rose up before them from that blinding water, they beheld an endless succession of meadows, the Cotentin country steeped in the breath of the ocean, bathed in a luminous vapour, which blurred the horizon with the delicate grey of a water-colour. Below them, beneath the colossal iron framework, in the silk hall, was the roar of business, the trepidation of the machine at work; the entire house vibrated with the tramping of the crowd, the bustle of the salesmen, the life of the thirty thousand persons hurtling there; and they, carried away by their dreams, thought they could hear the wind passing over the grass and shaking the tall trees, as they detected this deep dull clamour with which the roofs were resounding.

"Ah! Mademoiselle Denise," stammered Deloche, "why aren't you kinder to me? I love you so much!" Tears had come into his eyes, and as she signed to him to stop, he continued quickly: "No—let me tell you these things once more. We should get on so well together! People always find something to talk about when they come from the same part."

He was choking, and she was at last able to say kindly: "You're not reasonable; you promised me never to speak of that again. It's impossible. I have great friendship for you, because you're a nice fellow; but I wish to remain free."

"Yes, yes. I know," he replied in a broken voice, "you don't love me. Oh! you may say so, I quite understand it. There's nothing in me to make you love me. Listen, I've only had one sweet moment in my life, and that was when I met you at Joinville, do you remember? For a moment, under the trees, when it was so dark, I thought your arm trembled, and was stupid enough to imagine—"

But she again interrupted him. Her quick ear had just detected the sound of Bourdoncle's and Jouve's steps at the end of the corridor.

"Hark, there's some one coming."

"No," said he, preventing her from leaving the window, "it's in the cistern: all sorts of extraordinary noises come from it, as if there were some one inside."

And then he continued his timid caressing complaints. She was no longer listening to him, however. Rocked into a dreamy mood by his declaration of love, her eyes wandering over the roofs of The Ladies' Paradise. To the right and the left of the large glazed gallery, other galleries and other halls were glistening in the sunshine, between the housetops, pierced with garret windows and running along symmetrically, like the wings of a barracks. Metal ladders and bridges rose on all sides, describing a lacework of iron in the air; whilst the kitchen chimney belched forth as much smoke as a factory, and the great square cistern, supported aloft by cast-iron pillars, assumed the strange silhouette of some barbarous structure erected at this height by the pride of one man. In the distance, Paris roared.

When Denise awoke from this dreamy contemplation of space and the summits of The Ladies' Paradise, where her thoughts floated as in a vast solitude, she found that Deloche had caught hold of her hand. And as he appeared so woe-begone she did not draw it away.

"Forgive me," he murmured. "It's all over now; I should be too miserable if you punished me by withdrawing your friendship. I assure you I intended to say something else. Yes, I had determined to understand the situation and be very good." Then his tears again began to flow and he tried to steady his voice. "For I know my lot in life. It is too late for my luck to turn. Beaten at home, beaten in Paris, beaten everywhere! I've now been here four years and am still the last in the department. So I wanted to tell you not to trouble on my account. I won't annoy you any more. Try to be happy, love some one else; yes, that would really be a pleasure for me. If you are happy, I shall be happy too. That will be my happiness."

He could say no more. As if to seal his promise he raised the young girl's hand to his lips—kissing it with the humble kiss of a slave. She was deeply affected, and said simply, in a tender, sisterly tone, which softened somewhat the pity of the words: "My poor lad!"

But they started, and turned round; Mouret was standing before them.

For the last ten minutes, Jouve had been searching all over the place for the governor; the latter, however, was looking at the building of the new façade in the Rue du Dix-Décembre. He spent long hours there every day, trying to interest himself in this work, of which he had so long dreamed. There, amidst masons laying the huge corner-stones, and engineers setting up the great iron framework, he found a refuge against his torments. The façade already appeared above the level of the street; and indications of the spacious porch, and the windows of the first storey, a palace-like development in a crude state could be seen. Mouret scaled the ladders, discussing with the architect the ornamentation which was to be something quite new, scrambled over the heaps of brick and iron, and even went down into the cellars; and the roar of the steam-engine, the tic-tac of the trowels, the loud noise of the hammers and the clamour of the army of workmen in this immense cage surrounded by sound-reëchoing planks, really diverted him for an instant. He would come out white with plaster, black with iron-filings, his feet splashed by the water from the pumps but nevertheless so far from being cured that his anguish returned and his heart beat more loudly than ever, as the uproar of the works died away behind him. It so happened, on the day in question, that a slight diversion had brought back his gaiety: he had become deeply interested in an album of drawings of the mosaics and enamelled terra-cotta which were to decorate the friezes, when Jouve, out of breath, annoyed at being obliged to soil his frock coat amongst all the building materials came up to fetch him. At first Mouret cried out that they must wait; but, at a word spoken in an undertone by the inspector, he immediately followed him, trembling and again mastered by his passion. Nothing else existed, the façade crumbled away before being built: what was the use of that supreme triumph of his pride, if the mere name of a woman whispered in his ear tortured him to this extent!

Upstairs, Bourdoncle and Jouve thought it prudent to vanish. Deloche had hastened away; Denise, paler than usual, alone remained face to face with Mouret, looking straight into his eyes.

"Have the goodness to follow me, mademoiselle," he said in a harsh voice.

She followed him, they descended the two storeys, and crossed the furniture and carpet departments without saying a word. When he arrived at his office, he opened the door wide, saying, "Walk in, mademoiselle."

And, closing the door, he went to his table. The director's new office was fitted up more luxuriously than the old one; the rep hangings had been replaced by velvet ones, and a book-case, inlaid with ivory, occupied one whole side; but on the walls there was still no other picture than the portrait of Madame Hédouin, a young woman with a calm handsome face, smiling in a gilded frame.

"Mademoiselle," he said at last, trying to maintain a cold severe air, "there are certain things that we cannot tolerate. Good conduct is absolutely necessary here."

He stopped, choosing his words, in order not to yield to the furious anger which was rising within him. What! it was that fellow she loved, that wretched salesman, the laughing-stock of his counter! It was the humblest, the most awkward of all that she preferred to him, the master! for he had seen them, she leaving her hand in his, and he covering that hand with kisses.

"I've been very good to you, mademoiselle," continued he, making a fresh effort. "I little expected to be rewarded in this way."

Denise, immediately on entering, had been attracted by Madame Hédouin's portrait; and, notwithstanding her great trouble, was still pre-occupied by it. Every time she came into the director's office her eyes were sure to meet those of that painted lady. As a rule she was almost afraid of her, although she knew her to have been very good. This time, however, she felt her to be a kind of protection.

"You are right, sir," she said, softly, "I was wrong to stop and talk, and I beg your pardon for doing so. This young man comes from my own part of the country."

"I'll dismiss him!" cried Mouret, putting all his suffering into this furious cry.

And, completely overcome, entirely forgetting his position of director lecturing a saleswoman guilty of an infraction of the regulations, he broke into a torrent of violent words. Had she no shame in her? a young girl like her to fall in love with such a being! and he even made most atrocious accusations, introducing Hutin's name and the names of others into the affair, with such a flood of words, that she could not even defend herself. But he would make a clean sweep, and kick them all out! The explanation he had resolved on, when following Jouve, had degenerated into a violent scene of jealousy.

"Yes, your lovers! They told me about it, and I was stupid enough to doubt it. But I was the only one who did! I was the only one!"

Choking and bewildered, Denise stood listening to these frightful charges, which she had not at first understood. Did he really suppose her to be as bad as that? At another remark, harsher than all the rest, she silently turned towards the door. And, as he made a movement to stop her, she said:

"Let me alone, sir, I'm going away. If you think me what you say, I will not remain in the house another second."

But he rushed in front of the door, exclaiming: "Why don't you defend yourself? Say something!"

She stood there very stiff, maintaining an icy silence. For a long time he pressed her with questions, with a growing anxiety; and the mute dignity of this innocent girl once more seemed to be the artful calculation of a woman learned in all the tactics of passion. Had she desired it, which she did not, she could not have played a game better calculated to bring him to her feet, tortured by doubt, desirous of being convinced.

"Come, you say he is from your part of the country? Perhaps you've met there formerly. Swear that there has been nothing between you and this fellow."

And as she obstinately remained silent, as if still wishing to open the door and go away, he completely lost his head, and gave way to a supreme explosion of grief.

"Good heavens! I love you! I love you! Why do you delight in tormenting me like this? You can see that nothing else exists for me, that the people I speak about only touch me through you, that you alone can occupy my thoughts. Thinking you were jealous, I gave up all my pleasures. You were told I had mistresses; well! I have them no longer; I hardly set foot outside. Did I not prefer you at that lady's house? have I not quarrelled with her in order to belong solely to you? And I am still waiting for a word of thanks, a little gratitude. And if you fear that I should return to her, you may feel quite easy: she is avenging herself by helping one of our former salesmen to found a rival establishment. Tell me, must I go on my knees to touch your heart?"

He had come to this. He, who did not tolerate the slightest peccadillo among the shopwomen, who turned them out for the least caprice, found himself reduced to imploring one of them not to go away, not to abandon him in his misery! He held the door against her, ready to forgive her everything, to shut his eyes, if she merely deigned to lie. And he spoke the truth, he had quite reformed; he had long since given up Clara and had ceased to visit at Madame Desforges's house, where Bouthemont now reigned supreme, pending the opening of the new establishment, The Four Seasons, which was already filling the newspapers with its advertisements.

"Tell me, must I go on my knees?" he repeated, almost choked by suppressed tears.

She signed to him to cease speaking, herself quite unable to conceal her emotion, deeply affected by his suffering passion. "You are wrong, sir, to agitate yourself in this way," she at last replied. "I assure you that all these wicked reports are untrue. That poor fellow you saw just now is no more guilty than I am."

She said this with her brave, frank air, looking with her bright eyes straight into his face.

"Very good, I believe you," he murmured. "I'll not dismiss any of your comrades, since you take all these people under your protection. But why, then, do you repulse me, if you love no one else?"

A sudden constraint, an anxious bashfulness came upon the young girl.

"You love some one, do you not?" he resumed, in a trembling voice. "Oh! you may speak out; I have no claim on your affections. Do you love any one?"

She turned very red, her heart was in her mouth, and she felt all falsehood impossible in the presence of the emotion which was betraying her, the repugnance for lying which made the truth appear in her face in spite of all.

"Yes," she at last confessed, feebly. "But I beg you to let me go, sir, you are torturing me."

She was now suffering in her turn. Was it not enough to have to defend herself against him? Must she even fight against herself, against the gust of tenderness which sometimes took away all her courage? When he spoke to her like this, when she saw him such a prey to emotion, so overcome, she hardly knew why she still refused; and it was only afterwards that, in the depths of her healthy, girlish nature, she found the pride and prudence which maintained her intact in her virtuous resolutions.

Mouret gave way to a gesture of gloomy discouragement. He could not understand her. He turned towards his table, took up some papers and then at once laid them down again, saying: "I will detain you no longer, mademoiselle; I cannot keep you against your will."

"But I don't wish to go away," replied she, smiling. "If you believe me to be innocent, I will remain. One ought always to believe a woman to be virtuous, sir. There are numbers who are so, I assure you."

Denise had involuntarily raised her eyes towards Madame Hédouin's portrait; that lady so sensible and so beautiful, whose blood, they said, had brought good fortune to the house. Mouret followed the glance with a start, for he thought he could hear his dead wife pronounce that phrase, one of her own sayings which he recognised. And it was like a resurrection, he discovered in Denise the good sense, the mental equilibrium of her whom he had lost, even down to her gentle voice, sparing of useless words. He was struck by the resemblance, and it rendered him sadder still.

"You know I am yours," he murmured in conclusion. "Do what you like with me."

Then she resumed gaily: "That is right, sir. The advice of a woman, however humble she may be, is always worth listening to when she has a little intelligence. If you put yourself in my hands, you may be sure I'll make nothing but a good man of you!"

She smiled, with that simple unassuming air which possessed such a charm. He also smiled in a feeble way, and escorted her as far as the door, as he might have done with a lady.

The next day Denise was appointed first-hand. The dress and costume department was divided; the management creating especially for her benefit a children's costume department, which was installed near that of the cloaks and mantles. Ever since her son's dismissal, Madame Aurélie had been trembling, for she found the directors cooling towards her, and also observed the young woman's power increasing daily. Would they not shortly take advantage of some pretext or other and sacrifice her in favour of Denise? Her imperial countenance, puffed up with fat, seemed to have grown thinner from the shame which now stained the Lhomme dynasty; and she made a show of going away every evening on her husband's arm, for they had been brought nearer together by misfortune, and vaguely felt that the evil came from the disorder of their home; whilst the poor old man, more affected than her, a prey as he was to a sickly fear that he might himself be suspected of robbery, would count the receipts twice over with a great deal of noise, performing miracles the while with his injured arm. Accordingly when Madame Aurélie saw Denise appointed first-hand of the children's costume department, she experienced such delight that she paraded the most affectionate feeling towards her, being indeed really grateful to her for not having taken her own place. And so she overwhelmed her with attentions, treating her as an equal, often going to talk to her in the neighbouring department, with a stately air, like a queen-mother paying a visit to a young queen.

In fact, Denise was now at the summit. Her appointment as first-hand had destroyed the last resistance. If some still babbled, from that itching of the tongue which infects every assemblage of men and women, all nevertheless bowed very low before her face. Marguerite, now second-hand, was full of praise for her. Clara, herself, inspired with a secret respect for this good fortune, which she felt herself incapable of achieving, bowed her head. But Denise's victory was still more complete over the gentlemen; over Jouve, who now almost bent double whenever he addressed her; over Hutin, seized with anxiety on feeling his position giving way under him; and over Bourdoncle, at last reduced to powerlessness. When the latter saw her come out of the director's office, smiling, with her quiet air; and when on the morrow Mouret had insisted on the board creating the new department, he had yielded, vanquished by his terror of woman. He had always thus given in to Mouret, recognising him to be the master, notwithstanding his escapades and idiotic love affairs. This time the woman had proved the stronger, and he was expecting to be swept away by the disaster.

Yet Denise bore her triumph in a quiet, charming manner, touched by these marks of consideration, and desirous of interpreting them as sympathy for the miseries of her *débuts* and the final success of her patient courage. Thus it was with laughing joy that she received the slightest tokens of friendship, and this caused her to be really loved by some: she was so kind, sympathetic, and full of affection. The only person for whom she still showed an invincible repugnance was Clara, for she had learned that this girl had amused herself by leading Colomban astray, even as she had said she would do, for a joke; and he, carried away by his passion, was now becoming more dissipated every day, whilst poor Geneviève was slowly dying. The affair was talked of at The Ladies' Paradise, and thought very droll there.

But this trouble, the only one she had outside, did not in any way change Denise's equable temper. It was especially in her department that she was seen at her best, in the midst of her little world of babies of all ages. She was passionately fond of children, and could not have been placed in a better position. Sometimes there were fully fifty little girls and as many boys there, quite a turbulent school, all agog with the desires of budding coquetry. The mothers completely lost their heads. She, conciliatory and smiling, had the little ones placed in a row, on chairs; and when among the number there happened to be a rosy-cheeked little angel, whose pretty face tempted her, she would insist on serving her herself, bringing the dress and trying it on the child's dimpled shoulders, with the tender precaution of an elder sister. Bursts of clear laughter rang out, faint cries of ecstasy were raised amidst the scolding voices of the mothers. Sometimes a little girl, nine or ten years old, already a grand lady in her own estimation, would when trying on a cloth jacket stand studying it before a glass, now and again turning round with an absorbed air, while her eyes sparkled with the desire to please. The counters were littered with unpacked goods, dresses in pink and blue Eastern cotton for children of from one to five years old; sailor costumes in blue "zephyr" with plaited skirts and blouses trimmed with cambric; Louis XV costumes, mantles, jackets; a medley of little garments, stiff in their infantile grace, something like the contents of the cloak-room of a band of big dolls, taken out of the wardrobes and given over to pillage. Denise always had a few sweets in her pockets to appease the tears of some youngster in despair at not being able to carry off a pair of red breeches; and she lived there amongst these little ones as in her own family, feeling quite young again herself from the contact of all the innocence and freshness incessantly renewed around her skirts.

She now at times had long friendly talks with Mouret. Whenever she went to the office to take orders or furnish information, he would keep her chatting, enjoying the sound of her voice. It was what she laughingly called "making a good man of him." In her prudent, cautious Norman brain there sprang up all sorts of projects, ideas about the new style of business at which she had already ventured to hint when at Robineau's, and some of which she had expressed on the evening of their charming walk in the Tuileries gardens. She could not be occupied in any matter or see any work going on, without being moved by a desire to introduce some improvement into the mechanism. Thus, since her entry into The Ladies' Paradise, she had been particularly pained by the precarious position of the employees; the sudden dismissals shocked her, she thought them iniquitous and stupid, hurtful to all, to the house as much as the staff. Her former sufferings were still fresh in her mind, and her heart filled with pity every time she saw a new-comer with feet bruised and eyes dim with tears, dragging her misery along in her silk dress, amidst the spiteful persecution of the older hands. This dog's life made the best of them bad; and the sad work of destruction commenced: they were all devoured by the business before the age of forty, often disappearing, falling into unknown depths, a great many dying in harness, some of consumption and exhaustion, others of fatigue and bad air, whilst a few were thrown on the street, and the happiest married and buried themselves in some little provincial shop. Was this frightful consumption of human life for which the big shops were responsible every year, right and just? And she pleaded the cause of the colossal machine's gearing not from sentimental reasons, but by arguments appealing to the very interests of the employers. To make a machine solid and strong, it is necessary to use good iron; if the iron breaks or is broken, a stoppage of work, repeated expenses of restarting, quite a loss of power, ensue.

Sometimes she would become quite animated, and picture an immense ideal bazaar, the phalansterium of modern commerce, in which each would secure his exact share of profits, according to his merits, with a certainty of the future, assured to him by contract. Mouret would make merry over this, notwithstanding his fever. He accused her of socialism, embarrassed her by pointing out the difficulties of carrying out these schemes; for she spoke in the simplicity of her soul, bravely trusting in the future, whenever she perceived a dangerous gap underlying her tender-hearted plans. Nevertheless he was shaken, captivated by her young voice which still quivered at the thought of the hardships she had undergone, and was so instinct with earnestness as she pointed out reforms which would tend to consolidate the house; and even while joking with her he listened. Thus the salesmen's positions were gradually improved, the wholesale dismissals were replaced by a system of holidays granted during the dead seasons, and it was decided to found a sort of benefit club which would protect the employees against slack times and ensure them a pension. It was the embryo of the vast trades' unions of the twentieth century.

Moreover Denise did not confine her attention solely to the healing of the wounds from which she had herself bled; she conceived various delicate feminine ideas with which she prompted Mouret and which delighted the customers. She also made Lhomme happy by supporting a scheme he had long entertained, that of creating a band of musicians, of which all the members should be chosen from amongst the staff. Three months later Lhomme had a hundred and twenty musicians under his direction, and the dream of his whole life was realized. And a grand fête was then given on the premises, a concert and a ball, to introduce the band of The Ladies' Paradise to the customers and the whole world. The newspapers took the matter up, Bourdoncle himself, though staggered by these innovations, was obliged to bow before the immense advertisement. Afterwards came the establishment of a recreation room for the men, with two billiard tables and backgammon and chess boards. Then classes were held in the house of an evening; lessons were given in English and German, in grammar, arithmetic, and geography; at last too there were even riding and fencing lessons. A library was also formed, ten thousand volumes were placed at the disposal of the employees. And afterwards came a resident doctor, giving consultations gratis; together with baths, and hair-dressing and refreshment saloons. Every want of life was provided for, everything—board, lodging, clothing and education—was to be obtained without going out of doors. There, in the very heart of Paris, now all agog with the clatter of this working city which was springing up so vigorously amidst the ruins of the olden streets, at last opened to the sunshine, The Ladies' Paradise sufficed entirely for all its own wants and pleasures.

Then a further change of opinion took place in Denise's favour. As Bourdoncle, vanquished, repeated with despair to his friends that he would himself give a great deal to prevail upon Denise to accept Mouret, it was concluded that she still refused to do so, and that her all-powerfulness resulted from her refusal. From that moment she became popular. They knew for what indulgences they were indebted to her, and they admired her for the strength of her will. There, at all events, was one who could master the governor, who avenged all the others, and knew how to get something more than promises out of him! So she had come at last, she who caused him to treat the poor and humble with a little consideration! When she passed through the departments, with her delicate, self-willed head, her gentle, invincible air, the salesmen smiled at her, felt proud of her, and would willingly have exhibited her to the crowd. She, in her happiness, allowed herself to be carried along by this increasing sympathy. But was it all possible? She again saw herself arriving in a shabby dress, frightened, lost amidst the mechanism of the terrible machine; for a long time she had felt she was nothing, barely a grain of millet beneath the millstones which were crushing a whole world; and now to-day she was the very soul of this world, she alone was of any consequence, able at a word to increase or slacken the pace of the colossus lying at her feet. And yet she had not wished for these things, she had simply presented herself, without calculation, possessed of naught but the charm of her sweetness. Her sovereignty sometimes caused her an uneasy surprise: why did they all obey her? she was not pretty, she did nothing wrong. Then she smiled, her heart at rest, feeling within herself naught but goodness and prudence, a love of truth and logic which constituted all her strength.

One of Denise's greatest joys at this time was to be able to assist Pauline. The latter, now about to become a mother, was trembling, for she knew that two other saleswomen similarly circumstanced had been sent away. The principals did not tolerate maternity; they occasionally allowed marriage, but would admit of no children. Pauline, it was true, had her husband in the house; but still she felt anxious, and in order to postpone a probable dismissal, sought to conceal her state as long as she could. But Bourdoncle had observed that her complexion was getting very pale and one morning while he was standing near her, in the under-linen department, a messenger, taking away a bundle, ran against her with such force that she cried out with pain. Bourdoncle immediately took her on one side, made her confess, and submitted the question of her dismissal to the board, under the pretext that she was in need of country air. Mouret, who was not at the meeting, could only give his opinion in the evening. But Denise having had time to interpose, he closed Bourdoncle's mouth, in the interests of the establishment itself. Did they wish to wound the feelings of all the mothers and young married women amongst their customers? And so it was decided, with great solemnity, that every married saleswoman should, whenever necessary, be sent to a special midwife's at the Paradise's expense.

The next day when Denise went up to the infirmary to see Pauline, who had been obliged to take to her bed on account of the blow she had received, the latter kissed her heartily on both cheeks. "How kind you are! Had it not been for you I should have been turned away. Pray don't be anxious about me, the doctor says it's nothing."

Baugé, who had slipped away from his department, was also there, on the other side of the bed. He likewise stammered his thanks, disturbed in the presence of Denise, whom he now treated as an important person of a superior class. Ah! if he heard any more unkind remarks about her, he would soon close the mouths of the jealous ones! But Pauline sent him away with a good-natured shrug of the shoulders.

"My poor dear, you're always saying something stupid. Leave us to talk together."

The infirmary was a long, light room, containing twelve beds with white curtains. Those who did not wish to go home to their families were nursed there. However, on the day in question, Pauline was the only occupant. Her bed was near one of the large windows which looked on to the Rue Neuve-Saint-Augustin. And amidst the white hangings, in the calm atmosphere perfumed with a faint odour of lavender, they immediately began to exchange confidences in soft, affectionate whispers.

"So he does just what you wish him to, all the same," said Pauline. "How cruel you are, to make him suffer so! Come, just explain it to me, now that I've ventured to approach the subject. Do you detest him?"

Pauline had retained hold of Denise's hand, as the latter sat near the bed, with her elbow resting on the bolster; and Denise was overcome by sudden emotion. Her cheeks flushed red and, in a momentary weakness, her secret escaped her at this direct and unexpected question.

"I love him!" she murmured, burying her head in the pillow.

Pauline was astonished. "What! you love him?" And, after a pause, she asked: "So it's all to make him marry you?"

But at this, the young girl sprang up, quite confused: "Marry me! Oh, no! Oh! I assure you that I have never wished for anything of the kind! No, never has such an idea entered my head; and you know what a horror I have of all falsehood!"

"Well, dear," resumed Pauline, kindly, "you couldn't have acted otherwise, if such had been your intention. All this must come to an end, and it is very certain that it can only finish by a marriage so far as you are concerned. I must tell you that everybody here has the same idea: yes, they are convinced that you are riding the high horse, in order to make him take you to church. Dear me! what a funny girl you are!"

And then she had to console Denise, who had again sunk down with her head on the bolster, sobbing and declaring that she would certainly go away, since they attributed to her all sorts of things that had never even crossed her mind. No doubt, when a man loved a woman he ought to marry her. But she asked for nothing, she had made no calculations, she simply begged that she might be allowed to live quietly, with her joys and sorrows, like other people. Yes, she would go away.

At the same moment Mouret was crossing the premises below, seeking to forget his thoughts by visiting the works once more. Several months had elapsed, the façade now reared its monumental proportions behind the vast hoarding which concealed it from the public. Quite an army of decorators, marble-cutters, mosaic-workers, and others, were at work. The central group above the door was being gilded, whilst the pedestals destined to support statues of the manufacturing cities of France, were being fixed on the acroteria. Along the Rue du Dix-Décembre, lately opened to the public, a crowd of idlers now stood from morning till night, looking up, seeing nothing, but nevertheless interested in the marvels related of this façade, the inauguration of which was expected to revolutionize Paris. And it was beside this new building full of the fever of work, amidst the artists putting the finishing touches to the realization of his dream as commenced by the masons, that Mouret more bitterly than ever realized the vanity of his fortune.

The thought of Denise suddenly came upon him, that thought which incessantly pierced him with a flame, like the shooting of an incurable pain. And then he ran away, unable to find a word of satisfaction, fearful lest he should display his tears, and leaving behind him the disgust of triumph. That façade, which was at last erected, seemed but trifling in his eyes, very much like one of those walls of sand that children build, and it might have been prolonged from one end of the city to the other, elevated to the starry sky and yet would not have filled the void of his heart, which only the "yes" of a mere child could satisfy.

When Mouret returned to his office he was almost choking with sobs. What did she want? He dared not offer her money now; but the confused idea of marriage presented itself amidst his revolts. And, in the debility of his powerlessness, his tears began to flow. He was indeed very unhappy.

# XIII

One morning in November, Denise was giving her first orders in the department when the Baudus' servant came to tell her that Mademoiselle Geneviève had passed a very bad night, and wished to see her immediately. For some time the poor girl had been getting weaker and weaker, and had been obliged to take to her bed two days before.

"Say I am coming at once," replied Denise, feeling very anxious.

The blow which was finishing Geneviève was Colomban's sudden disappearance. At first, chaffed by Clara, he had grown very dissipated; then, yielding to the wild desires which at times master sly, chaste men, he had become her obedient slave; and one Monday instead of returning to the shop had sent a farewell letter to Baudu, written in the studied terms of one who is about to commit suicide. Perhaps, at the bottom of this freak, there was also the calculating craft of a man delighted at escaping from a disastrous marriage. The business was in as bad a way as his betrothed, so the moment was a propitious one for breaking with them both. And every one cited Colomban as an unfortunate victim of love.

When Denise reached The Old Elbeuf, Madame Baudu, with her small white face consumed by anæmia, was there alone, sitting motionless behind the pay-desk, and watching over the silence and emptiness of the shop. There was no assistant now. The servant dusted the shelves; and it was even a question of replacing her by a charwoman. A dreary cold hung about the ceiling; hours passed by without a customer coming to disturb the gloom, and the goods, no longer handled, became more and more musty every day.

"What's the matter?" asked Denise, anxiously. "Is Geneviève in danger?"

Madame Baudu did not at first reply. Her eyes filled with tears. Then suddenly she stammered: "I don't know; they don't tell me anything. Ah, it's all over, it's all over."

And she cast a dim glance round the dark shop, as if she felt that her daughter and The Old Elbeuf were disappearing together. The seventy thousand francs, produced by the sale of their Rambouillet property, had in less than two years melted away in the abyss of competition. In order to struggle against The Ladies' Paradise, which now kept men's cloths, even materials for hunting, shooting, and livery suits, the draper had made considerable sacrifices. But at last he had been altogether crushed by the swan-skin cloths and the flannels sold by his rival, an assortment that had not its equal in the market. Little by little his debts had increased, and, as a last resource, he had resolved to mortgage the old building in the Rue de la Michodière, where Finet, their ancestor, had founded the business. And it was now only a question of days, the crumbling away had nearly finished, the very ceilings seemed to be falling and turning into dust, even an old worm-eaten structure is carried away by the wind.

"Your uncle is upstairs," resumed Madame Baudu in her broken voice. "We each stay with her in turn for a couple of hours. Some one must stay here; oh! but only as a precaution, for to tell the truth—"

Her gesture finished the phrase. They would have put the shutters up had it not been for their old commercial pride, which still kept them erect in the presence of the neighbours.

"Well, I'll go up, aunt," said Denise, whose heart ached amidst the resigned despair that even the pieces of cloth themselves exhaled.

"Yes, go upstairs quick, my girl. She's expecting you, she's been asking for you all night. She had something to tell you."

But just at that moment Baudu came down. Bile had now given his yellow face a greenish hue, and his eyes were bloodshot. He was still walking with the muffled tread with which he had quitted the sick room, and murmured, as though he might be overheard upstairs, "She's asleep."

Then, thoroughly worn out, he sat down on a chair, mopping his forehead with a mechanical gesture and puffing like a man who has just finished some hard work. A pause ensued, but at last he said to Denise: "You'll see her presently. When she is sleeping, she seems to us to be all right again."

Again did silence fall. Face to face, the father and mother stood looking at one another. Then, in a low voice he went over his grief again, though without naming any one or addressing any one directly: "With my head on the block, I wouldn't have believed it! He was the last one, I had brought him up as a son. If any one had come and said to me, 'They'll take him away from you as well; you'll see him fall,' I should have replied, 'It's impossible, that can't happen as long as there's a God on high.' But he has fallen all the same! Ah! the poor fellow, he who was so well up in the business, who had all my ideas! And all through a young she-ape, a mere dummy fit for a window! No! really, it's enough to drive one mad!"

ÉMILE ZOLA

He shook his head, with his half-closed eyes cast upon the damp floor which the tread of generations of customers had worn. Then he continued in a lower voice, "Shall I tell you? Well, there are moments when I feel myself the most culpable of all in our misfortune. Yes, it's my fault if our poor girl is lying upstairs devoured by fever. Ought I not to have married them at once, without yielding to my stupid pride, my obstinacy in refusing to leave them the business in a less prosperous state than it had been before? Had I done that she would now have the man she loved, and perhaps their youthful strength united would have accomplished the miracle that I have failed to work. But I am an old fool, and saw through nothing; I didn't know that people fell ill over such things. Really, he was an extraordinary fellow: he had such a gift for business, and such probity, such simplicity of conduct, he was so orderly in every way—in short, my pupil."

He raised his head, still defending his ideas, in the person of the shopman who had betrayed him. Denise, however, could not bear to hear him accuse himself, and carried away by her emotion, on seeing him so humble, with his eyes full of tears, he who used formerly to reign there as an absolute and scolding master, she told him everything.

"Uncle, pray don't excuse him," said she. "He never loved Geneviève, he would have run away sooner if you had tried to hasten the marriage. I have spoken to him myself about it; he was perfectly well aware that my poor cousin was suffering on his account, and yet you see that did not prevent him from leaving. Ask aunt."

Without opening her lips, Madame Baudu confirmed these words by a nod. The draper turned paler still, blinded by his tears. And then he stammered out: "It must have been in the blood, his father died last year through having led a dissolute life."

And once more he looked round the dim shop, his eyes wandering from the empty counters to the full shelves and then resting on Madame Baudu, who was still sitting erect at the pay-desk, waiting in vain for the customers who did not come.

"Well," said he, "it's all over. They've ruined our business, and now one of their hussies is killing our daughter."

No one spoke. The rolling of passing vehicles, which occasionally shook the floor, seemed like a funereal beating of drums in the still air, so stuffy under the low ceiling. But suddenly, amidst this gloomy sadness peculiar to old expiring shops, several dull knocks were heard proceeding from somewhere in the house. It was Geneviève, who had just awoke, and was knocking with a stick they had left beside her.

"Let's go up at once," said Baudu, rising with a start. "And try to be cheerful, she mustn't know."

He himself as he went upstairs rubbed his eyes, in order to remove the traces of his tears. As soon as he opened the door, on the first floor, they heard a frightened, feeble voice crying: "Oh, I don't like to be left alone. Don't leave me; I'm afraid to be left alone." However, when she perceived Denise, Geneviève became calmer, and smiled joyfully. "You've come, then! How I've been longing to see you since yesterday! I thought you also had abandoned me!"

It was a piteous spectacle. The young woman's room, a little room into which came a livid light, looked out on to the yard. At first her parents had put her in their room, in the front part of the house; but the sight of The Ladies' Paradise opposite affected her so deeply, that they had been obliged to bring her back to her own again. And there she lay, so very thin under the bed-clothes, that you could hardly divine the form and existence of a human body. Her skinny arms, consumed by the burning fever of consumption, were in a perpetual movement of anxious, unconscious searching; whilst her black hair, heavy with passion, seemed thicker still, and to be preying with its voracious vitality upon her poor face, that face in which was fading the final degenerateness of a long lineage, a family that had grown and lived in the gloom of that cellar of old commercial Paris. Denise, her heart bursting with pity, stood looking at her. She did not at first speak, for fear of giving way to tears. However, she at last murmured: "I came at once. Can I be of any use to you? You asked for me. Would you like me to stay?"

"No, thanks. I don't need anything. I only wanted to embrace you."

Tears filled her eyes. Denise quickly leant over and kissed her, trembling at the flame which came from those hollow cheeks to her own lips. But Geneviève, stretching out her arms caught hold of her and kept her in a desperate embrace. Then she looked towards her father.

"Would you like me to stay?" repeated Denise. "Perhaps there is something I can do for you."

"No, no." Geneviève's glance was still obstinately fixed on her father, who remained standing there with a bewildered air, almost choking. However, he at last understood her and went away, without saying a word. They heard his heavy footsteps descending the stairs.

"Tell me, is he with that woman?" the sick girl then eagerly inquired while catching hold of her cousin's hand, and making her sit down on the edge of the bed. "Yes, I wanted to see you as you are the only one who can tell me. They're together, aren't they?"

In the surprise which these questions gave her Denise began to stammer, and was obliged to confess the truth, the rumours that were current at the Paradise. Clara, it was said, had already grown tired of Colomban, who was pursuing her everywhere, striving to obtain an occasional appointment by a sort of canine humility. It was also said that he was about to take a situation at the Grands Magasins du Louvre.

"If you love him so much, he may yet come back," added Denise seeking to cheer the dying girl with this last hope. "Make haste and get well, he will acknowledge his errors, and marry you."

But Geneviève interrupted her. She had listened with all her soul, with an intense passion which had raised her in the bed. Now, however, she fell back. "No, I know it's all over! I don't say anything, because I see papa crying, and I don't wish to make mamma worse than she is. But I am going, Denise, and if I called for you last night it was for fear of going off before the morning. And to think that he is not even happy after all!"

Then as Denise remonstrated with her, assuring her that she was not so bad as all that, she again cut her short by suddenly throwing back the bed-clothes with the chaste gesture of a virgin who has nothing to conceal in death. Her bosom bare, she murmured: "Look at me! Is it not the end?"

Trembling with mingled horror and pity, Denise hastily rose from the bed, as if she feared that her very breath might suffice to destroy that puny emaciated form. Geneviève slowly covered her bosom again, saying: "You see I am no longer a woman. It would be wrong to wish for him still!"

Silence fell between them. They continued gazing at each other, unable to find a word to say. At last it was Geneviève who resumed: "Come, don't stay any longer, you have your own affairs to look after. And thanks, I was tormented by the wish to know, and now am satisfied. If you ever see him again, tell him I forgive him. Farewell, dear Denise. Kiss me once more, for it's the last time."

The young woman kissed her, still protesting: "No, no, don't despair, all you want is careful nursing, nothing more."

But the sick girl smiled, shaking her head in an obstinate way, like one who will not be deceived. And as her cousin at last walked towards the door, she exclaimed: "Wait a minute, knock on the floor with this stick, so that papa may come up. I'm afraid to stay alone."

Then, when Baudu reached the little dismal room, where he spent long hours seated on a chair, she assumed an air of gaiety, saying to Denise—"Don't come to-morrow, I would rather not. But on Sunday I shall expect you; you can spend the afternoon with me."

The next morning, at six o'clock, Geneviève expired after four hours' fearful agony. The funeral took place on a Saturday, a dark cloudy day, with a sooty sky hanging low above the shivering city. The Old Elbeuf, hung with white drapery, lighted up the street with a bright speck, and the candles burning in the gloom seemed like so many stars enveloped in twilight. Bead-work wreaths and a great bouquet of white roses covered the coffin—a narrow child's coffin,—placed in the dark passage of the house close to the pavement, so near indeed to the gutter that passing vehicles had already splashed the drapery. With its continual rush of pedestrians on the muddy footways the whole neighbourhood reeked of dampness, exhaled a cellar-like mouldy odour.

At nine o'clock Denise came over to stay with her aunt. But when the funeral was about to start, the latter—who had ceased weeping, her eyes scorched by her hot tears—begged her to follow the body and look after her uncle, whose mute affliction and almost idiotic grief filled the family with anxiety. Downstairs, the young woman found the street full of people, for the small traders of the neighbourhood were anxious to give the Baudus a mark of sympathy, and in their eagerness there was a desire for a demonstration against that Ladies' Paradise, which they accused of having caused Geneviève's slow agony. All the victims of the monster were there—Bédoré and Sister, the hosiers of the Rue Gaillon, Vanpouille Brothers, the furriers, Deslignières the toyman, and Piot and Rivoire the furniture dealers; even Mademoiselle Tatin, the dealer in under-linen, and Quinette the glover, though long since cleared off by bankruptcy, had made it a duty to come, the one from Batignolles, the other from the Bastille, where they had been obliged to take situations. And whilst waiting for the hearse, which was late, all these people, clad in black and tramping in the mud, cast glances of hatred towards The Ladies' Paradise, whose bright windows and gay displays seemed an insult in face of The Old Elbeuf, which, with its funeral trappings and glimmering candles, lent an air of mourning to the other side of the street. The faces of a few inquisitive salesmen appeared at the plate-glass windows of the Paradise; but the colossus itself preserved the indifference of a machine going at full speed, unconscious of the deaths it may cause on the road.

Denise looked round for her brother Jean, and at last perceived him standing before Bourras's shop; whereupon she crossed over and asked him to walk with his uncle, and assist him should he be unable to get along. For the last few weeks Jean had been very grave, as if tormented by some worry. That morning, buttoned up in his black frock-coat, for he was now a full-grown man, earning his twenty francs a day, he seemed so dignified and sad that his sister was surprised, having had no idea that he loved their cousin so much. Desirous of sparing Pépé a needless grief, she had left him with Madame Gras, intending to fetch him in the afternoon to see his uncle and aunt.

However, the hearse had still not arrived, and Denise, greatly affected, stood watching the candles burn, when she was startled by a well-known voice behind her. It was that of Bourras who had called a chestnut-seller occupying a little box, against a wine shop opposite, in order to say to him: "Here! Vigouroux, just keep a look-out on my place, will you? You see I've taken the door handle away. If any one comes, tell them to call again. But don't let that disturb you, no one will come."

Then he also took his stand at the edge of the pavement, waiting like the others. Denise, feeling rather awkward, glanced at his shop. He now altogether neglected it; only a disorderly collection of umbrellas eaten up by damp and canes blackened by gas-light now remained in the window. The embellishments that he had made, the light green paint work, the mirrors, the gilded sign, were all cracking, already getting dirty, exhibiting the rapid lamentable decrepitude of false luxury laid over ruins. But although the old crevices were re-appearing, although the damp spots had sprung up through the gilding, the house still obstinately held its ground, hanging to the flanks of The Ladies' Paradise like some shameful wart, which, although cracked and rotten, yet refused to fall.

"Ah! the scoundrels," growled Bourras, "they won't even let her be carried away!"

The hearse, which was at last approaching, had just come into collision with one of The Paradise vans, which at the rapid trot of two superb horses went spinning along shedding in the mist the starry radiance of its shining panels. And from under his bushy eyebrows the old man cast a side glance at Denise.

The funeral procession started at a slow pace, splashing through muddy puddles, amid the silence of the omnibuses and cabs which were suddenly pulled up. When the coffin, draped with white, crossed the Place Gaillon, the sombre looks of the followers once more plunged into the windows of the big establishment where only two saleswomen stood looking on, pleased with the diversion. Baudu followed the hearse with a heavy mechanical step, refusing by a sign the arm offered him by Jean, who walked alongside. Then, after a long string of people, came three mourning coaches. As they crossed the Rue Neuve-des-Petits-Champs, Robineau, looking very pale and much older, ran up to join the procession.

At Saint-Roch, a great many women were waiting, small traders of the neighbourhood, who had wished to escape the crowd at the house of mourning. The demonstration was developing into quite a riot; and when, after the funeral service, the procession started off again, all continued to follow, although it was a long walk from the Rue Saint-Honoré to the Montmartre Cemetery. They had to turn up the Rue Saint-Roch again, and once more pass The Ladies' Paradise. It was a sort of defiance; the poor girl's body was paraded round the big shop like that of a first victim fallen in time of revolution. At the door some red flannels were flapping like so many flags, and a display of carpets blazed forth in a gory efflorescence of huge roses and full-blown peonies. Denise had now got into one of the coaches, being agitated by such poignant doubts, her heart oppressed by such cruel grief, that she had not the strength to walk further. In the Rue du Dix-Décembre just before the scaffolding of the new façade which still obstructed the thoroughfare there was a stoppage, and on looking out the girl observed old Bourras behind all the others, dragging himself along with difficulty close to the wheels of the coach in which she was riding alone. He would never get as far as the cemetery, she thought. However, he raised his head, looked at her, and all at once got into the coach.

"It's my confounded knees," he exclaimed. "Don't draw back! It isn't you we hate."

She felt him to be friendly and furious, as in former days. He grumbled, declared that Baudu must be fearfully strong to be able to keep up after such hard blows as he had received. The procession had again started off at the same slow pace; and, on leaning out once more, Denise saw her uncle walking behind the hearse with his heavy step, which seemed to regulate the rumbling, painful march of the cortège. Then she threw herself back into her corner and rocked by the melancholy movement of the coach began listening to the endless complaints of the old umbrella maker.

"The police ought to clear the public thoroughfares, my word!" said he, "They've been blocking up our street for the last eighteen months with the scaffolding of their façade—another man was killed on it the other day. Never mind! When they want to enlarge any further they'll have to throw bridges over the streets. People say there are now two thousand seven hundred employees, and that the turnover will amount to a hundred millions this year. A hundred millions! just fancy! a hundred millions!"

Denise had nothing to say in reply. The procession had just turned into the Rue de la Chaussée d'Antin, where it was stopped by a block of vehicles. And Bourras went on, with a vague expression in his eyes, as if he were now dreaming aloud. He still failed to understand the triumph achieved by The Ladies' Paradise, but he acknowledged the defeat of the old-fashioned traders.

"Poor Robineau's done for, he looks like a drowning man," he resumed. "And the Bédorés and the Vanpouilles, they can't keep going; they're like me, played out. Deslignières will die of apoplexy, Piot and Rivoire have had the jaundice. Ah! poor child! It must be comical for those looking on to see such a string of bankrupts pass. Besides, it appears that the clean sweep is to continue. Those scoundrels are creating departments for flowers, bonnets, perfumery, boots and shoes, all sorts of things. Grognet, the perfumer in the Rue de Grammont can clear out, and I wouldn't give ten francs for Naud's boot-shop in the Rue d'Antin. The cholera's even spread as far as the Rue Sainte-Anne. Lacassagne, at the feather and flower shop, and Madame Chadeuil, whose bonnets are so well-known, will be swept away in less than a couple of years. And after those will come others and still others! All the businesses in the neighbourhood will collapse. When counter-jumpers start selling soap and goloshes, they are quite capable of dealing in fried potatoes. 'Pon my word, the world is turning upside down!"

The hearse had just then crossed the Place de la Trinité, and from the corner of the gloomy coach Denise, who lulled by the funereal march of the procession still listened to the old man's endless complaints, could see the coffin ascending the steep Rue Blanche as they emerged from the Rue de la Chaussée d'Antin. Behind her uncle, who was plodding along with the blind, mute face of an ox about to be poleaxed, she seemed to hear the tramping of a flock of sheep likewise being led to the slaughter-house. It was the downfall of the shops of an entire district, all the small traders dragging their ruin, amidst the thud of damp shoes, through the black mud of Paris. Bourras, however, still continued, in a fainter voice, as if fatigued by the difficult ascent of the Rue Blanche:

"As for me, I'm settled. But I still hold on all the same, and won't let him go. He's just lost his appeal case. Ah! that's cost me something: nearly two years' pleading, and the solicitors and the barristers! Never mind, he won't pass under my shop, the judges have decided that such work as that could not be considered legitimate repairing. Just fancy, he talked of creating underneath my place a saloon where his people might judge the colours of the stuffs by gas-light, a subterranean room which would have joined the hosiery to the drapery departments! And he can't get over it; he can't swallow the fact that an old wreck like me should stop his progress, when all the others are on their knees before his money. But never! I won't have it! that's understood. Very likely I may be worsted. Since I have had to fight against the process-servers, I know that the villain has been buying up my bills in the hope of playing me some villainous trick. But that doesn't matter; he says 'yes,' and I say 'no,' and I shall still say 'no' even when I get between two boards like that poor child we are following."

When they reached the Boulevard de Clichy, the coach rolled on at a quicker pace and one could hear the heavy breathing, the unconscious haste of the followers, anxious to get the sad ceremony over. What Bourras did not openly mention, was the frightful misery into which he himself had fallen, bewildered by the worries which besiege the small trader who is on the road to ruin and yet remains obstinate even under a shower of protested bills. Denise, well acquainted with his position, at last broke the silence by saying, in a voice of entreaty:

"Pray don't stand out any longer, Monsieur Bourras. Let me arrange matters for you."

But he interrupted her with a violent gesture. "You be quiet. That's nobody's business. You're a good little girl, and I know you lead him a hard life, that man who thought you were for sale just like my house. But what would you answer if I advised you to say 'yes?' You'd send me about my business, eh? And so, when I say 'no,' don't you interfere in the matter."

Then, the coach having stopped at the cemetery gate, he alighted from it with the young girl. The Baudus' vault was reached by the first path on the left. In a few minutes the ceremony was over. Jean drew away his uncle, who was looking into the grave all agape. The mourners spread about amongst the neighbouring tombs, and the faces of all these

ÉMILE ZOLA

shopkeepers, their blood impoverished by living in damp, unhealthy shops, assumed an ugly, suffering look under the leaden sky. When the coffin gently slipped down, their blotched and pimpled cheeks paled, and their bleared eyes, blinded by the constant contemplation of figures, turned away.

"We ought all to jump into that hole," said Bourras to Denise, who had kept close to him. "In burying that poor girl they're burying the whole district. Oh! I know what I say, the old style of business may go and join the white roses they're throwing on her coffin."

Denise brought her uncle and brother back in a mourning coach. The day was for her dark and melancholy. In the first place, she began to get anxious at seeing Jean so pale; and when she understood that it was on account of another sweetheart she tried to quiet him by opening her purse; but he shook his head and refused, saying it was a serious matter this time, the niece of a very rich pastry-cook, who would not accept even a bunch of violets. Afterwards, in the afternoon, when Denise went to fetch Pépé from Madame Gras', the latter declared that he was getting too big for her to keep any longer; and this was another annoyance, for it would be necessary to find him a school, perhaps send him away. And to crown all, on bringing Pépé to kiss his aunt and uncle, Denise's heart was rent by the gloomy sadness of The Old Elbeuf. The shop was closed, and the old couple were sitting in the little dining-room, where they had forgotten to light the gas, notwithstanding the complete obscurity in which it was plunged that winter's day. They were now quite alone, face to face, in the house which ruin had slowly emptied, and their daughter's death filled the dark corners with a deeper gloom, and seemed like the beginning of that final dismemberment which would break up the old rafters, preyed upon by damp. Beneath the crushing blow, her uncle, unable to stop himself, still kept walking round and round the table, with his funeral-like step, seeing nothing and silent; whilst her aunt who said nothing either, remained huddled together on a chair, with the white face of one who is wounded and whose blood is running away drop by drop. They did not even weep when Pépé covered their cold cheeks with kisses. For her part Denise was choking with tears.

That same evening Mouret sent for the young woman to speak to her about a child's garment which he wished to launch, a mixture of the Scotch and Zouave costumes. And, still trembling with pity, shocked by so much suffering, she could not contain herself; and, to begin with, ventured to speak of Bourras, that poor old man who was down and whom they were about to ruin. But, on hearing the umbrella maker's name, Mouret flew into a rage. The old madman, as he called him, was the plague of his life, and spoilt his triumph by his idiotic obstinacy in not giving up his house, that ignoble hovel which was a disgrace to The Ladies' Paradise, the only little corner of the vast block that had escaped conquest. The matter was becoming a perfect nightmare; any one else but Denise speaking in favour of Bourras would have run the risk of immediate dismissal, so violently was Mouret tortured by the sickly desire to kick the old hovel down. In short, what did they wish him to do? Could he leave that heap of ruins sticking to The Ladies' Paradise? It would have to go, the shop must pass along. So much the worse for the old fool! And he spoke of his repeated proposals; he had offered him as much as a hundred thousand francs. Wasn't that fair? He never higgled, he gave whatever money was required; but in return he expected people to be reasonable, and allow him to finish his work! Did any one ever try to stop engines on a railway? To all this Denise listened with drooping eyes, unable on her side to find any but purely sentimental reasons. The poor fellow was so old, they might have waited till his death; a bankruptcy would kill him. Then Mouret added that he was no longer able to prevent things following their course. Bourdoncle had taken the matter up, for the board had resolved to put an end to it. So she could say nothing more, notwithstanding the grievous pity which she felt for her old friend.

After a painful silence, Mouret himself began to speak of the Baudus, by expressing his sorrow at the death of their daughter. They were very worthy and very honest people but had been pursued by the worst of luck. Then he resumed his arguments: at bottom, they had really brought about their own misfortunes by obstinately clinging to the old customs in their worm-eaten place. It was not astonishing that their house should be falling about their heads. He had predicted it scores of times; she must even remember that he had told her to warn her uncle of a fatal disaster, if he should still cling to his stupid old-fashioned ways. And the catastrophe had arrived; no one in the world could now prevent it. People could not reasonably expect him to ruin himself to save the neighbourhood. Besides, if he had been foolish enough to close The Ladies' Paradise, another great establishment would have sprung up of itself next door, for the idea was now starting from the four corners of the globe; the triumph of these manufacturing and trading centres was sown by the spirit of the age, which was sweeping away the falling edifices of ancient times. Little by little as he went on speaking, Mouret warmed up, and with eloquent emotion defended himself against the hatred of his involuntary victims, against the clamour of the small moribund businesses that he could hear around him. They could not keep their dead above ground, he continued, they must bury them; and, with a gesture, he consigned the corpse of old-fashioned trading to the grave, swept into the common hole all those putrifying pestilential remains which were becoming a disgrace to the bright, sun-lit streets of new Paris. No, no, he felt no remorse, he was simply doing the work of his age, and she knew it, she who loved life, who had a passion for vast transactions settled in the full glare of publicity. Reduced to silence, she listened to him for some time longer and then went away, her soul full of trouble.

That night Denise slept but little. Insomnia, interspersed with nightmare, kept her turning over and over in her bed. It seemed to her that she was again quite a little girl and burst into tears, in their garden at Valognes, on seeing the blackcaps eat up the spiders, which themselves devoured the flies. Was it then really true that it was necessary for the world to fatten on death, that it was necessary there should be this struggle for existence whereby humanity drew even increase of life from the ossuaries of eternal destruction? And afterwards she again found herself before the grave into which they had lowered Geneviève, and then she perceived her uncle and aunt alone in their gloomy dining-room. A dull sound as of something toppling sped through the still atmosphere; it was Bourras's house giving way, as if undermined by a high tide. Then silence fell again, more sinister than ever, and a fresh crash was heard, then another, and another; the Robineaus, the Bédorés, the Vanpouilles, were cracking and falling in their turn; all the small shops of the Saint-Roch quarter were disappearing beneath an invisible pick, with the sudden, thundering noise of bricks falling from a cart. Then intense grief awoke her with a start. Heavens! what tortures! There were families weeping, old men thrown into the street, all the poignant dramas of ruin! And she could save nobody; and even felt that it was right, that all this compost of misery was necessary for the health of the Paris of the future. When day broke, she became calmer, but a feeling of resigned sadness still kept her awake, turned towards the window whose panes were brightening. Yes, it was the needful meed of blood, every revolution required martyrs, each step forward is taken over the bodies of the dead. Her fear of being a wicked girl, of having helped to effect the ruin of her kindred, now melted into heartfelt pity, in face of these evils beyond remedy, which are like the labour pangs of each generation's birth. She finished by trying to devise some possible comfort, her kindly heart dreaming of the means to be employed in order to save her relations at least from the final crash.

And now Mouret appeared before her with his impassioned face and caressing eyes. He would certainly refuse her nothing; she felt sure that he would accord all reasonable compensations. And her thoughts strayed, seeking to judge him. She knew his life and was aware of the calculating nature of his former affections, his continual "exploitation" of woman, his intimacy with Madame Desforges—the sole object of which had been to get hold of Baron Hartmann—and with all the others, such as Clara and the rest. But these Lothario-like beginnings, which were the talk of the shop, gradually disappeared in presence of the man's genius and victorious grace. He was seduction itself. What she could never have forgiven was his former deception: real coldness hidden beneath a gallant affectation of affection. But she felt herself to be entirely without rancour now that he was suffering through her. This suffering had elevated him. When she saw him tortured by her refusal, atoning so fully for his former disdain for woman, he seemed to her to make amends for many of his faults.

That very morning Denise obtained from Mouret a promise of whatever compensation she might consider reasonable on the day when the Baudus and old Bourras should succumb. Weeks passed away, during which she went to see her uncle nearly every afternoon, escaping from her department for a few minutes and bringing her smiling face and girlish courage to enliven the dark shop. She was especially anxious about her aunt, who had fallen into a dull stupor ever since Geneviève's death; it seemed as if her life was quitting her hourly; though, when people questioned her, she would reply with an astonished air that she was not suffering, but simply felt as if overcome by sleep. The neighbours, however, shook their heads, saying she would not live long to regret her daughter.

One day Denise was coming from the Baudus, when, on turning the corner of the Place Gaillon, she heard a loud cry. A crowd rushed forward, a panic arose: that breath of fear and pity which suddenly brings all the people in a street together. It was a brown omnibus, belonging to the Bastille-Batignolles line, which had run over a man, at the entrance of the Rue Neuve-Saint-Augustin, just opposite the fountain. Standing up in his seat, the driver whilst furiously holding in his two black horses which were rearing cried out, in a great passion:

"Confound it! Confound it! Why don't you look out, you idiot!"

The omnibus had now been brought to a standstill. The crowd had surrounded the injured man, and a policeman happened to be on the spot. Still standing up and invoking the testimony of the outside passengers who had also risen, to look over and see the blood-stains, the coachman, with exasperated gestures and choked by increasing anger, was explaining the matter.

"It's something fearful," said he. "Who could have expected such a thing? That fellow was walking along quite at home and when I called out to him he at once threw himself under the wheels!"

Then a house-painter, who had run up, brush in hand, from a neighbouring shop-front, exclaimed in a sharp voice, amidst the clamour: "Don't excite yourself! I saw him, he threw himself under! He jumped in, head first, like that. Another one tired of life, no doubt!"

Others spoke up, and all agreed that it was a case of suicide, whilst the policeman pulled out his note-book and made an entry. Several ladies, all very pale, quickly alighted and ran away without looking back, filled with horror by the sudden shaking which had stirred them when the omnibus passed over the body. Denise, however, drew nearer, attracted by a practical pity, which prompted her to interest herself in the victims of all sorts of street accidents, such as wounded dogs, horses down, and tilers falling off roofs. And she immediately recognised the unfortunate fellow who had fainted away there in the road, his clothes covered with mud.

"It's Monsieur Robineau!" she exclaimed, in her grievous astonishment.

The policeman at once questioned the young woman, and she gave the victim's name, profession, and address. Thanks to the driver's energy, the omnibus had swerved, and thus only Robineau's legs had gone under the wheels; however, it was to be feared that they were both broken. Four men carried him to a chemist's shop in the Rue Gaillon, whilst the omnibus slowly resumed its journey.

"My stars!" said the driver, whipping up his horses, "I've done a famous day's work."

Denise followed Robineau into the chemist's. The latter, pending the arrival of a doctor who was not to be found, declared that there was no immediate danger, and that the injured man had better be taken home, as he lived in the neighbourhood. A man then started off to the police-station for a stretcher, and Denise had the happy thought of going on in front so as to prepare Madame Robineau for this frightful blow. But she had the greatest trouble in the world to get into the street again through the crowd, which was struggling before the door of the chemist's shop. This crowd, attracted by death, was every minute increasing; men, women, and children stood on tip-toe, and held their own amidst brutal pushing; and each new-comer had his version to give of the accident, so that at last the victim was said to be a husband who had been pitched out of window by his wife's lover.

In the Rue Neuve-des-Petits-Champs, Denise perceived, from a distance, Madame Robineau on the threshold of the silk warehouse. This gave her a pretext for stopping, and she talked on for a moment, trying to find a means of breaking the terrible news. The place wore the disorderly, neglectful aspect of a shop in the last agony, one whose business is fast dying. It was the inevitable end of the great battle of the rival silks; the Paris Delight had destroyed competition by a fresh reduction of a sou; it was now sold at four francs nineteen sous the mètre, and Gaujean's silk had found its Waterloo. For the last two months Robineau, reduced to all sorts of shifts, had been leading a fearful life, trying to avert a declaration of bankruptcy.

"I saw your husband crossing the Place Gaillon," murmured Denise, who had ended by entering the shop.

Thereupon Madame Robineau, whom a secret anxiety seemed to be continually attracting towards the street, said quickly: "Ah, a little while ago, wasn't it? I'm waiting for him, he ought to be back by now. Monsieur Gaujean came this morning, and they went out together."

She was still charming, delicate, and gay; but was in a delicate state of health and seemed more frightened, more bewildered than ever by those dreadful business matters, which she did not understand, and which were all going wrong. As she often said, what was the use of it all? Would it not be better to live quietly in some small lodging, and be contented with modest fare?

"My dear child," she resumed with her pretty smile, which was becoming sadder, "we have nothing to conceal from you. Things are not going well, and my poor darling is worried to death. Again to-day this man Gaujean has been tormenting him about some overdue bills. I was dying with anxiety at being left here all alone."

And she was once more returning to the door when Denise stopped her, having heard the noise of a crowd and guessing that it was the injured man being brought along, surrounded by a mob of idlers anxious to see the end of the affair. And thereupon with her throat parched, unable to find the consoling words she would have liked to say, she had to explain the matter.

"Don't be anxious, there's no immediate danger. I've seen Monsieur Robineau, he has met with an accident. They are just bringing him home, pray don't be frightened."

The young woman listened to her, white as a sheet, and as yet not clearly understanding her. The street was full of people, and cab-drivers, unable to get along, were swearing, while the bearers set the stretcher before the shop in order to open both glass doors.

"It was an accident," continued Denise, determined to conceal the attempt at suicide. "He was on the pavement and slipped under the wheels of an omnibus. Only his feet are hurt. They've sent for a doctor. Don't be frightened."

A great shudder shook Madame Robineau. She gave vent to a few inarticulate cries; then said no more but sank down beside the stretcher, drawing its covering aside with her trembling hands. The men who had brought it were waiting to take it away as soon as the doctor should arrive. They dared not touch Robineau, who had now regained consciousness, and whose sufferings became frightful at the slightest movement. When he saw his wife big tears ran down his cheeks. She embraced him, and stood looking at him fixedly, and weeping. Out in the street the tumult was increasing; the people pressed forward as with glistening eyes at a theatre; some girls, fresh from a workshop, were almost pushing through the windows in their eagerness to see what was going on. Then Denise in order to avoid this feverish curiosity, and thinking, moreover, that it was not right to leave the shop open, decided to let the metal shutters down. She went and turned the winch, whose wheels gave out a plaintive cry whilst the sheets of iron slowly descended, like the heavy draperies of a curtain falling on the catastrophe of a fifth act. And when she went in again, after closing the little round door in the shutters, she found Madame Robineau still clasping her husband in her arms, in the vague half-light which came from the two stars cut in the sheet-iron. The ruined shop seemed to be gliding into nothingness, those two stars alone glittered on this sudden and brutal catastrophe of the streets of Paris.

At last Madame Robineau recovered her speech. "Oh, my darling!— oh, my darling! my darling!"

This was all she could say, and he, half choking, confessed himself, a prey to keen remorse now that he saw her kneeling thus before him. When he did not move he only felt the burning weight of his legs.

"Forgive me, I must have been mad. But when the lawyer told me before Gaujean that the posters would be put up to-morrow, I saw flames dancing before my eyes as if the walls were on fire. After that I remember nothing. I was coming down the Rue de la Michodière— and I fancied that The Paradise people were laughing at me—that big rascally house seemed to crush me—so, when the omnibus came up, I thought of Lhomme and his arm, and threw myself under the wheels."

Madame Robineau had slowly fallen on to the floor, horrified by this confession. Heavens! he had tried to kill himself. She caught hold of the hand of Denise who was leaning towards her, also quite overcome. The injured man, exhausted by emotion, had just fainted away again. The doctor had still not arrived. Two men had been scouring the neighbourhood for him; and the doorkeeper belonging to the house had now gone to seek him in his turn.

"Pray, don't be anxious," Denise kept on repeating mechanically, herself also sobbing.

Then Madame Robineau, seated on the floor, with her head on a level with the stretcher, her cheek resting against the sacking on which her husband was lying, relieved her heart. "Oh! I must tell you. It's all for me that he wanted to die. He's always saying, 'I've robbed you; it was your money.' And at night he dreamed of those sixty thousand francs, waking up covered with perspiration, calling himself an incompetent fellow and saying that those who have no head for business ought not to risk other people's money. You know that he has always been nervous, and apt to worry himself. He finished by conjuring up things that frightened me. He pictured me in the street in tatters, begging— me whom he loved so dearly, whom he longed to see rich and happy." The poor woman paused; on turning her head she saw that her husband had opened his eyes; then she continued stammering: "My darling, why have you done this? You must think me very wicked! I assure you, I don't care if we are ruined. So long as we are together, we shall never be unhappy. Let them take everything, and we will go away somewhere, where you won't hear any more about them. You can still work; you'll see how happy we shall be!"

ÉMILE ZOLA

She let her forehead fall near her husband's pale face, and both remained speechless, in the emotion of their anguish. Silence fell. The shop seemed to be sleeping, benumbed by the pale twilight which enveloped it; whilst from behind the thin metal shutters came the uproar of the street, the life of broad daylight passing along with the rumbling of vehicles, and the hustling and pushing of the crowd. At last Denise, who went every other minute to glance through the door leading to the hall of the house came back: "Here's the doctor!"

It was a young fellow with bright eyes, whom the doorkeeper had found and brought in. He preferred to examine the injured man before they put him to bed. Only one of his legs, the left one, was broken above the ankle; it was a simple fracture, no serious complication appeared likely to result from it. And they were about to carry the stretcher into the back-room when Gaujean arrived. He came to give them an account of a last attempt to settle matters, an attempt moreover which had failed; the declaration of bankruptcy was unavoidable.

"Dear me," murmured he, "what's the matter?"

In a few words, Denise informed him. Then he stopped, feeling awkward, while Robineau said, in a feeble voice: "I don't bear you any ill-will, but all this is partly your fault."

"Well, my dear fellow," replied Gaujean, "it wanted stronger men than ourselves. You know I'm not in a much better position than you are."

They raised the stretcher; Robineau still found strength to say: "No, no, stronger fellows than us would have given way as we have. I can understand such obstinate old men as Bourras and Baudu standing out; but for you and I, who are young, who had accepted the new style of things, it was wrong! No, Gaujean, it's the last of a world."

They carried him off. Madame Robineau embraced Denise with an eagerness in which there was almost a feeling of joy at having at last got rid of all those worrying business matters. And, as Gaujean went away with the young girl, he confessed to her that Robineau, poor devil, was right. It was idiotic to try to struggle against The Ladies' Paradise. Personally he felt he would be lost, if he did not get back into its good graces. The night before, in fact, he had secretly made a proposal to Hutin, who was just leaving for Lyons. But he felt very doubtful, and tried to interest Denise in the matter, aware, no doubt, of her powerful influence.

"Upon my word," said he, "so much the worse for the manufacturers! Every one would laugh at me if I ruined myself in fighting for other people's benefit, when those fellows are struggling as to who shall make at the cheapest price! As you said some time ago, the manufacturers have only to follow the march of progress by a better organization and new methods. Everything will come all right; it is sufficient that the public are satisfied."

Denise smiled and replied: "Go and tell that to Monsieur Mouret himself. Your visit will please him, and he's not the man to display any rancour, if you offer him even a centime profit per yard."

Madame Baudu died one bright sunny afternoon in January. For a fortnight she had been unable to go down into the shop which a charwoman now looked after. She sat in the centre of her bed, propped up by some pillows. Nothing but her eyes seemed to be alive in her white face; and with head erect, she obstinately gazed upon The Ladies' Paradise opposite, through the small curtains of the windows. Baudu, himself suffering from the same obsession, from the despairing fixity of her gaze, sometimes wanted to draw the larger curtains. But she stopped him with an imploring gesture, obstinately desirous of looking and looking till the last moment should come. The monster had now robbed her of everything, her business, her daughter; she herself had gradually died away with The Old Elbeuf, losing some part of her life as the shop lost its customers; the day it succumbed, she had no more breath left. When she felt she was dying, she still found strength to insist on her husband opening both windows. It was very mild, a bright ray of sunshine gilded The Ladies' Paradise, whilst the bed-room of the old house shivered in the shade. Madame Baudu lay there with eyes fixed, full of that vision of the triumphal monument, those clear, limpid windows, behind which a gallop of millions was passing. But slowly her eyes grew dim, invaded by darkness; and when their last gleam had expired in death, they remained wide open, still gazing, and wet with tears.

Once more all the ruined traders of the district followed the funeral procession. There were the brothers Vanpouille, pale at the thought of their December bills, met by a supreme effort which they would never be able to repeat. Bédoré, accompanying his sister, leant on his cane, so full of worry and anxiety that his liver complaint was getting worse every day. Deslignières had had a fit, Piot and Rivoire walked on in silence, with downcast looks, like men entirely played out. And they dared not question each other about those who had disappeared, Quinette, Mademoiselle Tatin, and others, who, in the space of a day, sank, ruined, swept away by the flood of disasters: without counting Robineau, still in bed, with his broken leg. But they pointed with an especial air of interest to the new tradesmen attacked by the plague: Grognet the perfumer, Madame Chadeuil the milliner, Lacassagne the flower-maker, and Naud the boot-maker who were still on their legs, but full of anxiety at thought of the evil which would doubtless sweep them away in their turn. Baudu walked behind the hearse with the same heavy, stolid step as when he had followed his daughter; whilst in the first mourning coach could be seen Bourras's eyes sparkling under his bushy eyebrows and hair of a snowy whiteness.

Denise was in great trouble. For the last fortnight she had been worn out with fatigue and anxiety; she had been obliged to put Pépé to school, and had been running about on account of Jean, who was so stricken with the pastrycook's niece, that he had implored his sister to go and ask her hand in marriage. Then her aunt's death, this fresh catastrophe, had quite overwhelmed the young girl, though Mouret had again offered his services, giving her leave to do what she liked for her uncle and the others. One morning she had yet another interview with him, at the news that Bourras had been turned into the street, and that Baudu was going to shut up shop. Then, she went out after lunch in the hope of at least comforting these two.

In the Rue de la Michodière, Bourras was standing on the foot pavement opposite his house, whence he had been evicted on the previous day by a fine trick, a discovery of the lawyers. As Mouret held several bills, he had easily obtained an order in bankruptcy against the umbrella-maker and then had given five hundred francs for the expiring lease at the sale ordered by the court; so that the obstinate old man had for five hundred francs allowed himself to be deprived of what he had refused to surrender for a hundred thousand. The architect, who came with his gang of workmen, had been obliged to employ the police to get him out. The goods had been taken and sold, the rooms cleared; however, he still obstinately remained in the corner where he slept, and from which out of pity they did not like to drive him. The workmen even attacked the roofing over his head. They took off the rotten slates, the ceilings fell in and the walls cracked, and yet he remained there, under the bare old beams, amidst the ruins. At last when the police came, he went away. But on the following morning he again appeared on the opposite side of the street, after passing the night in a lodging-house of the neighbourhood.

"Monsieur Bourras!" said Denise, kindly.

He did not hear her for his flaming eyes were devouring the workmen who were attacking the front of the hovel with their picks. Through the glassless windows you could see the inside of the house, the wretched rooms, and the black staircase, to which the sun had not penetrated for the last two hundred years.

"Ah! it's you," he replied at last, when he recognised her. "A nice bit of work they're doing, eh? the robbers!"

She no longer dared to speak; her heart was stirred by the lamentable wretchedness of the old place; she was unable to take her eyes off the mouldy stones that were falling. Up above on a corner of the ceiling of her old room, she once more perceived that name—Ernestine—written in black and shaky letters with the flame of a candle; and the remembrance of her days of misery came back to her, inspiring her with a tender sympathy for all suffering. However, the workmen, in order to knock one of the walls down at a blow, had attacked it at its base. It was already tottering.

"If only it could crush them all," growled Bourras, in a savage voice.

There was a terrible cracking noise. The frightened workmen ran out into the street. In falling, the wall shook and carried all the rest with it. No doubt the hovel, with its flaws and cracks was ripe for this downfall; a push had sufficed to cleave it from top to bottom. It was a pitiful crumbling, the razing of a mud-house soddened by rain. Not a partition remained standing; on the ground there was nothing but a heap of rubbish, the dung of the past cast, as it were, at the street corner.

"My God!" the old man had exclaimed as if the blow had resounded in his very entrails.

He stood there gaping; he would never have imagined that it would have been so quickly over. And he looked at the gap, the hollow at last yawning beside The Ladies' Paradise, now freed of the wart which had so long disgraced it. The gnat was crushed; this was the final triumph over the galling obstinacy of the infinitely little; the whole block was now invaded and conquered. Passers-by lingered to talk to the workmen, who began crying out against those old buildings which were only good for killing people.

"Monsieur Bourras," repeated Denise, trying to draw him on one side, "you know that you will not be abandoned. All your wants will be provided for."

He raised his head. "I have no wants. You've been sent by them, haven't you? Well, tell them that old Bourras still knows how to use his hands and that he can find work wherever he likes. Really, it would be a fine thing to offer charity to those whom they assassinate!"

Then she implored him: "Pray accept, Monsieur Bourras; don't cause me this grief."

But he shook his bushy head. "No, no, it's all over. Good-bye. Go and live happily, you who are young, and don't prevent old people from sticking to their ideas."

He cast a last glance at the heap of rubbish, and then went painfully away. She watched him disappear, elbowed by the crowd on the pavement. He turned the corner of the Place Gaillon, and all was over.

For a moment, Denise remained motionless, lost in thought. Then she went over to her uncle's. The draper was alone in the dark shop of The Old Elbeuf. The charwoman only came in the morning and evening to do a little cooking, and help him take down and put up the shutters. He spent hours in this solitude, often without being disturbed during the whole day, and bewildered and unable to find the goods when a stray customer chanced to venture in. And there in the silence and the half-light he walked about unceasingly, with the same heavy step as at the two funerals; yielding to a sickly desire, to regular fits of forced marching, as if he were trying to rock his grief to sleep.

"Are you feeling better, uncle?" asked Denise.

He only stopped for a second and then started off again, going from the pay-desk to an obscure corner.

"Yes, yes. Very well, thanks."

She tried to find some consoling subject, some cheerful remark, but could think of nothing. "Did you hear the noise? The house is down."

"Ah! it's true," he murmured, with an astonished look, "that must have been the house. I felt the ground shake. Seeing them on the roof this morning, I closed my door."

Then he made a vague gesture, to intimate that such things no longer interested him. Each time he arrived in front of the pay-desk, he looked at the empty seat, that well-known velvet-covered seat, where his wife and daughter had grown up. Then, when his perpetual walking brought him to the other end, he gazed at the gloom-enveloped shelves, on which a few pieces of cloth were growing more and more mouldy. It was a widowed house; those he loved had disappeared; his business had come to a shameful end; and he was left alone to commune with his dead heart and fallen pride, amidst all these catastrophes. He raised his eyes to the black ceiling, he listened to the sepulchral silence which reigned in the little dining-room, that family nook which he had formerly loved so well, even to its stuffy odour. Not a breath was now heard in the old house, his regular heavy tread made the ancient walls resound, as if he were walking in the tomb of his affections.

At last Denise approached the subject which had brought her. "Uncle," said she, "you can't stay like this. You must come to a decision."

Without stopping he replied: "No doubt; but what would you have me do? I've tried to sell, but no one has come. One of these mornings, I shall shut up shop and go off."

She was aware that a failure was no longer to be feared. The creditors had preferred to come to an understanding in presence of such a long series of misfortunes. Everything paid, the old man would simply find himself in the street, penniless.

"But what will you do, then?" she murmured, seeking some transition in order to arrive at the offer which she dared not make.

"I don't know," he replied. "They'll pick me up all right." He had now changed his route, going from the dining-room to the windows; and every time he came to these windows he cast a mournful glance on the wretchedness of the old show-goods forgotten there. His eyes did not even turn towards the triumphal façade of The Ladies' Paradise, whose architectural lines ran right and left, to both ends of the street. He was thoroughly annihilated, and had not even the strength left him to get angry.

"Listen, uncle," said Denise at last, greatly embarrassed; "perhaps there might be a situation for you." And after a pause she stammered, "Yes, I am charged to offer you a situation as inspector."

"Where?" asked Baudu.

"Why, over the road," she replied; "at our place. Six thousand francs a year; a very easy berth."

He stopped suddenly in front of her. But instead of getting angry as she feared he would, he turned very pale, succumbing to a grievous emotion, a feeling of bitter resignation.

"Over the road, over the road," he stammered several times. "You want me to go there?"

Denise herself was affected by his emotion. She recalled the long struggle of the two shops, again saw herself at the funerals of Geneviève and Madame Baudu, and beheld The Old Elbeuf overthrown, utterly ruined by The Ladies' Paradise. And the idea of her uncle taking a situation over the road, and walking about there in a white neck-tie, made her heart leap with pity and revolt.

"Come, Denise, my girl, is it possible?" he asked simply, crossing his poor trembling hands.

"No, no, uncle!" she exclaimed, in a sudden outburst of her just and excellent nature. "It would be wrong. Forgive me, I beg of you."

He resumed his walk and again his step resounded amidst the funereal emptiness of the house. And, when she left him, he was still and ever marching up and down, with the obstinate locomotion peculiar to great despairs which turn and turn, unable to find an outlet.

That night also proved a sleepless one for Denise. She had discovered she really was powerless. Even in favour of her own people she was unable to find any consolation or relief. She must to the bitter end remain a witness of the invincible work of life which requires death as its continual seed. She no longer struggled, she accepted this law of combat; still her womanly soul filled with tearful pity, with fraternal tenderness at the idea of humanity's sufferings. For years past she herself had been caught in the wheel-work of the machine. Had she not bled in it? Had she not been bruised, dismissed, overwhelmed with insults? Even now she was frightened, when she felt herself chosen by the logic of facts. Why should it be she, who was so puny? Why should her small hand suddenly become so powerful amidst the monster's work? And the force which swept everything away, carried her along in her turn, she, whose coming was to be revenge. It was Mouret who had invented this world-crushing mechanism whose brutal working shocked her; he had strewn the neighbourhood with ruins, despoiled some, killed others; and yet despite everything she loved him for the grandeur of his work, loved him still more at each fresh excess of power, notwithstanding the flood of tears which overcame her in presence of the hallowed wretchedness of the vanquished.

The Rue du Dix-Décembre, quite new with its chalk-white houses and the last remaining scaffoldings of a few unfinished buildings, stretched out beneath a clear February sun; a stream of vehicles was passing at a conquering pace through this gap of light, intersecting the damp gloom of the old Saint-Roch quarter; and, between the Rue de la Michodière and the Rue de Choiseul, there was quite a tumult, the crush of a crowd of people who had been excited by a month's advertising, and with their eyes in the air, were gaping at the monumental façade of The Ladies' Paradise, inaugurated that Monday, on the occasion of a grand display of white goods.

There was a vast development of bright, fresh polychromatic architecture enriched with gilding, symbolical of the tumult and sparkle of the business inside, and attracting attention like a gigantic window-display flaming with the liveliest colours. In order not to bedim the show of goods, the ground-floor decoration was of a sober description; the base of sea-green marble; the corner piers and bearing pillars covered with black marble, the severity of which was brightened by gilded modillions; and all the rest was plate-glass, in iron sashes, nothing but glass, which seemed to throw the depths of the halls and galleries open to the full light of day. However, as the floors ascended, the hues became brighter. The frieze above the ground-floor was formed of a series of mosaics, a garland of red and blue flowers, alternating with marble slabs on which was cut an infinity of names of goods, encircling the colossus. Then the base of the first floor, of enamelled brickwork, supported large windows, above which came another frieze formed of gilded escutcheons emblazoned with the arms of the chief towns of France, and designs in terra-cotta, in whose enamel one again found the light coloured tints of the base. Then, right at the top, the entablature blossomed forth like an ardent florescence of the entire façade, mosaics and faience reappeared with yet warmer colourings, the zinc of the eaves was cut and gilded, while along the acroteria ran a nation of statues, emblematical of the great industrial and manufacturing cities, their delicate silhouettes profiled against the sky. The spectators were especially astonished by the central entrance which was also decorated with a profusion of mosaics, faience, and terra-cotta, and surmounted by a freshly gilt allegorical group, which glittered in the sun: Woman garmented and kissed by a flight of laughing cupids.

About two o'clock a special squad of police was obliged to make the crowd move on, and to regulate the waiting carriages. The palace was built, the temple raised to the extravagant folly of fashion. It dominated everything, covering a whole district with its shadows. The scar left on its flank by the demolition of Bourras's hovel had already been so skilfully cicatrized that it would now have been impossible to find the former place of that old wart.

In their superb isolation the four frontages now ran along the four streets, without a break. Since Baudu's retirement into a home, The Old Elbeuf, on the other side of the way, had been closed, walled up like a tomb, behind the shutters that were never now taken down; little by little cab-wheels had splashed them, while posters—a rising tide of advertisements, which seemed like the last shovelful of earth thrown over old-fashioned commerce—covered them up and pasted them together; and, in the middle of this dead frontage, dirtied by the mud from the street, and streaked with tatters of Parisian puffery, a huge clean yellow poster, announcing in letters two feet high the great sale at The Ladies' Paradise, was displayed like a flag planted on a conquered empire.

It was as if the colossus, after each enlargement, full of shame and repugnance for the dingy district in which it had modestly sprung up, and which it had subsequently slaughtered, had just turned its back to it, leaving the mud of the narrow streets behind, and presenting its upstart face to the noisy, sunny thoroughfares of new Paris. As now represented in the engravings of its advertisements, it had grown bigger and bigger, like the ogre of the legend, whose shoulders threatened to pierce the clouds. In the first place, in the foreground of one engraving, were the Rue du Dix-Décembre, the Rue de la Michodière, and the Rue Monsigny, filled with little black figures, and endowed with wondrous breadth, as if to make room for the customers of the whole world. Then came a bird's eye view of the buildings themselves, of exaggerated immensity, with the roofs of the covered galleries, the glazed courtyards in which the halls could be divined, all the infinitude of that lake of glass and zinc shining in the sun. Beyond, stretched Paris, but a Paris dwarfed, eaten away by the monster: the houses, of cottage-like humbleness in the immediate neighbourhood, faded into a cloud of indistinct chimneys; the public buildings seemed to melt into nothingness, on the left two dashes sufficed for Notre-Dame, to the right a circumflex accent represented the Invalides, in the background the Panthéon looked no larger than a lentil. The horizon crumbled into powder, became no more than a contemptible frame-work extending past the heights of Châtillon, out into the open country, whose blurred expanses indicated how far extended the state of slavery.

Ever since the morning the crowd had been increasing. No establishment had ever yet stirred up the city with such an uproarious profusion of advertisements. The Ladies' Paradise now spent nearly six hundred thousand francs a year in posters, advertisements, and appeals of all sorts; four hundred thousand catalogues were sent away, more than a hundred thousand francs' worth of material was cut up for patterns. It was a complete invasion of the newspapers, the walls, and the ears of the public, as if some monstrous brass trumpet were being blown incessantly, carrying the tumult of the great sales to the four corners of the earth. And, for the future, this façade, before which people were now crowding, became a living advertisement with its motley, gilded magnificence, its windows large enough for the display of the entire poem of woman's dress and its profusion of inscriptions painted, engraved and cut in stone, from the marble slabs of the ground-floor to the sheets of iron rounded off in semicircles above the roofs and unfolding gilded streamers on which the name of the house could be read in letters bright as the sun, against the azure blue of the sky.

Trophies and flags had been added in honour of the inauguration; each storey was gay with banners and standards bearing the arms of the principal towns of France; and right at the top, the flags of foreign nations, run up on masts, fluttered in the breeze. Down below the show of white goods in the windows flashed with blinding intensity. There was nothing but white; on the left a complete trousseau and a mountain of sheets, on the right some curtains draped to imitate a chapel, and numerous pyramids of handkerchiefs fatigued the eyes; while between the hung goods at the door—pieces of cotton, calico, and muslin, falling and spreading out like snow from a mountain summit—were placed some dressed prints, sheets of bluish cardboard, on which a young bride and a lady in ball costume, both life-size and attired in real lace and silk, smiled with their coloured faces. A group of idlers was constantly forming there, and desire arose from the admiration of the throng.

Moreover the curiosity around The Ladies' Paradise was increased by a catastrophe of which all Paris was talking, the burning down of The Four Seasons, the big establishment which Bouthemont had opened near the Opera-house, hardly three weeks before. The newspapers were full of details—the fire breaking out through an explosion of gas during the night, the hurried flight of the frightened saleswomen in their night-dresses, and the heroic conduct of Bouthemont, who had carried five of them out on his shoulders. The enormous losses were covered by insurances and people had already begun to shrug their shoulders, saying what a splendid advertisement it was. But for the time being attention again flowed back to The Ladies' Paradise, excited by all the stories which were flying about, occupied to a wonderful extent by these colossal establishments which by their importance were taking up such a large place in public life. How wonderfully lucky that Mouret was! Paris saluted her star, and crowded to see him still standing erect since the very flames now undertook to sweep all competition from before him; and the profits of his season were already being calculated, people had begun to estimate the increase of custom which would be brought to his doors by the forced closing of the rival house. For a moment he had been anxious, troubled at feeling a jealous woman against him, that Madame Desforges to whom he owed some part of his fortune. Baron Hartmann's financial dilettantism in putting money into both concerns, annoyed him also. Then he was above all exasperated at having missed a genial idea which had occurred to Bouthemont, who had prevailed on the vicar of the Madeleine to bless his establishment, followed by all his clergy; an astonishing ceremony, a religious pomp paraded from the silk department to the glove department, and so on throughout the building. True, this ceremony had not prevented everything from being destroyed, but it had done as much good as a million francs worth of advertisements, so great an impression had it produced on the fashionable world. From that day, Mouret dreamed of securing the services of the archbishop.

The clock over the door was striking three, and the afternoon crush had commenced, nearly a hundred thousand customers struggling in the various galleries and halls. Outside, the vehicles were stationed from one to the other end of the Rue du Dix-Décembre, and over against the Opera-house another compact mass of conveyances occupied the *cul-de-sac* where the future Avenue de l'Opéra was to commence. Public cabs mixed with private broughams, the drivers waiting about the wheels and the horses neighing and shaking their curb-chains which sparkled in the sun. The lines were incessantly reforming amidst the calls of the messengers and the pushing of the animals, which closed in of their own accord, whilst fresh vehicles kept on arriving and taking their places with the rest. The pedestrians flew on to the refuges in frightened bands, the foot pavements appeared black with people in the receding perspective of the broad straight thoroughfare. And a clamour rose up between the white houses, a mighty caressing breath swept along, as though Paris were opening her soul.

Madame de Boves, accompanied by her daughter Blanche and Madame Guibal, was standing at a window, looking at a display of costumes composed of made-up skirts with the necessary material for bodices.

"Oh! do look," said she, "at those print costumes at nineteen francs fifteen sous!"

In their square pasteboard boxes lay the costumes, each tied round with a favour, and folded so as to show the blue and red embroidered trimmings; and, in a corner of each box, was an engraving depicting the garment completed, as worn by a young person resembling some princess.

"But they are not worth more," murmured Madame Guibal. "They fall to pieces as soon as you handle them."

The two women had become quite intimate since Monsieur de Boves had been confined to his arm-chair by an attack of gout. His wife put up with the acquaintance, since in this way she picked up a little pocket money, sums that the husband allowed himself to be robbed of, being also in need of forbearance.

"Well! let's go in," resumed Madame Guibal. "We must see their show. Hasn't your son-in-law made an appointment with you inside?"

Madame de Boves did not reply, being absorbed in contemplation of the string of carriages, whose doors one by one opened and gave egress to more customers.

"Yes," said Blanche, at last, in her indolent voice. "Paul is to join us at about four o'clock in the reading-room, on leaving the ministry."

They had been married about a month, and Vallagnosc, after a three weeks' leave of absence spent in the South of France, had just returned to his post. The young woman already had her mother's portly appearance; her flesh seemed to be more puffy and coarse since her marriage.

"But there's Madame Desforges over there!" exclaimed the countess, looking at a brougham that had just pulled up.

"Do you think so?" murmured Madame Guibal. "After all those stories! She must still be weeping over the fire at The Four Seasons."

However, it was indeed Henriette. On perceiving her friends, she came up with a gay, smiling air, concealing her defeat beneath the fashionable ease of her manner.

"Dear me! yes, I wanted to have a look round. It's better to see for one's self, isn't it? Oh! we are still good friends with Monsieur Mouret, though he is said to be furious since I interested myself in that rival establishment. Personally, there is only one thing I cannot forgive him, and that is, to have urged on the marriage of my protégée, Mademoiselle de Fontenailles, with that Joseph—"

"What! it's done?" interrupted Madame de Boves. "What a horror!"

"Yes, my dear, and solely to annoy us. I know him; he wished to intimate that the daughters of our great families are only fit to marry his shop messengers."

She was getting quite animated. They had all four remained on the pavement, amidst the crush at the entrance. Little by little, however, they were caught by the stream and only had to yield to the current to pass the door without being conscious of it, talking louder the while in order to make themselves heard. They were now asking each other about Madame Marty; it was said that poor Monsieur Marty, after some violent scenes at home, had gone quite mad, believing himself endowed with unexhaustible wealth. He was ever diving into the treasures of the earth, exhausting mines of gold and loading tumbrils with diamonds and precious stones.

"Poor old fellow!" said Madame Guibal, "he who was always so shabby, with his teacher's humility! And the wife?"

"She's ruining an uncle, now," replied Henriette, "a worthy old man who has gone to live with her, since losing his wife. But she must be here, we shall see her."

Surprise, however, made the ladies stop short. Before them extended "the largest shops in the world," as the advertisements said. The grand central gallery now ran from end to end, opening on to both the Rue du Dix-Décembre and the Rue Neuve-Saint-Augustin; whilst to the right and the left, similar to the aisles of a church, the narrower Monsigny and Michodière Galleries, extended along the two side streets without a break. Here and there the halls formed open spaces amidst the metallic framework of the spiral staircases and hanging bridges. The inside arrangements had been all changed: the bargains were now placed on the Rue du Dix-Décembre side, the silk department was in the centre, the glove department occupied the Saint-Augustin Hall at the far end; and, from the new grand vestibule, you beheld, on looking up, the bedding department which had been moved from one to the other end of the second floor. The number of departments now amounted to the enormous total of fifty; several, quite fresh, were being inaugurated that very day; others, which had become too important, had simply been divided, in order to facilitate the sales; and, owing to the continual increase of business, the staff had been increased to three thousand and forty-five employees for the new season.

What caused the ladies to stop was the prodigious spectacle presented by the grand exhibition of white goods. In the first place, there was the vestibule, a hall with bright mirrors, and paved with mosaics, where the low-priced goods detained the voracious crowd. Then the galleries opened displaying a glittering blaze of white, a borealistic vista, a country of snow, with endless steppes hung with ermine, and an accumulation of glaciers shimmering in the sun. You here again found the whiteness of the show windows, but vivified, and burning from one end of the enormous building to the other with the white flame of a fire in full swing. There was nothing but white goods, all the white articles from each department, a riot of white, a white constellation whose fixed radiance was at first blinding, so that details could not be distinguished. However, the eye soon became accustomed to this unique whiteness; to the left, in the Monsigny Gallery, white promontories of cotton and calico jutted out, with white rocks formed of sheets, napkins, and handkerchiefs; whilst to the right, in the Michodière Gallery, occupied by the mercery, the hosiery, and the woollen goods, were erections of mother of pearl buttons, a grand decoration composed of white socks and one whole room covered with white swanskin illumined by a stream of light from the distance. But the greatest radiance of this nucleus of light came from the central gallery, from amidst the ribbons and the neckerchiefs, the gloves and the silks. The counters disappeared beneath the whiteness of the silks, the ribbons, the gloves and the neckerchiefs.

Round the iron columns climbed "puffings" of white muslin, secured now and again with white silk handkerchiefs. The staircases were decorated with white draperies, quiltings and dimities alternating along the balustrades and encircling the halls as high as the second storey; and all this ascending whiteness assumed wings, hurried off and wandered away, like a flight of swans. And more white hung from the arches, a fall of down, a sheet of large snowy flakes; white counterpanes, white coverlets hovered in the air, like banners in a church; long jets of guipure lace hung across, suggestive of swarms of white motionless butterflies; other laces fluttered on all sides, floating like gossamer in a summer sky, filling the air with their white breath. And the marvel, the altar of this religion of white was a tent formed of white curtains, which hung from the glazed roof above the silk counter, in the great hall. The muslin, the gauze, the art-guipures flowed in light ripples, whilst very richly embroidered tulles, and pieces of oriental silver-worked silk served as a background to this giant decoration, which partook both of the tabernacle and the alcove. It was like a broad white bed, awaiting with its virginal immensity, as in the legend, the coming of the white princess, she who was to appear some day, all powerful in her white bridal veil.

"Oh! extraordinary!" repeated the ladies. "Wonderful!"

They did not weary of this song in praise of whiteness which the goods of the entire establishment were singing. Mouret had never conceived anything more vast; it was the master stroke of his genius for display. Beneath the flow of all this whiteness, amidst the seeming disorder of the tissues, fallen as if by chance from the open drawers, there was so to say a harmonious phrase,—white followed and developed in all its tones: springing into existence, growing, and blossoming with the complicated orchestration of some master's fugue, the continuous development of which carries the mind away in an ever-soaring flight. Nothing but white, and yet never the same white, each different tinge showing against the other, contrasting with that next to it, or perfecting it, and attaining to the very brilliancy of light itself. It all began with the dead white of calico and linen, and the dull white of flannel and cloth; then came the velvets, silks, and satins—quite an ascending gamut, the white gradually lighting up and finally emitting little flashes at its folds; and then it flew away in the transparencies of the curtains, became diffuse brightness with the muslins, the guipures, the laces and especially the tulles, so light and airy that they formed the extreme final note; whilst the silver of the oriental silk sounded higher than all else in the depths of the giant alcove.

Meanwhile the place was full of life. The lifts were besieged by people; there was a crush at the refreshment-bar and in the reading-room; quite a nation was moving about in these snowy regions. And the crowd seemed to be black, like skaters on a Polish lake in December. On the ground-floor there was a heavy swell, ruffled by a reflux, in which nothing but the delicate enraptured faces of women could be distinguished. In the gaps of the iron framework, up the staircases, on the hanging bridges, there was an endless ascent of small figures which looked as if lost amidst the snowy peaks of mountains. A suffocating, hot-house heat surprised one at sight of these frozen heights. The buzz of all the voices made a great noise like that of a river carrying ice along. Up above, the profusion of gilding, the glass work and the golden roses seemed like a burst of sunshine, glittering over the Alps of this grand exhibition of white goods.

"Come," said Madame de Boves, "we must go forward. It's impossible to stay here."

Since she had entered, inspector Jouve, standing near the door, had not taken his eyes off her; and when she turned round she encountered his gaze. Then, as she resumed her walk, he let her gain ground, but followed her at a distance, without, however, appearing to take any further notice of her.

"Ah!" said Madame Guibal again stopping amidst all the jostling as she came to the first pay-desk, "that's a pretty idea, those violets!"

She referred to the new present made by The Ladies' Paradise, one of Mouret's ideas, which was making a great noise in the newspapers: small bouquets of white violets, bought by the thousand at Nice were distributed to every lady customer who made the smallest purchase. Near each pay-desk messengers in uniform stood delivering the bouquets under the supervision of an inspector. And gradually all the customers were decorated in this way, the building was filling with these white bridal flowers, every woman diffusing as she passed a penetrating perfume of violets.

"Yes," murmured Madame Desforges, in a jealous voice, "it's a good idea."

But, just as they were moving away, they heard two salesmen joking about these violets. A tall, thin fellow was expressing his astonishment: was the marriage between the governor and the first-hand in the costume department coming off, then? whilst a short, fat fellow replied that he didn't know, but that the flowers were bought at any rate.

"What!" exclaimed Madame de Boves, "is Monsieur Mouret going to marry?"

"That's the latest news," replied Madame Desforges, affecting the greatest indifference. "However, one's bound to come to that."

The countess darted a quick glance at her new friend. They both now understood why Madame Desforges had come to The Ladies' Paradise notwithstanding the hostilities attending her rupture with Mouret. No doubt she was yielding to an invincible desire to see and suffer.

"I shall stay with you," said Madame Guibal, whose curiosity was awakened. "We can meet Madame de Boves again in the reading-room."

"Very good," replied the latter. "I want to go up to the first floor. Come along, Blanche." And she went up followed by her daughter, whilst inspector Jouve still on her track, ascended by another staircase, in order not to attract her attention. The two other ladies soon disappeared in the compact crowd on the ground-floor.

Amidst the press of business all the counters were again talking of nothing but the governor's love matters. The affair which had for months been occupying the employees, who were delighted at Denise's long resistance, had all at once come to a crisis: since the previous day it had been known that the girl intended to leave The Ladies' Paradise, under the pretext of requiring rest, and this despite all Mouret's entreaties. And opinions were divided. Would she leave? Would she stay? Bets of five francs that she would leave on the following Sunday circulated from department to department. The knowing ones staked a lunch on it all ending in a marriage; yet, the others, those who believed in her departure, did not risk their money without good reasons. Certainly the girl had all the power of an adored woman who refuses to yield; but the governor, on his side, was strong in his wealth, his happy widowerhood, and his pride, which a last exaction might exasperate. At all events they were all of opinion that this little saleswoman had played her game with the science of a expert woman of the world and was now venturing on the supreme stroke by offering him this bargain: Marry me, or I go.

Denise, however, thought but little of these things. She had never imposed any conditions or made any calculation. And the reason of her departure was the very judgment which, to her continual surprise, was passed upon her conduct. Had she wished for all this? Had she shown herself artful, coquettish, ambitious? No, she had simply presented herself and had been the first to feel astonished at such a passion. And again, at the present time, why did they ascribe her resolution to quit The Ladies' Paradise to craftiness? It was after all so natural! She had begun to experience a nervous uneasiness, an intolerable anguish, amidst the continual gossip which went on in the house, and Mouret's feverish pursuit of her, and the combats she was obliged to wage against herself; and she preferred to go away, seized with fear lest she might some day yield and regret it for ever afterwards. If in all this there were any learned tactics, she was totally unaware of it, and she asked herself in despair what she might do to avoid appearing like one who is running after a husband. The idea of a marriage now irritated her, and she resolved to say no, and still no should he push his folly to that extent. She alone ought to suffer. The necessity for the separation caused her tears to flow; but, with her great courage, she repeated that it was necessary, that she would have no rest or happiness if she acted in any other way.

When Mouret received her resignation, he remained mute and cold, in the effort which he made to contain himself. Then he curtly replied that he granted her a week's reflection, before allowing her to commit such a stupid action. At the expiration of the week, when she returned to the subject, and expressed a determination to go away after the great sale, he did not lose his temper, but affected to talk the language of reason to her: she was playing with fortune, she would never find another position equal to that she was leaving. Had she another situation in view? If so, he was quite prepared to offer her the advantages she expected to obtain elsewhere. And when the young woman replied that she had not looked for any other situation, but intended first of all to take a rest at Valognes, thanks to the money she had already saved, he asked her what would prevent her from returning to The Ladies' Paradise if her health alone were the reason of her departure. She remained silent, tortured by this cross-examination. And thereupon he imagined that she was about to join a sweetheart, a future husband perhaps. Had she not confessed to him one evening that she loved somebody? From that moment he had been carrying deep in his heart, like the stab of a knife, the confession wrung from her. And, if this man was to marry her, she must be giving up all to follow him: that explained her obstinacy. It was all over; and so he simply added in an icy tone that he would detain her no longer, since she could not tell him the real cause of her departure. These harsh words, free from anger, upset her far more than a violent scene such as she had feared.

Throughout the remaining week which Denise was obliged to spend in the house, Mouret preserved his rigid pallor. When he crossed the departments, he affected not to see her; never had he seemed more indifferent, more absorbed in his work; and the bets began again, only the brave ones dared to risk a luncheon on the wedding. Yet, beneath this coldness, so unusual with him, Mouret hid a frightful attack of indecision and suffering. Fits of anger brought the blood seething to his head: he saw red, he dreamed of taking Denise in a close embrace, keeping her, and stifling her cries. Then he tried to reflect, to find some practical means of preventing her from going away; but he constantly ran up against his powerlessness, the uselessness of his power and money. An idea, however, was growing amidst his wild projects, and gradually imposing itself on him notwithstanding his revolt. After Madame Hédouin's death he had sworn never to marry again; having derived from a woman his first good fortune, he resolved in future to draw his fortune from all women. It was with him, as with Bourdoncle, a superstition that the head of a great drapery establishment ought to remain single, if he wished to retain his masculine sovereignty over the growing desires of his world of female customers; for the introduction of a woman to the throne would change the atmosphere, drive away all the others. Thus, he still resisted the invincible logic of facts, preferring to die rather than yield, and inflamed by sudden bursts of fury against Denise, feeling that she was Revenge and fearing he should fall vanquished upon his millions, broken like a mere straw by the Eternal Feminine on the day he should marry her. Then, however, he would become cowardly again, and discuss his repugnance: why should he tremble? she was so sweet-tempered, so prudent, that he could abandon himself to her without fear. Twenty times an hour the battle began afresh in his distracted mind. His pride tended to irritate the wound, and he completely lost his reason when he thought that, even after this last submission, she might yet say no, ever no if she loved another. On the morning of the great sale, he had still not decided on anything, and Denise was to leave on the morrow.

When Bourdoncle, on the day in question, entered Mouret's private room at about three o'clock, according to custom, he found him sitting with his elbows on his desk, his hands over his eyes, so greatly absorbed that he had to touch him on the shoulder. Then Mouret glanced up, his face bathed in tears. They looked at each other, held out their hands, and a hearty grip was exchanged by these two men who had fought so many commercial battles side by side. For the past month moreover Bourdoncle's manner had completely changed; he now bent before Denise, and even secretly urged the governor on to a marriage with her. No doubt he was thus manœuvring to save himself from being swept away by a power which he now recognised as superior. But beneath this change there could also have been found the awakening of an old ambition, a timid, gradually growing hope of in his turn swallowing up that Mouret before whom he had so long bowed. This was in the atmosphere of the house, in the struggle for existence whose continued massacres helped on the sales around him. He was carried away by the working of the machine, seized by the same appetite as the others, that voracity which, from top to bottom, urged the lean ones to the extermination of the fat ones. Only a sort of religious fear, the religion of chance, had so far prevented him from showing his own teeth. But now the governor was becoming childish, drifting into a ridiculous marriage, ruining his luck, destroying his charm over the customers. Why should he dissuade him from it, when he might afterwards so easily pick up the business of this weakling who fell at the feet of a woman? Thus it was with the emotion of a farewell, the pity of an old friendship, that he shook his chief's hand, saying:

"Come, come, courage! Marry her, and finish the matter."

But Mouret already felt ashamed of his momentary weakness, and got up, protesting: "No, no, it's too stupid. Come, let's take a turn round the place. Things are looking well, aren't they? I fancy we shall have a magnificent day."

They went out and began their afternoon inspection of the crowded departments. Bourdoncle meanwhile cast side glances at his companion, feeling anxious at this last display of energy and watching his lips to catch the least sign of suffering. The business was now throwing forth its fire, with an infernal roar, which made the building tremble like a big steamer going at full speed. At Denise's counter was a crowd of mothers with bands of little girls and boys, swamped beneath the garments they were trying on. The department had brought out all its white articles, and there, as everywhere else, was a riot of white fit for the garmenting of a troop of shivering cupids: white cloth cloaks, white piqué, nainsook and cashmere dresses, white sailor costumes, and even white Zouave ones. In the centre, for the sake of effect, for the proper season had not yet arrived, there was a display of confirmation costumes, white muslin dresses and veils and white satin shoes, a light gushing florescence like an enormous bouquet of innocence and candid delight. Madame Bourdelais, with her three children, Madeleine, Edmond and Lucien, seated according to their size, was getting angry with the smallest because he continued struggling whilst Denise tried to put a muslin-de-laine jacket on him.

"Do keep still! Don't you think it's rather tight, mademoiselle?" she said; and with the sharp look of a woman difficult to deceive, she examined the stuff, studied the cut, and scrutinized the seams. "No, it fits well," she resumed. "It's no trifle to dress all these little ones. Now I want a mantle for this young lady."

Denise had been obliged to assist in serving as the customers had besieged her department in great force. She was looking for the mantle required, when she set up a cry of surprise.

"What! It's you! what's the matter?"

Her brother Jean was standing before her, a parcel in his hand. He had been married a week before, and on the Saturday his wife, a dark little woman, with a provoking, charming face, had paid a long visit to The Ladies' Paradise to make some purchases. The young people were to accompany Denise to Valognes: it was to be a regular honeymoon trip, a month's holiday which would remind them of old times.

"Just fancy," he said, "Thérèse has forgotten a number of things. There are some articles to be changed, and others to be bought. So, as she was in a hurry, she sent me with this parcel. I'll explain—"

But she interrupted him on perceiving Pépé, "What! Pépé too! and his school?"

"Well," said Jean, "after dinner on Sunday I had not the heart to take him back. He will return this evening. The poor child is very downhearted at the thought of being shut up in Paris whilst we shall be enjoying ourselves."

Denise smiled at them, in spite of her suffering. She handed Madame Bourdelais over to one of her saleswomen and came back to her brothers in a corner of the department, which was, fortunately, getting clearer. The youngsters, as she still called them, had now grown to be big fellows. Pépé at twelve years old, was already taller and stouter than herself but still taciturn and living on caresses, looking, too, very gentle in his school-uniform; whilst broad-shouldered Jean, quite a head taller than his sister, with blonde hair blowing about in the wind, still retained his feminine good looks. And she, always slim, no fatter than a skylark, as she said, still retained her anxious motherly authority over them, treating them as children in need of all her attention, buttoning up Jean's frock coat so that he should not look like a rake, and seeing that Pépé had got a clean handkerchief. When she perceived the latter's swollen eyes, she gently chided him. "You must be reasonable, my boy. Your studies cannot be interrupted," said she. "I'll take you away at the holidays. Is there anything you want? But perhaps you prefer to have the money." Then she turned towards the other. "And you, youngster, it's your fault, you get making him believe that we are going to have wonderful fun! Just try to be a little more reasonable."

She had given Jean four thousand francs, half of her savings, to enable him to set up housekeeping. The younger one cost her a great deal for schooling, indeed all her money went for them, as in former days. They alone linked her to life and work, for she had again vowed that she would never marry.

"Well, here are the things," resumed Jean. "In the first place, there's a light brown cloak in this parcel that Thérèse—"

But he stopped, and Denise, on turning round to see what had frightened him, perceived Mouret standing behind them. For a moment he had been watching her acting the mother towards the two big boys, scolding and embracing them and turning them round as mothers do babies when changing their clothes. Bourdoncle had remained on one side, feigning to be interested in the sales; but he did not lose sight of this little scene.

"They are your brothers, are they not?" asked Mouret, after a silence.

He had the icy tone and rigid demeanour which he now assumed with her. Denise herself made an effort to remain cold. Her smile died away, and she replied: "Yes, sir. I've married off the eldest, and his wife has sent him for some purchases."

Mouret continued looking at the three of them. At last he said: "The youngest has grown very much. I recognise him, I remember having seen him in the Tuileries Gardens one evening with you."

Then his voice, which was coming more slowly, slightly trembled. She, much moved, bent down, pretending to arrange Pépé's belt. Both brothers, who had turned scarlet, stood smiling at their sister's employer.

"They're very much like you," said the latter.

"Oh!" she exclaimed, "they're much handsomer than I am!"

For a moment he seemed to be comparing their faces. But he could endure it no longer. How she loved them! He walked on a step or two; then returned and whispered in her ear: "Come to my office after business. I want to speak to you before you go away."

This time, Mouret went off and continued his inspection. The battle was once more raging within him, for the appointment he had just given caused him a sort of irritation. To what idea had he yielded on seeing her with her brothers? It was maddening to think that he could no longer find the strength to assert his will. However, he could settle it by saying a few words of farewell. Bourdoncle, who had rejoined him, seemed less anxious, though he was still examining him with stealthy glances.

Meanwhile, Denise had returned to Madame Bourdelais. "Does the mantle suit you, madame?" she inquired.

"Oh yes, very well. That's quite enough for one day. These little ones are ruining me!"

Denise, now being able to slip off, went to listen to Jean's explanations, and then accompanied him to the various counters, where he would certainly have lost his head without her. First came the brown jacket, which Thérèse now wished to change for a white cloth one of the same size and same shape. And the young woman, having taken the parcel, went to the mantle department, followed by her two brothers.

The department had laid out all its light coloured garments, summer jackets and capes, of light silk and fancy woollens. But there was little doing there, the customers were but few and far between. Nearly all the saleswomen were new-comers. Clara had disappeared a month before, and some said that she had altogether gone to the bad. As for Marguerite, she was at last about to assume the management of the little shop at Grenoble, where her cousin was waiting for her. Madame Aurélie alone remained there immutable, in the curved cuirass of her silk dress and with her imperial face retaining the yellowish puffiness of an antique marble. However, her son Albert's bad conduct was a source of great trouble to her, and she would have retired into the country had it not been for the inroads made on the family savings by this scapegrace, whose terrible extravagance threatened to swallow up the Rigolles property piece by piece. It was a sort of punishment on them, for breaking up their home, for the mother had resumed her little excursions with her lady friends, and the father on his side continued his musical performances. Bourdoncle was already looking at Madame Aurélie with a discontented air, surprised that she lacked the tact to resign: too old for business, such was his opinion; the knell was about to sound which would sweep away the Lhomme dynasty.

"Ah! it's you," said she to Denise, with exaggerated amiability. "You want this cloak changed, eh? Certainly, at once. Ah! there are your brothers; getting quite men, I declare!"

In spite of her pride, she would have gone on her knees to pay her court to the young woman. In her department, as in the others, nothing but Denise's departure was being talked of; and the first-hand was quite ill over it, for she had been reckoning on the protection of her former saleswoman. She lowered her voice to say: "It's reported you're going to leave us. Really, it isn't possible?"

"But it is, though," replied Denise.

Marguerite was listening. Since her marriage had been decided on, she had marched about with more disdainful airs than ever on her putty-looking face. And she came up saying: "You are quite right. Self-respect above everything, I say. Allow me to bid you adieu, my dear."

Some customers arriving at that moment, Madame Aurélie requested her, in a harsh voice, to attend to business. Then, as Denise was taking the cloak to effect the "return" herself, she protested, and called an auxiliary. This, again, was an innovation suggested to Mouret by the young woman—the engagement of persons to carry the articles about, thus relieving the saleswomen of much fatigue.

"Go with Mademoiselle," said the first-hand, giving the auxiliary the cloak. Then, returning to Denise, she added: "Pray consider the matter well. We are all heart-broken at your leaving."

Jean and Pépé, who were waiting, smiling amidst this overflowing torrent of women, followed their sister. They now had to go to the under-linen department, to get four chemises like the half-dozen which Thérèse had bought on the Saturday. But there, where the exhibition of white goods was snowing down from every shelf, they were almost stifled, and found it very difficult to get along.

In the first place, at the corset counter a little scene was collecting quite a crowd. Madame Boutarel, who had arrived in Paris from the south, this time with her husband and daughter, had been wandering all over the place since morning, collecting an outfit for the young lady, who was about to be married. The father was consulted at every turn so that it seemed they would never finish. At last they had stranded here; and whilst the young lady was absorbed in a profound study of some undergarments, the mother had disappeared, having cast her eyes on some corsets she herself fancied. When Monsieur Boutarel, a big, full-blooded man, quite bewildered, left his daughter to search for his wife, he at last found her in a sitting-room, at the door of which he was politely invited to take a seat. These rooms were like narrow cells, glazed with ground glass, and not even husbands were allowed to enter them. Saleswomen came out and went in quickly, closing the doors behind them, while men waited outside, seated in rows on arm-chairs, and looking very weary. Monsieur Boutarel, when he understood matters, got really angry, crying out that he wanted his wife, and insisting on knowing what they had done with her. It was in vain that they tried to calm him. Madame Boutarel was obliged to come out, to the delight of the crowd, which was discussing and laughing over the affair.

Denise and her brothers were at last able to get past. Every article of ladies' underwear was here displayed in a suite of rooms classified into various departments. The corsets and dress-improvers occupied one counter, there were hand-sown corsets, Duchess, cuirass, and, above all, white silk corsets, fan-pointed with divers colours, these latter forming a special display, an army of dummies without heads or legs, nothing indeed but busts; and close by were horse-hair and other dress improvers, often of fantastic aspect. But afterwards came articles of fine linen, white cuffs and cravats, white fichus and collars, an infinite variety of light trifles, a white foam which escaped from the boxes and was heaped up like so much snow. There were loose jackets, little bodices, morning gowns and peignoirs in linen, nainsook, and lace, long white roomy garments, which spoke of the morning lounge. Then appeared white petticoats of every length, the petticoat that clings to the knees, and the long petticoat which sweeps the pavement, a rising sea of petticoats, in which one lost oneself.

At the trousseau department there was a wonderful display of pleating, embroidery, valenciennes, percale and Cambric; and then followed another room devoted to baby-linen, where the voluptuous whiteness of woman's clothing developed into the chaste whiteness of infancy—an innocence, a joy, the young wife become a mother, amidst flannel coifs, chemises and caps like dolls' things, christening gowns, cashmere pelisses, indeed all the white down of birth, like a fine shower of white feathers.

"They are chemises with running-strings," said Jean, who was delighted with the rising tide of feminine attire about him.

However, Pauline ran up as soon as she perceived Denise; and before even asking what she wanted, began to talk in a low tone, stirred as she was by the rumours circulating in the building. In her department, two saleswomen had even got to quarrelling over it, one affirming and the other denying the favourite's departure.

"You'll stay with us, I'll stake my life. What would become of me?" said Pauline; and as Denise replied that she intended to leave the next day: "No, no," the other added, "you think so, but I know better. You must appoint me second-hand, now that I've got my baby. Baugé is reckoning on it, my dear."

Pauline smiled with an air of conviction. Then she gave the six chemises; and, Jean having said that he must next go to the handkerchief counter, she called an auxiliary to carry both the chemises and the jacket left by the auxiliary from the mantle department. The woman who happened to answer was Mademoiselle de Fontenailles, recently married to Joseph. She had just obtained this menial situation as a great favour, and she wore a long black blouse, marked on the shoulder with a number in yellow wool.

"Follow mademoiselle," said Pauline, and then returning to Denise and again lowering her voice, she added: "It's understood that I am to be appointed second-hand, eh?"

Denise promised, with a laugh, by way of joking in her turn. And she went off, going down the stairs with Jean and Pépé, all three followed by the auxiliary. On the ground-floor, they found themselves in the woollen department, a gallery entirely hung with white swanskin cloth and white flannel. Liénard, whom his father had vainly recalled to Angers, was talking to the handsome Mignot who was now a traveller, and had boldly reappeared at The Ladies' Paradise. No doubt they were speaking of Denise, for they both stopped talking to bow to her with a ceremonious air. In fact, as she passed through the departments the salesmen appeared full of emotion and bent their heads before her, uncertain as they were what she might be the next day. They whispered and thought she looked triumphant; and the betting was once more altered; they again risked bottles of Argenteuil wine and fish dinners over the event. She had entered the linen-gallery in order to get to the handkerchief counter, which was at the further end. The show of white goods continued: cottons, madapolams, dimities, quiltings, calicoes, nainsooks, muslins, tarlatans; then came the linen, in enormous piles, the pieces ranged alternately like blocks of stone: stout linen, fine linen, of all widths, white and unbleached, some of pure flax, whitened in the sun; next the same thing commenced once more, there were departments for each sort of linen: house linen, table linen, kitchen linen, a continual crush of white goods, sheets, pillow-cases, innumerable styles of napkins, table-cloths, aprons, and dusters. And the bowing continued, all made way for Denise to pass, while Baugé rushed out to smile on her, as on the good fairy of the house. At last, after crossing the counterpane department, a room hung with white banners, she arrived at the handkerchief counter, the ingenious decoration of which delighted the throng; everything here was arranged in white columns, white pyramids, white castles, an intricate architecture, solely composed of handkerchiefs, some of lawn, others of cambric, Irish linen, or China silk, some marked, some embroidered by hand, some trimmed with lace, some hemstitched, and some woven with vignettes; the whole forming a city of white bricks of infinite variety, standing out mirage-like against an Eastern sky, warmed to a white heat.

"You say another dozen?" asked Denise of her brother. "Cholet handkerchiefs, eh?"

"Yes, like this one," he replied, showing a handkerchief in his parcel.

Jean and Pépé had not quitted her side, but clung to her as they had done formerly on arriving in Paris, knocked up by their journey. This vast establishment, in which she was quite at home, ended by troubling them; and they sheltered themselves in her shadow, placing themselves again under the protection of this second mother of theirs as in an instinctive re-awakening of their infancy. The employees watching them as they passed, smiled at those two big fellows following in the footsteps of that grave slim girl; Jean frightened in spite of his beard, Pépé bewildered in his tunic, and all three of the same fair complexion, a fairness which made a whisper run from one end of the counters to the other: "They are her brothers! They are her brothers!"

But, whilst Denise was looking for a salesman, there occurred another meeting. Mouret and Bourdoncle had entered the gallery; and as the former again stopped in front of the young woman, without, however, speaking to her, Madame Desforges and Madame Guibal passed by. Henriette suppressed the quiver which had invaded her whole being; she looked at Mouret and then at Denise. They also had looked at her, and it was a sort of mute *dénouement*, the common end of many great dramas of the heart,—a glance exchanged in the crush of a crowd. Mouret had already moved off, whilst Denise strayed into the depths of the department, accompanied by her brothers and still in search of a disengaged salesman. But in the auxiliary following Denise, with a yellow number on her shoulder, and a coarse, cadaverous, servant's-looking face, Henriette had recognised Mademoiselle de Fontenailles, and relieved herself by saying to Madame Guibal, in an angry voice:

"Just see what he's doing with that unfortunate girl. Isn't it shameful? A marchioness! And he makes her follow like a dog the creatures he has picked up in the street!" Then she tried to calm herself, adding, with an affected air of indifference: "Let's go and see their display of silks."

The silk department was like a great chamber of love, hung with white by the caprice of some snowy maiden wishing to show off her own spotless whiteness. Pieces of velvet hung from the columns, forming a creamy white background against which silk and satin draperies showed with a metallic and porcelain-like whiteness; and there were also festoons of poult and gros grain silks, light foulards and surahs, which varied from the dull white of a Norwegian blonde to the transparent white, warmed by the sun, of a fair Italian or Spanish beauty.

Favier was just then engaged in measuring some white silk for "the pretty lady," that elegant blonde who was such a frequent customer at the counter, and whom the salesmen never referred to except by that name. She had dealt at the shop for years, and yet they knew nothing about her—neither her condition of life, her address, nor even her name. None of them, in fact, tried to find out, although every time she made her appearance they all indulged in suppositions just for something to talk about. She was getting thinner, she was getting stouter, she had slept well, or she must have been out late the previous evening; indeed every little incident of her unknown life, outdoor events and domestic dramas alike, found an echo at the Paradise, and was commented on. That day, she seemed very gay; and so, on returning from the pay-desk whither he had conducted her, Favier remarked to Hutin: "Perhaps she's going to marry again."

"What! is she a widow?" asked the other.

"I don't know; but you must remember the time she was in mourning. Perhaps she's made some money by speculating on the Bourse." A silence ensued. At last he ended by saying: "However, that's her business. It wouldn't do to take notice of all the women we see here."

But Hutin was looking very thoughtful, for two days before, he had had a warm discussion with the managers, and felt himself condemned. After the great sale his dismissal was certain. For a long time he had felt his position giving way. At the last stock-taking they had complained that he had not even transacted the amount of business fixed in advance; and moreover he was threatened by the appetites of the others, now slowly devouring him in his turn—by all the silent warfare which was waged in the department, amidst the very motion of the machine. Favier's secret undermining could be heard, like a muffled sound of jaw-bones at work underground. He had already received the promise of the first-hand's place, but Hutin, who was aware of it, instead of attacking his old comrade looked upon him as a clever fellow. To think of it! A chap who had always appeared so cold, so humble, whom he had made such use of to turn out both Robineau and Bouthemont! He was full of mingled surprise and respect.

"By the way," all at once resumed Favier, "she's going to stay, you know. The governor has just been seen casting sheep's eyes at her. I shall be let in for a bottle of champagne over it."

He referred to Denise. The gossip was going on more than ever, passing from one counter to the other, through the constantly increasing crowd of customers. The silk salesmen were especially excited, for they had been indulging in heavy bets on the affair.

"By Jove!" exclaimed Hutin, waking up as if from a dream, "wasn't I a flat not to pay court to her! I should be all right now!"

Then on seeing Favier laugh he blushed at this confession, and pretended to laugh himself, adding, as though to recall his words, that it was she who had ruined him with the management. Then a desire for violence seizing hold of him, he finished by getting into a rage with the salesmen whom the assault of the customers had disbanded. But all at once he again smiled, having just perceived Madame Desforges and Madame Guibal slowly crossing the department.

"What can we serve you with to-day, madame?"

"Nothing, thanks," replied Henriette. "You see I'm merely walking round; I've only come out of curiosity."

However, he succeeded in stopping her, and lowered his voice. Quite a plan was springing up in his head. He began to flatter her and run down the house; he had had enough of it, and preferred to go away rather than remain a witness of such disorder. She listened, delighted. It was she herself who, thinking to deprive The Ladies' Paradise of his services offered to get him engaged by Bouthemont as first-hand in the silk department when The Four Seasons should start again. The matter was settled in whispers, whilst Madame Guibal interested herself in the displays.

"May I offer you one of these bouquets of violets?" resumed Hutin, aloud, pointing to a table where there were four or five bunches of the flowers, which he had procured from a pay-desk for personal presents.

"Ah, no, indeed!" exclaimed Henriette, recoiling. "I don't wish to take any part in the wedding."

They understood each other, and separated with a laugh, exchanging glances of intelligence. Then as Madame Desforges began looking for Madame Guibal, she set up an exclamation of surprise on seeing her with Madame Marty. The latter, followed by her daughter Valentine, had for the last two hours been carried through the place by one of those spending fits whence she always emerged weary and bewildered. She had roamed about the furniture department which a show of white lacquered good had changed into a vast virginal chamber, the ribbon and neckerchief departments which formed white colonnades, the mercery and trimming departments with white fringes surrounding ingenious trophies patiently built up of cards of buttons and packets of needles, and the hosiery department in which there was a great crush that year to see an immense piece of decoration—the resplendent name of "The Ladies' Paradise" in letters three yards high, formed of white socks on a groundwork of red ones. But Madame Marty was especially excited by the new departments; they could indeed never open a new department but she must inaugurate it, she was bound to plunge in and buy something. And so at the millinery counter installed in a new room on the first-floor she had spent an hour in having the cupboards emptied, taking the bonnets off the stands ranged on a couple of tables, and trying all of them, white hats, white bonnets and white togues, on herself and her daughter. Then she had gone down to the boot department, at the further end of a gallery on the ground-floor, behind the cravats, a counter which had been opened that day, and which she had turned topsy turvy, seized with sickly desire in presence of the white silk slippers trimmed with swansdown and the white satin boots and shoes with high Louis XV heels.

"Oh! my dear," she stammered, "you've no idea! They have a wonderful assortment of bonnets. I've chosen one for myself and one for my daughter. And the boots, eh? Valentine."

"They're marvellous!" added the latter, with the boldness of one who is at last married. "There are some boots at twenty francs and a half the pair which are delicious!"

A salesman was following them, dragging along the eternal chair, on which a mountain of articles was already heaped.

"How is Monsieur Marty?" asked Madame Desforges.

"Very well, I believe," replied Madame Marty, scared by this abrupt question, which fell ill-naturedly amidst her rage for spending. "He's still shut up, you know; my uncle was to go to see him this morning."

Then she paused and exclaimed: "Oh, look! isn't it lovely?"

The ladies, who had gone on a few steps, found themselves before the new flowers and feathers department, installed in the central gallery, between the silks and the gloves. Under the bright light from the glass roof there appeared an enormous florescence, a white sheaf, tall and broad as an oak. The base was formed of single flowers, violets, lilies of the valley, hyacinths, daisies, all the delicate white blossoms of the garden. Then came bouquets, white roses softened by a fleshy tint, great white peonies slightly shaded with carmine, white chrysanthemums with narrow petals and starred with yellow. And the flowers still ascended, great mystical lilies, branches of apple blossom, bunches of white lilac, a continual blossoming surmounted at the height of the first storey by tufts of ostrich feathers, white plumes, which seemed like the airy breath of this collection of white flowers. One corner was devoted to the display of trimmings and orange-flower wreaths. There were also metallic flowers, silver thistles and silver ears of corn. And amidst the foliage and the petals, amidst all the muslin, silk, and velvet, in which drops of gum set drops of dew, fluttered birds of Paradise for the trimming of hats, purple Tanagers with black tails, and Kingbirds with changing rainbow-like plumage.

"I'm going to buy a branch of apple-blossom," resumed Madame Marty. "It's delicious, isn't it? And that little bird, do look, Valentine! I must take it!"

However, Madame Guibal began to feel tired of standing still in the eddying crowd, and at last exclaimed:

"Well, we'll leave you to make your purchases. We're going upstairs."

"No, no, wait for me!" cried the other, "I'm going up too. There's the perfumery department upstairs, I must see that."

This department, created the day before, was next door to the reading-room. Madame Desforges, to avoid the crush on the stairs, spoke of going up in the lift; but they had to abandon the idea, there were so many people waiting their turn. At last they arrived, passing before the public refreshment bar, where the crowd was becoming so great that an inspector had to restrain the outburst of appetite by only allowing the gluttonous customers to enter in small groups. And from this point the ladies already began to smell the perfumery department, for its penetrating odour scented the whole gallery. There was quite a struggle over one article, The Paradise Soap, a specialty of the house. In the show cases, and on the crystal tablets of the shelves, were ranged pots of pomade and paste, boxes of powder and paint, phials of oil and toilet vinegar; whilst the fine brushes, combs, scissors, and smelling-bottles occupied a special place. The salesmen had managed to decorate the shelves exclusively with white porcelain pots and white glass bottles. But what delighted the customers above all was a silver fountain in the centre, a shepherdess standing on a harvest of flowers, whence flowed a continuous stream of violet water, which fell with a musical plash into the metal basin. An exquisite odour was diffused around and the ladies dipped their handkerchiefs in the scent as they passed.

"There!" said Madame Marty, when she had loaded herself with lotions, dentrifices, and cosmetics. "Now I've done, I'm at your service. Let's go and rejoin Madame de Boves."

However, on the landing of the great central staircase they were again stopped by the Japanese department. This counter had grown wonderfully since the day when Mouret had amused himself by setting up, in the same place, a little "proposition" table, covered with a few soiled articles, without at all foreseeing its future success. Few departments had had more modest beginnings and yet now it overflowed with old bronzes, old ivories and old lacquer work; it did fifteen hundred thousand francs' worth of business a year, ransacking the Far East, where travellers pillaged the palaces and the temples for it. Besides, fresh departments were always springing up, they had tried two new ones in December, in order to fill up the empty spaces caused by the dead winter season—a book department and a toy department, which would certainly expand and sweep away certain shops in the neighbourhood. Four years had sufficed for the Japanese department to attract the entire artistic custom of Paris. This time Madame Desforges herself, notwithstanding the rancour which had made her vow not to buy anything, succumbed before some finely carved ivory.

"Send it to my house," said she rapidly, at a neighbouring pay-desk. "Ninety francs, is it not?" And, seeing Madame Marty and her daughter busy with a lot of trashy porcelains, she resumed, as she carried off Madame Guibal, "You will find us in the reading-room, I really must sit down a little while."

In the reading-room, however, they were obliged to remain standing. All the chairs round the large table covered with newspapers were occupied. Great fat fellows were reading and lolling about without even thinking of giving up their seats to the ladies. A few women were writing, their faces almost on the paper, as if to conceal their letters under the flowers of their hats. Madame de Boves was not there, and Henriette was getting impatient when she perceived Vallagnosc, who was also looking for his wife and mother-in-law. He bowed, and said: "They must be in the lace department—impossible to drag them away. I'll just see." And he was gallant enough to procure the others two chairs before going off.

In the lace department the crush was increasing every minute. The great show of white was there triumphing in its most delicate and costly whiteness. Here was the supreme temptation, the goading of a mad desire, which bewildered all the women. The department had been turned into a white temple; tulles and guipures, falling from above, formed a white sky, one of those cloudy veils whose fine network pales the morning sun. Round the columns descended flounces of Malines and Valenciennes, white dancers' skirts, unfolding in a snowy shiver to the floor. Then on all sides, on every counter there were snowy masses of white Spanish blonde as light as air, Brussels with large flowers on a delicate mesh, hand-made point, and Venice point with heavier designs, Alençon point, and Bruges of royal and almost sacred richness. It seemed as if the god of finery had here set up his white tabernacle.

Madame de Boves, after wandering about before the counters for a long time with her daughter, and feeling a sensual longing to plunge her hands into the goods, had just made up her mind to request Deloche to show her some Alençon point. At first he brought out some imitation stuff; but she wished to see real Alençon, and was not satisfied with narrow pieces at three hundred francs the yard, but insisted on examining deep flounces at a thousand francs a yard and handkerchiefs and fans at seven and eight hundred francs. The counter was soon covered with a fortune. In a corner of the department inspector Jouve who had not lost sight of Madame de Boves, notwithstanding the latter's apparent dawdling, stood amidst the crowd, with an indifferent air, but still keeping a sharp eye on her.

"Have you any capes in hand-made point?" she at last inquired; "show me some, please."

The salesman, whom she had kept there for twenty minutes, dared not resist, for she appeared so aristocratic, with her imposing air and princess's voice. However, he hesitated, for the employees were cautioned against heaping up these precious fabrics, and he had allowed himself to be robbed of ten yards of Malines only the week before. But she perturbed him, so he yielded, and abandoned the Alençon point for a moment in order to take the lace she had asked for from a drawer.

"Oh! look, mamma," said Blanche, who was ransacking a box close by, full of cheap Valenciennes, "we might take some of this for pillow-cases."

Madame de Boves did not reply and her daughter on turning her flabby face saw her, with her hands plunged amidst the lace, slipping some Alençon flounces up the sleeve of her mantle. Blanche did not appear surprised, however, but moved forward instinctively to conceal her mother, when Jouve suddenly stood before them. He leant over, and politely murmured in the countess's ear,

"Have the kindness to follow me, madame."

For a moment she revolted: "But what for, sir?"

"Have the kindness to follow me, madame," repeated the inspector, without raising his voice.

With her face full of anguish, she threw a rapid glance around her. Then all at once she resigned herself, resumed her haughty bearing, and walked away by his side like a queen who deigns to accept the services of an aide-de-camp. Not one of the many customers had observed the scene, and Deloche, on turning to the counter, looked at her as she was walked off, his mouth wide open with astonishment. What! that one as well! that noble-looking lady! Really it was time to have them all searched! And Blanche, who was left free, followed her mother at a distance, lingering amidst the sea of faces, livid, and hesitating between the duty of not deserting her mother and the terror of being detained with her. At last she saw her enter Bourdoncle's office, and then contented herself with walking about near the door. Bourdoncle, whom Mouret had just got rid of, happened to be there. As a rule, he dealt with robberies of this sort when committed by persons of distinction. Jouve had long been watching this lady, and had informed him of it, so that he was not astonished when the inspector briefly explained the matter to him; in fact, such extraordinary cases passed through his hands that he declared woman to be capable of anything, once the passion for finery had seized upon her. As he was aware of Mouret's acquaintance with the thief, he treated her with the utmost politeness.

"We excuse these moments of weakness, madame," said he. "But pray consider the consequences of such a thing. Suppose some one else had seen you slip this lace—"

But she interrupted him in great indignation. She a thief! What did he take her for? She was the Countess de Boves, her husband, Inspector-General of the State Studs, was received at Court.

"I know it, I know it, madame," repeated Bourdoncle, quietly. "I have the honour of knowing you. In the first place, will you kindly give up the lace you have on you?"

But, not allowing him to say another word she again protested, handsome in her violence, even shedding tears like some great lady vilely and wrongfully accused. Any one else but he would have been shaken and have feared some deplorable mistake, for she threatened to go to law to avenge such an insult.

"Take care, sir, my husband will certainly appeal to the Minister."

"Come, you are not more reasonable than the others," declared Bourdoncle, losing patience. "We must search you."

Still she did not yield, but with superb assurance, declared: "Very good, search me. But I warn you, you are risking your house."

Jouve went to fetch two saleswomen from the corset department. When he returned, he informed Bourdoncle that the lady's daughter, left at liberty, had not quitted the doorway, and asked if she also should be detained, although he had not seen her take anything. The manager, however, who always did things in a fitting way, decided that she should not be brought in, in order not to cause her mother to blush before her. The two men retired into a neighbouring room, whilst the saleswomen searched the countess. Besides the twelve yards of Alençon point at a thousand francs the yard concealed in her sleeve, they found upon her a handkerchief, a fan, and a cravat, making a total of about fourteen thousand francs' worth of lace. She had been stealing like this for the last year, ravaged by a furious, irresistible passion for dress. These fits got worse, growing daily, sweeping away all the reasonings of prudence; and the enjoyment she felt in the indulgence of them was the more violent from the fact that she was risking before the eyes of a crowd her name, her pride, and her husband's high position. Now that the latter allowed her to empty his drawers, she stole although she had her pockets full of money, she stole for the mere pleasure of stealing, goaded on by desire, urged on by the species of kleptomania which her unsatisfied luxurious tastes had formerly developed in her at sight of the vast brutal temptations of the big shops.[1]

"It's a trap," cried she, when Bourdoncle and Jouve came in. "This lace was placed on me, I swear it before Heaven."

She was now shedding tears of rage, and fell on a chair, suffocating. Bourdoncle sent the saleswomen away and resumed, with his quiet air: "We are quite willing, madame, to hush up this painful affair for the sake of your family. But you must first sign a paper thus worded: 'I have stolen some lace from The Ladies' Paradise,' followed by particulars of the lace, and the date. However, I shall be happy to return you this document whenever you like to bring me a sum of two thousand francs for the poor."

She again rose and declared in a fresh outburst: "I'll never sign that, I'd rather die."

"You won't die, madame; but I warn you that I shall shortly send for the police."

Then followed a frightful scene. She insulted him, she stammered that it was cowardly for a man to torture a woman in that way. Her

---

1. The manager of one of the great London drapery houses was telling me, recently, that the same kind of thing is far less infrequent than might be imagined among certain English women of fashion. And he added that these affairs are as a rule hushed up, even as they are hushed up in Paris. *Trans.*

Juno-like beauty, her tall majestic person was distorted by vulgar rage. Then she tried to soften him and Jouve, entreating them in the name of their mothers, and speaking of dragging herself at their feet. And as they, however, remained quite unmoved, hardened by custom, she all at once sat down and began to write with a trembling hand. The pen sputtered; the words "I have stolen," madly, wildly written, went almost through the thin paper, whilst she repeated in a choking voice: "There, sir, there. I yield to force."

Bourdoncle took the paper, carefully folded it, and put it in a drawer, saying: "You see it's in company; for ladies, after talking of dying rather than signing, generally forget to come and redeem these *billets doux* of theirs. However, I hold it at your disposal. You'll be able to judge whether it's worth two thousand francs."

But now that she had paid the forfeit she became as arrogant as ever. "I can go now?" she asked, in a sharp tone.

Bourdoncle was already occupied with other business. On Jouve's report, he decided on the dismissal of Deloche, a stupid fellow, who was always being robbed and who never had any authority over customers. Madame de Boves repeated her question, and as they dismissed her with an affirmative nod, she enveloped both of them in a murderous glance. Of the flood of insulting words that she kept back, one melodramatic cry escaped her lips. "Wretches!" said she, banging the door after her.

Meanwhile Blanche had not strayed far from the office. Her ignorance of what was going on inside and the coming and going of Jouve and the two saleswomen frightened her; she had visions of the police, the assize court, and the prison. But all at once she stopped short: for Vallagnosc was before her, that husband whom she had married but a month previously, and with whom she still felt rather awkward. And he questioned her, astonished at her bewildered appearance.

"Where's your mother? Have you lost each other? Come, tell me, you make me feel anxious."

Nothing in the way of a colourable fiction presented itself to her mind, and in great distress she told him everything in a low voice: "Mamma, mamma—she has been stealing."

"What! stealing?" At last he understood. His wife's bloated, livid countenance, ravaged by fear, terrified him.

"Some lace, like that, up her sleeve," she continued stammering.

"You saw her, then? You were looking on?" he murmured, chilled to feel that she had been a sort of accomplice.

They had to stop talking as several persons were already turning round. Hesitation full of anguish kept Vallagnosc motionless for a moment. What was to be done? He had made up his mind to go into Bourdoncle's office, when he perceived Mouret crossing the gallery. Thereupon, after telling his wife to wait for him, he caught hold of his old friend's arm and informed him of the affair, in broken sentences. The latter hastily took him into his office, where he soon put him at rest as to the possible consequences. He assured him that he need not interfere, and without appearing at all excited about this robbery, as if he had foreseen it long ago, he explained in what way it would all be arranged. Vallagnosc, however, even when he no longer feared an immediate arrest, did not accept the affair with this admirable coolness. He had thrown himself into an arm-chair, and now that he could discuss the matter, began to lament his own unfortunate position. Was it possible that he had married into a family of thieves? A stupid marriage that he had drifted into, just to please his wife's father! Surprised by his childish violence, Mouret watched him weeping, thinking the while of his former pessimist boasting. Had he not scores of times proclaimed the nothingness of life, in which wrong-doing alone had any attraction? And by way of diversion Mouret amused himself for a minute, by preaching indifference to his friend, in a friendly, bantering tone. But at this Vallagnosc got angry: he was quite unable to recover his philosophy, and with his middle-class breeding burst into virtuously indignant cries against his mother-in-law. As soon as trouble fell on himself, as soon as he was just touched by human suffering, at which he had always coldly laughed, the boastful sceptic collapsed and bled. It was abominable, they were dragging the honour of his race into the gutter, the world seemed to be coming to an end.

"Come, calm yourself," concluded Mouret, stricken with pity. "I won't tell you that everything happens and nothing happens, because that does not seem to comfort you just now. But I think that you ought to go and offer your arm to Madame de Boves—that would be more sensible than causing a scandal. The deuce! to think of it, you who professed such scorn for the universal rascality of the present day!"

"Of course," cried Vallagnosc, innocently, "when it is a question of other people!"

However, he got up, and followed his old school-fellow's advice. Both were returning to the gallery when Madame de Boves came out of Bourdoncle's office. She accepted her son-in-law's arm with a majestic air, and as Mouret bowed to her with respectful gallantry, he heard her saying: "They've apologized to me. Really, these mistakes are abominable."

Blanche joined them, and they soon disappeared in the crowd. Then Mouret, alone and pensive, crossed the shop once more. This scene, which had diverted his thoughts from the struggle going on within him, now increased his fever, and decided him to make a supreme effort. A vague connection arose in his mind: the robbery perpetrated by that unfortunate woman, that last folly of the conquered customer laid low at the feet of the tempter, evoked the proud and avenging image of Denise, whose victorious heel he could feel upon his throat. He stopped at the top of the central staircase, and gazed for a long time into the immense nave, where his nation of women was swarming.

Six o'clock was about to strike, the daylight decreasing out-of-doors was gradually forsaking the covered galleries, already dim, and even waning in the halls which gloom was slowly invading. And in this uncertain glimmer, the electric lamps lighted up one by one, their globes of an opaque whiteness studding with moons the distant depths of the departments. It was a white brightness of a blinding fixity, spreading like the radiance of a discoloured star and killing the twilight. Then, when all were lighted, there came a delighted murmur from the crowd, and the great show of white goods assumed a fairy splendour. It seemed as if this colossal orgie of white was also burning, itself becoming so much light. The song of the white seemed to soar upward in the flaming whiteness of an aurora. A white glimmer darted from the linen and calico department in the Monsigny Gallery, like the first bright streak which lights up the eastern sky; whilst along the Michodière Gallery, the mercery and the passementerie, the fancy-goods and the ribbons threw out reflections of distant hills—with the white flash of mother-of-pearl buttons, silvered bronzes and sparkling beads. But the central nave especially was filled with a blaze of white: the white muslin "puffings" round the columns, the white dimities and piqués draping the staircases, the white counterpanes drooping like banners, the white guipures and laces flying in the air, opened up a firmament of dreamland, a vista of the dazzling whiteness of some paradise, where the marriage of an unknown queen was being celebrated. The tent of the silk-hall was this heaven's giant alcove, with white curtains, white gauzes and white tulles, whose shimmer screened the bride in her white nudity from the gaze of the curious. There was now nothing but this blinding nucleus of white light

ÉMILE ZOLA

in which all other whites were merged, this snowy starry dust twinkling in the clear radiance.

And Mouret still continued to watch his nation of women, amidst the shimmering blaze. Their black shadows stood out vigorously against the pale backgrounds. Long eddies would now and again part the crowd; the fever of the day's great sale swept past like a frenzy through the disorderly, billowy sea of heads. People were beginning to leave; pillaged stuffs encumbered all the counters, and gold was chinking in the tills whilst the customers went off, their purses emptied, and their heads turned by the wealth of luxury amidst which they had been wandering all day. It was he who possessed them thus, who held them at his mercy by his continuous displays of novelties, his reductions of prices, and his "returns," his gallantry, puffery, and advertisements. He had conquered even the mothers, he reigned over all with the brutality of a despot, whose caprices ruined many a household. His creation was a sort of new religion; the churches, gradually deserted by wavering faith, were replaced by his bazaar, in the minds of the idle women of Paris. Woman now came and spent her leisure time in his establishment, those shivering anxious hours which she had formerly passed in churches: a necessary consumption of nervous passion, an ever renewed struggle of the god of dress against the husband, an ever renewed worship of the body with the promise of future divine beauty. If he had closed his doors, there would have been a rising in the street, the despairing cry of worshippers deprived of their confessional and altar! In their still growing passion for luxury, he saw them, notwithstanding the lateness of the hour yet obstinately lingering in the huge iron building, on the suspended staircases and flying bridges. Madame Marty and her daughter, carried away to the highest point, were wandering amongst the furniture. Madame Bourdelais, retained by her young people, could not get away from the fancy goods. And then came another group, Madame de Boves, still on Vallagnosc's arm, and followed by Blanche, stopping in each department and still daring to examine the goods with her superb air. But amidst the crowded sea of customers, that sea of bodies inflated with life and beating with desire, one and all decorated with bunches of violets, as though for the bridal of some sovereign, Mouret could now only distinguish the figure of Madame Desforges, who had stopped in the glove department with Madame Guibal. Despite her jealous rancour, she also was buying, and he felt himself to be the master once more, having them at his feet, beneath the dazzle of the electric light, like a drove of cattle from which he had drawn his fortune.

With a mechanical step, Mouret went along the galleries, so absorbed that he yielded to the pushing of the crowd. When he raised his head again he found himself in the new millinery department, the windows of which overlooked the Rue du Dix-Décembre. And there, his forehead against the glass, he made another halt and watched the departure of the throng. The setting sun was tinging the roofs of the white houses with yellow, the blue sky was growing paler, refreshed by a pure breeze; whilst in the twilight, which was already enveloping the side-walks down below, the electric lamps of The Ladies' Paradise threw forth the fixed glimmer of stars, lighted on the horizon at the decline of day. Towards the Opera-house and the Bourse were rows of waiting vehicles, the harness of the horses still presenting reflections of bright light, the gleam of a lamp, the glitter of a silver chain. At each minute the cry of a messenger was heard, and a cab drew near, or a brougham came forth from the ranks, took up a customer and went off at a rapid trot. The rows of conveyances were now diminishing, six went off at a time, occupying the whole street from one side to the other, amidst the banging of doors, the snapping of whips, and the hum of the passers-by, who swarmed between the wheels. There was a sort of continuous enlargement, a spreading of the customers, carried off to the four corners of the city, as the building emptied with the roaring clamour of a sluice. And the roof of The Ladies' Paradise, the big golden letters of the sky signs, the banners fluttering in the heavens, still flamed with the reflections of the setting sun, looking so colossal in the oblique light that they evoked the thought of some monster of advertising, some phalansterium whose buildings, incessantly multiplied, in turn covered up every district, as far as the distant woods of the suburbs. And the spreading soul of Paris, in a huge but gentle breath, sank asleep in the serenity of the evening, hovering in prolonged, languid caresses over the last vehicles which were spinning through the streets, now slowly deserted by the crowd as it disappeared into the darkness of the night.

Mouret, gazing around, had just felt something grand in himself; but, amid the quiver of triumph with which his flesh trembled, in face of Paris devoured and woman conquered, he experienced a sudden weakness, a defection of his strong will, by which in his turn he was overthrown beneath a superior force. It was an unreasonable longing to be vanquished amidst his victory, the nonsense of a warrior bending beneath the caprice of a child, on the morrow of his conquests. He who had struggled for months, who even that morning had sworn to stifle his passion, all at once yielded, seized by the vertigo which overcomes one on mountain heights, happy to commit what he looked upon as folly. His decision, so rapidly arrived at, acquired in a minute such energy that he saw nothing else useful and necessary in the world.

In the evening, after the last dinner, he sat waiting in his office, trembling like a young man about to stake his life's happiness, unable to keep still but incessantly going towards the door to listen to the hubbub in the shop, where the employees, submerged to the shoulders in a sea of stuffs, were now doing the folding up. At each footstep his heart beat. And all at once he experienced violent emotion, and rushed forward, for he had heard in the distance a deep murmur, which had gradually increased.

It was Lhomme slowly approaching with the day's receipts. That day they were so heavy, there was such a quantity of silver and copper, that he had been obliged to enlist the services of two messengers. Behind him came Joseph and one of his colleagues, both bending beneath the weight of the bags, enormous bags, thrown on their shoulders like sacks of plaster, whilst he walked on in front with the notes and gold, a note-book swollen with flimsies, and two bags hung round his neck, the weight of which made him sway to the right, the same side as his broken arm. Slowly, perspiring and puffing, he had come from the other end of the shop amidst the growing emotion of the salesmen. The employees in the glove and silk departments had laughingly offered to relieve him of his burden, the men in the drapery and woollen departments had longed to see him make a false step, which would have scattered the gold all over the place. Then he had been obliged to mount the stairs, and cross a bridge and then go higher still, turning about amidst the longing looks of the employees of the linen, hosiery, and mercery departments, who gazed in ecstasy at this fortune travelling in the air. On the first-floor the mantle, perfumery, lace, and shawl employees were ranged devoutly as for the passage of the Blessed Sacrament. And from counter to counter a tumult arose, like the clamour of a nation bowing down before the Golden Calf.

Mouret had opened the door, and Lhomme appeared, followed by the two messengers, who were staggering; and, out of breath though he was, the cashier still had strength to cry out: "One million two hundred and forty-seven francs, nineteen sous!"

At last the million had been attained, that million picked up in a day, of which Mouret had so long dreamed. But he gave way to an angry gesture, and with the disappointed air of a man disturbed by some troublesome visitor, he impatiently exclaimed, "A million! very good, put it there." Lhomme knew that he was fond of seeing the heavy receipts on his table before they were taken to the central cash office. The million covered the whole table, crushing the papers and almost overturning the ink; and the gold and the silver and the copper running out of the sacks and bursting the leather bags, formed a great heap, the heap of the gross receipts, such as it came still warm and palpitating from the customers' hands.

Just as the cashier was going away, heart-broken at the governor's indifference, Bourdoncle arrived, gaily exclaiming: "Ah! we've got it this time. We've hooked the million, eh?"

But on observing Mouret's febrile air he understood the situation and calmed down. His face was beaming with delight; and after a short silence he resumed: "You've made up your mind, haven't you? Well, I approve your decision."

All at once, however, Mouret planted himself before him, and in his terrible voice thundered: "I say, my man, you're rather too lively. You think me played out, don't you? and you feel hungry. But be careful, I'm not one to be swallowed up, you know!"

Discountenanced by the sharp attack of this wonderful fellow, who guessed everything, Bourdoncle stammered: "What now? Are you joking? I who have always admired you so much!"

"Don't tell lies!" replied Mouret, more violently than ever. "Just listen, we were stupid to entertain the superstition that marriage would ruin us. Why, is it not the necessary health, the very strength and order of life? Well, my dear fellow, I'm going to marry her, and I'll pitch you all out of doors at the slightest movement. Yes, you'll go and get paid like the rest, Bourdoncle."

And with a gesture he dismissed him. Bourdoncle felt himself condemned, swept away, in this victory gained by woman. He went off. Denise was just coming in, and he bowed to her with profound respect, his head swimming.

"Ah! you've come at last!" said Mouret gently.

Denise was pale with emotion. She had just experienced another grief, Deloche had informed her of his dismissal, and when she had tried to retain him, offering to speak in his favour, he had obstinately declined to struggle against his bad luck; he wanted to disappear, he said, what was the use of staying? Why should he interfere with people who were happy? Then Denise had bade him a sisterly farewell, her eyes full of tears. Did she not herself long to sink into oblivion? Everything was now about to finish, and she asked nothing more of her exhausted strength than the courage to insist on the separation. In a few minutes, if she could only be valiant enough to crush her heart, she would be able to go away alone, and weep unseen.

"You wished to see me, sir," she said in her calm voice. "In fact, I intended to come and thank you for all your kindness to me."

On entering, she had perceived the million on the table, and the display of that money wounded her. Above her, as if watching the scene, was the portrait of Madame Hédouin, in its gilded frame, and with the eternal smile of its painted lips.

"You are still resolved to leave us?" asked Mouret, in a trembling voice.

"Yes, sir. I must."

Then he took her hands, and, in an outburst of tenderness, after the long coldness he had imposed on himself exclaimed: "And if I asked you to marry me, Denise, would you still leave?"

But she rapidly drew her hands away, struggling as if under the influence of a great grief. "Oh! Monsieur Mouret! Pray say no more. Oh! don't cause me even greater pain than before! I cannot! I cannot! Heaven is my witness that I was going away to avoid such a misfortune!"

She continued to defend herself in broken sentences. Had she not already suffered too much from the gossip of the house? Did he wish her to pass in the eyes of others and his own for a worthless woman? No, no, she would be strong, she would certainly prevent him doing such a foolish thing. He, tortured, listened to her, repeating in a passionate tone: "I wish it. I wish it!"

"No, it's impossible. And my brothers? I have sworn not to marry. I cannot bring you those children, can I?"

"They shall be my brothers, too. Say yes, Denise."

"No, no, leave me. You are torturing me!"

Little by little he was losing his strength; this last obstacle drove him frantic. What! She still refused even at this price! In the distance he heard the clamour of his three thousand employees building up his immense fortune. And that idiotic million lying there! He suffered from it as from a sort of irony, he could have kicked it into the street.

"Go, then!" he cried at last in a flood of tears. "Go and join the man you love. That's the reason, isn't it? You warned me, I ought to have known it, and not have tormented you any further."

She stood there thunderstruck by the violence of this despair. Her own heart was bursting. And then, with the impetuosity of a child, she threw herself on his neck, sobbing also, and stammering: "Oh! Monsieur Mouret, it's you I love!"

A last murmur was rising from The Ladies' Paradise, the distant acclamation of a multitude. Madame Hédouin's portrait was still smiling, with its painted lips; Mouret had fallen on his table, on the million which he could no longer see. He did not quit Denise, but clasped her to his breast in a desperate embrace, telling her that she might now go, that she could spend a month at Valognes which would silence everybody, and that then he would go to fetch her himself, and bring her back, all-powerful, as his wedded wife.

THE END

# A Note About the Author

Émile Zola (1840–1902) was a French novelist, journalist, and playwright. Born in Paris to a French mother and Italian father, Zola was raised in Aix-en-Provence. At 18, Zola moved back to Paris, where he befriended Paul Cézanne and began his writing career. During this early period, Zola worked as a clerk for a publisher while writing literary and art reviews as well as political journalism for local newspapers. Following the success of his novel *Thérèse Raquin* (1867), Zola began a series of twenty novels known as *Les Rougon-Macquart*, a sprawling collection following the fates of a single family living under the Second Empire of Napoleon III. Zola's work earned him a reputation as a leading figure in literary naturalism, a style noted for its rejection of Romanticism in favor of detachment, rationalism, and social commentary. Following the infamous Dreyfus affair of 1894, in which a French-Jewish artillery officer was falsely convicted of spying for the German Embassy, Zola wrote a scathing open letter to French President Félix Faure accusing the government and military of antisemitism and obstruction of justice. Having sacrificed his reputation as a writer and intellectual, Zola helped reverse public opinion on the affair, placing pressure on the government that led to Dreyfus' full exoneration in 1906. Nominated for the Nobel Prize in Literature in 1901 and 1902, Zola is considered one of the most influential and talented writers in French history.

# A Note from the Publisher

Spanning many genres, from non-fiction essays to literature classics to children's books and lyric poetry, Mint Edition books showcase the master works of our time in a modern new package. The text is freshly typeset, is clean and easy to read, and features a new note about the author in each volume. Many books also include exclusive new introductory material. Every book boasts a striking new cover, which makes it as appropriate for collecting as it is for gift giving. Mint Edition books are only printed when a reader orders them, so natural resources are not wasted. We're proud that our books are never manufactured in excess and exist only in the exact quantity they need to be read and enjoyed.

# bookfinity™

## Discover more of your favorite classics with Bookfinity™.

- Track your reading with custom book lists.
- Get great book recommendations for your personalized Reader Type.
- Add reviews for your favorite books.
- AND MUCH MORE!

Visit **bookfinity.com** and take the fun Reader Type quiz to get started.

Enjoy our classic and modern companion pairings!

## Classic & Modern